Namaste - my daughters

Bettina Schulz

01.06.15

Dear Maisie,
This is as personal as it gets. So this is me in a nutshell :)
I hope you enjoy it, and thankyou for being the best friend ever.
  Love Melana x

Copyright © 2015 Bettina Schulz

All rights reserved.

ISBN: 1503392279
ISBN 13: 9781503392274

FOR MOHANA AND ASHA

Part One

Chapter 1

BETWEEN TWO WORLDS

Mumbai. Deep at night. Most flights from Europe arrive around midnight. It gives me some time to change worlds, to drift slowly into this ferocious city before she swallows me up with her hot breath the next morning.

Tired but relieved, I slump into the backseat of an old taxi. I roll down the window on my side and enjoy the warm breeze of tropical air. I quickly get the mosquito spray out of my bag and rub it on my feet and arms. Taxis have to queue for hours at the airport to wait for passengers. Mosquitoes get into the taxis while they're there and dance in the humid air of the cars. I already feel my ankles itching.

We leave the airport, but do not get very far on our journey. "There is something wrong with the car," the driver says. He's an old man. He slows down the car. We are just a few miles away from the airport. The roadside is dark, just bushes. There are no streetlights. I was not aware that anything was wrong with the taxi. I start to get worried.

"Why don't you drive on?" I ask. I suddenly remember that the security guard at the airport wanted to know where we were heading. The old man doesn't answer. He slowly stops at the roadside. Just a few meters away, I see another car waiting in the darkness. A shadow comes forward and walks toward us. It is another, younger man.

I am told by my driver to get out of the car. I get scared. Nothing like this has ever happened to me before in India. I always felt so safe in this country. I had never been robbed, never had any problems. Now this.

The men are talking to each other. They know each other well and have very obviously planned the stop. They ignore my protests and carry my luggage to the other car. The younger man swiftly lifts my bag onto the roof and ties down my luggage with a rope. For him, this is clearly routine. Both men must have done this over and over again. I complain. I am fed up. I don't want to watch my luggage being moved from one car to the other, waiting at the roadside in one of the darkest areas of Mumbai at four o'clock in the morning. And I am still frightened.

Now the younger man apologizes to me and asks me politely to get into his car. He will drive me to my hotel, he reassures me. Suddenly I understand. I even feel slightly sorry and embarrassed. These men work together and share passengers arriving at the airport; they might even be father and son. While the young driver takes people to their hotels, the old man returns to the airport and queues for hours for the next passenger. By the time he leaves the airport, his son has returned to their dark meeting point, ready to pick up the next guests from his father.

We get going at last. In the darkness, Mumbai stretches along the black roadside, battered, torn apart, and patched up again by heat, humidity, monsoons, and poverty.

The city seems exhausted, aching with the burden of millions of people at the very edge of existence. Slums line our route—squat heaps of metal and cardboard. On the potholed pavement and dusty traffic islands, people lie sleeping, huddled together under blankets and sheets of plastic. They are so worn out that nothing seems to wake them, not the traffic, not the mosquitoes, not the rats, not the stray dogs. Whole families lie motionless in the darkness, hole-filled blankets covering their bodies like shrouds as though death is just such a small step away.

I am confused, as I always am when I arrive in Mumbai. I stare out of the window and wonder, "Is it still as bad as last time, or is it even worse?" To me, it seems to be worse. But perhaps it's just its stark contrast against the clean, neat, and orderly world I had just left ten hours earlier. No, although I've been here so many times, I still cannot get used to the sight of Mumbai at night. It leaves me bewildered, baffled, and numb.

Wearily I answer the driver's questions. Then he falls silent. Driving through the darkness of Mumbai is not conducive to a nice chat.

We turn off into a dark neighborhood. Finally I signal the driver to stop. I get out of the taxi. Silence. In the dim glow of a few feeble streetlights, I see wooden carts lining the side of the street, packed closely together. On top of the old carts, on the pavement, and in the doorways of the houses, men are sleeping, breathing heavily under blankets and sackcloth. Tomorrow this will be a market again, full of noisy hustle and bustle and buzzing with colorful activity. But for now, it's quiet, with just the occasional wheezing cough.

I squeeze myself between the carts and knock on a glass door. It takes time, but a young man from the hotel opens the door, yawns, and smiles as he recognizes me. We instantly whisper. I pay the taxi driver, and the two men carry my luggage into the tiny hall of the hotel.

Through the door I can make out the little restaurant, all dark now so late at night. On two tables, men are curled up asleep. The man who answered the door takes me straight upstairs to the first floor. In the dimly lit passage, frighteningly large cockroaches scamper away. Some of the guests have eaten in their rooms and put the dirty dishes out in the hallway.

My room is tiny, the air sticky. I sink down on the bed and ask the young man if he could just quickly fetch me a towel, a sheet, toilet paper, and a plastic bottle of water. A broken air conditioner rattles beside me.

I'm happy. I'm finally here, and I'm content with this small hotel and my Spartan room. I couldn't search here—amid all the poverty and desolation in Mumbai—for a child to adopt, only to go back to a luxury hotel with a marble bath and a swimming pool. I deliberately wanted to retreat into a kind of austerity, to focus myself and not be distracted. How else can I immerse myself in this world, learn from its people, and understand them?

I decide to sleep without a mosquito net and turn off the light. Outside on the street, someone is having a coughing fit. The humidity is overwhelming. I listen to the street, to the coughing, to the barking dogs, and to the screeching trains.

I can't sleep in this oppressive heat, but still I feel liberated. I'm floating between worlds. Tomorrow I'll start my search for a children's home and a child. I'm finally taking my life into my own hands, as I've felt so powerless these last few months.

We've been discussing adoption with Sarah for many weeks now. She's our social worker—messy blond hair, dazzling blue eyes, and always a little bit disheveled. She works on our adoption report and advises us, drinking liters of black tea all the while. Sarah always gives us the impression that she understands us; perhaps she really does. The personal questions are a real intrusion into our private lives. It's always bothered Andreas and me, but we need to be pragmatic about it. We know that we'll have to put up with being assessed by a social worker if we want to adopt a child. Still, it's hard. It seems so hypothetical to discuss an adoption without a particular child in mind, not knowing if you'll be given a child at all.

I feel restless again, so I get up and gaze through the window of my hotel room onto the railway lines, which run right in front of the hotel. At night, families lie on the wide platforms, huddled together on the ground, covered up, all fast asleep. It does not matter how many trains shake the platforms, how much the floodlights cover the station in their glare.

I think of home. Back there, I neatly filed away the rejection letters from the Indian children's homes. Months ago. I had sent a whole stack of letters to orphanages in Mumbai, Kolkata, and New Delhi. In them, I introduced Andreas and myself, two people who were hoping to adopt an Indian child. I was careful to stress that we had already been assessed for foreign adoption by social workers. But by and by, the replies from the Indian homes landed on our doormat, almost twenty typewritten letters in total. "Although we're delighted to hear that you'd like to adopt… unfortunately we must decline your application" or "…unfortunately the best we can offer is to add you to our waiting list. At present the waiting time for a child is at least two or three years.…" I didn't want to accept this. With the widespread poverty in India, there surely must be plenty of children's homes that would be relieved to hear that someone wanted to adopt a child. And now I took heart in the fact that I would see for myself. I would find a home. I was sure of it. Perhaps even a child, too.

I couldn't have taken any more in the end, particularly after Sarah visited us with the questionnaire. She was always nice and levelheaded about it. The questionnaire was just part of the paperwork that every pair of prospective parents had to complete, she said. We were asked to check the appropriate boxes: Would we adopt a blind child or a visually impaired one? Would we accept a deaf child? Yes or no? Hard of hearing? A child with spina bifida? A child with AIDS? Mentally disabled? How far would we go? Please mark as applicable. Multiple choice. It was so cynical, cold, and calculating. How many children's fates were decided there on that form?

For each question, Andreas and I considered how far upside down we were prepared to turn our lives. Our egos crept into the check marks; we really wanted to lead a "normal life." We didn't want to have to let too many restrictions into our world. A visually impaired child? Yes. He or she could have an operation and wear glasses. A blind child? No. We were put off by the risks, the inconveniences, the complications.

Sarah understood us. She was even afraid, she said, that our sheer charitable nature and love of children would lead us down a road that would turn out to be more than we could handle. She advised us against adopting a disabled child, and I'm grateful to her for that. But every no from us was a decision against a child, a refusal to help someone who really needed it. The questionnaire left us no choice. It left us with guilty consciences.

That's why I'm here, I think, comforting myself. I lie down on the bed again. Starting tomorrow, I won't just sit and wait any longer; I'll search with my own eyes. I always tell myself that I've made the best progress whenever I've taken matters into my own hands.

Feeling confident once more, I fumble in the dark for the switch for the fan. I turn the dial carefully until the blades spin evenly and rhythmically above me, just enough to waft a gentle breeze over my body. I decide to sleep without the air-conditioning, so I turn it off.

Chapter 2

SLUMS OF MUMBAI

I awaken to a female voice announcing the suburban trains leaving for Mumbai during the morning rush hour. I look down from my hotel window at the bustle of people on the platforms below. The sleeping families have vanished. Trains pull in several at a time; the fast trains don't stop, but thunder through at high speed on their way to Mumbai Central. Commuters dangle out of the doorways in the wind; it's often the only way of getting on the train.

I head down to the hotel's foyer. In the hallway, last night's dirty plates have been cleared away, and the smell of sandalwood is beginning to drift through the hotel. The young man has just finished lighting a stick of incense on the family altar to the elephant god Ganesh. He soon spots me and waves to the newspaper boys blocking the entrance to let me through. The men use the shade of the hotel entrance to sort the papers and supplements.

I step onto the street. It is already pretty hot in the sun, even this early in the morning. Yet it's the hustle and bustle of the early day that dazzles me. The hotel is located in a popular quarter in the north of Mumbai. The streets are shaded by trees. Some orange-robed monks watch over a tiny temple nestled among the aerial roots of a holy banyan tree. At this time of day, groups of laborers line the streets, waiting to be hired for a day's work. Blackened by the sun and broken down by hard work in the heat, many of these men have nothing but the tools in their hands—a saw, for example. They crouch in groups, patiently waiting for the next job.

I need a moment to gather my strength before braving the crowds. I traveled to India on my own. Andreas couldn't join me; he had to work. He doesn't have as much vacation time as I do, and he's saving the weeks for our future trips to India, once we're actually in the process of adopting a child. All the same, it's a shame he can't be here to see the orphanage for himself, because which orphanage we choose and whether we even decide to adopt from India at all are such important decisions. Still, I will just have to do the groundwork on my own; we'll talk things over in the evenings over the crackling phone line.

Tourists are a rare sight in this part of Mumbai. The men on the street stare at me, at this Western woman standing outside the hotel, dressed in Indian dress—the salwar kameez—but otherwise so European, with her short hair and glasses, less feminine looking than Indian women.

I remember when I traveled through Rajasthan years ago. In those days I still wore long Western trousers instead of a salwar kameez. The children in the remote desert parts kept asking me if I was a man or a woman. They didn't know any other women with short hair who wore trousers and drove a car by herself.

Slowly I step between the lines of workers to the tea stand on the other side of the street with its huge aluminum pots bubbling with chai. I adore the smell, rich with cinnamon, cardamom, and cloves, heavy and sweet, infused with milk and sugar. The young man pours a stream of tea from one of the cooking pots into a teapot; it glistens like a metal streamer in the sun. He then pours me a glass, light brown and steaming. After a moment's hesitation, he gives me a nod and puts the glass inside another one so that I won't burn my fingers.

Now armed with my steaming tea, I push back through the workers again and stop at a stall to buy some bananas. The stallholder interrupts his morning shave to serve me. Like many others, he spent last night on the street. I point at some bananas. He feels them and pulls a face: not good enough. He gives me some others. Next door I ask for the *Times of India*. The shopkeeper pulls a clean newspaper from inside the stack, leaving the top copy to protect the rest from the dust and grime of the street. I pay and head back to my room, where I sip my tea and flip through the *Times*.

Before long, it'll be time for my first orphanage visit. I'll be traveling to Colaba, an area at the southernmost tip of Mumbai. I'd been able to arrange the appointment from home over the phone. It's more than a taxi ride away, so I've decided to take the train.

By the time I head back into the street, the laborers have disappeared. Now there are schoolgirls among the crowds, their oiled hair combed in braids with fresh jasmine. Around the corner, a market is in full swing, and the sellers have laid out their vegetables and fruits. Many of the fruits and vegetables are ones I've never seen before, all beautifully fresh and aromatic, carefully arranged in neat piles. Bunches of coriander and mint lie in the shade. Nearly every stall has a stick of incense burning. The sellers are proud of their goods and are doing a bustling trade with women, who use the mornings for shopping before the heat of the day drives everyone back inside.

At the station, I buy a ticket for the local train and cross the railway bridge to my platform. Suddenly,

I hear a woman screaming, the scream of a person who is beside herself with fury. Then, between the platforms, I see her. She is pointing and staring at a particular spot, what seems to be a hole between the rails. A boy tugs at her filthy kameez, and I wonder, "Why is his mother's head shaved?" Almost all Indian women wear their hair long, more often than not done into handsome braids. I watch while other commuters hurry past me to catch their trains. Slowly, I realize that a man has crawled halfway inside the hole under the rails. All of a sudden he reappears with a container full of water. There must be a broken water main running under the railway track.

Only then do I spot the two large canisters next to the boy. His mother seems to have lost her mind. She screams at the man like a madwoman and then climbs into the hole after him. Her son hands her a canister, and she vanishes with it into the darkness. Trains thunder past her all the while, often just a few feet away on the neighboring track. All at once, the mother jumps up, clears the hole with a single bound, and runs a few feet to the right, followed by the boy. Seconds later, the watering hole disappears beneath the heavy wheels of a train thundering past. The mother screams and curses as if deranged, and the boy pulls on her kameez again as if to calm her. No sooner have the wheels of the last carriage rolled into the distance than she scrambles straight back under the tracks. After all, the canister isn't full yet. Time and time again, her efforts are interrupted, and she clambers out of the hole. But she and the boy are used to it. By now, other people from the nearby slums have begun to arrive. They, too, want a share of the water. A circle forms around the mother and son, but the mother unleashes such a hysterical scream that the others keep their distance.

A few moments later, I hear a loudspeaker announce my train, and I run down the steps to the platform. Scanning the crowds, I find the section of the platform where the women are waiting, because trains in Mumbai have separate carriages for men and women. My train pulls in, and commuters are already jumping onto the platform from the still-moving cars. I have to take care not to be trampled underfoot. The first-class women's carriage comes to a stop right in front of me, and more commuters spill from the doorway. Before the last men and women have even left the train, the passengers on the platform begin to scramble aboard; anyone who doesn't get off quickly enough risks being trapped on the train. I find myself automatically swept into the carriage by the force of the women behind me. Peeking through a grille, I see the situation is even worse in the men's compartment; they're packed in like sweat-drenched sardines with no chance of a seat.

I manage to claim a few inches of a bench in the aisle. The airy seats by the open grilled windows are already taken. The women's colorful saris and dupattas flutter in the breeze of the already-speeding train. During the journey they take turns sitting by the window. Many of the women are reading, while others seem lost in their thoughts, gazing out of the window at the city as it slowly floats past us. They stare at the cramped slums along the embankment, endless rows of shacks made of wood, cardboard, and plastic sheeting. Each hut houses several adults, as well as the toddlers playing outside in the dirt. Between many of the shacks, bluish pools of brackish water glisten in the sun, plastic bottles and tubs bobbing on their surface. Some huts sit right on top of the trash itself. I see children and young people pulling scraps of plastic from among the waste and stuffing it into sacks, which they carry over the mounds of garbage. Here, the slums come so close to the embankment that mothers cook just several feet away from the passing trains, and toddlers play right beside the tracks. All along the embankment, men and women are answering the call of nature, and the stench of feces and chemicals is strong enough to sting our noses even inside the carriage. Large blue and white lettering adorns the brick walls that border the embankment—an education campaign for AIDS.

At the next station, a boy jumps into our compartment, dressed only in a pair of worn-out pants, his hair matted and his feet caked in dirt. He drops to his knees and begins to wipe the floor with a cloth. The women don't give him a glance. One of them pulls her sari aside. The boy gets to his feet, eyes the women in the first-class compartment, and then mops for a few more seconds. When this meets with no reaction from the women, he stands up again, holding out his hand, begging. Still nothing. The women stare out of the window. A lady opposite me shakes her head gruffly. Her gesture alone is enough, and the boy turns to me. I weaken; I just can't turn him away. *Anyone could have sent him*, I think, *and could be waiting to scold him for coming home empty-handed.* Under the women's disapproving gazes, I rummage in my bag for some nuts and hand them to the boy. No money, then. His disappointment is clear to see. Without a word, he shoves the nuts into his pocket and carries on, begging from the other women. His luck there is no better, so he jumps off at the next stop.

I arrive in Colaba with an hour to spare before my appointment at the first orphanage, so I wander down to the Gateway of India and from there along the waterfront. This is the Mumbai of picture postcards, a relic from colonial times, loved by Western and Indian tourists alike. Across the street, chauffeurs are pulling up in front of the Taj Mahal; I walk on, leaving the colonial splendor of this luxury hotel with its antique shops, sari boutiques, and private swimming pool behind me. Will my child come from the sort of family that holds an elaborate banquet at the Taj Mahal for their daughter's wedding, having earlier visited a top gynecologist to make sure a badly timed pregnancy doesn't spoil the happy occasion? Not likely.

When a woman gives up her child, when she's at the end of her tether, when she's given up hope, how often is poverty the real cause? Just a few blocks away, a view of the slums that run along the bay opens up before me. "Is this the world the mother of my future child calls home?" I find myself wondering. I decide to make my way in, slowly, but then I hesitate. I can't help but feel guilty. As a tourist, I don't really belong here. But then, I just let myself drift, wandering onward, straight into the warren of huts, shacks, and shelters made of plastic and wood, my tourist's camera hidden in a plastic bag.

From the moment I enter the slums, I'm attacked from all sides by mosquitoes and flies. Here, too, stale pools of standing water have formed between the huts. The air is sticky and moist; I can hardly breathe from the stench. From inside every hut, families peer after me, full of amazement. Then they return to their work. Only the children jump around me excitedly, their feet slapping in the dirt.

I'm surprised at how serious their faces are—their mouths set in sad, sometimes bitter lines—as well as by how sick they look, with their feverish eyes, the badly healed wounds and even scars on their skin, their injuries and allergies. Again and again, I see children with mental or physical disabilities. In between some huts, I spot a girl whose crippled legs only allow her to get around on all fours—polio, again. "And the polio vaccine has been around for how long?" I ask myself.

A group of women, weathered by the sun, have hitched their saris up around their hips and are crouching, legs apart, in the gutter, sorting fish and shrimp. The fishy smell mingles with the stench of feces. Nearby, little children are relieving themselves between the huts, while the adults go straight onto the litter-strewn beach of the bay. A few children are swimming in the foul mixture that laps onto the beach, whooping joyfully. The concept of sanitation simply doesn't exist here.

I keep walking with determination, as if I know where I'm going. "Leprosy is curable," a billboard informs. I suddenly remember a visit to Egypt ages ago, where I had wandered, just as unsuspectingly, into an unfamiliar area and found myself in the slums. I was just about to head back the way I came when I heard something rustling in a heap of garbage nearby—a man with a bad case of leprosy. He was kneeling in the trash, trying to shovel leftover food into his mouth with the stumps that were once his fingers. This was made even more challenging by the fact that someone had tied a cardboard mask over his face, perhaps to hide his deformed nose and mouth. For several seconds I stood staring at his face, rooted to the spot with horror. I didn't know what to do. Should I give him money? Help him up? His neighbors sitting nearby looked on, suspicious and unfriendly. It slowly dawned on me that I should go. The sick man turned away; he clearly didn't want to be seen like that. So, I went. I felt miserable, angry with myself. Why did I never know what to do in those kinds of situations? How could I be so incompetent?

In these moments, I just can't make a connection between this world and the world I call home; I simply can't understand why we live in such luxury while the people here live in misery. To my mind, there's absolutely no plausible reason why we have so much of everything, yet they lack the most basic resources. From my studies of economics and my work as an economic and financial journalist, I'm well aware of the many historical and socioeconomic explanations for our wealth and their poverty, but here in the slums, these theories become meaningless. Once again, I stand silently among the huts. It just makes no sense that we should have the choice of twenty-five different types of cold cuts at the local butcher while most people here live in such poverty. And why are we in the West so quick to come up with theories to explain and justify this misery? That's not to say that India hasn't seen huge socioeconomic improvements in recent years, yet here in the slums, it's hard to see any evidence for this. Standing here, it's a struggle to make sense of the life I have at home. I begin to question my own identity.

My thoughts are soon interrupted. A man approaches on a motorbike and wants to come past. I decide to make way for him. Gritting my teeth, I place one foot into the stinking sewage. The black filth curls between my toes—I'm wearing only light sandals—and it's all I can do to not let my disgust show. Suddenly, as I'm wiping the muck from my toes with a piece of paper, a little boy appears, thrusting a tin of water under my nose. From her hut, his mother smiles at me sympathetically. I nod a thank-you.

I stumble on through the slums in the searing midday heat until I suddenly find myself faced with a beautiful mountain scene; an invitingly cool river flows past shady palms, glistening in the sun. However, it's only a painted fantasy on a brick wall, a memory of paradise.

I'm just about to start making my way to the orphanage when a man calls out, "Madam, you're going the wrong way!" He tries to steer me back toward the Taj Mahal, but I instead point in the opposite direction, deeper into the slums, and ask him where that way leads. He shakes his head sadly. "There's nothing down there, madam," he says, adding, "Everything finished."

Chapter 3

HELP TO HELP THEMSELVES

Children shout and play in the crowded schoolyard—the same wild joyful noise I had heard on the phone at home when I made the appointment with the orphanage director, Mrs. Sudha. I look around eagerly for the entrance to her office. I have high hopes for this orphanage; after all, it's the only one that comes with a recommendation from some friends, who adopted a child from here years ago. I don't have this kind of endorsement for any of the other addresses on my list, and after all the rejection letters, I'm pinning all my hopes on Mrs. Sudha. She at least had been prepared to meet me, well aware of our intentions to adopt a child.

I warm to her at once, this little lady in dark glasses and a smart cotton sari, working away in her tiny office. Two women sorting letters ask me to wait a moment; Mrs. Sudha is on the telephone. The office is so small that they can't offer me a chair.

There's just enough room for their three desks and chairs, plus a fan that threatens to blow the papers off the desk. A framed poem hanging on the wall is the only clue to the adoptions that take place here:

Not flesh of my flesh,
Not bone of my bone
But still miraculously my own.
Never forget
For a single minute
You didn't grow
Under my heart
But in it.

Mrs. Sudha beams as I introduce myself, putting me so much at ease that I blurt out our adoption plans again, repeating what I'd already told her on the phone. I tell her that our social report is in the process of being prepared, and then, cautiously, I inquire about the orphanage.

"Oh, there's no orphanage here," she replies. "We place the children with foster parents nearby, but only as an absolute last resort." This is not at all the orphanage full of screaming babies I'd hoped for, but I try to keep my surprise to myself. As we sit down, I'm lost for words, which Mrs. Sudha notices.

"You see, poor as the people here are, we have to support them so that they can make it on their own. And with a little help, it can be done!" she tells me, confidently. I think back to my walk through the slums, just a few streets away from here. This office is helping the very people I saw there. They offer medical support, pay for countless children to go to school, and generally do everything they can to make sure families are able to stay together.

"There are so many women whose husbands have left them, who can barely provide for their children. Some of these women decide to give them away." Mrs. Sudha sighs, as if this fact always surprises her. Yet, she doesn't judge them for it. "We will always do everything in our power to prevent that," she continues, and offers me a glass of water.

"With medical support and help with their children's education from us, many of these women are able to keep their children. Once the children are able to read and write, they have every chance of getting themselves and their parents out of there." She waves a hand toward the slums.

As she explains the welfare program they are putting into place, I can't help but think of the neurotic mother with the cropped hair. In spite of her illness and her obvious, crippling poverty, she still had her son, who must have been five or six years old. I'm suddenly filled with admiration for that woman, for being able to support her son for all those years.

But how many other despairing mothers like her must there be? How many traumatized children?

"Even if a child is abandoned, we place them with Indian foster parents in the area as soon as possible. It's vital that these children remain in their social surroundings," Mrs. Sudha stresses. "We do the same with children who are neglected. Only where a mother makes it clear that she does not want to keep the child under any circumstances do we look for Indian adoptive parents."

The same goes for the babies given to them by unmarried mothers, she says, and of course I must know how catastrophic it was here for a young unmarried woman to find herself suddenly pregnant. "No girl will get a husband here once she has a child. It's over for her—no husband, no means of support. And she's brought shame upon her family. Unfortunately many parents still see things this way." Day in, day out, she tells me, young girls give birth in secret and give the babies up for adoption immediately afterward.

Just then, the phone rings and she has to interrupt our conversation. So far, everything she's told me fits with what I'd already learned about adoption in India. If a young mother leaves her baby at an orphanage to be put up for adoption, they must wait a few months in case she changes her mind. During this time, the mother has a legal right to demand the return of her child, no questions asked. Once this period is up, an orphanage can start looking for adoptive parents, but even then, they must be Indian. Only after every attempt has been made to find Indian parents can the orphanage apply for permission to open an adoption up to foreign parents. As a result, the vast majority of children who are available for foreign adoption have medical problems.

I can't help but admire this small, energetic woman for sticking to this policy with such determination and doing everything she can to help the women and children in her neighborhood. We could certainly adopt from here with clear consciences, I tell myself, because we would know that we were the child's only chance. We don't want to adopt a child who could have found parents that were just as good, or perhaps even better, in India. We don't want to tear a child away from his or her culture. I believe this can only be justified when there's no other way to help him or her. But then I think, *How sick of a child are we talking about? What would we be getting ourselves into?*

Full of anticipation, I wait for her to finish her call.

"You see, we're very proud to be able to help almost all of the children here. We only have to resort to foreign adoptive parents in a tiny number of special cases," Mrs. Sudha informs me with pride. I try to seem as enthusiastic as she is, but my heart sinks. She can see this.

"We do have a waiting list. We could put you on it," she suggests. "Then, when we have a child for you, we can let you know." I agree that I'd like that.

"How long would that take, roughly?" I ask tentatively.

"Oh, it's unlikely you'll get a child from here in under two years," she replies. There are other parents ahead of me on the waiting list. Her expression is serious, and she can see how disappointing this is for me.

I can hardly believe my ears—two years! Another two years. I've already waited years—first for a natural conception, then to conceive with hormone supplements, and finally to conceive via IVF. And now she's telling me I have to wait another two years, just like that. The disappointment is overwhelming. I'd honestly believed that here of all places, I had a real chance.

"Perhaps you should make inquiries in a few other places?" Mrs. Sudha offers. She's not just saying this to be nice. "The thing is, we're waiting for our license to be renewed; it's expired, you see. And with the best will in the world, we can't process adoptions without a license." I imagine all those months and years without a child. No, I can't wait that long.

I say a polite good-bye and remind her to put me on the waiting list, although both of us know full well that it will come to nothing.

Chapter 4

WE DON'T HAVE ANY CHILDREN!

In all honesty, it really doesn't matter which orphanage I visit next. I should have known that I wouldn't get a child handed to me on a silver platter at the very first address I visited.

The addresses come from a list put together by the Indian Ministry for Family Welfare for prospective adoptive parents. The orphanages on this list are the only ones that hold licenses allowing them to carry out international adoptions. I carry a copy with me at all times. I've already crossed off the names of those that sent me rejection letters; even so, there are still plenty left to try. With no referrals, recommendations, or connections to go on, the best I can do is to turn up unannounced and ask to speak to someone. So I decide to try one of the agencies I'd written to that hadn't replied to my letter.

It's an hour's taxi ride away through stifling traffic—an absolute torture in this scorching heat.

As we push our way in behind noisy trucks and buses, my patient taxi driver and I breathe in the diesel fumes. If there's not a huge bumper looming a few inches from my window, then there's smoky exhaust or a goods train with a leaky fuel tank. I take swigs from my plastic water bottle to try to wash the stale taste from my mouth, but before long, the water itself tastes like moldy dishwater.

Whenever we stop at a set of traffic lights, coughing children with matted hair squeeze their way between the cars, knock on the windshields with their dusty hands, and beg, egged on by their mothers who crouch lethargically on the pavement with babies on their laps. At one set of lights I see a toddler, perhaps three years old, standing on the road markings between two lanes of traffic flowing in opposite directions. He chatters away to himself while the traffic thunders around him, gesticulating with his little hands, completely unfazed by the huge trucks and buses roaring past just inches away. At the next crossing, a man pushes his stump of an arm through the window of my taxi, his eyes shine with a mixture of humility and bitterness. He's missing all the fingers on both hands; they appear to have been chopped off, perhaps the result of some horrific accident.

I can't help but feel sorry for him, so I give him some money. He takes the note between his stumps and holds them to his forehead in thanks. The taxi driver, on the other hand, seems less than impressed. After that, I roll up the window, telling myself I can't feed everyone in Mumbai, and I ignore the beggars at the next intersection.

One hour and countless coughing fits later, we pull up in front of a shabby tower block. The taxi driver gives me a questioning look, as if to ask whether I have any idea of where I'm trying to get to. But after a bit of poking around, and three dark, peeling stories higher, I find myself standing at the entrance to the "orphanage," which, in fact, looks more like a sparsely furnished office. It soon turns out that I'm in the wrong place at the wrong time. The disinterested Indian woman makes it pretty clear that I'm the last person she wanted to see.

At first, as I introduce myself politely and explain why I've come, she doesn't react at all. It's as if she hasn't heard me, even though I'm pretty sure she has a good command of English. She makes a point of shuffling the papers on her desk, trying to look busy. Then suddenly, she explodes.

"We don't have any children!" she exclaims. "You know, we don't give our children away—not even to the very best parents, like doctors from Ireland and Scotland."

I can't help but wonder why she thinks doctors from Ireland and Scotland would necessarily make the best parents. In any case, I wasn't aware that parents came in different categories, and find myself wondering which category Andreas and I would fall into. I start again, but she just talks over me.

"Thanks, but no thanks. We don't have any children for people like you."

I mention the letter I sent her some time ago.

"I get two letters from abroad every day," she snaps, trying to look busy again. "I stopped answering them long ago. You want a child? I can give you a child with a hole in the heart or a clubfoot!" I have half a mind to inquire about the child with the hole in the heart, but then I hesitate. There's no point. She's not interested. "The Indian government doesn't send children abroad anymore. Those times are gone," she rants.

Then, finally, I begin to understand. I can sense her resentment, her unwillingness, her rage, almost, toward me, this arrogant European who has just turned up out of the blue expecting to come away with a child. This takes exploitation and neocolonialism to a whole new level: first you wanted our cotton, and now you've come for our babies. I can almost see where she's coming from; I've seen the ads on the Internet. You only have to Google "adoption" and up pop lists of adoption agencies offering children from all over the world. Back at home, I remember surfing a website, popular with prospective adoptive parents. For many couples, it was clearly all about getting the youngest, healthiest baby as quickly and, of course, as cheaply as possible. This kind of parents really don't care whether the child's from China, Vietnam, Russia, or India. They just want a baby.

They're not interested in whether the child might have a chance if he or she stayed in his own country, and his cultural heritage doesn't factor into their plans either. They're also quite clearly in denial about the huge psychological impact that adoption has on a child. With that attitude, how can they possibly be prepared for the challenges of an international adoption? It's a recipe for disaster.

But I have neither the strength nor the energy to explain to this Indian woman that I'm different. I can't place my trust and my future in the hands of someone who dislikes me so intensely. I politely say good-bye, leaving her to sort her papers. She doesn't even reply.

I head back downstairs to the taxi, where I strike a big fat line through the address on my list. The driver notices my disappointment, so I explain to him why I'm asking him to ferry me all over Mumbai. It crosses my mind that he might now hate me, too. Quite the contrary, he's thrilled at the idea.

"That's such a kind thing you plan to do—to help a child! It's the best thing anyone can do in life," he exclaims in his broken English. But I wave his compliments away. He shouldn't be singing my praises. I'm hardly the Good Samaritan. No, a good dose of selfishness has influenced my decision to look for a child here. I make sure the taxi driver knows that the child will make Andreas and me happy, too.

"I'm helping the child, but the child will also be helping us. We'll all be happy. It's a situation that benefits everyone," I explain. He agrees, clearly hell bent on helping me any way he can. I can tell that he's a family man. He offers to drive me to a "proper" orphanage; he's sure I'd be able to adopt from there. I decide to take him up on this; after all, I'd like to see a "proper" orphanage.

Like the last place, it's "not far," which means another hour spent in noisy traffic, driving past building sites, slums, bridges, markets, saris, temples, and cows. The "proper" orphanage is another building that's seen better days, stained black and peeling from years of humidity, heat, and monsoons. I'm told the director is upstairs on the second floor, so the taxi driver and I climb the stairs to his office.

The whole place is so dark that I can barely see a thing. Yet the director's presence lights up the room. He's a tall, angular man, polite and calm. With great modesty, he explains that this is an orphanage for street children—for boys, to be precise—who were lost or had been given up by their parents. With that, he turns around and walks over to a parapet that overlooks the courtyard.

We look down onto an asphalt, covered yard where several youngsters are playing football, while others are sleeping, playing other games, or just hanging around the edge of the yard. Their clothes are clean, if shabby. They are all very thin, and there's not a single toy to be seen. "No one knows where all these children are coming from," the director says. This clearly troubles him, but I also sense that he is proud to be able to provide for these boys. "Here, they are safe, they have a place to sleep, and they are fed. We're even able to give them a basic education." I decide it's best not to ask about the "education." The poverty of the orphanage is plain to see. It's clear that the director is happy just to be able to feed these children.

Suddenly, I feel something wrap itself around my right leg. We break off our conversation, and I find myself looking down into the face of a little boy. His large, dark eyes glow back at me, somewhat feverishly. His face is gaunt, serious, and older than his years, and he smiles shyly at me, clutching my leg with his tiny hands. He can only be about three years old. He looks up at me so hopefully that it gives me a lump in my throat. I reach out and stroke his short black hair. Straight away, he grabs my hand. The director seems to have read my mind. "He was found a year ago at the station. We don't even know if he's from Mumbai. It may be that he came here by train from another town. He doesn't know himself."

I think back to the madness of the station—the rush to get to the trains pulling in, the crush of people, the running and shoving. Slowly, the platform empties, and some of the adults notice a little boy crying. In the chaos, who can say after the fact which train he arrived on, let alone where his parents have gone?

The director leads me through the bare rooms of the orphanage, through the dormitories with mats, blankets, and a few pallets. The little boy holds my hand tightly all the while. He seems so proud, as if he can hardly believe his luck. Gently, I ask the director what will become of him, and again, he seems to know what I'm thinking. "The boy stays here. We can't put him up for adoption; only his parents can do that. But they don't know where he is. Of course, it could be that they abandoned him."

This makes no sense to me. The little boy has already been in the orphanage for a year, and his parents have failed to find him. The director continues, "We have to assume that his parents are out there somewhere looking for him, and that means we can't give him up for adoption. It wouldn't be legal. Even if his parents never find him, or even if they aren't looking for him at all, we have to keep him here."

We've made our way back to the director's office as we talked. The little boy's hand is still in mine. I can hardly bear to let go of this shy little hand. Again and again the boy looks at me, pleadingly, almost as if he hopes that when we've finished talking, he'll be able to come home with me. I can't help but feel guilty. I ask if the children here have any toys—teddies perhaps. Teddies? The director turns to a young female employee and asks if she knows what a "teddy" is. I fix him with a stare.

"A teddy," I repeat, "a teddy to play with." The director and the woman look at me uncertainly and apologize. They're not familiar with the word *teddy*. I'm stunned.

The boy can tell that our conversation is nearly over. He clings to my salwar kameez and grips my pants tightly. I stare out at the courtyard, at the much older boys playing football, at the dark corridors, and imagine what life will hold for the boy, living here year after year. Carefully, I ask again if there's really no chance of adopting him.

"No." The director shakes his head and explains that the orphanage doesn't have an adoption license, not even for Indian adoptions. I have a feeling this orphanage for children who have lost their parents is just one of thousands across India. The children receive emergency care, but legal barriers and bureaucratic red tape deny them any chance of a new life.

It's so frustrating. I'm a mother who needs a child, and he's a child who needs a mother! We grasp each other's hands for a moment more…then the dream is shattered. I fight back the tears as I loosen his little hand from my clothing. I can hardly bear to look him in the eye. The director takes hold of the boy, and I hear him crying as I disappear down the stairs into the blackness below. I sit in the taxi, tears rolling down my face. What had the arrogant female director snapped at me earlier? "We don't have any children."

The taxi driver is watching me sheepishly in the rearview mirror. "Back to the hotel," I hear myself say. As if in a daze, I stare out at the rows of slum huts that line the roadside. It's rush hour, and we're creeping along at a snail's pace. The car is moving so slowly and the huts are so close to the curb that I can see into nearly every one. There's about ten feet between the huts and the traffic, and these ten feet are a whole world in themselves—a world where women try to cook with a can or two of water, if they cook at all.

I'm reminded of Ashok, a street boy who was once my guide around Old Delhi. I offered to buy him lunch, but he turned me down. He ate only three meals a week, he told me, and suppressed his hunger by chewing betel, skillfully spitting its red juice on street corners as we walked. He just couldn't get over how much I ate at each meal—three times a day at that!

The row of slum huts beside the street goes on and on. In the ten feet between the huts and the traffic, children play with old tin cans and plastic bottles while the elderly rest their weary bones on wooden pallets, all enveloped in a cloud of diesel gases. In these ten feet, men sleep like the dead, exhausted from day jobs that never earn them enough to feed their families.

I stare at a round-bellied young Bengal child who is standing beside the road screaming, while his mother tries to wash him with a can of water. And I think to myself that "luck" is a relative thing, indeed.

Near my hotel, I meet the cropped-haired woman again. She is lying curled up with her son under a sheet of plastic at the edge of the street. So deep is their sleep and so entwined are their bodies that not even the afternoon sun beating down on their heads can wake them.

Chapter 5

TEDDIES IN THE WINDOW

When I leave the next morning, the shack of the mother with her shaven head is empty. Only now do I realize how destitute her place really is: there is nothing more than sheets of plastic and blankets inside. The inside of another hut a few feet away looks more like a tiny living room, just seven square feet. Like all the other huts, this one is a construction of wood and plastic tarpaulins against the wall that runs between the railway tracks and the street, a strip of land that is only a few feet deep, yet offers just enough space for a few shacks. A picture of Ganesh is pinned on the wall inside the shack, and the floor and the area in front of the hut have been swept. In one corner, cooking pots have been stacked on top of each other, an onion sits on the lid of one. Otherwise the hut is empty.

I head to the bazaar near the hotel, where I buy three teddy bears to take to the next orphanage

I visit. I couldn't bear to face another poor child empty-handed, even if a teddy bear is all I can offer. And yet, I'm still not prepared for what awaits me today as I visit the next orphanage on my list.

This time it's a villa in a shady Mumbai side street lined with acacias. Several ceiling fans cool the office, where three elderly Indian ladies in saris stop their conversation as I enter. I have turned up unannounced, so as always I introduce myself, explain that I would like to adopt, and ask whether they can tell me more about international adoption. The women seem bored, totally disinterested, in fact. One of the ladies shuffles past me down a corridor and instructs a girl to come and talk to me. The girl is surprised, not at all prepared for the situation, and talks hesitantly about international adoption. It is obvious that she herself plays no part in the procedure at this orphanage. And then comes the familiar line: "We only very rarely have children with illnesses who we will send abroad," she tells me in her schoolgirl English.

I have the feeling she is only saying this to get rid of me, that the women are trying to avoid a conversation with me. I ask the young woman directly if I can look around the orphanage. She does not object.

She motions me to follow her. We climb a staircase to the second floor. A sudden stench surprises me—the acrid scent of urine. But the young woman is clearly used to it and continues down the corridor to a doorway. A wooden board is clamped in the doorframe, and I can see about ten children in the fairly dark room. The acacias in front of the building block out the sunlight, making it some time before I can see properly. Although the room is large, it is completely bare. The floor and walls are stone. The windows are barred.

Three little girls shake at the board in the doorway. Three dark little faces look at me, with hope.

"These are the two- to four-year-olds," I hear the young woman telling me. *So, even the children are put into groups with different categories*, I think.

The little girls take hold of my hand and pull so that I have to climb over the board into their room. They cling to me. One toddler babbles, "Mama, Mama." I fight to keep my composure. I expected Indian orphanages to be basic, simple places, but nothing like this.

As the children tug at me, I peer around the room. Only now do I notice the seven children lying at one end of the room, half naked on the stone floor. Three of them have managed to grab a corner of a baby's blanket that's far too small for them, but the others lie on the stone floor, huddled together in fetal position, some in a puddle of urine. The stench is terrible. Are they sleeping? I don't know, but they seem listless. I'm certain that two of them are just staring up at the ceiling. I'm struggling to cope.

Some of the toddlers have crept onto my lap. I put my arms around them, my eyes fixed all the while on the sleeping children. One of them taps his feet rhythmically in his sleep. I scour the room for toys—nothing. So I try to chat to the little ones, but they grab at my clothes, desperate to play. I sit there, waiting for a member of staff, for someone who's responsible for these children but who has perhaps just stepped out of the room for a while. However, no one comes. It dawns on me that apart from routine care, these children spend their days alone.

Just then, I remember my teddies and pull them out of my bag. But the young woman warns me, "All donations must be handed in downstairs."

I quickly put them away. There's obviously some reason why these children don't have toys, and it's clear they wouldn't get my teddies either. A feeling of uneasiness creeps over me. I detach myself from the little ones and step back over the board. I put on a brave face and play the moved, slightly naive Western tourist mommy.

And so the young woman leads me onward. We come to the newborn department. I thought babies cry a lot, but these are not crying...or not crying anymore. Rows of metal cradles lined with blankets stand under neon lights. It's only as I get closer that I can make out the tiny heads peeking out of the tightly swaddled bundles inside. Some of the babies are sleeping, others stare at the ceiling. Still others have rolled over, their heads up against the metal. None show any reaction.

An elderly worker of the orphanage smiles at me and points proudly at the babies, even though her duties probably only include feeding and changing soiled baby clothing. There's a pile of washed baby clothing on a table in the middle of the room.

I stroke one newborn on the cheek. The young woman from the office tells me that this baby has just arrived from the hospital and is only six days old. The baby opens its eyes grouchily. I had no idea anyone could look so untrusting at just six days old. The children here have obviously never been cuddled before. I feel guilty. What is our planet doing to its children?

So, here's where the babies are kept; this is where their life in the orphanage begins. How tiny they are! They can't even see properly yet, but already they're too much of a burden for others—unloved, rejected. Would it really have been such a terrible ordeal for the families of these little bundles to keep them and make sure they were fed and survived?

Next door is the department for babies up to three months old. I'm greeted by more rows of cots filled with more little parcels wrapped in blankets, but the parcels are larger this time, their heads rounder. A single baby is crying, but there's no reaction from the others, only blank stares. Two women are chatting in the corner of the room.

I go over to the cot with the crying baby, clearly writhing with pain in its blanket. *Perhaps it has colic?* I think. Neither of the women seems to care, though. I bend down over the screaming head and touch its cheek, talk to the little lost soul. The baby pauses, listens for a moment, and then, as if unable to process my attempts to soothe it, carries on screaming. I feel helpless, overwhelmed by the number of children, by the bleakness of this place, and it takes all my strength to control myself.

Then I notice the playpen in the back of the room. Inside are two little boys, perhaps two years old, just sitting there with no toys or blankets. I go over and touch one of the boys' faces. Immediately, he grabs my hand, and his face lights up, his eyes shining with pride. He takes my hand and holds it to his cheek, grasping it tight, like a trophy. He is clearly overwhelmed at being allowed to hold a hand. He revels in the sensation of my hand against his cheek, can hardly believe this is happening to him, and laughs with joy. I have to press my lips together and stare at the ceiling to stop myself from sobbing. At that moment I catch sight of teddies not unlike the ones I had brought with me, still wrapped in their plastic packaging; someone has tied them up high on the bars of the window.

The young lady takes me to the next room, the area for babies over three months. There are around twenty children here, all lying half naked in fetal position, either on the stone floor or on a blanket. Some lie in urine; the smell burns in my nostrils. Some of the children are sleeping, while others stare silently at the ceiling or into air. In one corner of the room, two older children with profound physical and mental disabilities lie on the floor, also half naked.

Most irritating of all are the two female employees standing nearby, presenting the children almost proudly, as if this was the way things should be, as if it was normal. A third woman gives me a helpless look as she rubs the back of a critically ill child lying on the floor. The child is motionless, as pale as death with tired eyes. *That child needs to go to a hospital*, I think, but I keep my comments to myself. I don't want to meddle. After all, I don't know how things are here, and from my Western perspective, it would be so easy to judge.

I'm shown two children who are potential candidates for international adoption. One has a bloated stomach and a bulge on his navel. Both children are lying, like the others, on the floor. A toddler in a playpen catches my eye. She is playing with a broken toy car and babbling to herself. I walk past the rows of playpens and cots in a daze.

Suddenly, I come to a halt. A young child is rocking back and forth on her knees. Professionals call this behavior "rocking" or "self-soothing." We have all these scientific terms for the attempt a desperately lonely child makes to calm him-/herself—"hospitalism" is another one. I stroke the girl's back. Nothing. She keeps on rocking in a trance. I prod her gently. Still nothing. She doesn't react in any way. I bend down to her level, stroke her arms, and talk to her. After a while, she raises her head. It's as if a fog has lifted from her eyes. She stops rocking and looks at me full of wonder. She touches my hand and my watch. As I keep talking to her, she begins to glow. She is so surprised and happy to be able to touch a human hand—just a hand, mind you, not a doll or chocolate or jelly beans. No, just a simple hand.

She smiles at me, and it's clear that she knows only loneliness and despair. She already knows more than

I do. I'd love nothing more than to hold her and stop her from falling back into that void. But as soon as I leave, she starts her monotonous rocking again. I cry, not just for these children, but also because I'm afraid that there could well be many, very many, orphanages like this one and many children like these. I hate to think that this orphanage is not an isolated case.

Passing through the office on my way out of the building, I spot a plastic bag under a desk packed with rattles, teddies, and toys. The women are still chatting away. The children will not get my teddies.

Back in the taxi, a wave of guilt washes over me, not because of the teddies, but because of the children. Because this is where we should be adopting from. From this orphanage, where children are suffering the most, where they are neglected, are sick from loneliness and distress, their souls shriveled to nothingness. But I'm just not brave enough to do it. I know that these children carry deep mental scars from their time here, that they will battle with the consequences of this traumatic experience for many years, perhaps forever. I'm afraid that if I adopt from here, tears, worries, and despair would be a certain part of our lives. I would already have failed before I'd even begun.

My phone call to Andreas that evening is a long one. I tell him about the day and pour my heart out to him. I just can't get the images of the orphanage out of my head. But Andreas feels the same way as I do, and so I cross another address off my list. Years later, I will discover that I can't erase these children from my memories, and I will wonder if I shouldn't have been a little braver after all.

Chapter 6

BUYING A BABY BOY

Every time I leave my hotel, he's there, this old man, sitting under one of the trees near the station. He has not even got a shack—nothing. Scrawny and haggard, he huddles at the side of the road and stares into space. The throngs of people on the streets, the motor rickshaws, honking cars, and the rumbling of the trains on the tracks—he seems to be oblivious to them all.

Not far from his tree begins the row of slum huts packed along the wall between the railway tracks and the street. The shaven-headed woman's shack is empty again, but her son is crouching in front of a neighbor's hut with another child. They take turns eating from a bowl of rice, licking their fingers with pleasure each time they pop a clump of rice into their mouths. The mother, whose hut it is, sits with them, feeding some of the rice to the baby on her lap, and from time to time they all help themselves to water.

I walk a few feet down the street, past the huts, to the Catholic orphanage next to my hotel. After spending a week dragging myself back and forth across Mumbai, it's a relief that I don't have far to go to get to the next place on my list.

"Just wait fifteen minutes, please. The sisters are praying. Soon they will finish," the porter tells me from behind the door, which he has opened a crack.

It's such a hot day that I decide to cross the road and wait outside the shop selling drinks, where I buy a lemonade. I am just about to sit down in the shade when a young Indian woman beckons me over.

"Come sit next to me," she says in broken English, throwing me a smile and patting the bench beside her. I'm struck by how pretty she is with her white teeth, proud eyes, and a heavy braid; her lime green sari contrasts with her dark skin. On her lap sleeps a baby. "My baby boy," she explains. "I'm too dark, but he is fair," she adds proudly. It's clear that she's here with her sister, a neatly dressed young woman who has a more serious air about her and is looking after a little girl—perhaps two years old—sitting in a yellow frilly skirt and sipping a soft drink.

The prettier sister comes right out and asks me why I knocked on the door of the orphanage, so

I cautiously explain our situation and tell her that we're hoping to adopt. I am quick to add that as foreigners, we're most likely to get a child with medical problems.

"We want to adopt, too. Well, she does," says the beauty, gesturing toward her sister. "But only a boy."

"Why only a boy?" I ask.

"Because otherwise her husband's family line will end, and the family name will die out," she explains. She then translates a little of our conversation for her sister. I ask her more about this.

"My sister has a daughter only," she tells me, nodding toward the little girl, who is still playing with the drink bottle. "When she marries, she will leave home and move in with her husband's family." I recall learning that many Indian girls are still taught that they are merely guests in their parents' houses, and that where they belong is in the family and home of their future husband.

"When the daughter goes, there will be no one left to care for the house and family or to carry on their name. So another family will take over, more likely than not, the in-laws or other relatives," the beauty explains.

Her sister gives us a questioning look; she can't follow our conversation.

"It is different with a son," the beauty continues, stroking her boy's head. "He'll get married and bring his wife home to live with us, and life will go on as normal. That's why we need a boy for my sister." She tells me quietly that since the girl, her sister has not been able to conceive another child.

Finally the beauty asks me the question I've been expecting: "Do you want a boy, too?"

"No, I'd prefer a girl. Well, actually I don't mind. But I'd be just as happy with a girl," I stress. I don't want to come across as the rich, arrogant Western woman, here to satisfy her desire for a child at the locals' expense.

"A girl? But why?" she asks in amazement. But before I can answer, she has already started translating for her sister, who then smiles at me, relieved. "A dark child would be fine, too," I add. More relief on their part—we're no competition.

The beauty goes on to complain about the orphanage. They make everything so complicated and ask too many questions; they even want to send someone to your house to see how you live so that they can write a report, she tells me with horror. As far as she's concerned, there are too many questions, and the whole thing takes far too long. It could be a year before the adoption goes through. They will not put up with this!

Then the beauty reveals her plan. "You see the gate to the orphanage over there?" she asks me with a nod toward the gate. "It will open again soon. We're going to sit here all day and wait for any woman who wants to give her baby to the orphanage," she explains. There were constantly women visiting the orphanage to leave their babies with the sisters, the beauty knows. "We just wait until a woman comes along with a baby boy. Then we buy the baby from her before she has a chance to give him to the orphanage." She tells me this and cuddles her own baby boy, who has just woken up and is blinking sleepily.

I am stunned, most of all with how casually she describes her idea of child trade. "And how much are you prepared to pay for the baby?" I probe.

"Between one thousand and two thousand rupees, depending on his condition," comes the prompt reply. I do some mental arithmetic; that's thirty to fifty dollars for a child.

"Yesterday a poor woman even wanted to give us her little girl for free." The beauty laughs. "But, of course, we don't want a girl." She goes on to say that the woman left the child at the orphanage after that.

I still can't quite believe my ears and ask her again if she really would pay for a baby.

"Of course," she confirms. "How much are you planning to pay?"

I can see in her eyes what she expects my answer to be. As a rich Western tourist, I'll probably pay a huge sum.

"Nothing. I'm not paying anything. Otherwise I'll end up in prison," I answer. She seems perplexed, and asks me again. Perhaps she has misunderstood? I repeat that it's illegal to pay for a child, that this is called child trafficking, whether it's in India, Europe, America, or anywhere else. She furrows her brow and discusses this with her sister.

"But you want a child! A child brings so much joy and saves the whole family. You have to be prepared to pay for that; you can't expect to get it for free!" she scolds. "You don't get anything for free."

I'm not sure how to respond to her raw logic. I talk about human dignity and child trafficking and international law, but she's having none of it. She's lost all respect for me, the rich Western woman who comes to India expecting everything for free, and a child of all things!

I change the subject. "Do you know anyone who's bought a baby this way?" I ask with interest. I want to know if anyone has been successful with this plan of buying a child in front of the orphanage.

"Oh, yes," she replies. The fact that she's waiting here so confidently seems to confirm this.

Across the street, the gate of the home swings open. We look at each other, and the beauty smiles, giving me a nod of encouragement. I stand up. When I look back after a few steps, she is smiling at me with what almost looks like pity.

I walk over to the gate, squeeze myself through the gap between the iron doors, and find myself in a different world. The noise, dirt, and commotion of the street are left behind, and in front of me lies a neatly swept courtyard. Rows of potted plants line the walls, and on the edge of the yard, among a few palms and bushes, there's even an old swing, a slide, and a merry-go-round.

I look up toward the sound of children, which carries down from one of the windows on the second floor of the pink-painted building, while from the first floor, the cries of younger children and babies spill out into the yard. In a corner, I discover scores of tricycles and baby walkers. A statue of Maria stands in an ornamental garden in front of the office building.

Now the porter is waving me toward the office, where I wait awhile. Religious pictures adorn the walls: Jesus with his halo, the pope. Then, on an office cabinet, I notice the photos taped to the iron door: Indian children in the garden; at the swimming pool; on the beach in France; in the snow in Switzerland; in their pajamas, tucked in bed with a teddy; with their little brothers and sisters on the carpet in an apartment somewhere in Europe; on a swing; and in a paddling pool. Little faces stare into the camera—curious, surprised, amused.

I'm still looking at the photos when an Indian nun walks into the office and introduces herself as Sister Lena. Dressed in a starched cotton sari with a silver cross on the shoulder, she sits down and listens to me after greeting me warmly in good English.

"I need to tell you that we give most of the children here to Indian parents. Almost 90 percent of them remain in India. The only children we send abroad are children with illnesses and children with dark color. They will not be adopted here," she tells me. "And they're almost always girls."

"I know, but I'm willing to adopt a child with illness or one with dark skin," I stress. I know this is my only chance. The nun nods thoughtfully.

"Has an official home study report already been completed back in Europe? Are your papers ready?" she asks.

Excitedly, I fish out the letter from our social worker back home. It confirms that our home study is complete and proves that the adoption preparations are progressing well on the European side. I push the letter across the desk toward her. She reads it.

"As a rule, we send all our overseas adoptions to Switzerland, France, or Italy; other orphanages send their children to other countries," she tells me. She must mean the other orphanages run by the Catholic order. All the same, the sister hasn't completely turned me down. She isn't as unfriendly as the workers at some other orphanages have been. She hesitates.

"I'll need to speak to Kolkata first and ask them if we can take on your case," she decides, handing the letter back to me. "Could you come back in a few days?"

"Yes, of course," I confirm politely. Her response gives me hope. Perhaps the head office in Kolkata will allow the sisters here in Mumbai to take on our case. A child from Mumbai! Yet I don't let my excitement show. I remind myself that I mustn't get my hopes up.

"Do you think I could see the orphanage?" I ask.

"Yes, of course." She smiles and beckons me to come with her. "You'll need to take off your shoes," she tells me, pointing at my sandals.

Barefoot, I follow her as she leads me into one of the wings of the orphanage. It's a hallway, where a warm breeze blows through the barred windows. Even here in the passageway, the cries of children can be heard. Sister Lena asks a younger nun, Sister Maria, to show me around. She is petite, with a great sense of inner peace and confidence radiating from her. She is obviously proud of her work.

Sister Maria leads me to the door of the room where the newborns live. Through the fly screen, I can see the little cradles packed closely together. I can even see an incubator in the corner. Every cradle holds a baby, wrapped in blankets in spite of the heat. The linen is fresh. The room is simple, but it's clean and doesn't stink, quite the opposite, in fact. Over on a table, a female staff member powders a baby and puts him in a new diaper. Next to her sits another woman, who is holding two infants in her arms and rocking them back and forth. Sister Maria explains that I'm not allowed into the room for reasons of hygiene.

Instead, she lets me into the next room, where most of the noise is coming from; it houses the babies up to six months old. Here, too, the rows of beds are packed, but the bed linen is fresh and each cot contains a toy or rattle. Fly screens cover the windows, and mobiles hang from the ceiling, drifting in the breeze. Pictures of toys, cats, teddies, and mountain views decorate the walls. In every cot there lies a baby, crying, gurgling, sleeping, playing, or screaming. Two girls are crouched on the floor; each holds two babies on her lap and is giving them bottles, talking to the children and rocking them. The girls are employed by the sisters, and in spite of the noise and crying, seem relaxed.

At a table laid out neatly with fresh cotton towels, powder, cream, baby oil, and medicine, a woman is putting a toddler into a clean dress, throwing the dirty washing into one of the nearby bins. *What a contrast to the shabby orphanage*, I think, hoping that that grim place was an isolated case after all.

Sister Maria leads me up a flight of stairs, past a picture of Maria, to the first floor, where a sister—an "earth mother" type—has her hands full with a group of small children. She laughs proudly as scores of toddlers tug and tear at her sari. Sister Martha is responsible for the children who are likely to be adopted by foreign parents soon, as well as some children the orphanage hasn't been able to place. Like the others, this room contains around twenty cots pushed up against each other and arranged in rows. The room and the beds are painted sky blue, and here, too, fly screens cover all the windows while fans maintain air circulation.

A toddler sits or stands in nearly every bed. One boy bears the scar from an operation on his cleft lip. Some of the older children look sickly; others appear disabled. I notice a child with deformed legs playing with a ball. Two young female employees change the babies' diapers and the bed linen. Again, this room doesn't smell bad, in spite of the number of children. Everything seems clean, if simple—almost humble, I decide. I know this is the right orphanage.

Out in the hall I notice two children who have been affected by polio and are feeling their way unaided along the windows in wooden walking frames. An old woman sits behind them, sewing on a Singer machine. Several children, perhaps between three and six years old, are playing in the hallway. As soon as they see us, they charge toward us, and they, too, tug at Sister Martha's clothing. They snuggle up to the nun and cling to her. The sister laughs, sweeps them up in her arms, and gives them cookies. Surrounded by children, she cuts a motherly figure, and it's clear that she enjoys her role.

She explains that the orphanage has around 120 children in its care and that these are not only children from Mumbai, but also from other areas of Maharashtra state, for example, from Amravati, an inland town.

Cautiously, I ask Sister Martha what kinds of children do people leave at the orphanage.

"They're nearly all newborns, brought here by their mothers when they're just a few days or weeks old," she tells me as she takes me back down the stairs to the newborn room. "I'm sure you know, it's hard for girls here when they have a child and aren't yet married. It ruins their chances of ever finding a man and getting married. So they bring their babies here. It's rare that children are given up for adoption simply as a result of poverty."

"How old are the children when they go to their new parents?" I ask.

She can tell what I'm thinking and says, "The children who go for international adoption are one to two years old. Indian cases move faster, and the children are younger." Children who are already a few years old when they arrive at the orphanage are one-off cases, she tells me, usually found by the police.

I change the subject.

"Is it true that mothers sometimes try to sell their children?"

She looks at me in surprise.

"Absolutely, but we won't pay a single rupee for a child. We have a saying: 'A child is a gift from God, and we are giving it back to Him.'" She sighs. We go back into the courtyard and retreat under the shade of the trees. It's baking hot in the midday sun.

"The mother does have two months to decide whether she would rather keep her child after all. During this time, she can pull her child out of the orphanage without giving us a reason," the nun says. "Sometimes the mothers realize that some hospitals will pay money for an infant and come to us asking for their babies back. We have no choice but to honor this, although we know that the mother will sell the baby at the nearest hospital," she adds with a bitter look. "Some hospitals will pay a hundred dollars for a baby. Of course, this is illegal." Again, I'm amazed at how openly the subject is discussed here.

I would have liked to say good-bye to Sister Lena, but she has just greeted an Indian couple and is ushering them into her office. So I promise Sister Maria that I will be back in a week. As I cross the yard, the children wave after me from the window up on the second floor.

I squeeze myself back through the gap in the gate and walk into the street, straight into the arms of the beauty, who is negotiating with a woman. I can't believe my eyes. The woman has a tiny newborn in her arms. I can't understand a single word of the conversation except for one: *charge*. My curiosity gets the better of me. I lurk on the other side of the street and wait. Finally the beauty and her sister come over to me, deep in conversation. Then the beauty turns to me.

"That woman is poor and can't afford to raise her child, but she says she won't give him away. She just wants help and money from the orphanage." Both sisters seem disappointed. Ten minutes later, the woman leaves the orphanage, still holding her baby, and disappears. The beauty and I say our farewells, wishing each other luck in our different quests for a child. In the morning, mine will lead me to New Delhi. In my luggage, I have a letter that makes a strange promise.

Chapter 7

THE THOUSAND-DOLLAR BABY

More and more birds circle in the morning sky over New Delhi. From the lawn of the Hotel Imperial, I can hear their cries. I am having my breakfast on the terrace. My waiter serves me tea while the gardeners water the plants in the flower beds and brass pots on the terrace. It is already warm, but an umbrella protects me from the sun.

I enjoy the hotel's colonial splendor, the gardens shaded by king palms. After the ordeal in Mumbai, I'm happy to relax in this luxury for a while, watching the staff set up lounge chairs around the swimming pool. The hotel is an oasis of calm, while just on the other side of the wall, traffic is roaring past on one of the main avenues leading to Connaught Circle, New Delhi's central roundabout.

I am exhausted from my stay in Mumbai. Over the last few days I have visited even more orphanages in Mumbai, traveling by train or taxi in the traffic, getting dusty and filthy; I seem to have a permanent cough from the diesel fumes. The visits were all equally dismal. The orphanages were similar, and the answer was always the same: adoption only after two or three years on the waiting list, if at all.

It all fitted in with the negative replies from the orphanages I had filed away at home. Just one letter had filled me with some hope as I took it out of the mailbox. The stamp showed it originated from New Delhi. It was a reply from a doctor, to whom I had written a few months before. I had been given her address by a couple that I had found with the help of an adoptive parents' group. The couple had already adopted a baby from this doctor in New Delhi.

"You want a baby, a very young baby? Then you need to contact this doctor," the woman had urged me during a phone call.

Now, again, I hold the reply from this doctor in front of me—handwritten, no formal letterhead. "I am sure you will be delighted to hear that we have already chosen a child for you," I read, still unable to believe my eyes.

This doctor is offering me a child, although our home study and adoption papers were not even completed when I contacted her, let alone sent off to the orphanage or the Indian authorities. I had not even put a letter from my social workers into the mail. The Indian doctor does not even know who we are. In her letter, she nevertheless asks me to bring whiskey, thermal underwear (winter nights in New Delhi are cold), blush, and lipstick, and she promises to pay me for the items once I visit her. Out of curiosity, I have decided to track this doctor down while I'm in New Delhi to visit other orphanages.

The hospital is in the city of Delhi in a building with signs at the entrance listing the medical services offered—a range of gynecological examinations among others. I can tell from the number of visitors that the clinic is busy, and it seems well equipped. Asking for directions, I eventually find myself face to face with a young woman, the senior doctor's daughter. She leads me along the hospital corridors to her mother, a tall lady in a sari, surrounded by a cloud of perfume.

The senior doctor welcomes me, seemingly overjoyed. She loves giving orders to the staff and holding their attention. Then she takes me to her private house, located next to the clinic. The living room, where we sit on plush sofas, is furnished in Western style. A painting on the wall shows horses galloping through waves on a moonlight beach.

I decide not to beat around the bush and quickly get out my plastic bag with the whiskey, blush, lipstick, and thermals. The doctor opens the bag, inspects the underwear, and indeed pays what I had spent on the shopping. I notice her red fingernails and her perfume again. The atmosphere is very matter of fact, and I have the feeling that we are watching each other, sizing each other up, the way business people do.

The doctor doesn't beat around the bush either; surprisingly quickly, she offers me this child again. She explains that adoptions from the hospital are officially carried out through a nearby orphanage. The orphanage is on the list of licensed orphanages approved by the Indian government for overseas adoption, she tells me, and the children live there.

"I only keep the children for overseas adoption here. Conditions aren't so good over there, and I can care for the children better here," she says, taking the whiskey out of the bag. "I can show you the child now," she continues. She waits for my joyful response, but she notices my cautious reaction. "Parents from everywhere are coming to me for adoption," she says proudly, fetching a letter from her desk. "Read this. You can write down the parents' address and check with them. They are in the process of adopting a little girl from here; I will show her to you also."

I take the letter and begin to write down the address, but at the same time, I scan the contents of the writing. I come across less-than-reassuring sentences such as "...unfortunately we cannot amend our papers" and "...would it be better to put my husband's age down as thirty-eight than forty-five?" I can already tell that I won't be adopting from here, but I am interested to find out how far the doctor will go.

"Where do the babies come from?" I ask.

"From young girls. They got pregnant out of wedlock—not married; they give birth in my hospital and then leave the baby here. It's my private clinic," she explains proudly.

"Do you pay for the children?" I ask bluntly. She hesitates with her answer and bites her lip.

"That depends on the girl's financial situation. We don't ask girls to pay for the delivery or their stay in the hospital, though; that is free," says the doctor. Somehow I get the feeling the clinic most probably pays the very poor women nothing, because they're just glad to leave the child at the clinic. Then again, maybe she does offer other families money for their babies if they're shrewd enough to ask.

"Don't you have to offer these babies to Indian adoptive parents first?" I press her further.

"Yes, but we put them off and tell them we haven't got any children or that they will just have to wait."

"But the authorities usually only approve foreign adoptions for children with illnesses or those with very dark skin, don't they?" I counter. She has moved on to the blush and lipstick.

"Oh, we just tell them there are medical problems with the child, even if that is not true," she says matter-of-factly. I am stunned by her chutzpah. "Then we get the *clearance*," she adds, by which she means the government approval to put a child up for overseas adoption. "We don't often have problems. Sometimes you get young girls working for the authorities; they are always so honest and diligent." She sighs. But she adds that normally the authorities don't make any trouble.

I grow braver and try to find out how far she will go. "How much should I pay for the child?" I know that it is illegal to even ask this question, yet the doctor doesn't hesitate for a moment.

"A thousand dollars," she replies. "But you don't pay until the child is out of the country. That is to say, we can't do that sort of thing beforehand." She does not mention that adopting directly from a hospital is strictly against the law in India and that, of course, her hospital does not have an adoption license. Instead she lists the administrative costs of an adoption, the solicitor's fees, the cost of the child's medical care and stay in the hospital. Compared to other Indian orphanages, the costs are excessive and run into thousands of dollars.

I pretend to want to see the child, so we go back into the hospital. In one of the rooms, the doctor flips open a file and runs her finger down a list of names and dates of birth. She then motions to one of the nurses to fetch a baby. When the nurse returns from the next room with an orphan in her arms, there is irritation. A discussion follows, and it seems that the women have different babies in mind. The nurse disappears again and comes back with another child, a pretty, sweet little baby—the Thousand-Dollar Baby.

"She's six months old. She was born premature, but she's in good order, pretty, and healthy." It's the senior doctor's sales pitch. The nurse cuddles the little one, who peers out from her blanket with curious dark eyes. I can hardly believe it, but I know there are countless Western parents who would not waste a second if they were in my shoes. It can be that easy.

In a nearby room, the nurses show me five more children in cots; all these children are reserved for overseas adoption to Europe and the United

States. But these children don't look happy. They are pale, sickly, and lethargic, and they barely react when I speak to them. The senior doctor notices my concern.

"You know, the orphanage isn't that good. That's why I bring the children here for a few weeks. I can't keep them here all the time because adoptions take place through the orphanage, so they have to spend most of their time there."

I say good-bye to the doctor, remain vague about the Thousand-Dollar Baby, and stop "over there" at the orphanage to have a look. A sorry scene meets my eyes. Too many children are packed into the rooms. The lack of caretakers and all the screaming is stressing out the children. Now I understand why the doctor was so embarrassed when I expressed an interest in seeing the orphanage and asked for directions. But I don't care; when I get home I will write *her* a letter turning down her offer of adoption.

I am unaware of what I would later learn from the married couple whose letter I saw: the social worker and the solicitor who were employed to work on the adoption were relatives of the senior doctor. They also told me that things didn't end with the list of expenses. During the adoption the doctor and her relatives demanded more and more money, always threatening that the adoption would not go ahead otherwise and the child would not arrive. Only after receiving the money would they insist that adopting directly from a hospital was illegal after all. I would only discover all of this when I visit the couple a year later, and I will only meet them and the daughter they acquired through the doctor once. They are not interested in further contact and clam up when the conversation turns to the Indian hospital. It is obvious to me that they did not ask too many questions at the time, and now they don't want to be reminded.

I follow my list of addresses, and on the same day, visit an orphanage run by the Church of North India. The director of the place shakes his head wearily when I talk to him about adopting. "You'll have to wait at least four years for a child. Even my waiting list for Indian parents is long," he says, pointing to a chart that he has pinned up on the wall of his tiny office. It shows that Indian parents who want to adopt a boy will have to wait for two years; for couples looking for a girl, it is six months. "You see, the problem is that more and more young mothers are selling their children on the black market. There they can get some money. A hundred dollars is a lot for a poor woman who doesn't know how else she'll get by." He seems to have sympathy for the women. "That's a lot of money. The women think, 'If I give away my child, I may as well give it to someone paying for the child.'" He seems almost resigned.

"Because more and more women are selling the children, fewer children can be legally adopted, and parents will just have to wait even longer." The problem is plain to see. The longer the parents have to hold out, the more frequently couples will bypass legal adoption and just get themselves a child illegally, because it is quicker and there is less red tape. Still, the man is bitter about his situation.

"We receive money from a German church organization," he says with a snort. As a German myself, I instantly recognize the name of that well-known charity. "But the people in charge don't want us to use the money to help prostitutes and their children, even though that is one of the biggest problems here. They say they won't give money to prostitutes." He curses the religious organization that makes senseless demands about how the money should be spent. "They do not want us to give children into overseas adoption! They say all children should be adopted in India. But nobody will tell me what to do with children with illnesses or handicaps or children nobody here wants to adopt."

He says he's had enough. He rails against unrealistic projects that he says the German aid organization wants to finance. They blow the money on festivals in the villages just so they can say it was used for "community initiatives," he claims. He has nothing good to say about the German organization. As a consequence of their behavior, he sends the children that he is able to put up for overseas adoption to the Netherlands or Scandinavia because he prefers the politics of the charities run by the churches there. "Those who have sensible foreign aid policies and give us more money get the children," he adds matter-of-factly. We have a good chat and drink tea, and in the end I leave—without being put on the waiting list.

Back in the hotel, I am exhausted. My cough from the smog and traffic has gotten worse; the dust and sweat of Delhi cling to my body. All I want is the swimming pool in the shade of palm trees and a cup of tea. I go to the pool, drift in the clear water, and feel as though my troubles are being washed away. I plunge my head into the water again and again, cooling off, and then swim a few strokes and float along on my back. The afternoon sun shimmers through the king palms and the birds are still circling in the sky. A waiter places a tray with a silver teapot beside my lounger. He has covered the bowl of melon so it doesn't attract the crows, which sit in the palms and on the roofs; they caw and head straight for the little side tables if someone leaves the lid off the sugar pot.

As I enjoy my tea, a new family at the swimming pool catches my attention: a blond couple with an Indian girl, around twelve years old, and a little

Indian toddler, perhaps around three years old. The parents stand proudly beside their loungers and are watching their elder daughter, who is holding the toddler in her arms. Carefully, the big sister sets the toddler down on the lawn. The little one grasps her sister's hand, and they both walk slowly toward the pool. As the little girl stares curiously into the water and clings on to her big sister's legs, I suddenly realize that the toddler is newly adopted and has only just come out from an orphanage. It is probably the first time she's seen a pool, grass, palm trees, lounge chairs, and swimsuits. Even walking on grass must be unfamiliar to her, because until now she's only known the stone floor of the orphanage or its sandy courtyard.

Then all of a sudden the little one turns round and trots slowly but determinedly toward the exit of the hotel. She doesn't look back once, although her new father is hurrying after her. Before she can disappear toward the street, he grabs her, picks her up, and brings her back to the family. Her mother, a Swede like her husband, is relieved.

"At least she slept right through last night," she tells me. The little one was found over a year ago at a railway station, left behind, perhaps on purpose. For six months the orphanage was required to place ads in newspapers and flyers in railway stations. They had to search for her parents. After this, the adoption process began and was expected to take five months. A year later, the Swedish family was allowed to adopt her. The mother tells me that the orphanage works with only Scandinavia for overseas adoptions.

I envy her, yet I'm happy for her. I ask myself if I'll ever get that far, if I'll ever experience the moment when I can show my child what grass is, what trees are.

Shortly afterward, we all join the other guests in the pool. The twelve-year-old has succeeded in gently getting the little one used to the water, and she carries her slowly down the steps to the pool, standing with her in the flat part of the shallow end. Nearby, another Indian girl is frolicking wildly in the water, sloshing, snorting, and diving; she is a good swimmer and splashes back and forth, scaring the little one, who has only just been brave enough to put her legs in the water.

"Would you mind swimming where it's a little deeper? The little one is still a bit frightened," I ask.

She is furious at this. "Well, I do actually mind! It's sunny over there and I'm not going home dark!" she says, throwing a disapproving glance at the twelve-year-old. Only then do I notice that the shallow end of the pool is in the shade of the palm trees, while the other part of the pool is in the glaring sun. It is obvious that the girl avoids swimming in the sun in order to avoid becoming darker, because her complexion is rather fair.

In India, large sections of the population still subscribe to the notion that fair is beautiful. It has long been part of Indian culture that fair complexion has been a symbol of divine beauty, of purity, of higher caste and a better social status. Many Indians with a dark skin color are still discriminated against today, beginning with adoption. In India, a child's dark skin color is recognized by the authorities as reason enough to put a child up for overseas adoption, even if the child is perfectly healthy. That is exactly how the staff at the orphanage in Mumbai explained it; it is just one side of the subtle racism that exists within the subcontinent. Suddenly I can put the swimmer's scornful glance at the Swedes' twelve-year-old daughter into context. The Indian daughter of the Swedish family stands at the poolside now, blissfully ignorant of her beauty, waiting to dive head first into the pool; droplets of water glisten on her black skin. It does not even cross her mind that someone could have a problem with her color here in India, in her homeland. Later I see her sunbathing in the afternoon sun, happily slurping a milkshake.

Chapter 8

IN THE DESERT

Drought-stricken land stretches into the glistening sunlight. I have left New Delhi and traveled out into the countryside, toward Gujarat in western India. Much of the land here is desertlike, dotted with thorny bushes in some places and covered with dry cotton fields in others. Drought envelops the little town on the edge of the desert where my train stops. I find myself standing in the street, wondering what to do next. My mechanical camera is broken—the film is stuck, the transport jammed. The man in the camera shop shakes his head; he has no idea how to fix it. Then, on a scrap of paper, he draws me directions to Mr. Rahoul, the local camera repairman. I trudge down alleyways in the heat until at last I find myself in front of a wooden door.

The door is open, and I can see into a neatly swept yard. A few potted plants stand in the shade. There's no one around, but as I step into the yard, a woman's voice calls out. Shortly afterward I'm greeted by Mr. Rahoul, a slender, elegant man. I show him my camera, and he invites me to follow him. We climb a staircase to an attic room. He ducks and I follow him into the room. It's fairly dark, but by the light of two lamps, I can soon make out a well-organized workshop. There's a table with bowls full of miniature tools—tiny brushes, tweezers, and screwdrivers. Over in the corner, I notice a darkroom, where another wooden table holds several old cameras.

We speak very little. He quietly inspects my camera and then reaches for his monocle and tiny tools. He begins to take it apart piece by piece. As he dismantles the body with experienced hands, he explains how reliable mechanical cameras are. Somewhere a dog barks, and someone walks past the house. The sound of footsteps fades into the distance. I'm enjoying the peace and the man's concentration as he works, and the stillness, breathing through the house, away from the heat outside. Time seems to stand still. I could watch him forever.

Eventually he puts the pieces back together and, finally, looks up, smiling quietly as the film transporter lets out the familiar sound of mechanical excellence. I want to pay him. I point to the rupee notes in my hand, but he pretends not to notice and nods, "No problem." Then he leads me back onto the street, where, with a bow, he thanks me as if it was I that had done him the favor instead of the other way around. *How much have we lost back home?* I think.

I manage to find a rickshaw driver, who, after a little searching, brings me to the orphanage in this desert town. It's certainly the prettiest one I've visited so far, with courtyards full of bougainvilleas and trees. It's not run by a religious order, but rather by an Indian organization. I've barely stepped into the front yard when I'm approached by a lady in a sari, her hair in a braid, eyes gleaming behind her glasses.

"You're very welcome here," she says, embracing me. I raise my hand in greeting; she returns the *namaste* and promptly leads me into her cool office. A picture of Gandhi hangs over the doorway to her room. The lady takes her seat behind her office desk; even though she is aged, her beauty is overwhelming. Two girls bring a glass of water. I feel at home, welcomed.

We talk. She tells me that nearly all their children are adopted within India and that foreign parents face a three-year waiting list. "More and more Indians are choosing to adopt themselves, you see."

She says she'd be more than happy to work with German parents, but she already has a long list of parents waiting for a child. Here, too, children are rejected by Indian parents for having too dark a skin color, because of medical problems, or simply on looks. She sighs. These children would be put up for international adoption. She is clear about the fact that she prefers children to be adopted within their own country.

To finish, she takes me on a tour of the orphanage. It's basic but clean, and there are plenty of young women taking care of the children. For the first time, children are introduced to me by name and are even lined up for a photo. There's a relaxed, almost jolly, atmosphere here; the women laugh. A few girls arrive back from school, and others sweep the yard. They all seem happy. Perhaps it's the purple bougainvilleas or the warm spirit of the director, who brings peace wherever she goes. The children are well dressed and healthy; they play and receive lots of attention—that counts for a lot.

A girl bounces around us; she is around eight years old, wild and boisterous. Now and again, the director puts her arms around her lovingly.

"Oh, yes, we'll find you some parents; don't you worry!" she says, and then the girl's off again, bouncing wildly around us. Suddenly she throws herself down in the dust, twists, and rolls high-spiritedly on the ground. She jumps up again and runs over to the other children.

"She tells us she was attacked by a bear," the director informs me. Then suddenly, it dawns on me, and I stare over at the girl. Her arms are missing. She jumps about, runs, and plays—yet she has no arms.

"You know those dancing bears they have in the villages? One day she got too close. The doctor couldn't help anymore, so he just amputated. Her parents abandoned her." The director sighs. I say nothing. A short, uncomfortable, heavy silence fell, accompanied by a crippling feeling of guilt. Everything remains unsaid. Then she changes the subject, behaving as if she'd never expected I would actually offer to adopt the girl. It was very tactful of her, yet I can't help but feel ashamed.

Later, I ask the director if there's anything she might like or need for the orphanage. Something she can use to boil lots of baby bottles is her only modest request. Once again, I return to my hotel empty-handed; once again, I cross an address off my list. I am getting tired of the search. I long for some rest. I decide to take a few days off to reflect. I search and try for something different.

Wearily flicking through my guidebook in my hotel room, an advert catches my eye. It's for a maharaja's palace out in the desert, not far from the town where I'm staying. It appears to be some sort of hotel—and it has a swimming pool. It looks like just the place. Everything's taken its toll on me: the heat; the endless, tedious city driving; the fumes; the grime; and the sad faces of all the children who've already been waiting for a miracle for far too long. I'm in desperate need of a break, so I go down to reception and ask them to book me a room there. The two young men behind the desk share a furtive glance.

"Hmm, we can't make any promises."

"We'll have to make some calls."

"It's not quite as simple as that."

My frustration grows.

I hail a rickshaw outside the hotel and ask the driver to take me to the bazaar. Night is falling, and the heat has died down to a pleasant warmth. The air is soft and smoky. Slowly the rickshaw rattles toward the bazaar. The wheels clank behind me, while in front of me the shoulders of the young man peddling me through the twilight heave up and down. He pants and pedals harder. It took me a long time to get up the courage to ride in a rickshaw. At first I saw it as exploitation. These days, I enjoy it, as I'm gently rocked down dusty alleyways past people, sights, and sounds, close enough to touch. The rickshaw driver does get paid for his work—it's his job.

I climb down from the rickshaw into the crowds and drift along the alleys filled with the smells and sounds of the Orient. This is the time when the desert town comes alive; the streets and alleyways are full to bursting. Women are buying supplies for the evening meal, while men stand in front of every shop and stall, haggling, trading, drinking tea, handling wares, and testing for quality. The smoky streets are a hive of activity, and movie soundtracks fill the air, blaring from banged-up tape recorders. Suddenly, through the music and the splutter of motorbikes and auto-rickshaws, the call of a muezzin rings out. It's time for evening prayers. Many men head in the direction of the mosque.

I could spend hours in a place like this, wending my way along the narrow alleys of the bazaar, losing myself in the atmosphere, diving deep into this world. At some point, I find myself pausing, quite by chance, in front of a shop selling textiles. Not the usual fabrics, saris, or salwar kameez, though, but embroidered wall hangings and quilts. Some are even vintage, handmade pieces. Before long, the two shopkeepers and I are sitting on the shop floor drinking tea while our hands fly through piles of old textiles. Although many items are worn, tattered, or ripped, there are a few pieces of beautiful handiwork. They are mostly wall hangings, quilts, and handicrafts of the sort that a young woman in this desert area would make to bring to her new husband's house as part of her dowry when she married. The incredible amount of work and patience it must have taken to make them is plain to see.

I run my hands over the pattern on a *chakla*, a square wall hanging. Thousands of tiny glass beads (in earlier times they even used Murano glass) have been hand stitched onto the cloth to form a picture. There's a white horse in the center, the steed the bridegroom traditionally rides to his wedding. All around the horse are animals: a peacock (the national bird of India), more horses, water buffalo, and camels—perhaps livestock belonging to the household of the sewer's future husband.

I imagine the anticipation, yet surely also the trepidation, that the bride who made this must have felt as she worked. Some girls never set foot outside their family home until their parents arrange a marriage with other parents from a neighboring tribe, the chief consideration being that the marriage respects the caste system. The Indian caste system has rules that often specify in minute detail who the children of a particular family are allowed and not allowed to marry. Even today, these rules have considerable influence with parents when they choose a spouse for their child. Thus, the rules underpin a network of thousands of castes that divide India's population into a hierarchy of various social groups.

In rural areas, marriages are arranged while the girls are still children. After the marriage has been formalized, the girl usually stays with her parents until she starts menstruating, at which point her in-laws take custody of her and become responsible for her well-being. This is often a very traumatic time for the bride-to-be, as she must leave behind everything she knows and go to live with a family of strangers. Once there, she will barely see her husband, working instead under the supervision of her mother-in-law. This arrangement often continues for years until the mother-in-law decides that the time is right to bring the young couple together to produce the next generation. Having children, particularly sons, is the bride's chance to improve her social standing within the family. Gradually the mother-in-law will take a backseat.

I buy the *chakla* and an old bag decorated with mirrors and knots, which would have held money for the bridegroom to shower over his guests on his wedding day. After much haggling, I also decide on an *odhni*, an old, bright red bridal shawl that the bride wears over her head and body. The cloth is woven from the best silk and then dyed red. Before the shawl was dyed, thousands of peppercorns were tied on with threads. The garment was dyed and the peppercorns removed, leaving behind a complex pattern of lotus blossoms and garlands of flowers. Finally someone, perhaps even the bride herself, finished the shawl with fine silver threads, so that it glistens in the twilight, a delicate red shimmer of silken splendor. It must have taken weeks, if not months, of work to create. As I travel back in the rickshaw carrying this precious treasure in my hands, I can't help but wonder if the moment will ever come when I'll pass it on to my daughter—perhaps even on her wedding day.

As I enter the hotel, the receptionist hands me the telephone, and a gentleman on the other end of the line tells me in perfect Oxbridge English that the maharaja's palace was not a hotel after all, but that I was invited to visit as a guest of the prince. I was expected the following day for lunch. I barely have time to stammer a "thank you" before the conversation is over.

"It's not really a hotel," the receptionist tells me with a smile of amusement. "But the family does take in paying guests from time to time. They stay there, eat with the family, and tour the palace. This must be arranged in advance, however," he tells me. "The palace will send a car to collect you tomorrow."

Chapter 9

THE FAIRY-TALE PALACE

Cotton fields as far as the eye can see. Drought has left the land dry, like a withered leaf. We bounce over the road in an Ambassador as the palace chauffeur concentrates on avoiding the potholes with the car, which has certainly seen better days a long time ago. Thornbushes, even rows of cacti in some places, line the roadside. We've been traveling in the heat for over an hour already, and the road is almost empty, apart from the occasional oxcart carrying cotton. In some of the fields, I can make out men and women working, picking balls of cotton by hand, scarves protecting them against the sun. It's blisteringly hot, even this early in the day.

After two hours of traveling, a village rises from the dust. A palace towers over the dry river valley. It is a castle with balustrades, domes, a clock tower, and sweeping roof terraces, surrounded by outbuildings. The chauffeur steers the car up a winding track. A doorman shuffles out of his hut and opens the iron gate. We enter a lost world of past glory. Withered grass spreads where there had once been a formal garden. Marble statues sigh in the glaring heat of the Indian sun. There are waterfalls and fountains dried under layers of dust. Ornamental ponds thirst for water, but shimmer brown from the nearby desert sand. The car slowly rolls up the drive, past one of the outbuildings: my suite, the estate manager explains most politely as he welcomes me. From the terrace of my suite, the parched landscape stretches all the way to the horizon. It is dotted with fields, thornbushes, and villages. A partly dried-up river cuts through it. I stand in the glazed doorway to my suite in a daze; my eyes need time to adjust to the shade inside. The room is cool. I slip off my sandals, and my feet are calmed by marble floor. My attention turns to two enormous four-poster beds with white lace covers and embroidered crests reading, "In God is my trust." Mosquito nets are hitched up on the bedposts. All the furniture is made of teak. Fascinated, I peek into the next room—the dressing room—where, exhausted from my journey, I rest in front of a mirrored cabinet and a dressing table. I see a spacious bathroom with an old-fashioned shower. It's peaceful; just the peacocks call from the garden.

I relish the peace. It's a pleasant change from the noise, dirt, and heat of the cities. This is India's other extreme, one of the last relics of colonial times. I can't help but wonder if the people down in the village even know what this palace looks like. The contrast between the prince and princess who live in this palace and the local population is stark; the villages are just another part of the landscape from up here.

Just then, the glass door swings open, and a servant comes in with hand towels and a tray laden with tea, sugar, and cookies on French china. He flicks a switch, and the fans under the ceiling start to move the air. Then he bows, and with a glance at the bathroom, tells me that when I'm ready, the *yuvraj* (prince) would like to welcome me.

Half an hour later, I find myself sitting on the palace's grand terrace, gazing through the archways of the balustrades onto the gardens below. The hills slope gently. At the turn of the twentieth century, all this would have belonged to the maharaja. Time has stood still in this palace. Through a glass door behind me, I can make out two elephant tusks holding a brass gong suspended between them. Nothing has changed here since the last English left after a tiger hunt.

Suddenly, a door opens behind me, and in walks the yuvraj, a gentleman in his midfifties dressed in a crisp white kaftan. His clothing contrasts beautifully with the deep, dark color of his skin. His hair is combed into a precise side part, and his green eyes sparkle pleasantly with a touch of curiosity. He greets me in perfect English, and has his servants bring us cool lemonade.

"Your life is like a fairy tale!" I exclaim in amazement.

"Ah, but it is like living in the past," he counters and launches into an inspiring discussion of economic and social policy. He studied and earned his PhD at Cambridge like his father, the former maharaja, and grandfather before him. "The British gave us a good education to keep our mouths shut," he tells me, with a touch of cynicism. He doesn't have much good to say about the British.

I'm hard-pressed to argue with his philosophical and political musings; after all, like many descendants of ancient Indian noble families, he was a politician for some years in New Delhi. He doesn't waste time with the usual questions.

"Can you believe my parents and grandparents used to sit on this terrace after sunset and listen to the wild animals? All the hills around here were covered in forest, and my ancestors used to go hunting. Now the trees have been cleared, and this is a wasteland. We're destroying our country!" he concludes bitterly, waving a hand toward the desolate fields and hills.

"You wouldn't believe how low the groundwater level has sunk already. And all the while, the population here is growing; the birth rate is soaring astronomically. Trees are being cut down for no good reason. The land is drying out, so the groundwater level sinks even lower. They're having to dig deeper and deeper to find water now," he insists wearily. The politicians weren't lifting a finger of course, because it wasn't good for their popularity. In one of his neighboring palaces, he couldn't even fill the swimming pool anymore. The pump was clogged with red mud.

"The Chinese have got the right idea, only allowing one child per family. But democracy is the order of the day here, and democracy bends to the will of the voter. Now, if we had a one-party state, things would be quite different," he explains, provocatively.

He is completely consumed by the fear that India's population explosion will one day be its downfall. India already has a population of over a billion, and in twenty to thirty years, it's set to overtake China as the world's most populous country. By that time, Mumbai, already one of our planet's great metropolises, with a population of sixteen million and the largest slums in Asia, will be home to around twenty-two million people.

Yet rural areas, too, are becoming increasingly populous. The forests are being cleared, placing the environment under great strain, particularly in areas that have already been plagued with drought for years.

It's around midday. The heat has become unbearable. The lemonade is long gone. A servant informs us that lunch is served. I follow the prince through the glass door and through the entrance hall of the palace into the great hall. Once again, it takes my eyes a moment to adjust to the darkness. Rhino and buffalo heads stare out from the walls, and a stuffed lion guards a corner—the previous maharaja's hunting trophies. The floor is covered with Persian rugs and the striped soft pattern of so many tigers, killed in the past triumph of the raj to serve as doormats. Tiger hunts on elephant back were a celebrated social pastime of the maharajas and the British.

No luxury was spared. Venetian crystal chandeliers dangle from the ceiling. The room has an air of time-honored splendor. You can still hear the past voices of colonial rulers echoing in the marble halls while the desert wind drifts through the palace.

Suddenly, I hear a rustling on the other side of the hall, and a tall, slender lady in a sari appears. The yuvraj introduces his wife, the *maharani*. A Labrador, soon to become my constant panting companion around the palace, nuzzles my leg. First the prince proudly shows me a majestic silver throne that belongs to his father, the maharaja, and then he asks me to write in the guestbook. From the previous entries, it would seem that small groups of tourists do, indeed, spend a few days here from time to time, but this is rare given the remoteness of the place.

The servants give us a signal, and we make our way into the adjoining dining hall. No sooner have we sat down than a servant leads a very elderly man into the room, his back crooked with age. He is the prince's father, the last maharaja, who was known as such until the title and the political influence that came with it were abolished by the British rule and later Indian governments.

I can hardly believe we're all sitting here together in the middle of the desert, making polite conversation over lunch, being served a four-course menu on fine French china, sipping from crystal glasses, and occasionally squinting in the desert light coming through the slightly open windows that look out onto the balustrades of the balcony. Schubert plays softly in the background. Although it's searingly hot outside, in here, the Labrador pants gently in the corner while we drink our soup. I sit under the beady stares of six tigers and four leopards (and that's just on one side of the dining room) listening to the prince's wife pondering how best to renovate the art deco guest wing. It's completely surreal. Now, even my search for a child seems unreal, as if it has no place in this world.

"And what brings you all the way out here?" the maharani asks, wrenching me from my thoughts.

"I'm visiting orphanages. I'm hoping to adopt."

"I see," she replies, but shows little interest.

"There's an orphanage here in the next large town." I elaborate and tell her about my visit.

"Indeed?" she inquires, polite yet indifferent. She's not interested in having this conversation. In fact, I almost have the feeling that it's uncomfortable for her. She pointedly changes the subject.

The yuvraj sits in silence while the maharani grumbles on about the renovation. Then he tells me he will have someone show me round the art deco palace after we've eaten.

"Then you'll be able to see the swimming pool as well," he says smiling, before segueing into environmental issues and social policy again. The old maharaja hasn't uttered a word throughout the entire meal, and as the yuvraj philosophizes about India and China for the umpteenth time, the maharani gets to her feet abruptly and excuses herself. The meal is over, and a servant escorts the maharaja from the hall.

"Do you play the piano?" my host asks suddenly.

"Yes," I answer with surprise.

"Then follow me," he replies and leads me back through the dining room and the great hall into another large room with more Persian rugs, teak furniture, and tiger skins. A Steinway grand piano stands by the window.

"Play a little," he urges, sinking down into an armchair with a cup of coffee. And so I find myself in the middle of the desert, sitting at a Steinway piano, playing passages from Beethoven sonatas, while the air outside shimmers in the desert heat. We're cocooned in a different world, totally set apart from the world outside, as far away from the poverty, the slums, and the orphanages as I am when I'm at home in front of the fire. Eventually, I run out of pieces to play, and we retire to the billiard room.

"So, you're hoping to adopt an Indian child?" the prince asks. I tell him our story.

"A boy or a girl?"

"A girl. That's to say, there isn't really a choice. It's pretty much only girls that are up for adoption anyway."

"Yes, of course. Boys are so important here." He sighs and tells me how, as a young maharaja's son, he came to be married.

"It was all arranged by our parents, naturally. They selected a girl from our caste from a certain family in another area—all strictly according to caste rules. I didn't meet her until our wedding day." The prince leads me to another room, which is laid out like a museum. I wonder at the assortment of beautiful textiles, costumes, and turbans belonging to the old maharaja. There are old sabers, daggers, pistols, rapiers, flags, banners, coats of arms, and family trees. The yuvraj shows me some silver pendants that elephants would wear during processions.

"These were used at my wedding. As the maharaja's eldest son and heir, I rode standing on an elephant, as tradition dictates," he recalls, his voice tinged with bitterness. The marriage was childless, and worst of all, there had been no son who could one day inherit the estate and the palace. The entire family was left without a son and heir. The whole thing had been a disaster, the yuvraj reflects. I think of the two beautiful sisters waiting in front of the orphanage in Mumbai.

The weight of expectation on him had been unbearable, he tells me, and it only got worse. The whole family had been in uproar, and eventually the marriage was dissolved, a total scandal in these circles.

The prince had thrown himself into politics in frustration. In the meanwhile, his younger brother married. His brother's wife finally became pregnant. An heir was on the way, and the whole family could relax again.

"But it was just a girl." The yuvraj sighs. "Girls don't count in inheritance terms, and the worst of it was that my sister-in-law wasn't able to have another child. So it was decided that I should marry again, as a last-ditch attempt to sire a son and heir." I can't begin to imagine the terrible arguments and discussions his family must have had back then.

"How strong must the family's influence be," I wonder, "how great the sense of duty and responsibility toward the entire family, when a grown man is forced into a marriage by his parents for the second time in his life?" We're not talking fairy tales from long ago here. I recall how a neighbor of mine from home, a young Indian who had mostly grown up in the West, traveled to his homeland and agreed to a marriage arranged by his parents. "I owe it to them," he insisted.

Thus, the prince married again. This time, finally, a son arrived—that precious, important child. The son was currently studying in England, and the prince hoped that he would become a worthy heir who would protect and continue the family line.

It's late afternoon now, and the enthusiastic palace manager drives me in the Ambassador to a nearby temple, a holy shrine. In the hazy, red evening light, farmers from the villages arrive with their wives. They pray there, devoutly, wholeheartedly, weary from their day's work in the dusty heat. The monsoon hasn't come for two years now, so the harvest will be poor again.

The temple stands next to a lake. The manager and I settle ourselves on the steps of the *ghat*, the sacrificial steps of the temple. The heat has died down, and the waters are still. Outlined against the sunset, I watch the silhouettes of the women along the banks as they collect water in copper pots and lift their burdens onto their heads. Buffalo snort in the lake, and the sound of the prayer gong carries down from the temple. Flocks of parrots circle in the sky. An offering bowl filled with flowers drifts gently across the waves.

"Can you see the crocodiles?" the manager asks.

"Excuse me?" I reply in confusion.

"There, in the lake. Can't you see them?" comes his puzzled reply, and he points with his finger. Only then do I spot the pair of eyes and swirls of water around a crocodile slowly gliding across the lake.

Chapter 10

THE CURSED SIP OF WATER

My mosquito bites are still itchy as I sit in the plane on the way back to Mumbai, the outline of India's west coast snaking below us in a haze. Subtly, I reach down under my seat and rub some cream onto my ankles. The insects got me on the wrists, too, even though I had carefully pulled the sleeves of my tunic right down over my hands at dinner in the palace.

The meal had been sinfully delicious and was accompanied by Beethoven's Fifth Symphony. It's hard to imagine a more fitting setting for the Fifth than this majestic palace with tiger, rhino, and buffalo heads staring menacingly down from the walls. However, the meal was somewhat spoiled by the mosquitoes, who perched on the damask tablecloth and attacked our hands and feet.

I put the anti-itch cream away and reach for the *Times of India*. Once again, I find myself reading the wedding announcements, which are split into two sections—one for parents seeking bridegrooms, and the other for parents looking for girls for their sons.

"Parents of son, computer science (IT) graduate, twenty-six, sporty, good looking, vegetarian, loves music and reading, seek young bride—twenty-four or younger; Brahmin, Jain, or Vaishnav caste; vegetarian; attractive; fair; and respectful of family traditions—for marriage. Please apply with photo via post or e-mail."

In long, deliberate paragraphs, parents describe every tiny detail of their child's future partner—which caste they should belong to, their career, that they must be vegetarian, and often that the applicant or bride must be "fair," by which they mean "light skinned."

Some of the ads explicitly state "caste no bar," meaning that caste is not important, while others explain that the child's first marriage has failed and that this is a second attempt. Some parents seek suitable partners from abroad, as far afield as London or Singapore.

"Why are you reading these adverts?" a voice next to me asks. I look up to see an Indian businessman (I will later learn that he works for a bank) watching me with interest. Until now, he had been reading a newspaper himself. He asks where I'm from, and I tell him my story.

"So you're hoping to adopt a girl? I have a daughter myself. We're looking for a husband for her at the moment, but she's already turned down some of our suggestions," he says with a resigned grimace.

"Have you been reading these adverts, too?" I ask.

"No, we're making our own inquiries through relatives, friends, and colleagues." He sighs. "I've found another candidate who seems a really good fit. He's a computer engineer like my daughter, but I have my reservations."

"Why? What kind of reservations?" I ask nosily.

"My daughter won't like him. He's a little on the chubby side…and too dark."

"Too dark?" I ask in amazement, thinking of the yuvraj with his almost-black skin.

"Yes, he's ever so dark. You wouldn't want to marry a black man, would you?" he asks, grumpily. Although I know our discussion is racist, I'm interested to find out more.

"Why not? What's wrong with dark skin?" I counter.

"Dark just isn't attractive."

"But why?"

"You wouldn't understand," he responds, annoyed. Does he see me as a naive, moralistic, Western tourist? "In the business world, there's no problem. But look closer, and you'll notice that every good hotel in Mumbai puts the fairest employees they can find behind their front desk," he tells me with a helpless gesture. He goes back to his paper.

He has a point. All the big Bollywood stars, fashion models, and sweet, laughing girls in the commercials on Indian TV are all so fair that they bear little resemblance to the average Indian on the street. I catch sight of the flight attendants serving coffee and little snacks—fair, every one of them, perhaps from Kashmir or at least northern India. Only yesterday, I was reading an Indian fashion magazine that had several pages featuring dark-skinned models, which they promoted as being particularly progressive. The subtle shade distinctions—"fair," "wheatish" (for medium brown), and "dark"—still permeate much of Indian society.

Perhaps it was once the same in Europe, in the days when upper-class ladies carried parasols and wore long gloves to protect their skin from the sun. Dark skin was long associated with manual work and poverty. But in India, it goes deeper than that. Three thousand years ago, so many sociologists believe, tribes from central Asia, the Aryans, pushed their way deep into the subcontinent and quickly put measures in place to assert their dominance over the darker-skinned Indian native tribes. Holy Hindu texts then cemented these measures in the divinely ordained caste system, and it followed that this hierarchy influenced people's perception of skin color. This theory goes some way toward explaining the discrimination against dark skin in India.

I remember the girl at the swimming pool in Delhi. Her mother must have drummed into her that she must protect her complexion to spare her from disapproving glances, as well as from disappointment when it came time to make wedding plans.

Worried now, I ask myself how much discrimination dark-skinned people really face here in India, and as a mixed-race family, I wonder how much racism we will experience in Europe and America. Many social workers in the States are fundamentally opposed to the idea of white parents adopting, for example, African American children, their argument being that white parents won't have experienced racism and will therefore be ill equipped to educate their children on this matter and help them through any issues they encounter. I respect their point of view, and to be completely honest, I do worry that we will be faced with racism and that we have no idea how to deal with it. In fact, I'm deeply afraid that our child could be psychologically affected by it while I stand by, powerless to help.

Andreas and I have already resolved to bring our children up to believe in themselves, so that they will be able to take racist comments in their stride. But I have no idea how much the racist comments we are yet to encounter will affect us, how unexpected they will be, or how badly prepared we will be to react in the right way.

At this point in time, I still believe that society is becoming increasingly tolerant and that we will be able to conquer racism. Even so, the Indian banker's comments have already made me realize that we will be asking a lot from our child. We will force her to live in a broadly Western society, expect her to just deal with racism and to live with it, on top of the trauma of not knowing her biological parents who simply abandoned her. At times like these, I lose my footing and question myself: am I doing the right thing, or just indulging my own ego? Am I so hell-bent on having a child that I haven't considered the consequences this will have for the child herself? Is my desperate search irresponsible, then? I really hope I find clear answers to these questions soon.

Waiting at Mumbai airport for my luggage, as so often happens in India, the family next to me strikes up a conversation with the same casual, friendly, curious questions I've heard many times before: Where are you from? Why are you here? Where are you headed? For what seems like the umpteenth time, I find myself telling the mother my adoption story.

"Our son is adopted," the mother says, pointing to the ten-year-old boy who is helping her husband to pull a suitcase off the luggage carousel. "I couldn't have children, you see, and my sister-in-law has six. So she just gave us one of her boys. Now he belongs to us; he's our son," she tells me, as if this transaction were the most normal thing in the world. I'd already heard that in India this sort of thing went on between families with lots of children and their relatives with none. In some ways, it seems so logical, so enlightened, and it appears to benefit everyone involved. Even so, I can't help but wonder if it won't lead to complications and arguments further down the line about where the boy really belongs.

Back in Mumbai, I return to my little hotel. As my luggage is unloaded outside, I look over at the slum huts nearby. The cropped-haired mother's hut is empty. The boy is gone, too. Next door, a woman sits on the floor in front of the neatly swept hut. Her legs are stretched out before her, and there is a naked baby on her thighs. Slowly and rhythmically, she massages and kneads the baby, whose skin glistens with massage oil. Next to that woman squats a young woman I assume to be the baby's mother. The women chat while the masseuse's hands slowly and gently run over the child's body. The infant doesn't cry, but calmly allows itself to be massaged. The masseuse's son sits in the entrance to the hut, shoveling the last remnants of some rice into his mouth with his hands. The confused old man is still sitting under his tree—motionless, hopeless, and frozen there in the same position as always. The row of slum huts has crept a little closer to him; a new hut has squeezed itself into the tiny space remaining by the tree.

Upstairs in my room, I throw myself down on the bed, tired, drained, and feeling a little hopeless. I've been traveling back and forth across India for two weeks now, and seeing all the children in the orphanages and the widespread poverty has left me even more determined to adopt at all costs. However, I want to do it legally, correctly, and cleanly. And I only want to adopt a child who has no other chance.

One thing has become clear to me after all the orphanages I've visited: if we're lucky enough to get a child at all, it will be a girl. In all my travels I hadn't encountered a single place that had suggested a boy for international adoption, so that must only happen very rarely. Similarly, it was no secret that it was mostly sick children who were selected to be adopted overseas. I find that strangely comforting, because that means we can be sure that this is the child's only hope.

After all my letters and travels, the best hope left to us is that the orphanage run by Catholic nuns will come through and find us a child. If not, we're stuck with the waiting lists and two or three years of patience. Just the thought of this frustrates me so much that I grab the remote and switch on the TV to distract myself. Almost every channel is an Indian Bollywood film, a talk show, or news in Hindi, Marathi, or Urdu that I can't understand.

Bored, I flip through the channels and pause on a fashion channel I've begun to notice over the last few days; it shows nothing but glamorous catwalk shows, twenty-four hours a day. Stick-thin, scantily clad models strut their stuff—bare midriffs, breasts bouncing merrily under see-through tops, and skirts so short they show more than a hint of bottom. I ask myself, "Who watches this channel here?" Is it the women, who, apart from an occasional glimpse of tummy button, go to great lengths to ensure their saris cover everything, even their armpits? Or the men, to whom the sight of a woman's upper arm, shoulder, or leg is quite vulgar enough? Or perhaps the young people, who are so progressive in their modern jeans and T-shirts, which they are quick to ditch in favor of salwar kameez or saris after their arranged marriages?

It's evening now. An asthmatic person gasps for breath outside. Even more frustrated than before, I turn off the TV and decide I may as well go to bed. When I go to brush my teeth, however, I find that I've run out of bottled water. I use only bottled mineral water to brush my teeth in India—it's safer. But my last bottle is empty, and I can't be bothered to go down to reception again. I need my peace.

So I take the thermos from my room and carry it to the sink in the bathroom. Then I hesitate. Every hotel room has a container like this to provide drinking water for its guests, but I don't know if it's fresh. Normally, I wouldn't touch the drinking water in Indian hotel rooms, but right now I'm too tired and grouchy. Besides, rinsing my mouth just once won't hurt, I tell myself, and I pour some water into a glass. I brush my teeth, take a sip, rinse, and go to bed. I will curse this moment and that sip of water for an entire year.

Chapter 11

KRISHNA'S PEOPLE

The next morning I awake to a pounding headache. It's already very light in my room; I've obviously overslept. I sit up and sink straight back down again. A crippling sense of exhaustion seems to throw me back onto the bed. The muggy heat of Mumbai has suddenly become unbearable. I try to sit up again and break out in cold sweat. With my head spinning, I drag myself to the bathroom—diarrhea. I sit there, shivering almost uncontrollably, cursing the sip I took from the thermos, as well as the mosquitoes buzzing incessantly around me. Everything annoys me. I hate that the hotel always gives me such a pathetically tiny roll of toilet paper, and I'm aggravated that I'm stuck here in this stuffy toilet in the first place, listening to the trains instead of out making progress.

Getting dressed seems to take forever. However, after some painkillers and a cup of spiced tea, I feel a little better. I'm not hungry, rather queasy, in fact. So I decide to stay away from food today and take some pills for my diarrhea. Such a shame that I had to get sick today. The Hindus are celebrating Krishna's birthday. It's a fabulous spectacle, and I am not sure whether I can manage to travel to Colaba, a neighborhood in southern Mumbai, to see it.

Slowly and painfully, I make my way out of the hotel. Walking down the dusty, noisy little street is torture for me now. There are no public restrooms, so the residents of the slum huts do their business in the gutter. For the first time, the stench of feces really bothers me. The noise of the auto-rickshaws, the trains, and the station announcements bore into my head.

Suddenly, I stop, perplexed. The shabby old man under the tree is reading the *Times of India*. I can hardly believe my eyes, yet there he sits, cross-legged, engrossed in the *Times*, a look of concentration on his face. He has expertly folded the paper, like the bankers I've seen on the Tube in London, and he reads with interest, deftly turning the page as if he's done it so many times before. I walk past him in disbelief. What did all these people do before ending up here on the street? *We should be very careful with our judgments*, I think to myself.

I feel slightly better, so I decide to take the train to Colaba. On arrival, the overwhelming sound of frantic drumming, loudspeaker announcements, and cries of celebration greets me from many streets away. I push my way through the roughly jostling crowds, tightly clutching my camera, until I finally find a spot from which to watch the festivities.

Just a few feet away is the hut where I trod in the mud and the little boy brought me a can of water to wash myself. This time, though, people fill the entrances to the huts, the streets, and every window and balcony on the block. At first I can't make out what's going on; all I can see is a group of around thirty young men dressed in red T-shirts, gesticulating wildly before suddenly bunching tightly together. They stand with their heads pressed together and then begin to climb onto each other's shoulders. Quick as a flash, more young men climb onto the shoulders of the first group. They, too, bunch together and lower their heads, and three more boys climb nimbly on top. The crowd cheers and yells in encouragement.

High above their heads, a rope has been strung across the street between the roofs of the houses; among flower garlands and little flags, a clay pot dangles from it. A young man manages to stand up on the backs of three of his team members, and another quickly pulls himself up the backs and shoulders of the rest. The pyramid sways and wobbles dangerously as he swings deftly onto the shoulders of the highest man and grasps at the rope with both hands. For a moment, the swaying pyramid looks as if it's about to collapse while the boy at the top fights to hold his balance. With full force, he slams his forehead against the clay pot. Saffron-red water and rice sprays over his face and the shoulders of the men. The crowd below goes wild with delight.

I'm just reaching for my camera when a jet of cold water shoots me in the face, leaving me soaked to the skin. Before I have time to work out where it's come from, two laughing women in colorful saris pull me under some plastic sheeting. As I follow their pointing fingers, I realize that the women on the balconies and at the windows are having fun pelting the crowd with little plastic bags of water. Their main target appears to be the men, who are climbing onto each other again to form a new pyramid under the next pot.

The whole street is filled with people dancing to drumbeats and their own joyful whooping. The young women pull me along. We follow the "Reds," the horde of sweat-drenched, sopping-wet, mud-caked young men, who are now already reaching for the next pot. This wild celebration is inspired by an event from Krishna's childhood, and the story is still a favorite of Indian children today. One day, Krishna's mother was playing with her son when she remembered a pot of milk boiling over in the kitchen and left hungry little Krishna alone. With his feelings hurt, Krishna reaches for the pot of butter his mother had churned earlier, eats some, and smashes the pot. Although Krishna runs quickly away when he hears his mother coming, she punishes the little rascal in the end.

All Colaba is in the grip of Krishna fever. I'm amazed by the men's team spirit. They can only succeed in smashing the jug if they all work together and if no one gives up, falters, or loses his balance. Their success depends on the discipline of every team member.

The Reds' numbers have swelled to more than forty men and boys, and now they're attempting their third pyramid. Already soaked, they wobble and shake as the cruel rain of water bombs continues from the upper stories. Three pots swing from the rope this time—a tempting prize. There are now thirty men in the bottom level of the pyramid alone; six men balance on their shoulders, and three more clamber over them. Quick as a monkey, one of the young Reds swings to the top, and this time one of the most talented boys gets to form the summit of the pyramid. Hand over powerful hand, he climbs the backs and shoulders of his teammates, balances for a short time on the shoulders of the highest man, and then reaches, both hands outstretched, for the prize.

At this very moment, the men lose their balance and the pyramid collapses. But the boy has already grasped the rope, and he now dangles from it, at least twenty-six feet above the street. The crowd stops cheering—this could be dangerous. It's too far for the boy to fall safely, so he just hangs there, about level with the third story of the surrounding houses. While the men beneath him try to rebuild the pyramid, the boy breaks the first pot with his forehead, and the red gunk drenches his head and shoulders. He continues to cling to the rope and even begins to swing athletically toward the next pot. Meanwhile, the pyramid below him has collapsed again; the men keep losing their balance.

The boy has reached the second pot now, cracks it against his forehead, and more of the red rice mixture shoots over his shoulders. The men make another attempt at a pyramid, but they just can't make it tall enough. Perhaps they're in too much of a panic; after all, the boy hanging above them is struggling with his grip. Some of the men call up to the boy, telling him to hold on. To my amazement, he's reached the third pot, and he smashes this one, too. The concoction spurts him in the face, runs over his shoulders, and down his back, leaving him dangling limply from the rope, exhausted and drenched. The men shout out from below, gesticulating. They just can't build another pyramid, and the situation seems dire. Then suddenly, all the men in the street stretch their hands up toward the sky. There are almost forty men—a carpet of eighty hands beneath the rope. In that moment, the boy lets go and falls backward, his arms and legs flailing wildly in the air. He lands in the sea of hands, which cushions his fall and places him back on his feet. The cheering and drumming is deafening. The high-spirited celebrations of this victory are a fiery, passionate sight.

Men crowd in front of my camera in wonder, posing like heroes—boisterous and sweaty, but beaming. They whoop with joy, confidence, red rice in their damp hair, red T-shirts clinging to their bodies, feet caked in mud.

I gaze into the amazed faces of the happy men, and suddenly, the adoption pops into my head. This child, this girl we're planning to adopt from here and remove from this culture—what are we taking away from her? She won't grow up here; she won't experience all of this. What are we depriving her of? How many festivals? How many hours spent wandering dreamily through bazaars bursting with color? How much music? How many sounds, sights, smiles? How much of the warmth of the people here? I'll be taking her away from the passionate celebrations, from the colorfulness, from the mystique of the temples, far away from her mother's beliefs, from her culture, from the year-round heat, from so many of the things that I love about India. These are the things that bring me back here time and time again. And, worst of all, I'd be taking her away from the people of India, from Indian friends, Indian teachers, Indian coworkers, and the Indian men of her future.

How can I make sure she experiences as much of this as possible? I decide that we will immerse our child in as much of her culture as we reasonably can. At home, we'll listen to lots of Indian music, we'll watch Indian videos, we'll eat curry, and I can read her Indian fairy stories. I'll read her the *Ramayana*, stories from the life of Krishna, and other myths. We'll visit Indian temples, and go to Indian music and dance events. She can take Hindi lessons. Yet all our efforts will just be a tiny taste, a poor imitation, of everything the real India has to offer.

Part Two

Chapter 12

LITTLE BINA

Just another few feet to the door of the orphanage. "Last chance," I tell myself. All the same, the sister did say I should come back; at the very least, maybe they will agree to let me adopt from here without it taking too long.

The gate has been left open, so I slip into the courtyard. Immediately, the noise of the street abates. I can already hear the cries of children from behind the windows of the orphanage. In the middle of the courtyard, some of the sisters and a few helpers struggle to heave canisters from a storeroom onto a truck while the security guard of the missionaries home stands on the back of the vehicle and carefully stacks them. Sister Maria recognizes me and calls me over to introduce me to the sister in charge of the orphanage. It is Sister Alissa, who is supervising the loading of the canisters.

"It's all for Gujarat," she says after welcoming me. A businessman has donated milk powder to be sent off to the area of a severe recent earthquake. Sister Alissa blinks from behind her spectacles and points to a storeroom, which is stacked to the roof with canisters of milk powder. As we talk, the sisters carry sacks filled with secondhand clothes to the truck. Sister Alissa tells me that the truck will be traveling to the earthquake zone in Gujarat later today. I remember seeing newspaper reports of the disaster in February, when powerful seismic tremors of 7.8 on the Richter scale destroyed villages and parts of the town of Bhuj in the north of the Indian state of Gujarat, leaving almost twenty thousand people dead. The earthquake hit one of the most remote and poorest areas of Gujarat, and the lack of coordinated help from the army and aid organizations meant that the population had been left to deal with the situation on their own for quite some time. "We've set up many camps and are helping locally," Sister Maria informs me.

"There will be many orphans and a lot of future adoptions," I reply, but I soon realize this is naive.

"Orphans, yes, but no adoptions," replies the sister. "We don't have the mothers' written permission for adoption," she explains. "We provide medical aid and a camp for the homeless." She asks to me to wait in the office while she calls Sister Lena.

As I wait on the sofa, listening to the sound of babies crying while staring first at a picture of the pope and then at a crucifix on the wall, I wonder whether I will ever adopt from here. After my last visit, I really hope so.

At that moment, Sister Lena enters the office, greeting me a little less enthusiastic than last time. She sits down with a sigh. She's not a young woman anymore. I can tell that the heat is taking its toll on her, too.

"I take it you had no luck elsewhere," she says, looking at the copy of our letter from social services.

"No, most orphanages have long waiting lists," I hesitantly admit.

"Well, it is not very different here. We don't have many children to give to adoption either," she says, her voice suddenly a little harsher.

"Yes, I know," I reply, and my heart sinks. I had hoped so badly that her conversation with Kolkata had come to something, that we might have had a chance.

"Tell me, what about the complexion—what complexion should the child have?" she asks all of a sudden, throwing me a quizzical glance. I stare back at her. I need a moment to pull myself together, to grasp the situation.

"It doesn't matter," I stammer. "It really doesn't. We're happy to adopt any child, including a child who is dark." Is she thinking something over? She seems relieved, and her expression is friendlier.

"Would you also adopt a child with illness?" she asks. I can hardly believe what I'm hearing. I can feel my heart thumping, my thoughts racing.

"Yes, yes, of course," I say, trying to keep calm. So it might be a child who is ill. I can't help but feel a little scared. On the other hand, this is exactly what we wanted; we knew that most of the children put up for overseas adoption are ill or even physically disabled. "As long as it's not disabled," I add cautiously.

"No, no," the sister replies, looking thoughtful at the letter. She first hesitates, but then looks me firmly in the eyes. My heart is beating so fast that I can almost hear it ringing in my ears. I frantically wonder how I should respond to whatever illness the child might have.

"Would you adopt a child with problems with its eyes—a child with a squint that needs to be operated on?" She looks at me, almost hopefully.

"Oh, yes, of course," I say with relief. *An eye problem*, I think to myself, *not the legs or stomach issues, not polio or spina bifida, but eye operations*. "But the child isn't mentally disabled?" I ask, worried. Hopefully, the sisters are being honest with me.

"No, no." She waves my question away. "She's not disabled; she's just got a squint and can't focus properly," she explains, pointing to her eyes to demonstrate the squint. "Also, she's dark, but she is available for international adoption. She's ten months old." She looks at me with questioning eyes again. I realize it is a girl, and the joy of anticipation sweeps over me. I'm thrilled and just stare at the sister. "Just don't mess up now and say the wrong thing," I tell myself.

"Would you be prepared to adopt the child? Should I get her?" asks Sister Lena. She makes it quite clear that she wants to know how serious I am about her suggestion.

"Yes, yes, absolutely," I tell her, although I'm so excited that I can hardly string two words together. Slowly, the nun gets to her feet.

"Right, then," she says, giving me an earnest look. "I'll go and get her, OK?"

"Yes, yes, please," I repeat. As soon as I say this, she disappears down the hall where the babies' cries are coming from.

I bite my lip. "The child the sister is just about to bring into this room will be my daughter," I tell myself. There is no turning back now. We want to adopt. We are looking for a child. We are prepared to accept a child with an illness, and now someone is offering exactly this kind of child to me. What reason could I possibly have to reject that child? That I don't like the tip of her nose or the way she looks? No, absolutely not. I couldn't do that to the child or to Sister Lena. And how could I possibly justify that kind of response to myself? "I have to see this through," I tell myself. This child is going to be my daughter. Yet my mind is full of doubts. What if she's ugly? What if I just don't like her? I perch on the sofa, powerless, excited, and confused all at once.

Suddenly, there she is in the doorway, the sister with a little bundle in her arms. At first all I can see is a pink frilly dress and a tuft of black hair.

"Bina." Sister Lena beams expectantly. And at that very moment, the little girl turns her face toward me—a small, pretty, but slightly frightened little face. She has a tiny nose and beautifully curved lips—not an ugly face at all. One could even say it is dainty. I breathe a sigh of relief. Her dark eyes scan the room unsteadily. Straight away I notice that she can't see properly, that her eyes can't find a focal point. I worry that she might be blind or perhaps have more serious issues with her eyes. I can tell the little one is confused. She clings to the sister nervously.

I want to get up.

"No, no, stay seated. I'll pass her to you," the sister says. She carries Bina over to me and gently sets her down on my lap. I'm amazed at how light she feels, at how delicate and small her little hands are. Bina turns her face away and I feel frightened, particularly as Sister Lena is watching my every move. As I hold Bina tightly, I feel as awkward as she does.

"She just needs a little time," says the sister to both of us. Soon, the feeling overwhelms me that this is going to be my child, and I become emotional and motherly toward her. I give her a long kiss on the forehead, humming softly as I do. Bina sits still and enjoys my kisses and then, for the first time, she looks in my direction. All of a sudden, she grabs my necklace with her little fingers. So she's not blind, I realize with relief. I chatter away to her, tell her that I wear glasses and that maybe she'll have to wear some, too, one day. Then the whole family will have glasses. My babbling seems to cheer her up. I feel so comfortable that I carry on; I even talk to Bina about adoption. I laugh. She laughs, too. I discover that she's already getting two little teeth in her bottom jaw. Bina pokes her fingers into the tiny mirrors of my salwar kameez—yet more proof that she can see. Although her squint is painfully obvious, I'm optimistic that an operation could help.

I gaze at her in wonder—her fine black hair, the gentle curves of her eyebrows and long eyelashes, the downy black hairs around her hairline on her dark brown skin, her pink palms. I notice that she has large, unevenly spaced ears. Suddenly, I'm overcome with emotion. I've waited for this moment for so long. Tears well in my eyes; I wipe them away.

"You need time, too. Take your time, both of you," I hear the sister say. She's smiling and seems relieved. She's much friendlier now. Maybe she was afraid that I was yet another Western woman who only wants the perfect child.

As I stroke the little one's hair, I notice that she has big bald patches on her head, caused perhaps by long hours spent lying in her cot without being let out. I suddenly think of the long rows of barred cots, and in that moment, I vow to myself that this will be my daughter. We are going to adopt her, and we will fight to do this, whatever it takes. Whatever is wrong with her eyes, we will figure it out and help her.

"So, will you take her?" Sister Lena asks me. "She's just got the eye problem, a few moles, and the uneven ears. And she's dark. Those are the reasons for overseas adoption given in her papers."

I'm excited, yet scared. I want to adopt Bina, but I hardly know anything about her and want to learn more.

"Where did she come from? Do you know anything about her parents?"

"Sadly not. Her mother gave her up—she was born out of wedlock. I can tell you her mother was young, but we don't know anything about the rest of the family, about the pregnancy, or about the father," answers Sister Lena. "We don't know much, and I'll tell you the little we do later when you take Bina home. She's healthy; you'll receive a medical report from our doctor."

I stand up, holding Bina gently in my arms. It's a huge risk adopting a child when you don't know anything about her life; it seems reckless to me. I know nothing of the congenital diseases she might face, nothing about any pregnancy complications, nothing about her mother, nothing about her birth and very little about her life since—ten short months of life shrouded in mystery. Yet in this moment, none of this matters to me. I want to help Bina, and anyway, I know I have no other choice.

I think Bina is sweet. Will she be pretty? I couldn't say. She has a lovely high curved brow, stunning eyes, and a delicately formed mouth. However, she also has the uneven protruding ears and thinning hair, and the back of her head is not quite round somehow, perhaps from lying down so much. I have no idea what she will look like in the future, and I don't know anything about her personality. All I have is this little bundle of sadness in my arms and the knowledge that she has no parents in the world.

"Will you take her?" the sister asks again. She makes no mistake about the fact that she's offering me Bina and only Bina—that is, I have no choice. I can't help but thank her for that.

"Yes," I answer decisively, nodding. "Yes, I'll take her. Of course, I can't speak for my husband. He'll need to make up his own mind, but I think it'll be fine. Can we take a photo of her?" I ask, thinking of Andreas, who is on a business trip at the moment. Suddenly, I have a terrible thought that he might reject Bina, that he might not want her for some reason or might feel that I'm forcing him into it. It's a shame he couldn't make this journey with me, and perhaps he doesn't fully understand exactly how difficult it is to get a child in the first place.

Sister Lena and I take Bina outside into the courtyard. By now the truck has rolled off down the street. The gate has just been closed after it. The heat is unbearable out here, and the sunlight dazzles Bina straightaway. She blinks in my arms, winces as if the bright light is hurting her eyes, and starts to cry. I pass Bina back to Sister Lena, and immediately the crying stops as she buries her little face in the sister's white linen sari. Luckily, Sister Lena is happy to have her picture taken. I come away with a lovely shot of Bina in Sister Lena's arms.

"It's time to take her back inside now. You can come, too. Then you'll see where she spends her time," the sister remarks. I follow her back into the orphanage to the room where the children between three and ten months are kept. Eventually, the sister stops beside a tiny cot in a long row two-cots deep and puts Bina down. She begins to cry bitterly straightaway. She shoves her fist into her mouth and sobs. Tears fill my eyes. I fight the urge to pick her up again. We have to go; if we keep standing there, it will only make matters worse. I turn around and can hear her crying behind me, not in anger or defiance. It's just a deeply sorrowful, lonely crying. It's the saddest cry I've ever heard a child make. It's the crying of my daughter.

As we walk away from the cot, I turn around and see Bina roll onto her knees. She starts to rock her body back and forth, rhythmically and monotonously. I'm overcome with a sense of panic; I stare at the long rows of cots, the crying babies, the dark, barred windows covered with fly screens, and all of a sudden, the heel-dragging bureaucracy that is our adoption process seems unbearably drawn out and demoralizing. It's as if Sister Lena can read my mind.

"Make sure your papers are prepared and arrive quickly," she urges once we're back in the office. "Then you'll receive Bina's papers and her medical report; you'll need these for the notary. You will have to sign all the papers in front of the notary, and then they will send everything back to us. From here, they go to the ministry in New Delhi and then to the court."

"How long will all that take?" I ask nervously. I'm concerned. I can't help but think of all the adoption books I've read over in recent months—books written by parents, by doctors, by experts in child psychiatry and developmental psychology. They all agree on one thing: the longer a child spends in an orphanage, the greater the chances that his or her behavior and development will be affected. Some scientists go so far as to say that just being separated from the mother after birth causes profound trauma for the child. And that's not to mention the effects of an unhappy pregnancy.

Most scientists and doctors believe that an infant is extremely likely to show behavioral issues if he or she remains in an institution longer than the first few months of life. The longer the time spent there, the more traumatic it becomes for the child and the more the (often-tragic) experiences and shortcomings of life in an orphanage affect his or her behavior.

After reading all these books, I remember telling myself that I wouldn't adopt a baby that was more than six months old. I had read terrifying reports of children who were left completely incapable of integrating into normal family life and who needed years to work through the consequences of their traumatic experiences. Some would never manage to do so. This was particularly likely when children had been through several orphanages and caregivers early on in their lives and had been looked after by multiple people, preventing them from forming a close relationship with a single person. A child learns about the world through a deep and intimate relationship with his or her parents or with another caring person who protects him or her.

I know now that my hope of adopting such a young child was unrealistic, at least if I want to adopt from India. Bina is already ten months old, and the wheels of bureaucracy turn slowly, both on the Indian side and my own. Am I already too late?

"Now, don't you worry," says Sister Lena. "Bina is absolutely fine here. The main thing is that you get your papers ready quickly. And make sure you call me straightaway when your husband has agreed."

The joy of having finally found my daughter overwhelms me again, and I push all doubts aside. I can't afford to waste time. I'll need all my strength, energy, and courage to see Bina's adoption through. I've made up my mind and am relieved that a decision has been reached so that finally the time of worrying and not knowing is over. We've found a child! I know that no matter what life decides to throw at us now, we can deal with it. I'm so happy and can hardly believe this is happening. I'll call Andreas straightaway; he'll be over the moon!

"Thank you so much," I tell Sister Lena. "You can't possibly know how much this means to us, to me. You've given us a child." I am deeply touched.

"God wanted it this way. Thank you for being willing to help Bina," she replies.

We say our good-byes. I go back out into the courtyard and leave the orphanage in a daze.

I stumble out into the street into the whirlwind of clattering auto-rickshaws. In front of me lie the slum huts. A train wails nearby. A cow trots through the chaos, unperturbed by the scooters swerving around it. The men are still brewing their spiced tea at the side of the street. Suddenly, I feel a deep connection to this country. As if through some pact or contract, I feel bound to it, adopted by it, swallowed into it, part of this maelstrom. My daughter comes from here, from this bubbling melting pot, this cruel metropolis, this terrible yet beautiful country. I feel as if I've been set free. I smile with relief and can feel myself glowing as I make my way back through the street. We've found a child, and I'll do everything I can to get the adoption through as quickly as possible. I just hope with all my heart that Andreas accepts Bina. She shouldn't have to spend any longer waiting in her cot.

I walk determinedly into the little bazaar. Last time I was there, I saw a man selling Indian children's clothes in dazzling colors—red and orange, with little mirrors embroidered onto them, in the style of traditional costumes from Rajasthan. I buy two sets, a dress and a tiny salwar kameez, along with some of the bangles that mothers put on their children's wrists—a few things to get us started.

Back at the hotel, I try to get hold of Andreas, but he's caught up in a meeting. When he calls back,

I tell him everything. I'm so excited that I can't help but overwhelm him with the news. "We haven't just found the right orphanage but a child. We have a child. Can you believe it?" I talk and talk, and as I describe Bina to him, I just hope so much that he won't come up with any arguments against her. I'm afraid that he might feel forced into it. But Andreas is positive, if cautious; he wants to see photos, wants to be sure that I'm not making decisions without him. I can tell it's hard for him, being so far away from it all. I notice something else, too: the sense of responsibility is already there in him. He wants to provide for Bina, to care for her. He knows her fate depends on him, and he is brushing all manner of questions and doubts aside because of this. I'm relieved. I'm convinced that Andreas will accept Bina, and I count my blessings that I have a husband who is prepared to go through this with me and who has so much trust in me. It's so good to know we're in this together. I couldn't do it any other way.

I lie awake for hours that night, listening to the trains, the monotonous loudspeaker announcements, the rattle of the auto-rickshaws, and the cawing crows. At one point the clatter of drink crates cuts through the darkness; the hotel must be getting a new delivery. Later still, barking dogs and the asthmatic wheezing of the merchants, wrapped up outside in their blankets, are the only sounds left to hear. I wonder what Bina hears, just several feet from here in her little cot in the orphanage. Can she hear the trains? The barking dogs? The constant coughing? But then, perhaps the babies never stop screaming? I begin to worry. If she cries in the night, does someone come to her? And in the daytime, would anyone even be able to hear her over the cries of the other babies?

Once again, I see the long rows of baby beds and hear Bina's long, drawn-out, deeply sad crying. How long will it be until I can finally take her away from that cage of a cot? I'm flying home tomorrow. Our case will have to go through so many authorities. Until now there have been nothing but delays, and that's just from the Indian side.

Once I get home tomorrow, I will do everything I can to hurry the adoption along. I'm determined that Bina will be out of the orphanage for good by her first birthday.

Chapter 13

A MODERN ODYSSEY

"Squint." "Strabismus." "Ophthalmology." "Cross-eyed." I've been sitting in my office at home for almost two hours now, typing these search terms into my laptop. During the day, my job leaves me no time to surf the Internet; but now, late in the evening, I sit here feeling my way through a maze of websites.

I hadn't expected to find so many different sites: ophthalmic clinics from all corners of the world, research centers, eye specialists answering questions posted by worried patients, even forums where parents of children with squints discuss treatment methods. I flip through the pages, still warm from my printer—a whole bundle of academic articles on squinting in children and its treatment.

All this surfing comforts me. I'm finally doing something productive now, unlike before my trip. There's nothing holding me back.

I catch a glimpse of Bina's photo. I have it lying here on the desk in front of me. Her fine hair is plastered against her sweaty head in the heat, her dark squinting eyes barely visible under her long, black lashes.

Andreas didn't like her ears at first, but that was his only complaint when I placed this photo of a child he'd never even seen before in his lap. Now he thinks she's as cute as I do and is desperate to fly to Mumbai together so he can meet her. I've already phoned Sister Lena to confirm that Andreas has agreed—that we'd definitely like to adopt Bina. Consequently, she's in the process of preparing the paperwork.

I've also called Sarah, our social worker, to tell her about Bina. Although she congratulated us, I could sense the hesitation in her voice as she asked us to send over Bina's medical reports as soon as they arrived. She also warned me not to get too emotionally attached to Bina. After all, she wasn't legally our child yet, and who knows what could happen?

She has a point. I haven't been able to bring myself to frame Bina's photo and put it on display in the living room; it could be tempting fate. I'd rather wait until we've signed the adoption papers from our lawyer. All the same, I feel like a huge weight has been lifted; the inner conflict I've had for the last few years has vanished into thin air because finally, at long last, we have a decision. After years with no success, Andreas had been right to be reluctant to continue trying to conceive a child through fertility treatment. We'd already wasted far too much time! We should have gone down the adoption route much sooner.

In fact, we'd already toyed with the idea of adoption years ago. Sunnita would always be on our minds. After my first trip to India, I'd written to the charity SOS Children's Villages to ask if I could sponsor a little girl. They soon replied, offering me a newborn baby in a small Indian town. I'll never forget the moment I opened the letter and stared in shock at the black-and-white photo inside: it was a portrait of the tiny infant, starved to the bone, her closed eyes swimming in huge gaping sockets. She'd been found by the police, abandoned—or more accurately, dumped—by the side of the road. Every Christmas since then, they sent me a photo of Sunnita, still sickly, delicate, and cautious, but alive at least, posing stiffly in her Sunday best with her nine adoptive siblings, also orphans. In the middle of the photo, framed by the children, stood the Children's Village "mother" of this family of ten.

One day, on one of our trips to India, we arrived unannounced at the reception of the SOS

Children's Village and asked to see Sunnita, wondering whether she even existed. Yes, of course, the village leader replied and shyly led us to the small house where the family lived. There was Sunnita. I recognized her from her photo. She was as sickly and feverish as ever, but also safely snuggled in her mother's arms and doted on by her nine siblings. Back then, the village leader told us that they were having to turn children away; there were so many abandoned babies that there was simply no other option but to send some of them to "regular" orphanages. This had affected us deeply, and we promised each other that one day when we started a family we would also adopt a child from an Indian orphanage.

But then I made things difficult for us. The idea of adoption frightened me, and I convinced myself that somehow pregnancy would work out. School, studies, career, marriage—I'd never had to admit defeat before in anything I did, and I could not and would not accept that my body didn't work the way I wanted it to.

I became impatient. I had worked hard, and until now my efforts had always been rewarded. It seemed so unfair that I couldn't have a child. I felt that having children was my right, and every woman with a baby bump I saw filled me with resentment.

I knew these thoughts were irrational and that getting pregnant had nothing to do with how hard you tried. It's quite the opposite, in fact. When I saw my gynecologist, he asked me bluntly whether by any chance I had a stressful, demanding career with tight deadlines. Then he just nodded knowingly and gave me a look that said, "Ah, another one." He was trying to say that having a stressful, pressured job and trying to get pregnant weren't a good combination. But I wouldn't take the hint; I tried to force my body into getting pregnant. I've lost track of the number of months I spent taking my temperature every morning to find out when I was ovulating and pinpoint my most fertile days. I found these temperature graphs comforting; they reminded me so much of the technical analysis charts used in investment banking. All my uncertainty was summed up in numbers, confined to a range, and pretty soon I was able to see a pattern in the temperature curve. These charts and curves gave me a little bit of security and rationality—until my next period anyway.

Then I slowly I let myself be led on a merry dance of curiosity, hope, and disappointment by gynecologists who promised me what I wanted to hear—that I could become pregnant. I just needed a little medical help, they said. This "help" was relentless. There was no end in sight. For years I believed the gynecologists, who dangled hope in front of me like a carrot—just one more examination, just a few more weeks of hormones, just another blood test... and then it would be very likely that I'd be pregnant. I should be excited and just relax—that was very important. Everything would be fine.

Andreas and I had many discussions about how far we wanted to take this. It was always on our minds, and of course it was uncharted territory for us. Andreas was more inclined to accept that having children just wasn't going to work out for us. I, on the other hand, was obsessed with the thought that it simply had to work, that success was just out of reach. After all, fertility treatment had worked for so many of our friends.

Andreas stood by me. He accompanied me on my odyssey through gynecologists' offices and shared the hope, disappointment, and tears that colored my life for many years.

In all this time, not one of the five gynecologists I saw mentioned the word *adoption*. This was not their field. The journey from the world of gynecologists to the world of adoption was one we would have to discover for ourselves and make alone.

The first chapter of our odyssey was a trip to the hospital for a laparoscopy, a surgical operation to investigate the organs of the abdomen and pelvis. It was a small, simple procedure, as my gynecologist put it, quite routine. "Everything's in perfect working order. Completely normal. You'll get pregnant, just be patient," the doctor assured me—an optimistic misdiagnosis.

On the next stage of our journey to completing our family, I was prescribed hormones to help my eggs mature faster and to improve their quality, making them more fertile. We took it in good spirits and hoped—until my next period arrived. I didn't get pregnant, even with the hormones.

After many months of trying all these methods and failing, we were presented with the next level of technology: artificial insemination. We talked until we were blue in the face about whether this was the right thing to do or whether we should just give up and adopt instead. But success seemed just around the corner; friends of ours had conceived their children this way.

To go down this path was to abandon all hope of conceiving naturally. The act of conception would be transported from the privacy of our bedroom to a sterile operating room at the clinic and chance would be taken out of the equation. An instrument would be used to inject the man's sperm directly into the woman's uterus. Making a baby would no longer take place in a man's loving arms, but on the gynecologist's examination table under the bright lights of the operating room, the procedure carefully monitored by an ultrasound. Any small part of the process that was still in nature's hands was more of a curse than a blessing because it was unpredictable and couldn't be controlled.

First of all, I had to have hormone injections, which mostly took place at our local doctor's surgery. I found it incredibly embarrassing, and always wondered what the doctors and receptionists there must think of me. Perhaps they thought, "Why is she putting herself through this? Why doesn't she just let it go?" Or maybe they thought it would come to nothing anyway, but were too polite to say so. Trying to get pregnant the technical way seemed so affected; I was extremely uncomfortable with the situation and never really came to terms with it, even on the day of the operation.

I insisted that Andreas go to the office as normal, against his will, and went into the operation room alone. I would immediately realize that this was a mistake. As the friendly nurse called me into preop, my eyes filled with tears and I began to sob. I found it so unbelievably tragic to conceive a child this way, alone on the operating table, surrounded by medical equipment and doctors. The nurse, a lovely Indian woman, asked me why I was so upset. I told her it was the situation.

"I know, I know," she said soothingly, holding my hand.

The doctor comforted me, too. "Only the result matters."

I let them get on with it, silently raging at myself. How could I be desperate enough to put myself through this procedure? Every last scrap of fun, the humanity, and everything natural had been stripped away, and all that remained was shame at being completely at the mercy of technology. When the bleeding started two weeks later, showing that I wasn't pregnant, it only served to confirm my pessimistic premonitions.

From then on, Andreas was dead-set against any more medical interventions. I believe that he just couldn't take it anymore, watching me suffer psychologically as well as physically. It was emotionally draining for him, too; he had always been more willing to accept that we couldn't have children naturally. It was different for me; I felt as if I had failed, that this somehow made me less of a woman. It was a matter of self-esteem.

Also, the idea of taking a strange child into my life scared me in ways I couldn't quite define. It took some time for me to understand that the only way to put these fears to rest was to throw myself into the topic of adoption and learn as much as I could about it. In those days, though, I shied away, let myself be put off by friends' stories of adoptions that had "gone wrong," and believed the warnings that we'd have less trouble with our "own" children. There was no place in our lives for social workers, psychiatrists, experts in children with physical or learning disabilities, special schools, or drug counselors, of that I was sure. These were the sorts of things I associated with the phrase "gone wrong," and they represented a risk that I didn't want to take, didn't want to have in my life. I never really thought about what they might actually entail. I was terrified of spending the rest of my life blaming myself.

All these uncertainties and fears meant that after a month's break, I tried to bully Andreas into letting us have a go at IVF, even if only once. The procedure involved harvesting some of the woman's eggs during an operation, mixing them with the man's sperm in a petri dish, and then, once the cells began to divide, implanting one of the resulting embryos back into the woman's body.

This time our arguments at home were more heated. Andreas was against IVF.

"If it doesn't work, your back's against the wall. You'll have no other choice. I don't want adoption to be a last-resort option for us. I want us to do it willingly, to make a positive decision to adopt a child, not just do it because it's the only option we have left."

His argument made sense to me, and I began to warm to the idea of adoption. All the same, I still didn't have quite enough confidence to go down this route. What if the adoption went wrong? If we didn't at least try IVF, would I always mourn for the biological child I could have had? In the end, Andreas agreed, but he left me in no doubt that he would do this once, and only once.

But as we prepared for the in vitro procedure, our doubts grew. Why go to such great lengths to force a pregnancy and bring a child into the world when there were already thousands of children in orphanages without parents? We couldn't find a satisfactory answer to this question, and it became the main reason for our ever-increasing interest in adoption. In spite of all the misgivings we had about adoption, we couldn't help but see artificial insemination as a kind of betrayal of a child in an orphanage. Somewhere in the world there was a child who had missed out on parents or who would have to wait longer to find some, all because I wouldn't take the risk and make a decision. I was running from myself, and gynecological technology was helping me to do it. I found myself half hoping that the IVF procedure would fail and the choice would be made for me.

I started reading books on adoption again. I spent my evenings sitting with my laptop, surfing the Internet and ordering even more adoption literature on Amazon, most of it from the United States. No other country has produced such a diverse, interesting, and professional range of books on the subject. The deeper I buried myself in these books, the more convinced I became that adoption was the right thing for us, particularly once I understood that no child comes out of an orphanage unscathed and that parents and children have to learn to live with these consequences for a lifetime.

Meanwhile, the preparations for my artificial insemination continued. I was pumped full of hormones. The side effects were miserable: my head ached, I was permanently tired, I struggled to concentrate, and I could barely keep up with my job.

Slowly, I began to get the feeling that perhaps I simply wasn't meant to get pregnant. Although I'm not particularly religious, I longed for some kind of explanation. It felt as if I was meddling with my body in ways I shouldn't—the words *And lead us not into temptation* echoed in my head. I was afraid that God, if he existed, was no longer on our side, that he had stopped helping us. This was the only way I could explain to myself why everything had failed.

We decided to go for a long weekend in the country to recharge our batteries. I realized too late that I hadn't brought enough vials of hormones for my injections. The pharmacist in the village didn't stock them, and there was a three-hour wait at the local clinic due to emergencies. We had no choice but to cut our weekend short, so I drove us home through the heavy traffic. Once there, I spent another hour waiting to see the duty doctor. This was the final straw. I lost it completely and flew into a sobbing rage. I couldn't take it anymore. I was exhausted and disappointed. I felt as if everyone had abandoned me.

My fears only grew as the day of the operation approached. I was terrified that God might punish us with a disabled child. Of course, I knew I was being ridiculous, and Andreas laughed at me. All the same, I felt differently about the operation now. My heart wasn't in it. I buried my nose in my adoption books, and it really helped. It calmed me. An adoption was a huge undertaking, but it was something to aim for—an alternative.

I dreaded the operation, dreaded the anesthetic, dreaded everything, and I was glad that Andreas stayed with me this time. After the operation came the bad news: the gynecologist revealed that I had endometriosis, a medical disorder that drastically reduced the chances of successful fertilization. He recommended that we go ahead with the IVF this time. However, if it failed, I would need an operation before trying again, as this would be the only chance of further IVF attempts resulting in a pregnancy. At first I was shocked and disappointed, but then I took his diagnosis as confirmation of the fact that pregnancy simply wasn't meant to be for me. I was almost relieved. Finally it looked like things were going to work out in favor of adoption.

The clinic called me the next morning to tell me my eggs had already been fertilized in the petri dish. That afternoon I had a receptionist on the phone, babbling excitedly at me that three embryos had formed. All systems were go. I remained skeptical, however, knowing that there was still a good chance it would all come to nothing.

Perhaps that explains why I was calmer this time: our situation was not hopeless. Even at this point, I was half hoping that the IVF procedure would be unsuccessful.

It also helped that Andreas was there at the clinic with me and that I had gotten to know the staff, as well as the principles of the procedure. The doctor recommended that we implant all three embryos. He explained that the probability of my getting pregnant at all was around 20 to 25 percent and that, when this was adjusted for the risk of miscarriage, my chances of giving birth to a healthy child were only around 12 to 15 percent (not taking into account my endometriosis). So they implanted all three embryos. We even got to see them beforehand—three translucent bubbles under the microscope.

The doctor spoke encouragingly of our chances. Of course, he knew nothing of our adoption plans, but I was tired of hoping, tired of disappointments, tired of uncertainty. When we got home, I told Andreas, "Don't get your hopes up." Andreas, however, was optimistic.

"I'm not. I just know it's going to work this time," he said, but only after first musing that "It's a shame, really. Adopting an Indian girl would have been much more exciting."

The days that followed were unbearable. I was exhausted and flat—pregnant, perhaps? Gradually, I began to hope again. But a few days later, the sickness had passed, and my stomach began to ache. I felt as if my period was going to arrive at any minute and trample my hopes of pregnancy in the dust. I was shocked and silent, too exhausted to even cry.

To us, the last few weeks seemed like a cruel joke. I was just as far from being pregnant as I had been when we started. Even though he said nothing, I could tell Andreas was disappointed. He had hoped so very much, even more than I had.

Finally, the day came when the clinic had told me to call for my blood test results. "We're terribly sorry, but the test has come back negative," the receptionist said in her singsong voice, trying hard to sound sympathetic while other telephones rang in the background.

"Thank you," I replied cheerfully, hiding my disappointment, and I hung up.

My God, we'd been so close! We'd seen the embryos under the microscope—they could have become three children! Why was I so damned infertile? I cried, and this time I cried bitterly. I stood in the kitchen and stared out into our little yard. Earlier, while tidying my desk, I'd come across a picture of Andreas as a child. A little rascal had grinned back at me, all cheeky eyes and dimpled cheeks. I already saw a little child like him playing on the lawn.

I was glad when that year was over; it had taken so much energy to get through it. I once heard that we die when all our life force has been drained away. The past few weeks had cost me a lot of life force and significantly reduced my life expectancy, at least I imagined so. But all things considered, it was also a big relief; the subject was moot. I wouldn't be having the operation, wouldn't be continuing down the gynecological route. It would have taken too much time, strength, courage, and energy—all things I would need for the adoption.

As I sit here, looking at the photo of Bina, I'm glad this tortuous year is behind us and that we chose to adopt. We wasted so much time, ran ourselves into the ground, and came within an inch of missing out on a child like Bina. Now, after my trip to India and meeting Bina, I find it hard to make excuses for the way I behaved back then.

Chapter 14

INDIAN NEFERTITI

Nefertiti sits opposite me in the café. This is exactly how she must have looked—the straight, graceful nose, the gently sweeping eyebrows, the high forehead, the finely chiseled features.

I can hardly believe that this young Indian looks so much like her, only her glowing complexion is darker than the Egyptian statue's. She keeps pushing a strand of her black, curly hair out of her face, her dark eyes peer curiously around the restaurant.

I met this girl—Inka is her name—through friends. They'd contacted her as soon as they heard about our Indian adoption; after all, what could be better than to meet an Indian girl who is older now and can tell me her side of the adoption story? Inka is a student at a language college.

People at the neighboring tables are watching us, I notice, staring at her exotic beauty. Inka prods at her salad Niçoise, thoughtful. "Of course, I always tell them that I'm Swedish," she says. Because of her striking looks, people are constantly asking where she's from. "But then, people always think I'm joking. They say, 'Seriously? You can't be from Sweden! Tell us where you're really from.'"

She begins to ponder. "At home in Sweden, no one asks me that anymore. We live in a small village, and everyone there knows that my two sisters and I were adopted from India. We were still very little when we came to live with our parents," she recalls and then goes on to tell me about her Swedish home, her life there in the countryside, and her Swedish boyfriend. This was why I'd been so keen to meet her—I wanted to hear what a now-grown young woman had to say about her adoption, the conclusions she'd reached about it, whether she had any advice for me.

"Then I came here and all of a sudden people are telling me I can't be Swedish. It's the first time anyone's said it so openly to my face. So I make a point of telling them that I originally come from India. But that's ridiculous, too—I don't even know the place."

I ask whether her parents have told her about India, whether she'd ever been there. "No. If we had questions, my parents would answer them, but we didn't really have many," she replies. "If she'd never been introduced to India, how would she know what to ask?" I wonder. Questions don't appear out of thin air; they come in response to a stimulus.

"Now, for the first time, I find myself in a foreign country surrounded by curious people who keep beating me over the head with the fact that I'm Indian," she says uncomfortably. "I don't even know what it means to be Indian! I don't know the first thing about India."

I had already sensed Inka's confusion earlier when I was telling her about India. She hadn't even heard of the Indian greetings *namaste* or *namaskar*. I was amazed to think she wouldn't even be able to greet the people of her native land.

"I sometimes go out for Indian food with my friends here," Inka tells me. After all these years, she's slowly starting to become interested in learning about India. "It's too much, though. It's such a big country, and the culture's so foreign and different. I don't know where to start," she says quietly, looking around helplessly.

I feel sorry for her, although I can understand her parents, too. How were they supposed to teach their children about Indian culture in a Swedish country, particularly in a time before the Internet, videos, Amazon, or satellite dishes? What lengths should they have gone to? At what point does one's own culture become more important and take precedence over everything else? These thoughts aside, not all adoptive parents are convinced that their children should be familiarized with their native cultures. I've met parents who stand by that attitude. "My children are German. Everything else just confuses things."

"Have you thought about going to India?" I ask Inka, carefully. *It would be a shock for her*, I think, *but a place to start*. She doesn't feel ready to take that step, however.

"I have thought about it. Perhaps with someone else. I wouldn't want to travel alone. I wouldn't know where to start or how to arrange it, though."

I'm not convinced it's just a matter of logistics that's holding Inka back from traveling to India. Could it also be that she's afraid of seeing what she's missed out on, that she might realize she belongs there and yet she doesn't fit in? Afraid that then she won't feel she really belongs anywhere?

"It wasn't until I turned twenty that I realized I didn't know who I was anymore," she confesses.

"I'm only just starting to think about it now." She tells me she feels alone on this journey, that she is deeply insecure. She sips her coffee pensively and then lights a cigarette.

We continue to talk for a long time. I give her a book in which adopted young people discuss their experiences of being adopted from another country. Some feel thankful, fortunate, and positive about their adoption. Others are indifferent. Still others are full of frustration and hate and are deeply critical of their adoptive parents. Many of these young people have profound feelings of displacement, particularly those who weren't allowed to keep their original birth name, who had a completely new identity forced upon them, and whose heritage was ignored by their adoptive parents.

Inka herself holds no grudges toward her parents or her adoption. "Why would I? She is, and always will be, my mum. She's the person who looked after us." She's thankful for her idyllic childhood in Sweden, is looking forward to going back and seeing her sisters and parents again, and has never wanted to meet her biological mother, even if it were possible.

We say good-bye and plan to meet again someday. But I would never hear from her again.

I make my way home, deep in thought. Why do so many parents ignore their children's roots? Is immersing oneself in another culture too difficult, too strange? Are the parents themselves afraid of becoming insecure? Why are other cultures so often perceived as threatening to our lives, rather than enriching to them? Or are those people who insist it only complicates matters for children perhaps right after all?

Personally, I'm very much enjoying learning about India at the moment: listening to traditional Indian music and reading the stories of the *Mahabharata*, an ancient Indian epic. Andreas and I enjoy browsing antiques fairs for old books of Indian fairy tales and accounts from British colonial India. I've even taken up yoga, which has done me a world of good, and I often make curry. I feel as though I'm on the edge of a vast sea, wading into it; right now, the water comes up to my ankles. It will be a long time before I'm fully submerged, and I will never be able to swim in this sea. Our knowledge will always be a hodgepodge—incomplete, learned from books, and observed from the outside, never lived or experienced for ourselves. Even so, we've made a commitment to give Bina enough of a taste that she will be able to continue this journey by herself, so that she will be able to become closer to her birth country and roots in a natural and unforced way. We want to raise her with a sense of her Indian identity—at least, as much as we can.

Sorting through the mail at home, I find a letter from our lawyer; she was recommended to me by an organization for adoptive parents. Andreas and I have an appointment with her in a few days' time to sign the legal documents that the Ministry for Family Affairs requires in order to send our adoption papers to India.

Speaking of the ministry, there's a letter from them, too. They are preparing our papers to send to the orphanage and to the Central Adoption Resource Agency (CARA), the New Delhi–based authority responsible for adoptions. When I open the letter, my heart leaps into my mouth. I sink down on a chair and stare at the letter in surprise. Then my surprise turns into anger.

"Unfortunately, we are unable to process your case at this time, as we are awaiting the following papers from the Youth Welfare Office..." the letter informs me. I can hardly believe my eyes and start to panic. I had thought our papers were almost ready to be sent off, and now I find that the ministry hasn't even started processing them. We're at least two weeks behind where we should be. Distraught, I run to my office and rummage through my files for telephone numbers. My stomach begins to ache; recently, I've found that stressful situations bring back the aftereffects of the amoebas I swallowed from the thermos that night in Mumbai.

Although the Youth Welfare Office had indeed sent the social report via us to the ministry, it appears they had not done the same with our criminal background checks and medical records. Other documents are missing, too. I drop everything and grab the phone. As is typical, I can't get hold of the caseworker I need at the Youth Welfare Office and have to keep calling around, explaining myself each time. My entire afternoon is a write-off. Here we go again, more of the familiar torture we've been going through for almost a year now.

It appears our friends were right. When they told us about their adoptions and recommended the orphanage in Mumbai, the husband had taken me aside into his study and pointed at his files. "See here, two files for each adoption—and they're crammed. It's like doing a PhD; you should prepare yourself for that."

My two files are already full of correspondences with the authorities as well as a host of duly notarized and certified documents and certificates that we had to enclose with our social report—all in English, of course—for the Indian authorities. In some cases, even the official stamp of the German authority has to be translated into English, and this translation in turn must be stamped. I've lost count of the number of telephone calls I've made, of the number of weeks I've spent researching how a private, independent adoption—that is, one that doesn't involve a professional adoption agency—even works in the first place. Then we had to provide medical records, criminal background checks, and references from friends and family. Our friends and my mother-in-law had to complete detailed questionnaires with written references. Among other things, they wanted to know if our marriage was stable, how we resolved conflict, and whether we were violent.

Then followed an hour-long interview with our social worker, Sarah. We spent late nights at parents' meetings, despite being tired from our days at work. Finally there was all the documentation we had to produce and the never-ending letter writing, phoning around, paying for translations, and chasing up authorities this entailed. I sorted out references and letters of confirmation from our employers, banks, insurance companies, and the tax office; deeds from the land registry; our birth and marriage certificates—all in English, all rubber-stamped. I even had to provide an "infertility statement," a medical confirmation of the fact that there was no chance of my becoming pregnant. The Indian authorities insist on this before they will allow a couple to adopt a child.

I often find myself sitting up late at night, working on the adoption. For months now, it's been almost like a part-time job, especially as we have to complete our "homework" of reports and provide comprehensive résumés and family trees. It's never ending, and my only consolation is having a good moan about it with the other adoptive parents in the parents association.

I realize that it's important to keep a close eye on prospective adoptive parents. Criminal activity does go on—there are cases of corruption, child trafficking, and abuse by pedophiles. And when it comes down to it, some couples are simply not suited to adopting a child. The authorities' red tape has a purpose: it's there to protect the adoption process from abuse.

Yet the flipside of this is that the process has become so complex that even the authorities themselves make mistakes, which complicates matters and creates delays. This situation had annoyed me before, but now every time I think of Bina, I despair because I know that every mistake means she will spend longer in the orphanage than she otherwise would have.

The next few weeks are a tortuous waiting game as we wait for the ministry to proceed with our case.

So many excuses over the telephone. They're short staffed; people are on sick leave or on vacation. Andreas and I make use of the delay to combine our offices into one room, freeing mine up for a nursery. I can't bring myself to start decorating it, though; I'm afraid that our case will drag on and on. My nagging and hassling the authorities can only do so much. We're dependent on them to get the work done, so we'll simply have to wait, which is something I'm finding very difficult to do.

I wake in the night, drenched in sweat, and stare into the darkness that fills my room. I think of Bina. Are we already too late? The crushing fear lies heavy on my chest in the gray light of morning; there's no escape from it. I can't sleep any more. I think about how much fuss we make here when a child has to spend a few days in hospital, of how often mothers and fathers are allowed to stay in with their child overnight, so desperate are we to protect that child from ever feeling abandoned. And yet, my daughter has already spent a year alone in the orphanage—every day, every night. Almost two months have passed since I saw her last. *I should have gone back long ago*, I think. *I should be helping her now.* But there's no telling how much longer the adoption will take to process, and I can hardly drop my work for months on end and disappear to India. I lie anxiously in bed, listening to my own long, miserable sobs.

The weeks go by. I struggle through my job, and then the day arrives—Bina's first birthday. I don't know what to do. Our papers are still with the caseworker at the Ministry for Family Affairs. Our lawyer has stamped them all, but the documents still need to pass through the Foreign Office and the Indian Embassy before they can be sent off.

I decide to phone the orphanage in Mumbai, which takes several attempts because of poor connection. At last, someone picks up, a sister who tells me she will fetch Sister Lena. I hear her footsteps fade into the distance. The line falls silent. Then suddenly, I hear the crows cawing, and in the background I can hear children crying and the familiar rattle of auto-rickshaws. All at once the orphanage seems so near—the heat, the traffic outside its walls, and the sight of Bina sitting in her cot. I long so much to see her again, to get her out of there.

Sister Lena comes on the line, says she's pleased to hear from me, and immediately asks when our papers will arrive. Bina's documents are almost ready, she tells me, and soon everything can go off to the Indian ministry. We chat about the adoption, and then I ask anxiously after Bina. I know I need to be careful what I say. I don't want to hurt Sister Lena.

"Oh, she's fine, of course. She's well looked after here; she has everything she needs. There's no need to worry." She seems a little indignant that I even needed to ask. In her eyes, she does everything she can to ensure the children in the orphanage are well cared for. They are fed, watered, and cleaned; they receive medical care; and someone plays with them from time to time. Everything's fine. And when I think of the conditions in the slum huts along the railway embankment a few feet away from the orphanage, I really can't hold the nuns' attitude against them.

I thank her politely and say good-bye. There is silence on the line again—the connection goes dead. Tears well up in my eyes. Andreas tries to comfort me, but doesn't quite succeed, especially when we light a candle for Bina's first birthday without her. I think of the extravagant birthday parties some of my friends throw for their children—the invitations, the balloons, the gifts, every moment captured on video. But Bina has spent a year alone in the orphanage and doesn't have any parents or even someone to give her a hug. She certainly has no one who would realize that today is her first birthday. I place her photo next to the candle and can only hope that she at least got the cuddly duck, the blanket, and the music box I sent her.

"I'll buy the tickets tomorrow," I tell myself, no matter how far along our papers are. Andreas and I are flying to Mumbai together to see Bina.

Chapter 15

A NEW FAMILY

My eyes are fixed on the doorway. Any moment Sister Lena is going to walk into the yard with Bina in her arms. She'd said it would take her only a moment to change Bina and get her dressed.

We are waiting in the shade. The caws of crows from the palm trees mingle with the cries of the babies of the orphanage. Mumbai is hell, as ever, an urban nightmare. Andreas feels it has gotten worse—the slums, the grime, the stench, and the crowds. It's something that gives us cause for thought every time we visit.

We arrived in Mumbai this morning in the early hours and stayed at the little hotel by the railway tracks. We could hardly wait for the orphanage gates to open. Andreas is meeting Bina for the first time today, and I hope to get to know her a little better—I held her for such a short time before. In fact, I can hardly remember what she was like; it all went so quickly. Will she have changed in the last two months? I wonder how she will be coping with the orphanage now that she has just turned a year old. And how will Andreas react to her?

"Stop biting your fingernails!" Andreas's voice grumbles beside me. He's right. I am nervous and tense. I sigh; I've noticed that I sigh so deeply these days, as if I'm struggling for breath. Andreas bites his bottom lip; it's a strange feeling for him, standing in this courtyard in Mumbai waiting to hold our little daughter.

There's Sister Lena now, holding Bina tightly in her arms. Bina is a vision in pink ruffles again. I stifle a laugh; I can't help but wonder if Sister Lena has dressed her to match the orphanage, with its fresh coat of pink paint.

Then my sense of humor vanishes. I hold my breath as Sister Lena approaches. Bina seems very disturbed, much thinner, and more sickly than I remember. She turns her worried face toward us, and I realize that she can barely see.

"She's not used to this. She needs a little time," says Sister Lena as she hands Bina to me. "It's better if I leave you alone, otherwise she'll just keep wanting to come back to me." And with that, she heads in the direction of her office. Bina immediately turns her head to follow her, sobs, and then clings stiffly to my arms.

"Come on, let's sit down for a bit," Andreas suggests, and we settle ourselves on the stone bench between the ornamental plants. I try to lift Bina up a bit so he can get a better look at her, but she clings to my clothes, her eyes fixed ahead of her in distress. Suddenly, she begins to cry fearfully and looks around again for the sisters and the orphanage.

"Do you want to take her?" I ask Andreas. However, when I try to place Bina in his outstretched arms, her crying becomes louder, panicked, and utterly desperate. I set her back on my lap again, gaze into her tiny, frightened face, see how the corners of her mouth quiver, and notice the big bald patches in her hair and her large ears. She won't look at us, but stares blankly at my clothing until eventually she collapses onto my tummy in exhaustion and lies there like a little frog. She's stopped crying now and has gone completely stiff—*rigid with shock*, I think. I talk to her in a soft, calming voice, but I can't help but feel that she's not taking it in. So I gently stroke her back. I'm moved, extremely happy to finally hold her in my arms, and yet I feel so guilty. It's plain to see that the past couple of months have been hard on her, that she is suffering here and needs to leave. *Every day counts*, I think.

How many more weeks must she spend here while the wheels of bureaucracy slowly turn? Once again, I worry that we're already far too late.

"It's too much for her," says Andreas. He bends over her, stroking her hair while I pat her back soothingly. Then suddenly, he exclaims, "She's asleep." It's true. Her eyes are closed, and she seems to be sleeping. Sweat streams down from her hair over her temples. I have to keep batting the mosquitoes away. So Andreas rubs her with some insect spray. I notice a rat creeping through the bushes behind our bench. Everything's so much more squalid than I remember it, and I realize that I must have gotten used to the way things are here during my last trip.

"She's really not doing well, Andreas. Last time she was calmer, more secure somehow. Now she's just not reacting to us at all," I tell him. Am I afraid that he will reject Bina? "I'm just not sure she's OK," I continue. I'm distraught. Bina's behavior doesn't make sense to me.

"What did you expect? She's still here in the orphanage. She just needs to get out!" Andreas replies. "She'll be better then. You'll see." Andreas is always so much more confident about things than I am. Perhaps he has a point.

We sit there, sweating, listening to Bina's deep regular breathing. She's lying, straddling my tummy. I can feel her back rising and falling beneath my hands. She's sleeping. "Is this some kind of shock-avoidance tactic—simply sleeping through the situation?" I wonder. I gaze at her head with concern—the bald patches at the back, her large, uneven ears. Come to think of it, I don't know what dimensions are normal for a one-year-old, and I have absolutely no idea how a child of this age should behave either.

Suddenly, Bina awakes. She sits up and looks around as if in a trance. This time I give her to Andreas, who takes her carefully in his arms and talks to her quietly. But she doesn't respond; she becomes poker stiff and stares into thin air, blanking everything out. Then she begins to cry. Andreas hands Bina back to me. A cloud of thoughtfulness and helplessness descends over us. Bina has stopped crying on my lap and stares stiffly at my stomach, completely devoid of reaction, despite my attempts to stroke and talk to her. It's as if she can't hear me, as if she's not really there. When she does react, it's delayed, as if she's in slow motion, as if she's paralyzed somehow. She gazes in the direction of the sisters again. We decide that it's too much for her, that it's time for her to go back. We take her to Sister Lena.

As soon as we walk into the baby room and she's in Sister Lena's arms, a change comes over Bina. All of a sudden she can see clearly, looks around with interest, and snuggles into Sister Lena's shoulder. It's such a relief, and I reassure myself that perhaps it was just the unfamiliar situation. I look around at the rows of cots, at the babies inside grasping at the bars and the two young women changing, feeding, dressing, and making the beds of this gaggle of babies, which they do in a routine, friendly, but also brisk manner. Instead of modern diapers, the babies have simple cotton cloths that need to be changed as soon as they get wet. This visit, the orphanage seems more primitive, harsher, and more stressful for the children. However, I must remember that this time I don't have the contrast of the other orphanages and have come straight from our rich, clean, perfect world.

I look at Bina, who looks quite at home in the sister's arms, even smiling and babbling now as the nun plays with her. I see the deep, almost tender, connection between them. Perhaps Bina never leaves this room. Perhaps this is why she's incapable of dealing with other situations. And, of course, she doesn't know what to do in the arms of these strange new people.

We arrange with the sister to come back and see the children after they've had their lunch and nap.

Outside the home, Andreas comforts me. "She's a sweet little thing. She's just scared of us. Once our child is home with us, she'll soon recover. Just you wait and see." I'm touched. Andreas said it without thinking: Bina—our child.

And yet, at what point does Bina actually become our child? It's so tricky to pinpoint in an adoption. Is it the moment when you see the child for the first time, or when the parents make the joint decision to adopt? Maybe the day when you go to the lawyer's office to sign the papers, or the day when the Indian court grants custody? Perhaps it's better to wait until you bring the child home to celebrate, or a year later when the German courts confirm the German adoption. Or is it the day when the child receives his or her German passport, granting him or her the nationality and the last name of the parents? It's a long process with many individual steps, and with every one you complete, you just find yourself worrying and hoping for the next one.

Even so, as we slowly make our way back through the busy streets to our hotel and as we sit eating our curries and drinking sweet lassi, a cool yogurt drink, in the little vegetarian restaurant there, we both suddenly feel that we're parents. I sense this feeling bringing us closer together, and we draw new strength from this closeness.

That afternoon, Andreas and I go back to the orphanage. On the way I notice that the slum huts are more tightly packed together than they had been two months ago. They now run the full length of the wall. I even see the cropped-haired woman again in her hut, huddled under blankets with her son; she appears to be in a trance—dazed, bent forward in exhaustion. The son seems to be searching her hair for lice.

This time we're allowed to go straight to Bina and visit her in her cot in the baby room. She sits there, the cotton cloths wrapped around her already wet, and is reaching through the bars trying to steal a plastic bear from the baby in the cot next to her. As the little girl yanks the toy away out of Bina's reach, I suddenly remember the blanket, the music box, and the cuddly duck I'd sent her from home. There's no sign of them here. When I ask the sisters about it later, they have no idea what I'm talking about. They never received a parcel from us.

One of the young women in the room takes Bina out of her cot and wraps her briskly in new cotton cloths. Bina calmly puts up with this and watches us curiously, less fearfully than this morning. Yet when the young woman hands Bina to me and we leave the room of crying babies, she nervously clings to me again. Outside in the yard, she buries her face in my clothes as if the sunlight is blinding her, as if she can hardly focus. Her body freezes and stiffens once more, and she shuts down. I give her to Andreas, who sits her on his tummy and squeezes himself carefully into the dusty children's swing among the tropical plants. Yet as soon as Andreas slowly starts to swing with her, Bina begins to cry and shake with fear. She clings to Andreas in shock, staring blankly ahead of her. It's obvious that she's never been on a swing before, so Andreas sits down beside me with her on the bench. It takes just a few minutes before she falls asleep again. When she wakes up a little later, she goes back into slow-motion mode and stops responding altogether. I start to worry that there's really something mentally wrong with her. I just can't make sense of her behavior; she can't be so tired that she keeps falling asleep all the time. Andreas and I agree that, at the very least, being here has affected her behavior.

"Do you think we could ask them if we could take her to the doctor? After all, we've got no idea what's wrong with her," I suggest.

"Sure, we could certainly do that. But she needs parents, Bettina, whatever's wrong with her. And don't forget, we could have just as easily brought a disabled child into the world. Then we would have just had to deal with it." I know he's right, and I'm annoyed with myself for not being able to accept

Bina as she is. I have to know exactly what's wrong with her eyes, whether she's mentally healthy. I'm already wondering how she'll keep up with other children later in life. Bina isn't even our daughter yet, and already I'm turning into the competitive parent. I am worried, though. I can't be sure if the sisters are being honest with me when they say that Bina's only problem is her eyes. Somehow her whole head, her eyes, and her ears appear to be asymmetrical and a little off. What if something went wrong during her birth? I stop myself. There I go again, so afraid of having a disabled child, of the massive responsibility this brings and the child's lifelong dependency on me. Andreas is right, of course, when he says Bina needs parents, especially so if she turns out to have special needs. However, I would be the one who would have to give up so many things and who would be caring for the child most of the time. Andreas would still have his job.

We can only spend a little time with Bina in the yard before she begins to cry again, heart-wrenchingly this time. We take her back to her little bed, but her crying doesn't stop. She suddenly begins to rock monotonously back and forth, as if in a trance. I look to one of the young women for help, but they're both busy giving other babies their bottles. They're different women than the ones who were here even this morning, I notice. Deeply concerned, we leave Bina there alone.

"Get our papers ready. She needs to get out of there," Andreas snaps in irritation.

We find Sister Lena buried behind a pile of files in her office, discussing adoption cases with another sister, who is filling out forms on an old typewriter. Delicately, I ask if we might take Bina to see a doctor. She agrees that we can do so the following day. She even seems to understand our concerns.

"But Bina is fine. She's very healthy, in fact." Sister Lena laughs.

I'm still not so sure myself. As we join the tourists traveling to Colaba late that afternoon, we ponder the best way to go about finding a pediatrician with no connections to the orphanage. Then I catch sight of the Taj Mahal, the luxury hotel on the bay here near the Gateway of India. This time, instead of avoiding the place, we cross the street and go into the lobby. We're greeted with a rush of ice-cool air. Through a glass wall, we catch a glimpse of the luxurious swimming pool where tourists recover from the dusty heat of the city.

I make my way to the front desk and ask if they can recommend a pediatrician.

"A pediatrician? I'm afraid not," the receptionist replies apologetically, but then he seems to pause for thought. I'm just about to turn away when his face brightens and he cries out, "Of course, my uncle! My uncle is a pediatrician, but not here. He works further away in the north of Mumbai." I can hardly believe my luck as he explains to me that his uncle works in the exact part of town where the orphanage is. I use the Taj Mahal's phone to call the pediatrician and make an appointment for tomorrow.

The next day, the sisters put Bina in a sky-blue dress with sky-blue socks and a matching sky-blue hat. She seems much calmer than before, and is even up to playing with us for a while, putting her arms up and down, and rocking in our arms along with nursery rhymes. Little does she know that two trips to the doctor await her today. Her first appointment is with an eye specialist at the local hospital, accompanied by Sister Maria; the second is with the independent pediatrician. Bina remains in Sister Maria's arms, and the four of us travel together in an auto-rickshaw to the hospital. As soon as we leave the gates of the orphanage, Bina is frightened again, even in the sister's arms, and she clings to her like a frog. We have an hour's wait at the hospital. Then the specialist has to put drops in Bina's eyes to dilate her pupils so that he can do a thorough examination. Now we have to sit tight and wait for the drops to take effect. Bina clings ever tighter. I'm holding her now. Sister Maria has gone off to visit other children from the orphanage who are in the hospital at the moment. Suddenly, Andreas and I find ourselves sitting alone with Bina in the cramped, stuffy corridor of this Mumbai hospital. Mothers huddle with their young children on the floor, tightly packed together outside one of the tiny consultation rooms. There's obviously a vaccination clinic running today. The hospital reeks of disinfectant, and there's the constant crying of children. Bina slowly relaxes—she seems to feel at home in these noisy, cramped surroundings—and plays with my pen. Not once does she cry, as I'd feared she might when Sister Maria disappeared down the corridor.

The Indian mothers and their children watch us with interest. One of the women asks me, with the help of much gesturing, whether this is our child. I nod, and she responds with an approving version of the Indian headshake and an encouraging smile.

We could really use a smile right now, as Bina's good mood comes to an abrupt end when we're called in and the doctor begins the eye examination. Luckily, Sister Maria arrives at that very moment, but it's awful for Bina all the same, because the doctor has to get right up close to her eyes. She tosses her head from side to side in fear, so violently that the doctor has to call in several assistants to hold her steady. Bina screams her head off. The men are drenched in sweat—it's baking hot in here—and I fight back the tears, wondering whether to ask the doctor to stop the examination. I really feel that the child suffering in front of us is our daughter and I feel so terribly sorry for her.

Once the torture is over and she's back in Sister Maria's arms, Bina calms down, and the doctor gives us his diagnosis. He doesn't have much equipment at his disposal, and his "practice" is just a tiny room with just enough space for a couch, a small desk, and a chair. We barely have room to turn around, and can hear the children having their jabs in the next room scream blue murder. However, the doctor seems used to all this and he strikes me as being very experienced as he raises his voice over the crying babies.

"No evidence of muscle weakness, no neurological damage, just a standard squint. She can have an operation to correct it at some point." We all breathe a sigh of relief, the doctor included, and decide there's no need for any further eye examinations.

We drop Sister Maria back at the orphanage and set off for the pediatrician's office. There we sit, Andreas and I with Bina on my lap, traveling through the bustling traffic in the auto-rickshaw. Once again, I get the feeling that we're parents now. Bina clings to me, goes stiff again, and falls asleep. I stroke her head and her dark hair, gazing down at the long lashes that cover her eyes. She is so unbelievably sweet and tiny, so fragile, innocent, and vulnerable.

After searching for a while, we find the entrance to the doctor's practice in a run-down building in a back street. As we climb the stairs, I almost want to leave again. I don't like this dark stairwell and feel sure we must be in the wrong place. Yet, when we finally reach the top of the stairs, we actually do find ourselves in a waiting room, although it's so dark that we can only make out the patients and the receptionists once our eyes have adjusted. I hand Bina to Andreas. She wakes up, fresh and lively in the dark atmosphere. A little boy is playing on the floor of the waiting room. Bina snuggles up to Andreas, and then suddenly sits up and starts babbling. A little later she even takes her first shaky steps across the room, holding Andreas's hands. Her eyes suddenly fill with pride, and I feel like an idiot for ever thinking that she could have a mental disability.

We're called in to see the doctor. Bina prods at his telephone with a pen. He's patient with her. He sees lots of children from orphanages he tells us. He works for another orphanage nearby. Then he examines Bina slowly and very sensitively, speaks to her kindly, and concludes that her development is perfectly normal—very tall for her age, a little bit light of weight, but otherwise healthy. "You can adopt her without any worry," he says with a smile.

We arrive back at the orphanage with time to spare, so we sit on the bench again. Straightaway, Bina stiffens again, her movements slow down, she blinks as if she can hardly see, and then drops straight off to sleep on Andreas's tummy. We agree that she is somehow unable to cope with the world outside the orphanage. But of course, how can we expect her to when this is all she knows? This should not prevent us from adopting her. No matter what's wrong with her, she needs parents; if there is something wrong, then she needs them all the more. I hope that everything works out.

With heavy hearts, we take her back to her little cot, where she immediately falls into a trance and begins her monotonous rocking. As we leave, I suddenly hear her crying sorrowfully. I can make out her individual cry, even over those of the other children. I would dearly love to pack her up and take her home with us, but we can't do that until the Indian courts have granted us custody, and that's a very, very long way away.

But there is a glimmer of hope. Since we arrived in Mumbai, I've spoken to the Ministry for Family Affairs, which has told me that our papers are ready and will be sent to India in the next few days. Then we will receive Bina's adoption papers in return to give to our lawyer to sign—a moment I have been working toward for almost a year. Sister Lena is also relieved when I tell her about our progress. Andreas and I board the plane that evening, happy, in spite of having to leave our daughter behind. Everything's suddenly become serious and exciting all at once—we're a step closer to adopting Bina.

Chapter 16

THE MISSING FIVE CENTIMETERS

The waiting is unbearable. At five thirty this morning, I was already in my study, sitting at my desk in my bathrobe with a cup of tea, on the phone to Sister Lena in Mumbai. Because of the four-hour time difference, this is the best time to reach her. Our papers have finally arrived in India, and the sister has put Bina's adoption papers—court documents and medical certificates—in the mail today. Once they arrive, we need to take the originals of these documents to our lawyer and confirm our intention to adopt by signing them.

I have gone to great lengths to arrange an international courier service to collect the papers from the orphanage and send them to us and have made countless phone calls to their helpful young employee in Mumbai to check that everything was going to plan.

The international courier has a website that provides detailed tracking information for every shipment. I'm so on edge that I decide to go online to check where my package is now. I type in the long shipping bill number and then furrow my brow as the information pops up: "collected in Mumbai, in transit via air to New York, Bronx distribution center." Thinking I must have made a typo in my excitement, I enter the number again. But there it is again on the screen: "collected in Mumbai, in transit via air to New York, Bronx distribution center." A shiver runs down my spine as I check the numbers again. They match.

I have one last try. Once again the destination comes up as "New York, Bronx distribution center." My stomach starts to ache with tension and worry. It doesn't help, of course, that I'm on my third type of antibiotics. I've had to cut lots of different foods from my diet and have lost several pounds. I reach for the phone and call the courier in Mumbai. Please, not another problem—surely we can't be that unlucky.

"That's right, the shipment is on its way to New York. We did tell the orphanage that you don't live there, but they insisted the address was correct," the worried young man confirms. A hot wave of anger and despair rises inside me.

"But we haven't lived in New York for two years now. I did explain several times…" I already see the courier riding through Manhattan on his motorbike and handing the letter to the porter at our old apartment on the Upper West Side. By the time the porter has discovered that we no longer live on the twentieth floor…It doesn't bear thinking about. Bina's precious papers!

I call the orphanage and speak with Sister Lena. At first she doesn't seem to understand what I'm talking about, and then she remembers that for some unexplained reason, she must have used one of our old addresses. I become very short with her and blame her for the delay. I remind her that we've no time to waste. Then she loses her patience.

"I suppose you think you're the only case we have to deal with. We're very busy, and everyone has to wait their turn. Stop hassling us! If Bina has to stay with us a bit longer, so be it. It wouldn't be the end of the world. She's absolutely fine here, and the little bit more love she would get with you won't make that much difference anyway."

I'm so furious that I can barely speak. The "little bit more love"? How can she say that? Tears fill my eyes, but I force myself to stay calm, control myself, and say nothing. We need to work together with the orphanage, and whether our case progresses quickly, or even at all, is completely dependent on them. I simply can't risk our case and Bina's fate being shoved on the back burner all because of my stupid comments, so I apologize.

Many phone calls later, the courier's employee in Mumbai and I arrange for the shipment to be intercepted at an airport in Europe on its way to New York. As promised, the courier company manages to fish the letter out. I have the papers in my hand that very same evening.

I tear open the envelope right away. In among the documents is a photo of Bina. She squints dreamily into the camera, small, delicate, and sickly. Curiously, but also with a touch of unease, I pick up the papers. These few pages contain what little we know about Bina's past, perhaps all we will ever know.

She was born in Mumbai, and her mother gave her to the orphanage when she was nine days old. "Handed in by unmarried mother," reads the form from the orphanage, and a little further down, "The mother gives up her child for adoption due to the child being born out of wedlock in order that the mother and the child might have a better life and future."

So, Bina's mother wasn't married and brought her child to the orphanage herself a good week after the birth to provide a better future for them both. At least that's how it reads—one of the "typical cases" Sister Lena had told me about. There are no details of relatives, and the mother requested that no attempt be made to contact her—this is noted explicitly on the form. As the papers state, the mother has given a written statement of her consent to surrender Bina for adoption.

What happened back then, over a year ago? What became of the mother described in these few short lines? What is she like? Who is Bina's father? I have so many questions. The faces are missing. The voices, the arguments, the explanations—everything's missing. Maybe Sister Lena will be able to tell me a little more, although I know that the Indian authorities keep the identities of biological parents top secret. It would be in no one's interest if a Western woman were to show up on an Indian family's doorstep out of the blue and turn their world upside down, not to mention potentially putting a young woman's life at risk. I completely understand their position, yet I still stare at the form, trying to spot the little clues between the lines, knowing that there are many questions about Bina that I will not be able to answer. The information here gives nothing away; there's too little to go on. She will never know what her parents looked like; there's not even a little passport photo of her mother—nothing. We have no names, no faces, and crucially, no answer to "Why? Why did she give me away?" This question will remain unanswered her whole life long.

The papers make particular mention of Bina's squint and also include a rough assessment of her physical development. There is a separate medical report as well that briefly summarizes her current development as "normal" and contains a short description of her squint and different-size ears. The doctor writes that she cannot sit unaided and that her physical development is a little behind where it should be. That evening, Andreas and I go through the papers together. There's even a list of around ten different vaccinations, the results of scores of blood tests, including some for HIV, and the medical details of X-rays of her chest and lungs. Everything seems normal to us, and our GP confirms this the following day. His amazement and approval is plain to see as he analyzes the papers of our "little lady," as he calls her.

"Well, what are you waiting for?" he asks with a grin. He tells me he's looking forward to the day when we all come to see him together.

The next day, I send copies of all these documents to our social worker, Sarah, so that she can forward them to a specialist doctor, who will assess the papers on behalf of the Youth Welfare Office. I've already sorted out an appointment with the lawyer as well. That evening, for the first time in almost a year, Andreas and I sit down for a lovely candlelit dinner together, relieved, confident, and relaxed, dreaming of our future with Bina. After so many years we finally feel like the end is in sight, and we're in the mood to celebrate. We've got our strength back. Over the next few days, we decorate the nursery, buy a cot, bottles, and fun, colorful clothes that look about the right size for Bina. Friends that we've told about Bina send us gifts—toys and clothes that their children have outgrown; their kind gestures do us a world of good. There's such a happy feeling of anticipation. Bina's moving into our home and into our lives!

But then comes the letter. After I've read it, I sit on the sofa, numb, torn between fear and anger, crying because of it and also because I'm at my wit's end.

"Having assessed Bina's medical documents, we are sorry to inform you that we have reached the following conclusions," the letter from the social worker's specialist doctor states. "Bina's development is equivalent to that of a seven- or eight-month-old child, which represents a severe developmental delay." Furthermore, "she is completely unable to form clear words, which at this age is a further sign of delayed development." The next paragraph warns that "the uneven ears could indicate abnormalities in the middle and inner ear," and further down, it adds that "although cosmetic improvement of the squint is possible, visual problems cannot be ruled out. The child would then suffer from various long-term problems with her sight." The most serious problem, however, according to the letter, was the circumference of Bina's head. Not only was Bina severely underweight, but her head circumference was only forty-one centimeters. When taken into account together with her age and height, this was "microcephalic"—that is, abnormally small, disabled. "Although such a child is occasionally found to be of normal intelligence, it is far more likely that she will experience learning difficulties, particularly as developmental delays have already been established." The letter concludes, "In light of the risk that the child has a learning disability, we must ask ourselves whether this adoption should proceed. This will depend on whether the parents are prepared for the potential challenges ahead and will be subject to them being approved to adopt such a child."

Hysterically, I scan Bina's medical reports, struggling to make out one word from another through my tears. The form from the orphanage does indeed state that her head circumference is forty-one centimeters. I have no idea what size a child's head should be, but Bina's head hadn't seemed small to me—quite the opposite, in fact. But then the doubts creep in: her behavior in the courtyard at the orphanage—could this have been a sign of mental problems after all? Had something happened during her birth? But Bina had been so happy at the doctor's, and we couldn't all be that wrong, especially not the Indian doctors.

I feel worked up. The specialist's letter is so depressing. She even recommends that several blood tests be redone, as if to imply that Indians can't be trusted. Even if something is wrong with Bina, that only means she needs us more than ever. Why would people make it more difficult for us to adopt her? In complete hysterics now, I phone Andreas at work.

"She's crazy," is his opinion. "Of course Bina can sit up on her own, and besides, when we were at the doctor's she even walked a little holding my hands. Phone the orphanage and tell them to measure her head again." *That will go down well after my run-in with Sister Lena*, I think. They probably have so many forms to fill out there, so many children's heads to measure, that a few centimeters off here or there doesn't matter. And then a superpedantic doctor comes along and turns the minor inaccuracies of an Indian form into a disabled child. It's the only way, though; we need to dispute the letter, point by point.

At six the next morning, I'm already on the phone to Mumbai again, trying to convince Sister Lena. She seems really quite miffed about it, but all the same, she does promise to remeasure Bina's head. The result is forty-six centimeters—five centimeters more than before. Straightaway, I write a letter to the social worker, pointing out the progress in Bina's development and telling her about the forty-six centimeters. When I call the head of the Youth Welfare Office a day later, I can hardly believe my ears. She's completely on our side, she stresses at the beginning of our conversation. Having said that, the doctor had warned her that the documents from India weren't necessarily to be trusted; after all, the orphanage knew exactly where they were going. But I needn't worry, she said assuringly; everything was fine. If we felt we could adopt Bina, we should go ahead as planned and visit the lawyer. I put the phone down, exhausted. Another battle won, but I have a feeling it won't be the last.

I can hardly wait for our appointment with the lawyer. Once we've signed the papers, at least no one can stand in our way from that perspective. In a sense, it's a notarial reservation of Bina, and no one can argue with it.

The mood at the lawyer's is suitably formal. As the appointment is a meaningful milestone, we've dressed in our best clothes and are a little nervous. I'm sighing again. When we get to the office, two women who work in the chambers are there in addition to the very professional young lawyer to act as witnesses.

We are presented with six documents with which we commit ourselves to adopting Bina, to bring her into our home as our child, to raise her, to fully acknowledge her as our legal heir, and to provide for her welfare in any way that we could. There are deeds in which we promise that for the next five years, we will send social worker reports to India documenting Bina's development. These reports are to be completed quarterly for the first two years and biannually for the remaining three. And there are still more papers in which we commit to adopting Bina before the German authorities according to German law within two years. Only then will the Indian Supreme Court in Mumbai grant us custody of Bina according to Indian law. There's even a document where Andreas and I confirm that neither of us suffers from tuberculosis, a mental illness, or any other illness. We even swear on the Bible at one point. The Indian authorities require all these documents, complete with signatories and a lawyer's stamp, in order to bring our adoption of Bina before the Ministry for Social Affairs in New Delhi and the Supreme Court in Mumbai.

We sign everything very conscientiously, neatly, and ceremoniously—not with a ballpoint pen, but a fountain pen. With every signature I feel Bina's adoption coming closer, and I feel that she's more and more our child. We even have to sign our names on a photograph of Bina. As I write my last name across her delicate little face, I pause, almost aghast. With our signatures, we adults are deciding an infant's fate. Bina doesn't have a say in the matter. At the moment, she has no concept of what's happening here. It will be many years before she understands. Will she blame us for this one day? I don't know. All the same, I have the feeling that our signatures give Bina security. She will finally have parents and a home.

Once all the papers have been signed, the lawyer and her witnesses congratulate us. We stand outside on the pavement after our appointment, Andreas and I, staring dazedly at the traffic. Then we fall into each other's arms, overcome with joy and relief. It's a new beginning for Bina and for us—our big break.

Chapter 17

HOPE AND DISAPPOINTMENT

The final countdown. I'm finding it hard to concentrate on my job. At home, I spend my time getting everything ready for my trip to India to bring Bina home with me. A lot has changed in our house: I've moved the furniture around, decorated the nursery in bright colors, and put up cheerful pictures. Andreas has installed a safety gate on the steep stairs to stop Bina from falling down and hurting herself. Our house looks like we already have a toddler—toys everywhere, the blue stroller in the hallway, the high chair at the table, and the child car seat in the vehicle. Everything's ready. We visit our friends and both sets of parents one last time. I will be in India for many weeks, and when I get back with a nervous child, there won't be much time for traveling.

I'm still waking up in the night. Every time I lie there counting the days since our trip to Mumbai in my head—another month now that Bina has spent alone in her cot, crying, with no one to spend much time with her, descending back into her monotonous rocking. She is now thirteen months old. A quarter of a year has passed since I first met her, and I keep worrying that I might already be too late to save her. I don't get much sleep these days. At work in the editorial department, I find the daily press conferences boring and the glorified way in which the politicians, bankers, and companies present themselves almost unbearable. It doesn't help that I'm physically weakened by nerves and the aftereffects of the amoebas—my weight has dropped to 117 pounds.

In the evenings, I surf the Internet and often visit a chat room where American parents discuss the problems they've had in adopting their children from India. They're not finding it any easier than I am, even those who have paid thousands of dollars to professional adoption agencies. From time to time, there are happy posts, parents celebrating the fact that their child has finally arrived. Some of the people using this board have never once visited the country they're adopting from, and many parents pay an agency to accompany their child on the journey from India. Financial or logistical reasons prevent some of them from making the trip, but others choose not to travel to India because they see it as a dangerous, dirty, and terrible place. Whatever their reasons, both groups of parents meet their children for the first time at the airport, armed with a video camera, balloons, and a teddy bear. When I think of Bina, I can't imagine what a shock this must be for the child, but lots of these Americans write that everything's "great" and that the child is adjusting "wonderfully."

One evening I log on to see the chat room flooded with messages of condolences. After investigating with a few clicks, I learn to my horror that they are for an American couple who had been hoping to adopt a little girl. The orphanage in Kolkata had called them the day before yesterday to say that, sadly, the girl had died of a lung infection. The only consolation for the parents, apparently, was that the orphanage was doing its best to find another child for them to adopt. "How guilty must those parents be feeling," I wonder. If only they'd been there… Should they have pushed harder for the adoption to go through quicker? Then she would already have been home. Such a nightmare.

Our case, thank goodness, is making good progress. One day during one of my weekly phone calls, Sister Lena tells me that CARA, the department of the Indian Ministry for Social Affairs that deals with international adoptions, has approved our adoption of Bina. We need this consent in order to apply to the Indian court for custody of Bina. Sister Lena is proud, and we're over the moon! Our adoption's been given the green light—another huge step forward! I cheer and do a little dance for joy.

I can even check online that approval has been granted. CARA has a website, which is updated every month, and there in a long list of orphaned children, I find Bina's name, her date of birth, the name of the orphanage in Mumbai, and our Youth Welfare Office. Now the orphanage can instruct its solicitor in Mumbai to apply to the Supreme Court of India for custody of Bina, which means it won't be long before I go to India.

I've already got it all planned. I told my boss about Bina's adoption long ago. He has been super supportive, although I could tell he was disappointed when I told him I'd have to take a break from the editorial team for a while. Even with an adopted child, I'm entitled to a certain amount of parental leave, for which I have applied. I don't want to tear Bina away from the orphanage and the arms of the sisters without giving her time to get to know me. So I've decided to hole up in the little hotel near the orphanage for several weeks and visit her every day. I plan to learn as much as I can about Bina's life in the orphanage and slowly build a relationship with her. I won't take her away from there until she has gotten to know me and learned to trust me. She's already been through enough shocks—first being separated from her mother shortly after birth and then being looked after by so many different sisters and caretakers in the orphanage. I need to make Bina's transition from the orphanage to the scary, unknown world outside as painless as possible. But even then, it will still be a traumatic adjustment for her, regardless of how much time I spend with her in the orphanage beforehand.

I call Sister Lena again to find out if she's contacted the solicitor. No sooner has she picked up the phone than she launches into a grumpy tirade.

"Finally, you decide to ring! I've been waiting ten days to hear from you. Why didn't you get in touch sooner? You need to ring the solicitor right away—the court has rejected the case." She tells me she doesn't know why.

It's all I can do to stammer back, "Yes, yes, I'll do it right away."

I hang up and dial the solicitor's number. My stomach suddenly aches, my knees go weak. Rejected—but why? For the love of God, why have they rejected it now? A thousand questions shoot through my head as I desperately try to get through to someone. Three times the connection breaks, and the fourth time all I get is the noise of a fax machine. I'm at my wit's end, so frustrated that I slam down the receiver and lose it completely. I scream with anger and bang my fist on the table so hard that my knuckles hurt. I yell so loudly that I'm still hoarse two days later. I just can't take it anymore—the endless waiting and this roller-coaster ride of hope and disappointment, heaven and hell.

On the fifth try, I finally get on the line someone who works at the solicitor's. The situation isn't as bad as I'd feared. While the court was inspecting our papers, they noticed that all the original copies of the references written by our friends and family were missing. Also Andreas hadn't signed my written confirmation that I had applied for parental leave to care for Bina.

"You need to send the documents over right away—preferably by fax—so that we can try for another court date. But you must hurry, the court will be in recess soon and will be closed," the office worker in Mumbai explains to me over the crackling connection. Anxiously, I phone the Youth Welfare Office to ask about the references, but our caseworker is on leave and no one in the office can find our file. I call Mumbai again, and they suggest that our friends and family write out the letters again.

There's no time to lose. The following two days are a hectic blur. I hang on the phone, requesting new questionnaires from the Youth Welfare Office about our marriage, and hastily sweet-talk my friends into writing yet more letters about our "wonderfully stable marriage," our "exemplary tolerance," and our "enormous fondness for children." I also make another appointment with the lawyer to have Andreas's signature stamped. Then all these papers are sent to Mumbai by courier. This time they meet with the court's approval, and I hope that it won't be long before we get a court date. I decide that I will fly to India in two weeks; I've already updated the visa in my passport.

After more than ten years' employment, my final days in the office have arrived. I'd never realized I'd find it so difficult, no matter how much Bina fills my thoughts. Suddenly, I can understand those men who are reluctant to retire. I'm glued to my desk day and night writing just a few more articles, fastidiously tidying my office, archiving my files, and updating my computer. My last day at work finds me sitting numbly at my desk with a cup of tea, sorting my mail and placing the invitations I've received on my colleague's desk. There's a lump in my throat as I record my new voice mail message: "Please don't leave a message. Instead, call my colleague…" I suddenly catch myself clipping my articles out of the newspaper again, something I haven't done for a long time—my last articles. All at once, my mind is overflowing with so many topics for articles. For weeks I have had to summon up the will to write, waiting desperately for my last day. I couldn't think of anything to write about; I felt uninspired. Yet as I leave this evening, I'm fighting back the tears. I've packed my business cards as a memento. I hand in the key to my company car. I've decided not to say good-bye to my colleagues on the other floors for fear of crying. Then I leave the office for the last time and take a taxi home through rush hour. As the door to my house closes behind me, I collapse in tears. I know that once I have a child I will never be able to work as intensively, with as much dedication, and without compromise as I have until now. Those days are gone forever.

I wait for Andreas to come home, pack the last few items in my suitcase, and get everything ready for my flight to Mumbai. Andreas and I still have two evenings to ourselves. Then I will be gone, and I will spend weeks, perhaps months, in Mumbai staying next to the orphanage, visiting Bina, playing with her, and waiting for my appointment at the Mumbai Supreme Court. Only then will we be granted custody of Bina in the eyes of Indian law. That will give us the right to remove her from the orphanage and apply for her passport and visa for the trip home. Because of work commitments, Andreas won't be able to join me for a few weeks. So, unfortunately, the first few steps with our daughter are ones I'll have to take by myself.

Part Three

Chapter 18

HOME AND NO HOME

I'm feeding her too slowly. Bina wriggles on my legs with every pause. The heat is stifling in Mumbai, as usual, and the ceiling fans in the orphanage just make no difference. Sweat streams down my back. My glasses slide down my nose, and the moment I try to push them back, Bina hits the spoon with her hand and spatters my salwar kameez with porridge. I finish every mealtime with my clothes clinging to my body, drenched in sweat, and covered in baby food.

The caregivers don't give the children the chance to behave like this. The young helpers Didi and Camilla sit on the floor to feed, placing the children lengthwise on their legs with their heads in their laps. That way the children can kick their legs and flail their arms around as much as they want. There's no escaping the spoon until the bowl is empty; anything they spit out is just shoveled into their mouth again, as quick as a flash. The children have just enough time to swallow before the next spoonful of porridge arrives. At the end of the day, there are twenty children to feed in this room alone, and four times a day at that. Didi and Camilla often feed them two at a time.

After a few days, I was able to feed Bina myself. She refused to take any food from me at first, and Didi had to help me feed her, as she was Bina's favorite. *Didi* is the Hindi word for *sister*—I never discovered her real name. For the first few meals, Didi and I took turns with the spoon, but now Bina lies on my outstretched legs looking up at me curiously, her head on my feet so that we can look each other in the eyes and slowly get to know each other's faces. I sit on the floor between the cots. The room is so packed full of cots that there's no space for a table and chairs.

I chatter away to Bina. At least she can hear me, now that the babies have stopped crying. The other little ones lie in their cots, their tummies full, sucking on their bottles of rice water, and slowly dozing off to sleep in the heat. The orphanage is relatively quiet at this time of day. In these midday hours, the children's earsplitting cries let up for a while, and peace descends over the rooms while the sisters retire for their midday meal and prayers.

Suddenly, I can hear the rumble of the trains, the auto-rickshaws, the traffic, and the crows in the branches of the trees that cover the barred windows. Bina watches my lips and moves her lower jaw as if trying to imitate my speech. She already recognizes me; she smiles when I arrive at the orphanage in the mornings and come over to her cot—fourth row from the window, second cot from the left. She has quickly realized that I only ever play with her, that I'm there just to see her and take her out of her cot, and she watches nervously if I give attention to any of the other children.

I was so excited to see her again when I arrived a few days ago. My feet couldn't climb the steps to the second floor fast enough. I kicked off my sandals and raced to find her in her cot among all the other babies. From now on, nothing would come between us. There she sat, playing with a little rubber duck. As I approached her cot and bent down, her face lit up. It was not because she had recognized me—too much time had passed for that—but rather because all the children here are thrilled when someone spends a bit of time with them, distracts them from the monotony of their daily lives, plays with them. Every song, every game, every cuddly toy, however small, every picture book is a little bit of comfort to them and is wrenched from my hands in amazement.

For the first few days, I was shocked by the conditions here. The orphanage seemed more primitive than I remembered—the long rows of cots in the bare rooms, just a few small pictures on the walls. Then there was the constant noise of children crying and the friendly but ultimately very hurried and sometimes crude way in which the women change and feed all these children and give them their medicine before its time to change them again. Even the sounds of the trains, the helicopters, and the traffic seem louder than the last time I was here. The climate seems hotter, the dirt on the streets more disgusting. The barred windows on one side of the orphanage look out over the slum huts along the railway embankment and the rows of tracks running into Mumbai. On the other side, there's the courtyard with the rickety swing and slide, and beyond this, the neighboring church.

Bina's behavior, however, has been a pleasant surprise. She is much friendlier and more outgoing than three months ago. This time we're taking things very slowly and gently. I've since realized how terrifying it must have been when we carried her out into the yard—we were total strangers to her. Infants her age almost never leave the room where they sleep, so the fact that we carried her out of her dark room into the glaring sunlight in the yard with no warning at all must have been very upsetting for her.

Only children who have passed their first birthdays are allowed into the yard to ride tricycles and play on the slide, and even they are out only once or twice a week. For that reason, I've decided to play with Bina up here for the time being, in her familiar little world of cots and changing tables. And slowly I notice she is beginning to make progress: she lets me hold her for a little bit longer; she even allows me to change her diaper. The cotton cloths the babies wear round their nether regions are in the diaper changing room, piled high on the table. The first time I dressed and undressed Bina, my hands shook with nerves, but things are already much better. Bina snuggles up to me, enjoying my kisses, and she squeals with delight when I play with her. She is so desperate for every little bit of tenderness and love.

I use one of the cotton cloths from the changing table to wipe the porridge off myself and am just about to give Bina another spoonful when I notice little Kabir standing next to me. He's one of the big ones, the slightly older children who sleep across the hall in a different room. These are children who have either been found abandoned by their parents by the railway tracks and have been brought in by the police or have been given up for adoption because they're too sick, disabled, or ugly, or because their parents have died—complex cases, and very difficult to process due to the children's traumatic pasts and their illnesses and disabilities. Kabir is pasty, always sick with something, and much too small for his age, fragile almost. Silently, he watches me feed Bina, and then suddenly he points at a small teddy bear that has fallen out of one the children's cots. He gives me a questioning look. I nod back as if to say, "In a minute, when I've finished." Lots of the big ones steal from the little ones—they pinch their toys—but not Kabir. Instead of grabbing the teddy, he just stands there, gentle soul that he is, waiting for me to help the other child. Then he points at Manika, a stocky little girl who is standing in her cot, clutching her bottle of rice water, and tugging insistently at the bars. Her diaper is wet. Once again I nod at Kabir. "In a minute, when I'm finished."

Slowly, he toddles over, sits down next to me, and gently places his little hand on my hand holding the porridge spoon. He looks at me pleadingly, points to his tummy, and opens his mouth—a shy request for food, not aggressive, but tentative. I pop a spoonful of porridge into Kabir's mouth, and he beams, swallowing the food with obvious pleasure. So now I have two mouths to feed—one spoonful for Bina and one for Kabir. He opens his mouth wide every time, giving me a hopeful, almost beseeching look.

But suddenly, Camilla, the helper, bursts into the room and shouts at Kabir furiously in Marathi, the regional language in these parts. She points at his tummy and shakes her head, indicating that I shouldn't feed him. Then she pulls Kabir roughly off the floor, gives him a further telling-off, and drags him out of the room after her. He quickly turns to me as he goes and smiles, a little sad to have mixed me up in his scheme to get to the porridge, but there is also a mischievous gleam from having managed to get one over on Camilla.

What a poor hand fate has dealt these children. A fat, young boy who is a little slow mentally and is teased and bullied by the other big ones spends nearly all his time crying in the corner. A thick scar runs across his neck from ear to ear, as if someone had tried to slit his throat. One young boy in Bina's group has a deep hollow in his abdomen, as though half his organs are missing; he can't keep any food down and just spits everything up. It takes the helpers half an hour just to feed him because he simply brings up the food again, crying and gurgling as they mercilessly shovel it back into his seething mouth, again and again.

One of the older girls is crude, aggressive, disturbed; she is perhaps around seven years old and a real screecher. She's always fighting with the other children, and sometimes when she can't take it anymore, she crawls into the darkness under her bed and screams and screams. She screams with every fiber of her being, and deep, gurgling, roaring sounds come from within her—animalistic, raw, so loud that her ears must ring. It seems as if her head must be about to burst, her vocal cords ready to snap, and yet still she screams. The whole orphanage rings with the sound, and the other children fall silent in horror. She screams so loudly that it can be heard out in the street.

Manika is another one, a chubby little girl, just eighteen months old, but already so full of hatred. I have to take care not to stand too close to her cot, otherwise I get a sharp pain in my arm or back as she stabs at me with all the furious strength her little fingers can muster or pulls at my hair. And when I turn around, she throws me murderous looks, narrows her eyes almost theatrically to menacing slits, desperately trying to kill me with her evil glares. She hates everyone, even the other children; she pushes and hits them and knocks them over until Didi and Camilla put her back in her cot. There, she shakes the bars and screams in fury until Didi or Camilla hisses a sharp "Stop it!" which is enough to shut up even Manika. But even then, she just uses her eyes to project her anger into the room.

Bina has eaten her porridge now and is tired. So I take her in my arms, my precious little child, and rock her to sleep. Then I carry her out into the shady corridor of the stairwell. It's cool here, and the wind blows up from the courtyard through the bars of the windows; the sun rays can't reach us in here. I sit down on the floor. An old woman in a sari sits at the end of the hallway, working on a battered old Singer sewing machine. She sits here for hours on end every day, sewing new cotton cloths for diapers, little dresses, and sheets. I enjoy the peace and quiet and the rhythmic sound of the sewing machine. Almost all the children are sleeping now, and I can hear the crows cawing out on the window ledge.

Suddenly, I hear quiet footsteps padding toward me. It's Leela, one of the big ones. She has already woken up and sits down beside me; she watches Bina sleeping in my arms and then looks up at me, pleadingly, beseechingly. I slowly stroke her hair. She holds still and moves her head closer to me without a word. I stroke rhythmically through her hair, massage her head gently, lovingly—she hardly dares to breathe in case I stop. She looks at me gratefully. She says nothing, but tilts her shock of hair toward me. She has short hair, oiled to prevent lice, like the other children here. Leela is around eight years old and wears the signs of her life in the orphanage like a shroud—eight years spent in the darkness. She waits here in the orphanage in a kind of limbo between two lives. Every day she lines up with the other big ones to be combed. She sits beside them on a long bench to eat her curry, goes to sleep with them at night, packed bed to bed beneath the picture of Jesus that hangs on the wall, and waits to see what kind of parents Sister Lena downstairs in her office will find for her.

"We can't offer these girls to Indian parents; they will just use them as cheap labor," Sister Martha had explained to me yesterday.

Bina is sleeping deeply now. I carry her back to her room again and lay her down on the mattress of her cot. The fans whir above the beds. The blankets are piled in a tall stack as they're needed only at night—it's far too hot during the day. I leave Bina to her midday nap, go into the hallway, slip my shoes back on, leave the orphanage, and make my way slowly through the hot, heavy traffic back to the little hotel.

Up in my room, I peel the sticky, stinking clothes from my body, shower in my tiny bathroom, and pick out a fresh salwar kameez. I bought a supply of these thin cotton kaftans during my first few days here, and in this heat I need at least two per day. The heat really takes it out of me. I shower three times a day, and within a few days, I'd lost even more weight.

Downstairs in the little vegetarian restaurant where I eat lunch daily, the waiters are already expecting me and bring me my usual sweet lassi, a bell pepper curry, and papadums, those delicate discs of chickpea flour. I write in my diary and recover in the air-conditioned restaurant, barely noticing that the tablecloth hasn't been changed in days and that there's yet another huge cockroach sitting on the back of one of the seats behind me.

After lunch, I go for a lie down in my little room, watching the fan spinning on the ceiling above me, listening to the rattle of the motorbikes and auto-rickshaws, the whines of the trains, and the calls of the men from the tea stands. I doze a little and gather my strength for the afternoon.

Roars and cries greet me as I return at three o'clock and climb the stairs to the second floor. The big ones have awoken and are sitting on the long bench, sobbing. They're always this upset after their midday nap, and it takes a beaker of cool water and a few pieces of papaya, pineapple, and banana to calm them down. In the baby changing room, I find Sister Martha, who always seems happy, no matter how much the children scream and cry. She presses all the children gathered around her to her enormous bosom, and her warm, powerful voice carries over any amount of nagging and crying. She loves the children, every one, however ugly, disabled, disturbed, or sick they might be. She comforts them, feeds them, cares for them, kisses and hugs them in a wonderful "earth mother" kind of way. If the children survive the atmosphere and way of life of the orphanage in relatively one piece, they have her efforts to thank for it.

Bina sits in front of her on the changing table, as naked as the day she was born, enjoying her daily routine. With experienced hands, Sister Martha powders her chest and back against the heat, spreads coconut oil on her hair to protect her from lice, and wraps her in a fresh cotton cloth. Then the sister selects a kitschy, light green, frilly dress for Bina with a matching green headband and deftly combs Bina's black hair into a little topknot that sticks up in the middle of her head. Finally, she dips a cotton bud in *kajal* and presses it against Bina's forehead between her eyebrows to form a black bindi "to protect her from the evils of the world"—a little sign of protection Sister Martha paints on the forehead of every child each day, although she herself is deeply Catholic and always sports a silver cross of Jesus on her shoulder. Once she's finished, Bina sits there in the baking heat, surrounded by the smell of sour milk and urine-soaked diapers, neatly combed and gleaming with coconut oil—a real bundle of joy, at least until life in the orphanage messes her up again.

While Bina was having her makeover, I was watching Nirav and Aisha. Aisha tugs at my clothing, and whispers, "Auntie." I put my arm around her.

"They left her here at the railway station," says Sister Martha, nodding toward Aisha. Our conversation is in English, as I don't speak Marathi, and the children don't understand a word we're saying. "Her heart was so bad that her hands had turned blue. We paid for her first operation, but she needs another one. That's for the parents to arrange, if we find any—it's difficult with a child like her." The sister sighs. Aisha is not an attractive child; her hands are no longer blue, but her arms and legs are like twigs, too thin for her slightly crooked body. Her body is topped by her irregular head and neck. She can't move her head properly. An aura of sadness surrounds her, always. She follows the sisters around and helps them whenever she can. Again and again, I hear her soft, pleading voice behind me: "Auntie." I am painfully aware that she would far rather say "Mommy."

And then there's Nirav, whose teeth have nearly all fallen out or rotted away. He has outward-squinting eyes and a slightly misshapen head. He's a child who never stops; he's always on the go, bouncing wildly down the corridors. Really, he could do with a soccer pitch to run around on. Sister Martha grabs Manika and makes a start on her hair, and the big ones go back to their games. Someone has brought Hula-Hoops into the orphanage. They must be a donation. The children broke them in two as soon as they arrived, and now they hurl them noisily against the tiled floor and walls. It's not long before the rest of the big ones take the pieces of Hula-Hoop away from the fat boy with the scar on his neck and the screaming girl. Soon, the noise of the bouncing hoops is peppered with the boy's crying and the girl's bestial screams.

I steal away with Bina and take her on our familiar circuit of the orphanage, down into the dark room where she laid when we visited her a few months ago. But when we reach the door of the room, Bina hesitates; she clings to me and struggles, unwilling to enter the room where she lay in a cot six months ago. So, slowly, we carry on. Bina has just started walking and toddles forward cautiously. Even though she still falls down a lot, she's improving all the time and is so proud of herself. She walks to the kitchen, with its mirrored medicine cabinets, and stands in front of them amusing herself, sticking out her tummy, fascinated by her own reflection.

Suddenly, someone calls out, "Maharani"—"little queen"—and Sister Alissa, the head of the orphanage, enters the room. "She's going to be a pretty one," she says, and Bina races into her arms. Although Sister Alissa rarely comes upstairs to see the children, Bina is as attached to her as a grandmother. There are always many tears when it's time for them to part. The two of them have a deep, intimate bond, and I respect that. Bina crawls into

Sister Alissa's arms and throws me a questioning glance, so I encourage her. I don't want her to feel that she has to choose between the sisters and me; she will make that decision later for herself. Right now, the sisters are still more important to her than I am.

Sister Alissa pops a caramel into Bina's mouth, and after a few minutes she hands her back to me. I need to distract Bina straightaway, because she's already begun to sniffle as the sister walks away. So we go to see the washerwomen who work at the massive stone troughs behind the kitchen, washing hundreds of cotton diapers, sheets, and dresses. The sweat runs down their faces in the heat. Later on, they will balance the baby baths full of clean laundry on their heads and carry them up the many stairs to the flat rooftop, where the items will be hung out to dry in the blistering heat.

Bina and I pay a short visit to Sister Lena, who is poring over a mountain of documents as usual. After that, I'd planned to take Bina out into the yard, but she blinks. The light is too bright for her; she hasn't quite got used to sunlight yet after so much time spent living in a darkened room. So we stay in the shade so as not to hurt her eyes.

When we go back up to the children's rooms, Sister Martha has gone. Usually she just comes up for half an hour or an hour to comfort the little ones, but then she has to get back to sorting out the care packages for the areas affected by the earthquakes in Gujarat.

Meanwhile, the older children are playing in the passageway that looks out over the courtyard, the one where the old lady sits at the end sewing. The passageway has a long row of windows, all barred and so high that the big ones have to stand on their tiptoes to catch a glimpse of the courtyard. Anita, who must be the oldest girl here at around eight years old, lifts one of the little ones up so that she can have a peek, too. Anita is a sweetheart, always happy in spite of the scars and weeping spots on her face. She chatters away excitedly to me whenever I see her, and the fact that I can't understand a word she says doesn't seem to bother her. She is just happy to have someone to talk to.

The children have lost interest in the Hula-Hoops, and in the absence of anything else to play with, they amuse themselves by trying to pull themselves up on the bars of the windows. Down in the yard below, a young Indian couple is being shown a tiny baby. With all his strength, Nirav has managed to pull himself up so high that even his feet rest on the bars of the window. Nimbly, he clambers up to the very top of the bars where he has the best view and can look out over the whole yard, almost close enough to touch the crows on the window ledge. His face fills with sorrow as he watches the scene below. How often must the older children here stand by and watch as babies are brought out for young parents to adopt while children like Nirav, Aisha, and Anita are left behind?

Suddenly, the droning noise of a helicopter fills the air as it flies low over the orphanage; there must be a helipad nearby because many helicopters fly over the orphanage every afternoon, before disappearing behind the church. Nirav and the other children wave to the helicopter from their perches on the windows and look to see if the men inside wave back. Anita even calls out to them.

Later on, once I've laid Bina back in her cot with a bottle of milk, given her a kiss, and left her with the other children and the helpers for the night, I look up and see Nirav dangling from the barred window, waving after me. He waves until I disappear through the gate and out into the street.

Chapter 19

BINA'S MOTHER

Sister Lena's in a good mood. She isn't always, though. The heat takes it out of her, and sometimes she seems to suffer from pain in her back and legs to the extent that she can hardly move. But today I'm lucky, and she smiles conspiratorially as I enter her office. I've been hanging around her office for days now, and she knows exactly what I'm after. I want to learn more about Bina's mother—every clue, every tidbit. I want to drink everything in, to treasure it, so that one day I can share it with Bina. I know that there won't be much to tell, but there must be more than I read in Bina's papers.

I don't need to ask the question. Sister Lena has already read my mind and grabs Bina's file. It's a tricky situation. Indian law strictly states that the details of the biological parents must not be released to adoptive parents, particularly their names and addresses—anything that could be used to identify the mother or father. All the same, I need to find out as much as I can, because everything I learn now will help me to answer Bina's questions in the future.

"You're in luck. She brought Bina to the orphanage herself. I met her in person," says Sister Lena.

"What did she look like?" I ask.

"Tall, slim, dark—very dark. She was young."

"What was she like? What did her laugh sound like?" I ask, and immediately realize how stupid this question is.

"This was no laughing matter. She was very solemn. It's a sorry situation when a woman has to give up her child." The sister puts me in my place. "Her name is Ragini."

In this moment, it was as though a huge weight had been lifted. A name! At least now I have a name, even if it's only a first name and even though I know that I will never discover her last name or where she lives—I can hardly search the whole of Mumbai for one particular Ragini. But when I talk to Bina, it will make a world of difference to be able to refer to her as "Ragini" instead of "your mother in India." Suddenly, she has a name, something personal, individual, and unique.

"That's why I gave Bina a name with a musical meaning—in honor of her mother," Sister Lena explains. "Bina means a musical instrument. And Ragini is the melody. Both are destined to be together, but Bina will be able to play different melodies wherever she will find love, your love," says Sister Lena with a friendly nod.

This moves me deeply. Now I know that thought went into choosing my daughter's name, and I know the meaning behind it. I would never dream of changing it, unlike the parents of so many other children adopted from foreign countries.

"So, Ragini didn't choose Bina's name?" I inquire.

"No. The mothers aren't allowed to name their babies. We do the naming," says Sister Lena. I can guess the reason why: it's to prevent mothers from tracing their children later down the line in the same way that I would be prevented from tracking down Ragini.

"It says here in the file that Ragini was twenty-five years old," Sister Lena reads. "That's nonsense, of course. She was quite obviously nowhere near twenty-five, more like seventeen. But that's often the way here. Women pretend to be older than they are—that is to say, of legal age. Sex with minors is illegal here, and if a seventeen-year-old turns up with a child, it's really a matter for the police. Also, she would need to be accompanied by her parents so that they could sign the papers giving the child up for adoption. Still, as many young women keep their pregnancy secret and don't want their parents to find out, they come here alone and tell us they are much older. I would say Ragini was seventeen at the most," she summarizes.

"What does it say in the forms the women sign? Could I see one?" I ask.

"No, they're not meant for you. Those papers are for the court's eyes. It's a two-sided document, which confirms that, after a cooling-off period of three months, the mother gives up all rights to the child."

"How did Bina's mother seem? Was she poor?"

"No, not particularly. But she wasn't educated. She didn't sign the papers; she used her fingerprint instead. And she gave the impression that she didn't want to spend a moment longer here than she had to. She left Bina here, and then she would have gone to the lawyer where we send all the women. He lives alone with his mother, so there's no risk of anyone seeing them. That's where they sign the papers to give up the child."

I ask a few more questions and discover that Ragini is Hindu. "She wasn't married, and, well, you already know—once a girl has a child, there's no chance of her finding a husband. It's all over," says Sister Lena decisively. "You know, sometimes a girl actually believes she is already married. She falls in love, and the man drags her off to some temple where they hang garlands of flowers round their necks and walk around a fire seven times to get 'married'—a sort of secret love marriage. The man uses the girl for a few months, and when she falls pregnant, he vanishes. Then the girl is stuck with a child, but without a marriage certificate. Indian women have no rights in these situations, and as far as the law is concerned, they are unmarried but with child."

"And the father?"

"Nothing. We know nothing about the father. Ragini didn't tell us much, only that he came to visit her twice beforehand and that on the third visit she went with him." It's clear that not even the Indian authorities know the identity of Bina's father.

"But it wasn't rape?"

"No, no, not rape," says Sister Lena.

"I had never seen Ragini before that day. She brought Bina to us, and I haven't seen her since. She was from Mumbai, but not from this neighborhood."

I ask myself how these girls must feel when they give up their children, what they must go through.

"They just want to put it behind them as quickly as possible and make a new start. In all of the three hundred adoptions I've processed here, there have only been two cases where the women have come back," says Sister Lena, looking at the wall in front of her with the collage of baby photos from Switzerland, France, Italy, and Spain.

"Are the girls under pressure at home to give up their illegitimate children?"

"No, they do it because they want to. They have no other choice. In our society, no one will marry them if they have a child." I think back to the wedding ads in the newspaper with their precise criteria of caste, career, and skin color that all had to be met before the parents would even seriously consider allowing someone to marry their child. And then their daughter suddenly comes home with a big belly—it didn't bear thinking about. It's really a credit to these girls that they didn't decide to abort.

When I ask exactly why Ragini gave up her child, what things must have been like for her at home, Sister Lena gives me a wave that indicates she isn't prepared to tell me any more.

"We don't like to ask too many questions here. It's hard enough for the girls as it is. They're under unbelievable pressure, and some of them carry the children in secret."

Then she tells me, "You might want to consider visiting the other institution we run: a nursing home for elderly women. It's two neighborhoods away. There are also lots of young women there waiting to give birth. Afterward, they give the children up and disappear again. It's all very secret," she explains and tells me how to get to the home.

"Did Ragini stay there during her pregnancy?"

"No, no, not her. She didn't turn up until Bina was a week old. We'd never met her before then."

Sister Lena answers my other questions, but can't tell me about Ragini's pregnancy, about genetic conditions in her family, or about her father; she just doesn't know.

I decide then and there that at some point over the next few days I will visit the nursing home where pregnant girls go to wait for their babies to be born. That way, I can gather images to illustrate the story of Bina and Ragini—faces, eyes. Although I haven't got a picture of her, perhaps I can get an idea of what Ragini might have been like.

Sister Lena snaps the file shut. It's clear that she has nothing more to say. That file contains Ragini's full name, perhaps her address, too, and the declaration with which this young woman had given up her child. The judge will need it during the adoption hearing—the adoption can't take place without it. And yet I will never see it. These are all the details I will ever have and Bina will have to live with them. These few scraps are all I have been able to find out about her mother; her father will remain a complete mystery.

Still, I'm grateful that Sister Lena was able to tell me this much. If I hadn't come here, I would never have discovered these details about Ragini. In particular, I would never have known her name. When all's said and done, I would have to accept this; I would have to put my trust in Sister Lena. I would never be able to stand face-to-face with Ragini and ask her what really happened back then.

I go back upstairs to the children's room. The staircase rings with the noise and cries of the big ones, who are jumping around on the dinner benches. Sister Martha is not there, and the young helpers are downstairs in the kitchen preparing porridge. The little ones are still in their cots. It's afternoon, and Didi and Camilla haven't yet had time to take them out and put them down to play on the floor. Bina beams and tries to climb out of her bed when she sees me. She bites my shoulder with joy as I carry her over to the changing table, change her wet cotton cloths, and put her in a fresh dress.

She has deliciously dark eyes, so big and warm; it's impossible to tell where the pupil ends and the iris begins. Her lashes are amazingly long, and her eyebrows curve gently. She gives off a gentle, happy vibe; she laughs and smiles more often each time I see her. In the beginning, her face was often mask-like, a closed book, but now she often has a smile on her face. I play with her and cuddle her before putting her down on the floor, where she immediately toddles off toward the stairs without looking back. I follow her slowly and open from behind the little gate that stops the children from climbing the stairs down to the yard. Without looking to see if I'm following her, Bina totters unsteadily down the steps and waddles slowly down the hall to the kitchen. She still doesn't turn around. I've noticed that a lot; she's just happy if I'm there. But if I'm not there, that's OK, too, and she doesn't look for me.

This time I take her out into the yard, which is partly shaded at the moment. She's slowly learning to tolerate this level of light. She runs back and forth from the entrance of the orphanage chasing the crows. The heat is too much for me, even this late in the afternoon. So I sit on the wall between the flowerpots and have a rest. Bina keeps running over to me and throwing herself joyfully into my salwar kameez. She's so happy to have escaped the room of cots for a while.

Suddenly, the gate leading to the street opens, and a schoolgirl rushes through in a dark red school uniform and snow-white blouse, her hair in two long pigtails tied with red ribbons. She makes a beeline for Sister Alissa and Sister Lena's office. A little later, a woman who must be her mother arrives and makes her way slowly across the courtyard. While Bina plays over by the gate, the mother and her daughter greet the nuns, and Sister Martha takes them on a tour of the orphanage. After that, Sister Alissa disappears with the girl into the building where the nuns live. Having seen the head nun, Bina runs after them in hopes of candies and juice.

The schoolgirl's mother comes over and sits down next to me between the hibiscus plants.

"Are you adopting the little one?" she asks and straightens her sari. She speaks good English and seems very elegant and pensive.

"Yes, I'm still waiting for the court date. Three weeks to go," I reply.

"When are you going to tell her? Have you already thought about it?"

"Tell her what?"

"That she's adopted. When are you going to tell your child that she's adopted?" the mother asks.

"I've already told her—on the very first day," I reply, thinking back to a week ago when I first arrived and took Bina on my lap. I explained that she's here in the orphanage at the moment, but that I was going to adopt her and be her mommy. I told her everything that was in my heart. I knew that Bina couldn't understand a word, but it wasn't about that. It was the fact that I'd said it. I needed to learn to talk about it, to get over my fear of telling her the truth.

"I haven't managed to tell my daughter; I just can't. I keep meaning to, but I just don't have the heart," stutters the mother beside me. As I see her wipe the tears from her cheeks, suddenly I understand: she adopted her daughter from the orphanage here.

"I keep bringing her here so that she gets to know the orphanage and understands that there are children who don't have any parents," she tells me. "And yet I can't bring myself to tell her that she came from here herself."

We look at her daughter, who is now crossing the yard, her hands filled with candies. She is sharing them with Bina, who is sure to spit them out again, as the caramels are huge, sticky, and so sweet that they glue your mouth together. That's too much, even for Bina.

"Tell her this evening. The sooner you tell her, the easier it will be. It only gets harder as the child gets older. Please say you'll do it this evening," I urge her, but it's easy for me to talk. I have no choice but to tell Bina the truth: anyone who sees us will know straightaway that she isn't my biological child, that she must be adopted. We need to be open and honest with this topic from the start for that very reason.

Things are different for the Indian mother next to me. If she doesn't say anything, no one will be any the wiser—except one day when her daughter finds out, she will see it as a huge betrayal and lose faith in her parents.

"You have to understand, your society is more tolerant; they accept things like that. It's not like that here—Indian society is very different. Things aren't so easy," the mother says. And she's right—many things are different. In India, there's still a far greater stigma attached to a woman who can't have a child than there is in the West.

Once again the wedding ads come to mind, where so much importance was attached to the caste of the future spouse. Children from the orphanage don't belong to a caste—or at least not the right one. It's impossible to know which caste they ever belonged to or if they had one at all. And it's not important to the sisters. When I asked about caste, Sister Lena had answered with a decisive "no caste."

"These children don't belong to any particular religion. We do bless them, but in the end, the children will be brought up in the religion of their future parents. We can't make any assumptions," Sister Lena explained. For that very reason they don't baptize the children either, although the order itself is deeply Catholic.

Next to me, the mother is lost in thought as she watches her daughter playing with Bina without a care in the world. She fights back the tears again. "I just don't know how she'd react, and that frightens me."

Chapter 20

IT'S A SECRET

We've been searching for nearly half an hour now, but the auto-rickshaw driver is patient. The sisters did tell me the way, but in this busy quarter of Mumbai, the home isn't so easy to find. At last, our rickshaw comes to a stop in front of a gate. It's closed, and the high walls block our view of the courtyard and the building beyond. A large sign at the entrance offers the only clue to what lies within: "Home for the Dying and Sick."

I pay the driver and walk over to the gate. There's no bell. Through the bars I can make out the entrance to the building and an ambulance standing in the yard. I wait until an old man comes limping out of the building toward me. He nods expectantly. When I tell him that I've come from the orphanage across town, he lets me inside.

The courtyard is pleasantly shady; tall king palms stand nearby, three stories tall, their leafy tops bowed toward the building. It's almost silent here—no children's cries greet me, just the constant squawking of the crows. As I slip off my sandals at the entrance, I'm greeted by a petite sister, who introduces herself as Clara. She asks after the other nuns at the orphanage and about Bina. The other sisters had told her to expect me, Clara says, and she'd be proud to show me her "work."

Sister Clara invites me into the building, yet I stand in the corridor, rooted to the spot by shock. Both sides of the hallway are lined with elderly women huddled close together on the floor, serving themselves curry from an aluminum plate offered by a sister. Some of the old ladies give me an irritated look and seem to grumble about what this young woman is doing here.

"We're all these women have," says Sister Clara. I follow her down the corridor until we find ourselves in a spacious hall. "We're all they have" rings in my ears as I stare around the room at a sea of stretchers, so closely packed that it's almost impossible to pass between them.

"We're full to bursting. We can't take in any more women; we just don't have the space." I hear Sister Clara sigh behind me. I look at all the crooked, tired, frail bodies around me, bedded down for their final rest—120 elderly women. Some crouch on the floor and stare blankly ahead; others have sunk down onto their beds, exhausted. Some lie on their stretchers as if dead or paralyzed, their strength, their energy, their life almost gone, just waiting for the end. I see women who have perhaps lost their husbands and families, or perhaps they never even had families. There are women no one cares about. I wonder if some of them chose their own path in life, risking rejection from their families, being pushed aside by society because their choices were unacceptable. Here in their loneliness and helplessness, the end of their lives shrink to the size of a stretcher, their mealtimes to a plate of curried rice, their community to other dying women and a few hardworking sisters. Their lives are already over; they have no contact with the outside world, with the comfort of family, with chattering relatives and gossiping neighbors.

Yet in this one building, the circle of life is complete; as the women lie dying downstairs, upstairs new lives are beginning. The second floor provides a refuge for girls who need to keep their pregnancy a secret because families, relatives, and neighbors must not discover the consequences of their "accidents." Now Sister Clara leads me up the dark stairway. There are even a few old women sitting here on the steps, waiting for their plates of rice.

All the time I'm with the young women up here, I'll be searching for one face: Ragini's.

I know that I'll never know what she really looks like. All the same, I hope to take an impression with me from the young women who will give up their babies here. What laughter and tears, what hopes, fears, and joys might I find written in their faces? As I climb the stairs behind Sister Clara, I can feel my heart beating; it's beating hard, as if I were about to meet Ragini herself. I know that this visit is enormously important because it will teach me things that I will later share with Bina. Even if Ragini was never here, it will help me to better imagine the kind of person she is.

Up on the second floor, I suddenly find myself in the doorway of a bright, friendly, airy room. Sunbeams dance through the tops of the palm trees and fall onto the small number of stretchers and mattresses, packed as closely as the ones downstairs. The room has windows on three sides and seems to float among the treetops. Five pregnant young women sit on the beds; two of them are reading, while two of the girls break off their conversation in surprise at a Western woman barging into their secret hideaway. They had obviously believed no one would find them here.

"They come here in the fourth or fifth month of their pregnancies—before it starts to show," Sister

Clara whispers to me. "They carry their babies to term here. After that, they go home again, and leave the babies with us."

Before she leaves, each girl signs a legal document, confirming that she gives her child up for adoption. The babies are then taken to the orphanage and are put up for adoption there.

I am grateful to Sister Clara for allowing me to come up here. With the five young women smiling politely at me, it's hard to find words for what I want to say. Yet all at once, I pluck up my courage and babble forth, in English, as I don't know any Marathi or Hindi. I tell the young girls everything I would want to say to Ragini if I ever had the chance: that I'm a young mother who can't have children herself, but that my husband and I feel so lucky and blessed to be able to adopt a child from here, that we will love our child with all our hearts and will go to the ends of the earth for her. I tell them the child will have a good life and that even though we live in another country, we will visit India whenever we can, because we love and respect this country. And I reassure them again, for good measure, the child will have a good life.

The girls smile back at me, as friendly as ever, and I wonder if they have understood a word of what I've just said. Then suddenly, one girl, who almost looks relieved, asks me how old the child will be when I adopt her. With a start, it dawns on me that I'm not the only one worrying about children spending too long in the orphanage and who feels that families should be found for them as quickly as possible. Both of us fear for our children.

"She'll be around one to two years old," I tell her, and she seems pleasantly surprised. Perhaps she had imagined that the adoption process would take much longer. We look each other in the face, a deep, searching look, memorizing every inch, because it seems to go some way to answering our questions: Did she love her child? Will she love her child? We see the other mothers around us, and it comforts us both; it's so important for both of us to see what the other person is like—even if that person is only a substitute.

The mothers here aren't poor and desperate women from the slums; they're the ordinary, friendly girls I've seen on the streets with books under their arms, shopping in the market with their mothers, choosing fabric in the shops for a new salwar kameez, munching candy at the snack stand, or picking out a few colorful headbands at the bazaar. Some of them speak English. At least two of the girls here can read books. I'm sure that they all hope to marry well, and they give the impression that abortion is not an option for them on moral and religious grounds.

Still, these girls come from homes where being pregnant out of wedlock is cause for scandal. "With a child in tow, marriage is out of the question," Sister Lena told me, and Sister Clara confirms this is the case. The fear of being shunned and of the shame they will bring upon the family in the eyes of their parents, as well as bullying at home, even leads some pregnant girls to commit suicide. What did my Indian neighbor at home tell me?

"In times gone by in our villages, those were the girls who would throw themselves down the well." I know these wells; there's one in the middle of the bazaar. The fruit traders have set up their stalls around it. With its thick stone wall, it must be at least sixteen feet across, and deep—frighteningly so—particularly long after the monsoon season when I can barely make out the murky black water far below. You'd need a long rope to draw water here, and anyone jumping in would be lost forever, especially if they couldn't swim. There's nothing to hold on to down there.

This is why the sisters take the young girls in. "When they realize they're four or five months along, they come. Sometimes their parents even bring them," Sister Clara says. "It's all very hush-hush," she whispers to me.

I'd rather not hear about the family dramas, despair, tears, and accusations that have gone before, but ultimately the girls and their parents have decided that the girls will spend their pregnancy here with the sisters. Until the birth, the girls stay up here in this bright room, united in their shared fate, supporting each other—for months on end. An ambulance is already waiting in the yard for when labor starts. There are plenty of hospitals around here. The newborns stay with the sisters.

"No religion. No name." Sister Clara, too, confirms that the girls aren't allowed to name their babies.

"Do the girls not want contact with their babies, then? They never want to see them again?" I ask gently. This sister hesitates.

"Even if they did, we don't allow it." Each girl signs the adoption declaration, and after a three-month window, during which she can change her mind, there's no going back. The girl loses all rights to her child and any connection with it. Further contact is not allowed.

"These are their own babies, their own blood, you see. It could cause problems," the sister says. There's clearly the worry that a child might not understand who his or her real mother is, or that the mother might have regrets. Even if at a later date a mother just wants to know where her child has ended up, she won't receive any information. No contact is allowed—not a letter, not a phone call. Nothing.

"We just tell them the children will be sent to England, France, or Switzerland; that's all." In theory, then, there are two mothers in the world who would like to learn more about each other, but the sisters and the authorities forbid it.

After the birth, the girl returns home. Perhaps the rest of the family is told she has spent the last six months visiting relatives in Kolkata. There are gynecologists who can even restore her virginity. Now the girl's marriage prospects are good once more, and she's not a burden to her family. Everything's peachy.

I ask myself whether, by deciding to adopt, I'm not guilty of supporting this entire system; perhaps these families' secret escape route only works because there are mothers like me who are willing to adopt the girls' babies? Am I helping to support this society's old ways, and in doing so, unintentionally making myself the girls' enemy when what they really need is a society that will treat their mistakes with more tolerance? After all, by adopting one myself, am I not the very person who allows these girls' parents to make a baby disappear instead of working through the girls' "accident" openly and honestly and accepting the child? By adopting, am I not reinforcing Indian society's definition of what constitutes a "mistake" in a girl's life, to be hushed up and erased? And who thinks of the impact this dishonest solution has on the child? Am I lending my support to a system that values a young girl's welfare and marriage prospects above a child's need to stay with his or her mother?

Doubtless, it would never occur to these Indian girls and their families that a young woman could raise her child alone. In spite of my age, I'm often asked if my mother-in-law and other relatives will be at home to help me with the child. My answer of "No" is met with looks of disbelief. A woman handling a child and a job by herself seems to be inconceivable to most Indian parents.

I won't stay and chat with the women any longer; I don't want them to feel spied on or threatened by my presence. The young women seem quite different to me. One is more serious, older, and standoffish; perhaps she'd like to keep her child if she could. Heavily pregnant, she looks unhappy and desperate; she will have been able to feel her baby moving around inside her for some time now. Perhaps she's under enormous pressure from her family to give up her baby—and I'm part of their scheme. The face I'll remember most, though, seemed to glow; this young girl was clearly relieved and pleased to have found a way out.

I say my good-byes, and we wish each other all the best, mother to mother, from the mother who gives to the mother who receives. Meeting each other will have to be enough for us. I will never stand face-to-face with Ragini and be able to ask her why she gave Bina up, and this beautiful girl will never know the mother who adopts her child and be able to ask her if she loves the child or if the child is happy. We will carry this uncertainty, and all the worries it brings, with us every day for the rest of our lives.

Chapter 21

FRAGILE BONDS

Easy come, easy go. Today is the first time I've realized just how superficial Bina's relationship with me is. I was stupid to let myself think she could get used to me so quickly, that she accepted me as her mother. I'd only been gone one day, to visit the home for pregnant girls, and already the fragile bond of trust between us has shattered. She just couldn't cope with it.

That morning, when I walk into her room and go to greet her in her cot, my daughter doesn't even look at me. I know she knows I'm there, but she ignores me. I bend down to her, stroke her head, cuddle her, but Bina just stands up, raises her arms to be picked up, and stares out the window. No sooner have I lifted her up than she wants to be put down, and she trots off through the older children's room toward the stairs without looking back. She acts as if I'm not there. This goes on all morning. I try to get her attention, but she toddles stubbornly down the steps to the first floor and totters into the kitchen where she finds Sister Alissa—ignoring me completely all the while.

Sister Alissa greets Bina and takes a large jar of caramels from the medicine cabinet. So, a little later, Bina sits smugly in Sister Alissa's arms, caramel and chocolate sauce dripping from her mouth, joyfully snuggling into her beloved sister with her whole sticky body.

"That's children for you!" Sister Alissa laughs, enjoying Bina's affections. As she cuddles my little one, I do my best to accept the situation and not to let my disapproval show, but I don't really succeed.

I'm in a bad mood today. For ten days now I've been chasing around after Bina in this dark, noisy orphanage, feeding her porridge and trying to make the children's lives a little brighter with nothing but broken pieces of toys. I'm constantly treading in bits of banana, puddles of urine, or squashed caramels, cuddling children with dirty diapers, getting milk spattered on my salwar kameez and porridge on my glasses. I feel as if I'm sinking into a mushy mess of porridge, urine, milk, and rice water. I'm constantly sweating, losing more and more weight, and battling diarrhea. Now I stand here, awkward and insecure, in the presence of the head sister, and my daughter won't even look at me.

I need to get a grip. I know that I'm being unfair and that I can't expect to make up for a year spent in the orphanage in just ten days. The very reason I came here was so that Bina's attachment to the sisters could be gradually transferred to me, to avoid tearing her away from her orphanage-porridge-sisters routine in one fell swoop. There would be setbacks—I had read this many times in my adoption books. Two steps forward, one step back. Today was just a "step back" day. All the same, when theory turns into practice, it hurts.

"I mustn't take Bina's behavior personally," I tell myself as I watch her snuggling up to Sister Alissa. She looks at me almost pleadingly, asking me whether this is OK. I give her a nod: yes, it's fine. You go ahead and cuddle the sister. I'll get my turn at some point.

Of course, I mustn't be unfair to the sisters either. It must be hard for them to sit back and watch as Bina slowly distances herself from them, abandons them, and grows closer to this European woman. The sisters are more attached to individual children than you might think. Sister Alissa has taken Bina to her heart, and I'm glad that she has this grandmother figure in her life because the deeper her relationship with the sisters, the better her relationship will be with me, once this bond has been gradually transferred. But this process will take time—many weeks, not just ten days.

I leave Bina with Sister Alissa, who carries my daughter off to the nuns' quarters, and go back to the children on the second floor, planning to retreat to the solitude of the cot room. At this time, all the children are normally running around in the big ones' room.

I want to be alone. I am hoping for some peace and quiet, but the room is not quite empty; Sister Martha stands over one of the cots, gazing sadly at the little girl inside. I'd noticed the little one from the start. She is deathly pale, very slight, and she spends all day standing in her cot, her hands tightly gripping the bars, jerking her head from left to right, rhythmically, endlessly, as if in a trance. Her whole body rocks from side to side with incredible force. She is the only child this badly affected by hospitalization; she shuts everything out.

"She won't even look at me; she won't react to me at all. I just can't get through to her," says Sister Martha, sighing as she tries to hold the child's head steady. The girl's little face is contorted with the constant strain.

"Is she disabled? Surely there must be something wrong with her," I say to Sister Martha.

"Apparently, she's completely healthy, at least so the doctor says. He tells us she's normal." I notice the doubt in her voice.

"I don't believe that," I reply.

"I don't think she's healthy either; something's not right with her. But the doctor even says we can put her up for adoption."

"But there's nothing normal about her behavior," I point out, knowing how alarmed and shocked I would be if I was given a child like this.

"Yes, I know. Something's not right with her, at least I think so. That's why I won't give her away. I can hardly offer her to prospective parents without knowing what's wrong with her. I'm going to wait and see; often abnormalities are easier to spot when the child's a little older. I make a point of never giving a child away if I can't tell the parents exactly what's up with them. That would just be wrong."

We watch in horror as the little girl continues her rocking.

"Do you remember little Ashok?" Sister Martha asks. I know exactly the boy she means. He is around five years old, skinny, and really quite vicious, devious almost—always unkind to the other children. But it's no wonder. He appears to be mentally disabled and can't hold his own against the other children, particularly the big ones, who abuse and bully him, rejecting him at every turn.

"He came to us when he was still very little, and we already had adoptive parents for him," Sister Martha tells me. "On the day when these parents came to collect him, Ashok was lying in his cot. I was passing by and saw him there. I suddenly noticed the funny way he was holding his hand—it was like a kind of intuition. I stopped the adoption the very same day."

"What about the parents?"

"We sent the parents away. As time went by, we realized that Ashok has a physical disability, that his physical development is delayed." Sister Martha turns away from the little girl's cot, and we go into the diaper changing room, where she prepares a bottle of rice water for her.

"Much later, we had managed to find parents for Ashok who were prepared to take him in spite of his physical disability. They were from Switzerland. Once again—it was just before the adoption—I was walking through the room as before and saw Ashok. I suddenly said to myself, 'Something's not right here.' So I stopped that adoption as well. He's not just disabled in a physical sense, I thought; he's mentally disabled as well. And as it turned out, he really is mentally disabled."

I'm moved as I listen to Ashok's story. To think his adoption had been stopped twice—two sets of parents turned away. What would have become of Ashok with these Indian or Swiss parents? Perhaps the parents might have been shocked at first, but then they might have helped him. Then he wouldn't be here now, in this orphanage, getting beaten up by the other children, having to fight for his place by poking, pushing, and hitting, never really standing a chance. But this would have meant deceiving the parents, tricking them. The orphanage's reputation would have been damaged, and with it the chances of finding homes for other children. The sister's decision makes sense, and yet I notice how Sister Martha seems to wrestle with her thoughts sometimes. Does she feel guilty? Or is she reminding herself that in the long term, being honest with parents is the only way to secure a future for as many children as possible?

"What happens to the children who are so disabled that no parents can be found for them?" I ask the sister.

"Most of the time it just takes longer to find parents for these children. But the difficult cases are sent to another orphanage over in Santa Cruz," she says and then falls silent. Santa Cruz is another district of Mumbai. I throw her a questioning look.

"You can go there if you like. Yes, you should see it, really. It's a home for the disabled and for AIDS sufferers. It's huge. I worked there for a long time; it's a very challenging place to work. But I enjoyed it. I would even say I was happy there. Don't hesitate to visit if you feel like it," she says, eyeing me carefully.

I admire Sister Martha. I admire her commitment. The sisters don't have any kind of private lives; they give up their lives completely and dedicate all their efforts to the order, to their work here. They don't even have their own possessions. They don't get time off. They get nothing. And yet, they are happy, fulfilled. They have found their mission—their calling—and they seem completely balanced, generally content, and yes, even joyful.

Yet the work here is so hard, so inhumane sometimes, and tragic. I remember how three days ago, Sister Martha had stood in the infants' room, the dark room where Bina had spent six months. She was pointing at a cot that I'd often peered at in horror. There lay a baby, a little girl who was really quite pretty, just a few months old. She has very intelligent, warm eyes, but her arms and legs are completely crippled. One little leg is now just an amputated stump.

"We've already had to have one of her legs amputated; in a few weeks, the other one will have to come off as well." Sister Martha sighed. "And later on, probably one of her arms, too," she added. We both stared at the girl, who was holding a teething ring in one of her crippled hands. I shuddered at the thought of the child's limbs being amputated, one by one.

"She is very intelligent. She watches everything that goes on here and really responds to us when we spend time with her," Sister Martha had stressed.

Perhaps that's why the sisters spend so many hours of the day praying. They work and help without question. They don't blame anyone. They don't involve themselves in the ways of the world. I couldn't do it. I would always be looking for someone to blame, someone to hold responsible. I would want to solve problems right away. But perhaps this kind of attitude makes it impossible to concentrate selflessly on serving others; perhaps it distracts you from the real purpose.

"Where's Bina?" Sister Martha asks suddenly.

"She's downstairs playing with Sister Alissa," I answer indignantly. "She won't have anything to do with me. Today I'm just a means to an end, a way to get out of her cot; she's not interested in me at all."

"But that's not true! Yesterday while you were out, although Bina played up here, she kept stopping to look for you. She's really very attached to you," the sister assures.

She's right, of course. I decide to go and bring Bina back upstairs. Passing through the older children's room, I'm surprised to see a European sitting there with the children. He's brought along some cookies, and the children are happily munching away, spraying crumbs everywhere. He tells me that he's adopting one of the girls and points to Leela, the girl who had recently let me stroke her hair. I don't know whether she understands who this man is or that he will be her future father. She sits munching cookies with Anita, Nirav, and the other children.

Downstairs, Bina actually seems happy to see me when I collect her from Sister Alissa's arms. She looks bored, so I take her back upstairs. A little later, Bina sits on my lap shoving shortbread into her mouth and gasping with delight with the other children.

At noon, after her cookie binge and another porridge food fight, I leave Bina in her cot with a bottle of rice water for her afternoon nap. I go back to the hotel, have something to eat, and then sneak up to the roof of the hotel where the trash is stored. I discovered the way up there a few days ago. You just have to open the door at the end of my corridor, which leads into a narrow staircase. If you follow the stairs down, you'll find yourself in the hotel kitchen, a blackened room that stinks of oil and curry, where the kitchen boys crouch on the floor chopping spices, onions, and vegetables and huge pots simmer away over big fireplaces. The first time I ended up there, the sweaty men stared at me in disbelief, and I ran straight upstairs again.

If you go up the stairs, however, you'll need to clamber over a few sleeping young men, who are taking a break from their work in the hotel. They are snoring away on the landings, curled up on their newspaper mattresses. They lie here, even though there's little space for them on the landings and in spite of the baking-hot air and the stench coming up from the kitchen. Having reached the top, I push open the door to the roof of the hotel and find myself standing next to the water tank surrounded by broken chairs and empty beverage crates. I've set up a chair and pushed the garbage aside a little, and there I sit, high above the railway tracks and the flat roof of the orphanage, where the children's laundry is drying. The only other things this high up are the top of a blossoming tropical tree and the cawing crows, which sometimes perch on the water tank next to me. Over the rooftops of the houses on the other side of the railway tracks, children's paper kites dance in the hot tropical breeze, and the helicopters almost graze the tops of the trees. Sitting in the shade of the treetop, I can cope with the heat a lot better than in my small, stuffy room.

At three o'clock that afternoon, I head back to the orphanage. I've barely reached the second floor when I hear Nirav's cries. No one knows where he's got to. Aisha is looking after the little ones, playing Ring a Ring o' Roses with them, and Anita is helping. The little girl who always screams is hiding crossly under the table. A new girl has arrived; she is around six or seven years old and is standing against the wall as if in a trance. She stares in disbelief at the grouchy, fretting children, playing or teasing each other; her big black eyes are full of bewilderment. She doesn't react to any of the children; she is stone faced, as if she's had a dreadful shock. She's as pretty as a picture, but crippled and silenced by fear and confusion.

I search for Nirav. At some point my intuition tells me to open a door I've never opened before; I'd always thought it was a cupboard. But it's not a cupboard—it's a door to an attic room full of junk. In the half light, I make out a crying, quivering Nirav. Someone—I have no idea who—had locked him in here as punishment. Carla and Sivana, the second shift of helpers, have gone downstairs to fetch the pans of hot milk bottles. Sobbing, Nirav pushes his way past me and runs to the barred balcony where a few dresses are sometimes hung up to dry; it looks out toward the train tracks. There's another way up to the roof of the orphanage from here via a steep staircase, but Nirav just crawls up against the balcony and begins to tear rhythmically and repeatedly at the bars. He rocks back and forth, crying. Deep sobs come from his chest. His face, with its outward-squinting eyes, is swimming with tears. They drip down onto his scrawny chest. Spit runs down his chin, and his wobbling lips reveal what's left of his rotten teeth. I slowly approach him and lay a hand on his arm.

"Nirav," I say softly, but he lets out a furious howl, scurries away from me, crawls up against the bars again, and resumes his monotonous rocking. I can't get through to him. I fight back the tears. I would love to take him in my arms, comfort him, and hold him tight. As it is, the best I can do is be nearby and show him that I'm there for him. However, he would rather be alone; he stares out at the tracks, at the trains thundering past, at the slum huts beside the street below, and at the kites dancing over the rooftops in the distance. He cries and cries.

Suddenly, I feel a tug on my salwar kameez. It's Bina. She grabs my hand, gives me a questioning look, and pulls me away. She pulls me to the other children, and I'm extremely moved. It's the first time that Bina has reached out to me, grasped my hand, given me a clear sign that she wants to play with me. I take her on my lap and sit among the screaming, frolicking children. I begin to sing. I sing children's songs at the top of my voice and rock Bina on my lap. I couldn't have done this at first; in the early days I would look at the children, and my voice would fail me. But now I can sing, while Bina sits on my lap rocking her head rhythmically from side to side along with the songs. I can sing, despite all the scars and spots, the ulcers and disabilities, the fear and aggression of the children. I see the joy in their eyes as they clap their hands and laugh, and suddenly it doesn't seem so bad that shy little Kabir is lying on the floor at the back of the room crying or that across in the cot room, Sivana is feeding the little boy who spits everything up again. At some point, Nirav comes back into the room.

All of a sudden, Anita lets out an excited shout and runs back into the corridor overlooking the yard. The children rush out and stand at the barred windows on tiptoe. I follow them. Nirav has climbed right up to the top of the bars again. Aisha and Anita yell something down into the yard, and then I see the European, who is just saying good-bye to

Sister Alissa and Sister Martha. He is holding Leela's hand, and both of them turn around to go. Leela is wearing a pretty dress, and her hair is neatly combed. She looks up as the children cry out—but only briefly and hastily. The children fall silent as she disappears through the gate with the European. Nirav waves and then lets his hand fall and stares blankly ahead. Aisha whispers, "Auntie," and slips her hand into mine. I go back into the room with Bina and the other children, but somehow I can't sing as lightheartedly as before.

Chapter 22

A LACK OF TRUST

I can't stop thinking about Leela—how her heart must have hammered as she followed her new European father through the gates of the orphanage and out into the street. It all happened so quickly that she'd barely had time to say good-bye to Nirav, Anita, and Aisha. She was so confused that she daren't even wave to her friends at the window above.

I'm sure the sisters must have explained to her that this strange man was her new father and that her new mother and perhaps even siblings were waiting for her at his house. But what was Leela to make of this man? What were these strange sounds coming from his mouth? Was he nice or nasty? How long would she stay with him—just a few months, or years? How long would it be before this person sent her away, too?

There had been no one there to ask as she left the orphanage. The nuns and her friends Nirav, Aisha, and Anita, with whom she'd always played—she'd had to leave them all behind. In one day, her whole life in India became null and void; her world collapsed around her. But then, she had already known it was a world in which nothing could be trusted, where nothing was permanent or reliable.

Every child in this orphanage had experienced this; each and every one had learned that the world was an unpredictable place. In Bina's case, as with all babies in the orphanage, this traumatic experience began shortly after she was born. Just a few days after she came into the world, the warmth and security of her mother, her voice, suddenly vanished. Instead, Bina was thrown into a strange world full of many different voices, screaming children, and unknown hands that shoved a bottle of milk into her mouth.

After just a few weeks, this world was exchanged for another as she was moved from the infant room to the one where the young babies were kept. There, the voices and the cries of the other babies were even louder, and the women who appeared from time to time with porridge and bottles of milk didn't have the same familiar faces. Once again, it was different women who worked with Sister Maria to care for Bina, often in shifts—some in the morning and others in the afternoon and night. They have so many children to look after that they never had much time for Bina. Strange children crawled in the cots around her, and unfamiliar noises came from outside—the drone of the helicopters and the wail of the trains. Just a few months later, Bina was moved again, this time upstairs to the second floor, to another new set of caregivers and Sister Martha.

And yet, Bina was one of the lucky ones. Many of the children aren't from Mumbai, and they spend the first few months of their lives in orphanages in the country or in other towns in the Indian state of Maharashtra.

Every child here has already learned one thing: the world around them is not to be trusted. It's unpredictable. People come and go. They might give you food and drink, but ultimately you're alone. Even the women who play with you only stay for a little while, and then they put you back in your cot and walk away, no matter how much you cry.

Things are so different for a baby born into a loving family. This child is only cared for by his or her mother and father at first, perhaps also siblings and close relatives. The number of caregivers is small and manageable, and over time the baby learns that the behavior of these people is predictable and that the world is a safe and dependable place. As soon as the child shows signs of hunger or thirst, Mother or Father is there with food or drink and a cuddle. This continual satisfaction of the child's needs shapes his or her development and behavior. In the course of his or her daily, interpersonal relationships with his or her parents, a child learns to copy others' gestures and speech, and above all, he or she learns to trust. After a while, the child has learned that he or she can depend on his or her parents and trust them, that they are figures of stability. This is the source of a child's basic sense of trust and his or her capacity to form attachments; a child needs this subconscious sense of security so that he or she can later detach him-/herself from his or her parents and venture into the outside world.

A child learns how to bond with and trust other people in the first year of life. If he or she is not able to form this bond with an attachment figure at this formative time, he or she misses out on an important part of childhood development, which is necessary to help him or her to grow up into a well-balanced and confident adult.

The trauma of separation that the orphanage children have already experienced when their biological mothers gave them away and the subsequent upheaval of constantly changing caregivers rob them of the opportunity of ever forming a bond with a single attachment figure and jeopardize their chances of psychologically healthy childhood development. Crucially, there's only so much that can be done further down the line to make up for these shortcomings. If a child misses out on important milestones in his or her psychological development in the first year, there is then very little chance that he or she will ever achieve these. This results in the behavioral problems that affect many orphanage children for many years, in some cases their entire lives.

When a child experiences a world that is constantly changing, uncertain, and fragile, he or she feels threatened and tends to adopt behaviors he or she hopes will protect him or her from the chaos and the pain. These mechanisms are deeply rooted, and correcting them, if they can be corrected at all, often takes a long time and a great deal of trust and understanding from future parents.

When Bina is unable to look me in the eyes, it's because she never had a close, intimate relationship with her mother and because, subconsciously, she's afraid of this new, unusually close relationship. In her experience, people are unreliable and unpredictable, so it's only logical that she would try to protect herself from the risk of forming another bond, which could easily be shattered, by not even looking at me. After all, we form emotional bonds with other people through eye contact.

When Manika pokes, scratches, and bites me, it's really a desperate cry for attention and love. Although she doesn't get love when I defend myself and scold her, she certainly gets my undivided attention, and even this negative attention is better than being ignored. By doing this, she can make sure I'm paying attention to her and not to the other children.

When the older girl in the room across the hall lies under her bed and roars so loudly that her whole body shakes, it's a sign that the sense of fear and anger she feels toward this chaotic world is too huge for her to bear. Children who have a stable relationship with an attachment figure know that others will help them and that they don't have to be overwhelmed by their fears. Through their parents, they learn how to express and control feelings like joy, anger, and fear. Children who have never experienced this are often unable to moderate feelings like fear and become overwhelmed by their emotions.

The same goes for an appropriate response to pain. If a child has never learned that it's OK to show that he or she is in pain and that others will react with cuddles, comfort, and bandages, eventually he or she will hardly respond to pain. Here at the orphanage, I have seen children fall down a stone staircase and land on their heads, run into a door while playing and hit their foreheads, or cut their knees, and they do not react in any way. There were no screams, no tears—every child just rubbed his or her head and carried on playing. At first glance, one might think they were just being brave, but it's actually a sad demonstration of the fact that these children have never learned that a cry of pain can elicit a sympathetic reaction from another person.

When Nirav stood beside me on the balcony and rocked rhythmically back and forth, tearing at the bars and slipping into a trance, it was his way of getting rid of the deep inner turmoil and fear that he feels in this chaotic world. It was a helpless attempt to calm himself, because he didn't know how else to do so and because there was no one there to help him. Even when I tried to interact with him, Nirav was unable to allow me to help, as he has learned that he's alone in this world and must look after himself because no one else will.

Even Aisha's behavior is symptomatic. The fact that she hangs on the nuns' apron strings and looks after the other little children like a good fairy and that she so obviously plays the Goody Two-shoes is no reason to admire her. She has been deeply affected by being sent away and abandoned. "Why?" she wonders. "Was I bad? Did I do something wrong? Was it because I didn't help enough?" She looks for reasons to blame herself. She's determined that this will never happen to her again, and so she plays the good fairy. She's doing it out of pure fear—the fear that she will be sent away for not behaving correctly. It's a preventive measure.

The terrifying reality is that all these children's worlds will come tumbling down again; none of them will stay in this orphanage forever. One of two fates awaits them: either they will experience the trauma of adoption, in which they will be catapulted into completely unfamiliar surroundings to live with total strangers, or they will be sent to another institution. Either way, it will confirm their beliefs that the world is dangerous and unpredictable and that, sadly, even the sisters can't protect them from it.

This is exactly the reason I came here. I don't want Bina to experience her adoption as her world shattering around her. I don't want there to be any more traumas in her life that show her that people are not to be trusted. Although I know that the changes ahead will be a shock for Bina, I hope that I can soften the blow and instill a little bit of trust in her. I want Bina to get to know me and gradually get used to me so that she feels safe with me when we finally leave the orphanage together.

Fortunately, the nuns and the young women who help here at the orphanage understand this.

While I was still at home, Sister Lena had called to tell me I didn't need to come to Mumbai, that Bina was doing fine. However, since I've been here, the sisters have come to appreciate why I am doing this: so that the bond that Bina has with the sisters can slowly be transferred to me.

That's why the nuns let me visit Bina every day and are allowing me to take on the roles of the people she is most attached to, bit by bit. First, Sister Martha and the female care workers had to show me how to feed and change Bina, and it took some time before Bina accepted my doing these things. Now, I have completely taken over, and they are hardly involved in Bina's care.

I have tried to do things the way they have always been done here in the orphanage. After washing and changing Bina, I oil her hair with coconut oil the same way that Sister Martha does with all the children. I tie her hair into the same topknot, dust her skin with the same white powder to guard against heat rash, and place a black dot of kajal, a bindi, on her forehead the way Sister Martha taught me. Bina is familiar with these little rituals, so I'd like to continue them after we get home. I don't yet realize that putting coconut oil on her hair and painting a bindi on her forehead would become the little touches that would still make my daughter happy years later.

I still feed Bina on the floor, as is the custom here in the orphanage, but I like her to have her bottle of milk in my arms so that we can make eye contact and gaze at each other.

I have memorized the times when Bina goes down for her afternoon nap and I know that instead of a pacifier, the children in the orphanage go to sleep with a bottle of milk or rice water in their mouths. Because it's so hot, they sleep without covers, so I will not be surprised to find that Bina still sleeps without one a year or two later, no matter how cold our winters get in the north.

As the weeks have gone by, I've learned to hum an Indian melody that Sister Martha sings to the children. At some point, I noticed that the children here love to play Ring a Ring o' Roses; this will be Bina's favorite game for years.

All these little things are important to my daughter and will help us one day when we take her out of the orphanage.

If I hadn't come here, I would never have discovered that the sisters don't call Bina by her name, but by a nickname they've given her. I would never have learned the Hindi words the sisters use when it's time for the children to eat or go to sleep. Over the weeks, I have picked up a small vocabulary that I will use for years at home.

I'm making sure to take lots of photos and videos. Later, I will hang the photos of the sisters on the wall in Bina's room. I've also put together a little album for her with photos of the orphanage, which I got developed in the bazaar here. Bina already looks at the book with interest. She taps the sisters' faces with her fingers and babbles away. At this point, I can't know that the video I'm taking of daily life in the orphanage will still hold Bina's interest years later and will encourage her to ask questions about her past in India.

The most important thing, though, is that my daughter doesn't feel as if she has suddenly been torn away from the sisters and the orphanage. Every day, we both go down to visit the sisters in the courtyard, the office, and the infant room. The nuns make a fuss of Bina, and the fact that I'm watching her being happy, cuddling, and being fed candies shows her both that the sisters aren't pushing her away and that I'm not trying to rip her out of their arms. She has time to slowly detach herself from the sisters and get closer to me, little by little. In this way, Bina sets the pace at which she's ready to trust me and take the next step in her life.

These days, Bina cries as I pack my bag to go at the end of the day. She is more and more attached to me; I can hardly give her a kiss in the evening for fear that she will cling to me and cry.

All the while, my feelings toward Bina are developing as well, deepening. In the early days, they could best be described as a huge sense of responsibility toward her. Now I notice that I'm seeing her more and more as my daughter and becoming more concerned that something might happen to her. She becomes more precious to me with every passing day.

My hope is that, one day, we will both have become so used to each other that we'll be able to say good-bye to the sisters in peace. That's my dream. I'd like Bina to leave the orphanage in my arms without panicking that the rug is being pulled out from under her again. Maybe then she'll realize that she can trust me, that she can feel safe with Andreas and me; only then will she develop the confidence to navigate the wider world with ease. That's why these weeks we're spending together in the orphanage matter so much—for the rest of her life.

Chapter 23

OF JOY AND HAPPINESS

Three weeks have already passed since I arrived. I have gotten used to India again, and now I hardly remember the issues that had at first shocked me so much about Mumbai. I am not bothered by the dirt and stench anymore; I'm actually impressed by how clean the city is. When I step out of my little hotel in the mornings to bring my empty glass back to the tea stall, the men from the work crew are long gone, and the streets have been swept clean. In the market, the traders have arranged their vegetables in tempting piles; the smell of fresh coriander mingles with the scent of sandalwood from incense sticks.

Even the slums nearby are neat and tidy in the morning. In recent weeks, they have been joined by another new hut, where a mother lives with four young children. She often feeds her little ones from a large shared bowl of rice. A public restroom has even been installed under the steps up to the railway bridge. Ever since it was built, the stench near the wall of the orphanage has slightly improved.

Out in the street, the baby masseuse's little boy is frolicking about. He has lathered himself up, poured a bucket of water over his head, and is now standing at the side of the road, stark naked. With his smart, short haircut, he looks as though he is about to get dressed for school. His mother is wearing a fresh sari, neatly wrapped around her body, her hair coiled in a freshly oiled bun. Only the shaven-headed woman's hut is empty; she has left her tattered blankets bunched up in the corner.

As I enter the street to the orphanage, I stop, surprised. I find my way blocked by a large crowd of people—bitterly poor women, gaunt and haggard, most of them carrying malnourished children—surging against the locked metal door. Nearly all have worn-out, cheap, outdated cotton saris slung around their scrawny hips and chests. Many of the women have given up fighting for a place at the gate and are squatting almost apathetically in the dust on the street, right next to the deep gutter full of stinking trash and discarded plastic. Two toddlers with matted hair and snotty noses, wearing little jackets that are old and full of holes, crawl dangerously close to the passing cars. However, this doesn't seem to bother anyone.

As they catch sight of me, their excited talk dies away, and they move to the side a little so that I can push my way through. Then the women call out something. They beat on the gate, which soon opens. The porter recognizes me, pulls me by the hand into the courtyard, and quickly closes the door behind me.

The courtyard, too, is densely crowded, and the babble of voices is just as loud. Nirav and Anita are clinging on to the barred window above, observing the scene. A long line of women and a few frail men are waiting, all clutching plastic bags expectantly. As I near the head of the line, I realize what is causing all the commotion in and around the courtyard and the orphanage: food is being handed out. Next to the offices and entrances, the sisters have piled mountains of bags of clothes and foodstuffs. One sister collects the pink food tickets, given out beforehand in the slums and on the streets. Then the women file past the heaps of rice, sugar, salt, flour, lentils, powdered milk, and cookies, not to mention the parcels of secondhand clothes. Several sisters hand each woman a bundle of old clothes, food parcels, and a plastic bottle filled with cooking oil.

Sister Lena catches sight of me and waves me over.

"Now you can take over for a while. It'll be like this all day." She asks me to take her place giving out the rice. It's already hot; the food is being handed out in the blazing sun. Sister Lena has clearly got a backache again. Before I know it, I find myself standing in a row with the nuns. I am responsible for an enormous mountain of bags of rice. Sister Martha is passing out bags of lentils on my left, whereas on my right Sister Maria is putting one small bag each of sugar and salt into the plastic bags the women hold out to us.

The line is dealt with quickly; after all, as Sister Martha tells me, we're expecting one thousand families here today. No sooner are the women and children let back out into the street with their bags than the next group is allowed into the courtyard to line up and collect their food.

An Indian businessman stands in the courtyard, eagerly chatting away and rubbing his hands together in amazement. He has donated most of the food and makes no secret of the fact that he is happy and proud to be able to help.

I dig in and hand out the rice as if I'm working on a production line. Things move so quickly that I often only see the hands of the people holding out the plastic bags to me—haggard, hard hands; thin hands; frail hands that have spent a lifetime being worked to the bone; lots of tattooed arms. Every now and then, I look into the alarmingly old and furrowed faces and see the black-tanned skin, the dark eyes, which are often sad, but always grateful, almost shy. So much joy over a bag of rice! Some of the women reach out to me and say, "Thank you so much, sister." They don't notice that I'm not a sister at all. I turn my gaze back to the bony, calloused, wrinkled hands in front of me, often so weak that they cannot hold the plastic bags open without shaking. For some, the bags of food are already too heavy, and their children have to help with the carrying. Soon, the bag of lentils bursts, and as they leave the courtyard, the oil sloshes out of the cheap plastic bottle that won't close properly. I can hardly bear the women's grateful glances, and tears start to well in my eyes, even though I had always longed for a chance like this: to help the poor, just to help, to give—without thinking about it, just give, give, give. It's such a refreshing change from my job back home.

And so, I keep staring at the tattooed hands that file past me, the colorful saris—the gaudier the sari, the poorer the woman—and the smiles bearing teeth stained red by the betel folks chew to abate their hunger. People glide past me—beautiful faces, proud, but also humiliated faces, sad and desperate. There are jaded and determined faces, yet unemotional faces, too. And tired ones—a great many very tired faces. My back starts to ache, but there's no time for a break. The line surges onward;

every woman, every child, and every old man wants rice and powdered milk, a bag of clothes, and a bottle of oil.

All at once, it dawns on me why the shaven-headed woman wasn't in her hut today, even though at this time on any other day she would still be lying among her blankets with her son, asleep. She stands near the line at the edge of the yard and gestures; she doesn't want to line up with her food ticket. Once again, she's too agitated, exasperated. Sister Lena, who has organized the food drive with military precision and is supervising the courtyard, motions to the woman's son to join the line with the food token. We give him a bag of food, clothes, and oil. Suddenly, an unkempt young man forces his way past the porter and storms into the yard. He starts talking at the shaven-headed woman. It seems that he wants to join the line with her.

"No!" scolds Sister Lena. "Not again; he's already had his turn. Out with you! One lot each—I won't have any begging. Get out at once!" And with the porter's help, she shoos the man from the yard. Meanwhile, the little boy has gotten his food. Sister Lena sends him away along with his disheveled, shaven-headed mother. "Some people always have to push their luck," the sister shouts. She makes sure that no one else tries any shenanigans: no begging, no pushing, no shoving, and no cheating.

After this interruption, the operation continues without incident. "Assalamu Alaikum," I hear an old lady in front of me say. She has a handsome, kind, gentle face and is so pleased with the rice that she keeps repeating "Assalamu Alaikum" over and over again. I carry on handing out bags, and then I espy the caregiver Camilla leading Bina by the hand. I see my daughter stumbling toward me over the bags of rice, and I stop in my tracks, holding up the line. Sister Lena signals to me to take a break; she'll carry on in my place.

"Bina's court case is in two weeks' time," she calls after me. "The courts have accepted the case, and all the paperwork is done. We still need passport photos of Bina. Get some taken this afternoon." Sister Lena nods to me. It is a relief when a case moves on to the next step for her, too.

I'm happy—happy about the rice I have given out, happy about the progress in the adoption case, and happy about Bina, who climbs babbling into my arms. She snuggles into me and doesn't bother with the sisters. Even her favorite, Sister Alissa, who is watching the food distribution from the inside of her cool office, cannot call her away from me. I am so happy with Bina in my arms in the shade near the busy scene.

"You're taking the little one?" I suddenly hear a voice next to me. It's an Indian lady in a pretty sari. A few gold bangles adorn her wrists, a red bindi graces her forehead, and her parting has a slight red tint, a sign that she is married. She is clearly proud of the food donation as well; she points out the businessman, her husband, and informs me that he has donated some of the food.

"Yes, I am. This is Bina. In two or three weeks we'll be able to take her out of the orphanage," I reply. As I say this, I have a vague sense that Bina is not squinting as badly as she was three weeks ago. Could it be that taking her out of her dark room and playing with her so often in the daylight has helped?

"Couldn't you get a boy?" she asks and looks at me like Indian mothers probably look at their daughters-in-law when family matters have to be discussed.

"No, I won't be able to get a boy, and I don't want one. I'm very happy with a daughter. I love girls, and she is a very brave one," I stress, hugging Bina.

"Naturally!" the Indian mother-in-law agrees. "You always see inside a child's heart. And girls *are* cute. That's true—*definitely*," she coos. "And it's so kind of you to adopt this child. You know, here nobody would have taken her. She's so dark, you see." She makes a helpless hand gesture. "But you look into her heart; that's good," she adds, giving me a sympathetic smile.

There it is again. I am stunned. Bina has her little lime-green dress on and looks adorable. I just don't get it. What's wrong with her skin color? A few days ago, Sister Alissa tried to convince me that even though Bina might be dark now, she would obviously become fairer once she joined us in Europe. "Then she will have a normal complexion, because it's cold where you live," she said. Of course, this was made-up nonsense. But why on earth did she feel the need to persuade me that Bina would become fair? And what is a "normal" complexion anyway? Sister Alissa was very dark herself. Had she suffered prejudice like this? Was she constantly reminded of her dark skin color?

I pick Bina up, say a polite good-bye to the woman, and go upstairs to the children, because it must be time for Camilla and Didi to bring the little ones' porridge soon.

Nirav is hanging on to the window bars, watching the food being handed out from a bird's eye view. The other children have given up; they are too small, and it's too tiring for them to keep balancing on their tiptoes to steal a glance into the courtyard.

Aisha and Anita have now moved on to playing Ring a Ring o' Roses with the little ones, although they can barely hear themselves sing over shy Kabir and the boy with the scar on his throat, both of whom are crying loudly. As I arrive, they all rush at me and pull at my things. They want me to sing with them and want to play "horsey" on my knee. Each and every one of the children loves playing "horsey," both because they like being dropped off my lap and because they get to snuggle so close to me when I pull them up out of the "ditch" again.

I decide I will buy the children a big sack of toys today during the lunch break. Books, too. I can hardly bear watching them being so bored anymore.

Once Bina has finally dozed off in her cot, after her porridge and rice water, and the big ones have been sent to their room for their midday nap, I take a stroll through the bazaar. Some of the businesses have closed for lunch, but most of the little shops are open. The place is tightly packed, but despite this, the heat is bearable because the bazaar is covered and the walkways and shops are shady. In a small shop ahead of me by the entrance of the bazaar, a large number of women are hunting for the right color bangles to match their saris. The shopkeeper has hundreds of loose plastic bangles in stock, in all sizes and all colors of the rainbow. Even Sister Martha keeps bringing the colorful bracelets back to the orphanage and is always putting new bangles on the children's wrists; their multicolored sparkle and the way they clack on their wrists delights the children and lends a joyful, carefree note to their appearance.

In the next alley, I find a toy shop, whose owner can hardly believe his luck today at selling so many plastic cars, rubber ducks, spinning tops, and other toys all in one go. I'm careful to make sure that each toy is as tough as possible and looks as if it could withstand a tantrum from Nirav or Ashok. In the end, for the cost of few rupees, I come away with a whole sack full of the stuff of children's dreams. In another shop, I find some really lovely picture books featuring animals, cars, and airplanes.

I could hardly wait for the lunch break to end that day. All the same, I hadn't bargained for what would happen when I approached the children with my bag of goodies. Nirav, two other boys, Anita, and Aisha realize at once what I've got in the sack. Before I realize it, they are pulling roughly at the bag. They are afraid of missing out on the toys. I wrench the sack from their hands, hold it high above my head, and call out to them to sit down. Only then do I hand out one toy to each child; I'd counted them beforehand in the bazaar to make sure that there's exactly the right number. But instead of being pleased, each child clutches his or her toy and peeks at what the others have got. Only when they understand that everyone has gotten a toy do Nirav and the boy with the scar on his throat dare to have a look at their own plastic cars. Anita tries out her spinning top with Aisha, and Kabir plays with his nodding, red plastic bear, pulling it along behind him. It's just Ashok who can't get on with his building blocks; he doesn't understand that he can stack the individual pieces to form a tower, and he throws the bricks on the floor in frustration. All the others are playing, but they are rough, almost aggressive, with the toys. I fear that their fun will not last long.

As I approach the cots, Bina genuinely dances for joy when she sees me. When I pick her up, she nestles into my shoulder and gently nibbles my neck. I kiss her and hug her tight. It's the first time Bina has shown such sincere joy at the sight of me. I'm slowly getting the feeling that she really looks forward to seeing me as a person and that she doesn't just see me as a means to get out of her cot so that she can reach the sisters. I believe she's starting to enjoy her moments with me and that our time together makes her happy. Even though we're still taking things slowly, we've come such a long way in three weeks. I know my stay here has been worthwhile.

Bringing Bina with me, I go over to the older children and pull one of the children's books from my bag. I sit Bina on my lap, and the other children, particularly the bigger ones, crowd around me. Silence and speechless wonder follow. Nirav, Aisha, and Anita whisper as they see the pictures of airplanes, cars, motorbikes, and boats. Nirav lays his finger carefully on each picture, mumbling in amazement. At this, the other children ask me to tell them the words to go with the pictures, repeating them very slowly back to me. They're so keen! In deep concentration and with obvious effort, they repeat each word in their broken English. It becomes clear to me just how hungry they are for pictures, language, learning, and school; how they long for the world outside; and how terribly little of it they experience inside the orphanage.

I flick through one of the books and pause, irritated. One page shows opposites, such as big and small, fat and thin, high and low, as well as beautiful and ugly. There is a picture of a blue-eyed, blond European girl; underneath her picture is written the word "beautiful." Alongside is a dark Indian woman in a sari; this picture bears the caption "ugly." I can hardly believe it: this is a book for children! How can Indian women and girls gain self-respect, pride, and a positive image of themselves if even a children's book, which is presented as an educational schoolbook, labels them as "ugly"? In moments like this I think that maybe it wouldn't be such a bad thing at all if I took Bina away from these prejudices, these mothers-in-law, and this social pressure. All the same, who knows what kind of discrimination she will face in my country?

One of the other books has an alphabet printed in it, and it gives me an idea. In a cupboard in the diaper changing room, I manage to find some paper and a few pens. Soon, Nirav, Anita, Aisha, and a couple of other children are sitting on the long bench at the dining table, trying to draw letters, while Bina sits eagerly beside them, chewing on a pen and excitedly beating her fist on a book. Nirav is trying his very best to write the A and the B; the letters are large and clumsy, but he's doing it so seriously that he sighs in concentration and presses much too hard with the pen in his effort and enthusiasm. Meanwhile, Anita has managed to draw a whole row of As, slowly and in a somewhat spidery hand. Upon seeing the children's joy and the light shining in their eyes, I promise myself to look at books and draw letters and numbers more often with them. Their frustrated aggression, which usually wears them down and causes them to lay into one other, has disappeared.

Suddenly, Sister Martha comes in. "You can come down; we're in the yard," she calls. As soon as the children hear this, they rush down the stairwell. It is late afternoon, and the heat has eased up a bit. The food donation is over. Some of the sisters are packing what remains of the secondhand clothes and a few canisters of cooking oil away into the storeroom. The porter has washed the courtyard down with water so that it now smells fresh, with the scent of tropical plants. Sister Alissa and Sister Maria have seated themselves down in the shade on the little wall among some potted plants, while Sister Martha is helping the children to carry the dented and bent tricycles and baby walkers out of a shed into the yard.

Anita, Aisha, and Nirav are already clambering between the tropical plants onto the rickety swing-boat. Moments later, they are swinging through the air, giddy with joy. The smaller children have a go on the tricycles. Sister Martha has lifted Bina into a round walker, in which she pushes herself eagerly across the yard. I sit down next to the sisters and enjoy the peaceful, shady atmosphere. The crows caw from the surrounding palms, the children play with gay abandon, and the sisters watch with amusement as their charges tumble and trip over each other with enthusiasm or ambitiously try to ride across the yard on the tricycles and walkers.

I think about how much other adoptive parents miss by not coming here. Many of the young children will soon be going to their new parents in Europe, yet these parents will not be able to imagine the world their children have lived in; they will have no idea of their joys, fears, and worries. To them, these are children without a past, without a history. Of course, it simply wouldn't be practical for all adoptive parents to stay in the orphanage for weeks on end, bugging the sisters, but it would be so valuable for the children. For days now, I've been photographing Bina's orphanage life, making video recordings, making sure that I have a picture of every sister and of every caregiver holding her; it will become a valuable memento for her later on.

I am taking photos now of the children riding their tricycles across the courtyard. The nuns know their children well, each one's individual personality, and they laugh at their antics, slip them caramels now and then, and are clearly satisfied with the day.

I can see how a life like this can be fulfilling. The sisters have worked with all their might to ensure that a thousand families can eat properly for at least a few days, and they have gotten the children through another day. They set themselves certain requirements and are satisfied with how the day has gone. The joy in their eyes at having been able to help is visible. Perhaps that's why they have this unbelievable aura of inner peace.

How different an impression they make than the faces I have seen in my working life: the permanently harassed, stressed look on the faces of Western people, the constant look of dissatisfaction on their lips, and the eternal worry that things are never enough, that nothing brings true fulfillment. Here, the rewards are much more modest, but the fulfillment can be all the greater.

Chapter 24

THE HOME IN SANTA CRUZ

We crawl slowly through the traffic. I've already made the long train journey to Santa Cruz, but the home for the disabled is still quite a journey from here. So I've hired an auto-rickshaw. I want to see what becomes of the children whose mental and physical disabilities are so severe that no one wants to adopt them, in India or anywhere else. I'm thinking of the child who rocks his head constantly back and forth and the little girl who will be losing her second leg in the next few weeks.

Santa Cruz is in the center of Mumbai and is more densely populated than the area around the orphanage. The traffic is more hectic, the buildings more run-down, and the slums bleaker; the huts at the side of the road are packed with so many people that most have a board at head height to create another floor. The elderly, exhausted men or older children sleep upstairs, while downstairs, mothers sit apathetically on the floor surrounded by a swarm of younger children, trying to cook a little rice, arguing with the neighbors over a few inches of string used as a washing line. There's not an inch of space here between the rickety, plastic-and-cardboard shelters and the tires of the cars and trucks rolling by. Compared to these slums, the masseuse from the railway embankment and even the cropped-haired mother live in luxury.

The driver jostles our rickshaw through the traffic, which has come to a standstill. The trucks, buses, and cars can't go any further and sit there filling the huts with their diesel fumes. Motorbikes and auto-rickshaws, on the other hand, are able to weave their way between them. We squeeze so close to the other vehicles that I could reach out and touch their hubcaps and exhaust pipes.

Suddenly, the driver hangs a left. Moments later, we're clanking across the courtyard of an industrial estate. I can see several spacious factory buildings.

"I'm looking for a home for disabled people, not a factory!" I grumble to the driver, pointing to a faded sign bearing the name of a company.

But the driver shakes his head and points to another sign hanging from a smaller building near the factory. He's right; it's the same Catholic order that runs

Bina's orphanage. After asking the driver to wait for me, I walk over to the entrance of the small building.

The front path and the steps are lined with pots filled with blooming hibiscus and oleander. Flowers cover the area beside the home and the wall of the nearby factory—a miniature paradise garden. Even the veranda is in bloom, an oasis in this concrete desert of factories and the gray, corrugated metal and plastic of the slums.

I knock on the door. When there's no answer, I open it and call into the dark hallway. After a few minutes, a young nun appears. I introduce myself and tell her about Sister Martha.

"She said it would be OK for me to look around the home," I say. I tell the sister that I'm adopting a child from the orphanage.

"Yes, of course," the sister replies. "But you'll have to wait until our lunch break and prayers are finished." With that, she disappears inside again and shuts the door. I suddenly realize that it's already lunchtime and I'll have to wait until three o'clock when the nuns finish their break. Given that the sister hadn't exactly seemed pleased to see me and hadn't seemed willing to show me around during the lunch break, I'm left standing helplessly on the veranda.

At first, I wait; I don't want to give up and have traveled all this way through the traffic for nothing. But it soon becomes too hot for me out on the veranda. The midday sun beats down on the yard between the factories and the sisters' quarters. The heat takes my breath away, and my head begins to ache. I'm not feeling well today as it is; my diarrhea has come back, and I've been taking antibiotics again for the past three days. Worrying that the amoebas are flaring up again, I've been taking the tablets I still have, even though I'm beginning to think that the drugs are actually making me weaker.

I can see I won't last much longer on the veranda, certainly not the two hours I still have left to wait. My rickshaw driver is lying in a shady gateway, fast asleep. So I decide to explore the home on my own.

I'd always thought of hell as hot and fiery and full of loud screams. I didn't know that it's slow and deathly quiet, that it cuts off your air supply and stops your heart, leaving you frozen and silent, like Lot's wife.

Cautiously, I approach the barred door of the first factory hall, not knowing what awaits me inside. The fly screen on the door is so thick and the hall beyond so dark that I can't make out anything at all. I open the door and step inside. Slowly, as my eyes get used to the dim light, I make out the cots—long, endless rows of them. They're packed side by side, filling the entire vast hall. Some of the cots are empty; others contain young children. As I slowly make my way down the path between them, I notice that every child is disabled. An eerie silence hangs over this room and every movement is slow. Out of the darkness, I see a girl coming toward me in slow motion, shuffling and limping; she gives me a confused smile and takes my hand. I stare into her smiling face and the curious emptiness of her eyes and then I turn back to stare at the sea of cots. The girl snuggles up to me as if she knows me. Then slowly, limping, she pulls me deeper into the hall—it's as if she's been expecting me.

A long changing table stands at the end of the hall where a caregiver is laboriously dressing a physically disabled child; another young woman carries a large disabled child in both arms. The women don't notice me and show no reaction; they weren't expecting me. The woman slowly carries the child down the rows of cots to the left side of the hall. This is the only part of the hall where daylight falls through narrow windows high up on the wall. In the light, I can make out an area of the floor covered with mats. Children lie there who are too disabled to sit; their bodies writhe on the floor, contorting and stretching in the faint shaft of light shining down through the darkness. Around the mats and the dark mass of bodies, the caregivers have set up little chairs for the children who are just about capable of keeping themselves upright. They slump in the chairs, moving and twisting like a confused audience watching the grotesque performance at its feet. The whole scene is so ghastly that it chokes me up. I start to feel trapped in this dark underworld, as if I'll never escape.

The girl tugs at my hand, but I can't go on; I'm so horrified I can hardly move. As I stare at the awkwardly writhing limbs and heads, the twisted hands and legs, one thought fills my head: how do the children get out of here? Do they ever get out? What if this is the end for these children? What if they have to spend forever here in the dark in a vast hall full of other disabled children? What if this is their final destination?

I can't take it anymore, and I pull my hand away. The girl turns around, gives me a confused smile, and sadly lets go of my hand I retrace my steps, walking backward, not daring to turn around. I slowly feel my way along the hallway back toward the entrance, toward the light, toward the other side of the bars where the flowers grow, the sky is blue, and the sun shines. It couldn't shine too brightly or be too hot for me now. I leave the girl standing between the cots in the darkness and slam the barred door shut behind me, pulling my hand away as though the metal had burned my fingers. I turn around, and then I notice myself going weak at the knees. I'm not sure what's to blame for this feeling: the sudden heat, the antibiotics, or the hall.

I look over at the next building, and suddenly I realize with horror just how many of these halls there are here. I make my way slowly around the flower beds and a few pots of hibiscus toward the door to the second hall. This time, I press my nose to the fly screen and wait for my eyes to get accustomed to the darkness.

Women—here are the women. This hall is as full as the last one, this time filled with makeshift beds crammed so close together in some places that there's barely enough room to squeeze between them. On every bed, a disabled woman is sitting, lying, or sleeping. Once again, I find their slow-motion movements upsetting. A mentally confused woman kneels on the floor between the beds in her nightdress, scrubbing the tiles like a woman possessed—always the same few tiles. She crawls around the floor between the beds, cleaning and polishing endlessly. I decide not to enter. I pull my head away from the fly screen. The scene fades away.

I turn around and spot another hall on the other side of the flower bed–lined path; this one doesn't have a barred door, though, but a heavy one made of iron. I approach the door and hesitate. Should I go inside? I can't stop now; I want to see what's hidden inside this hall, unseen and unknown to our sunny side of the world.

I open the door and am hit by a deafening wall of noise—the same screaming that emanates from the girl in our orphanage along the embankment, an ear-piercing roar. I stare at the jumble of screaming bodies making its way toward me, falling and trying to stand again—young people. Several helpers are doing their best to lay a wide table, but the horde of boys and girls running and falling into each other is uncontrollable. The women have to keep stopping to help them or put them in their place. I notice that many girls and boys are unable to walk because they're half lame and their crutches keep slipping on the tiled floor. Some of them are still shuffling and limping toward me, but I just can't do it. I retreat, walk backward across the hall, and slam the door. In the same moment, the cries fall silent, and I'm back in the peaceful heat among the factory buildings and flower beds. My driver is still asleep under the archway. I look around at the other halls. Surely there can't be more of them. Then I realize I haven't yet found the AIDS sufferers.

I wend my way through the flower beds to hall number four, whose entrance is at the end of a shady courtyard. I pause for a moment and notice a number of men sitting and lying there.

Then it dawns on me: of course, these must be the disabled men. The barred door is open, allowing the men to leave the hall and sit outside in the shade, to see the sky and the flowers in the distance. Here, too, everything is in slow motion. One of the men has spotted me and is clumsily shuffling toward me. I hesitate, wondering what to do. Now the other men in front of the hall have noticed me as well; two of them have heaved themselves off the floor and are also limping in my direction.

The first man has reached me now and stands there barefoot and smiling, dressed simply in pants and a vest. He is big, very big. He tries to talk to me, but I can't understand a word, as his speech is slow and gurgling. In any case, it would be Marathi or Hindi, of which I know neither. At first, I wonder if I should go with him, but as the other two men begin to circle me, fear kicks in. I suddenly wonder whether it's really such a good idea to be wandering around here alone. I don't know these men; they may not be as friendly and harmless as they seem. I decide to leave. I raise my hand and utter a friendly namaskar. The men continue to speak to me, as if trying to persuade me to stay, but I carefully step away. I am glad that they don't try to follow me.

I walk between the flower beds toward the exit and don't turn around until the men are out of sight.

Then I turn my back on these halls, this slow-motion hell, and rush back to the auto-rickshaw. The driver has already seen me coming. Soon, we're clattering out of the courtyard and into the street.

When I reach the orphanage, I can't get to Bina quickly enough. I take her out of her cot and hold her close. I stand with her on the balcony in silence, looking out at the railway tracks. I'm not sure if I'm comforting Bina or vice versa. I bury my face in her hair, enjoying the scent of coconut oil.

Then I notice Nirav standing beside me, his hands clenched around the window bars. The balcony is littered with the broken remains of the car I had given him. Over in the corner, I glimpse Kabir's plastic bear lying ruined in the dust. Nirav rocks rhythmically from one foot to the other with the same confused expression as before; his cheeks are still wet with tears, and spit runs from his mouth. I watch him anxiously as he rocks in his trance and stares out at the trains thundering by. I can't get the home for the disabled in Santa Cruz out of my mind. As I look at Nirav, I'm racked with guilt as I think, *Andreas and I have made it so easy for ourselves with Bina. She only has a little squint, and it's already getting better, becoming less noticeable. Otherwise, Bina is healthy and slowly starting to blossom. We really have made it easy for ourselves.*

Chapter 25

THE WASHERWOMEN ON THE ROOF

It's nine o'clock in the morning, and I'd like nothing better than to stay in bed. I've been lying here for half an hour now, listening to the calls of the merchants and tea sellers down on the street, the loudspeaker announcements from the station, and the wail of the trains. The sun is already shining into my room, and it's getting hot. But I just can't face getting out of bed.

I barely slept a wink last night. My heart was racing, and I had stomachache and diarrhea. I lay shivering in bed, listening to the barking dogs and coughing men outside.

A heavy exhaustion has been creeping over me for days now, numbing my muscles and bones. I awoke to a throbbing headache. Even though I've been taking antibiotics for two weeks, my diarrhea shows no signs of letting up. I've lost more weight; I can almost count my ribs if I breathe in. I'm so emaciated that when I lie on my side in bed, my thighs don't even touch anymore.

I force myself to stand. My knees shake. Still, I manage to get dressed and drag myself to the orphanage. I know something's not right with me. I should really go to the doctor, but I don't know any doctors here.

I sit on the orphanage floor between the cots with my back against a wall and roll a ball for Bina to crawl after. The other children are still in their cots, but one of the cots is empty. Until recently it had been the bed of a particularly sick little girl, who did nothing but spit and had constant diarrhea. Yesterday, she lay there white as a sheet, listless and motionless. Now she is gone.

"We're worried she has typhoid, so we sent her to hospital," Sister Martha tells me when she arrives a little later. She seems tense and concerned. A case of typhoid is always worrying—the child's life is at risk, as are the lives of the other children.

"By the way, the social worker is coming this afternoon. Hopefully, we won't have any problems with Bina," she adds. I've been waiting a long time for this visit. The social worker needs to see Bina and prepare one last report on her for our adoption hearing at the high court in Mumbai.

"Why would there be problems?" I ask with surprise.

"Well, Bina is squinting less now, but her squint is one of the reasons she was put up for international adoption. If her squint has improved, it's one fewer reason why she should be adopted by you."

Words fail me. First, Bina had squinted too much to be adopted by Indians, so she was offered to us. Now she isn't squinting enough.

"But we've already told the social worker that you've been here for a month looking after the little one, and we're praying for you. Don't worry," Sister Martha reassures me.

But I am worried. I've already noticed that Bina's squint has improved enormously since I first met her. All the same, almost five months have passed since then; time enough for a childhood squint to correct itself to some extent. It had never occurred to me that this progress could become Bina's undoing—first too sick, then not sick enough.

Once Sister Martha has excused herself to visit the typhoid patient, I sit back down between the cots and play with Bina. I hold her little head, kiss her two huge, gentle eyes and her long eyelashes, and suddenly find myself wishing that, for this afternoon at least, she will squint really badly. Bina doesn't understand, of course, and just shoves the mushy remains of a banana into my mouth.

Over in the diaper changing room, I see Manika running after the helper Camilla. Camilla has spent a lot of time playing with grouchy Manika over the past two weeks. I think the helper has realized that Manika's aggressiveness will only improve with a lot of attention. I tried a few times last week in the lunch break, but it had been a stupid idea. As soon as Bina was asleep, I played with Manika, who would otherwise try to annoy me with her poking, hair pulling, and angry glares. She was stunned by my sudden attentions and immediately tried to monopolize me for herself. As soon as I went back to my daughter again, Manika would attack her furiously. Of course, how was she supposed to understand that her turn was over? Playing with both children was out of the question, as Manika would bully Bina with her aggressive ways, and Bina was clearly terrified that I would leave her again.

That's the tricky thing with orphanage children: they crave tenderness and human attention, but if you care for them and then turn away, it confuses them all the more.

I watch Bina playing, and Camilla going about her routine of changing the little beds. We can't communicate with each other, as the helper can't speak a word of English; she only speaks the regional languages, Marathi and Gujarati. I'm in awe of the young women who work tirelessly day and night, changing diapers and bed linens, feeding porridge, dispensing juice and medicine, mopping the puddles of urine off the floor, and washing and changing the children when they get dirty or sick or have one of their regular bouts of diarrhea. In spite of all the screaming, of Manika's and Nirav's tantrums, and of the children's various illnesses, little ways, and meltdowns, I've never seen one of the women give a child so much as a smack on the bottom in all the weeks I've been here. They never shout at the children; their worst punishment is putting a child back in bed so he or she can't get out. Having said that, here in the orphanage I haven't yet seen the terrible consequences that follow when a child views the bed as a punishment and a prison.

Unexpected visitors enter the room. Today, it's two Indian ladies and their teenage daughters; the mothers are dressed in silk saris, while the daughters wear freshly starched salwar kameez. Camilla sends the ladies straight back out into the hallway, as they haven't taken off their shoes. In the interest of hygiene, we all go barefoot here in the orphanage, and that goes for visitors, too. The ladies slip off their shoes and hand Camilla a plastic bag of candies, chocolate, and lollipops. They keep some of the first two to hand out there and then to the "sweet children," who they pass and comment on as they move from cot to cot, chatting away.

We get a lot of visitors here in the orphanage—usually classes of schoolchildren or well-off Indian men who are interested in making a donation. Sometimes, though, it's Indian women like these ladies, who want to show their spoiled daughters that there's more to Mumbai than Bollywood. Besides, a visit could lead to an educational discussion on where babies come from and what can happen to a girl if she's not careful.

Since I arrived, these visits have begun to irritate me more and more. As one of the ladies grills me on why I couldn't have adopted a boy instead, the daughters go from cot to cot, stroking the children's cheeks and hair. Then they try to pick the babies up and play with them a little. When the little ones react in terror, the girls dump them back in their cots, offended. It reminds me of a zoo. When one of the mothers gets hold of Bina and goes to pick her up, my patience finally snaps. Perhaps I'm oversensitive today, because I really do feel jealous. I feel it's my duty to protect Bina from the women's attentions, so I carry her off to Nirav and the older children. When the ladies leave the little ones some time later, the children scream after them for chocolate. Camilla doesn't bat an eyelid—but then, she never does.

The screaming and the big ones' boredom are really starting to get to me. The toys I brought lie broken in the trash can or under the beds in pieces. Outside on the tin roof, I can see the damaged red plastic bear and a few pieces of the toy car. Perhaps Nirav pushed them through the bars of the balcony in a fit of rage.

I can't sit here much longer with Bina. We can't play or sing in peace. The noise is deafening, the children are being too aggressive with each other, and I can hear the ear-piercing cries of the little girl from the bedroom next door. She must have crawled under one of the beds again.

It's too rough for Bina here with the big ones. Every few minutes, someone runs into her or knocks her over. Toys are ripped from our hands. It's so noisy that Bina can't concentrate, and she runs around in confusion. I've also noticed recently that she is picking up on the older children's aggressive behavior and has begun to lash out at other children when a game doesn't go her way.

So I pack up my bag, which I bring every day with toys for Bina—eight stacking plastic cups, a few Lego

Duplo bricks, a fabric cube, and an empty lipstick—and I carry this and my little girl up the steep wooden steps to the flat roof of the orphanage. Exhausted, I sink down with her in the shade of a corrugated iron shelter. It's baking hot on the roof, but in the few feet of shade, it's just about bearable. The view, on the other hand, is very refreshing. Looking toward the street, one can see treetops swaying gently in the coastal breeze; the other side looks out over the railway tracks to the surrounding buildings.

We're not alone up here. Two washerwomen stand on the street side of the roof, bent over in the heat, laying out freshly washed sheets and diapers on the hot concrete floor. I have no idea how they manage to stand on the scorching-hot floor; my feet would burn straightaway.

I enjoy the peace, although I'm finding it harder to stay upright; I long for quiet and a cool bed. Bina sits beside me in the shade, plunging her little hands into the bag, curiously packing and unpacking the toys, and contentedly babbling away. She sighs with concentration, totally absorbed in her world of play. Everyone's happy—Bina with her game, I with the peace and quiet, and the ants with the cookie crumbs that my little girl drops on the floor.

Bina has her back to me, and not for the first time, I notice that she's been playing for half an hour without looking at me—not once. If she wants me to help her—for example, to put the old lipstick back together—she holds it out to me but stares at the floor, not at my face.

I've also noticed how she sometimes stands up and toddles off toward the stairs without looking back for me; at that moment, I don't exist in her world. She sometimes seems so hard of hearing when I call her name that last week I asked Sister Martha in all seriousness if her hearing was OK. Sister Martha had simply laughed and reassured me that it was.

All the same, I am a little worried. After a month of visiting Bina every day and spending mornings and evenings with her, I feel I've gotten to know her well. She has grown used to me and is attached to me—but only to a certain extent. I have the feeling that she's not completely letting me in, as if she's not quite sure of things yet. She's only protecting herself, of course. The more she opens up to me, the greater the danger that she wouldn't be able to cope with the loss if I were suddenly to leave. On a subconscious level, she's protecting herself from this potential disappointment. On days like these, I can clearly see that there's a long way to go before we've grown together. I have to appreciate that these few weeks are not going to make up for the entire first year she has lost—particularly the vital, formative first year of her life.

By now, the washerwomen have finished laying out the sheets and have come walking across the baking hot roof toward us. Perspiration streams down their faces, which are tanned almost black by the sun, and their saris are soaked with sweat. The women give us a friendly nod and then go under the metal shelter. They peel their saris from their bodies, enjoy the breeze, and then take fresh saris from plastic bags.

When one of the women notices me secretly watching, she shows me how she wraps her red sari, a piece of cloth almost twenty feet long. She expertly drapes it three times around herself, and it flows so lightly and airily around the body that it's barely noticeable in this heat. After wiping the sweat from her brow, she bends down to Bina and says, "You lucky girl." At first, I think it's the typical hymn of praise, that fate has been kind to Bina, but then she slowly continues in her broken English.

"No mommy, no daddy, no brother, no sister, no auntie—but now you have mommy and daddy," she says and hesitates. Then she taps herself with her finger and says, "No mommy, no daddy, no brother, no sister, no auntie—and never mommy or daddy." Suddenly, the scales fall from my eyes: the washerwomen were children who had lived here in the orphanage and were never adopted. And what chance would they have had? Back then, hardly anyone would have wanted a "dark baby" from an orphanage, especially not a girl, healthy or otherwise. In those days, international adoptions were almost unheard of.

I now understand that some of the staff here were once orphanage children themselves—maybe even the big porter at the entrance and the hunchbacked woman who works downstairs with the infants. And I remember what Sister Martha had hinted to me about Aisha with her heart condition; the nuns were worried that they wouldn't find adoptive parents for her and she would have to stay here with them as a helper.

The washerwoman explains to me in her broken English that both she and her colleague were now married; she herself had four children, and the other washerwoman had one. I'm amazed: in spite, or perhaps because of, their children, they come here every day and work so hard in the blistering heat.

Together, we climb the steps down from the roof. The midday heat is now too hot to bear. My vision is starting to blur. As I carry Bina down the stairs, I feel almost dizzy. When we reach the cot room, I sink straight down on the floor. Camilla hands me Bina's lunchtime bottle of rice water. I'm thankful that Bina drinks it quietly on my lap so we can look into each other's eyes. I have an overwhelming urge to lie down beside her on the stone floor.

"You're not well," Sister Martha says as she appears in front of me. She's back from the hospital; the little girl didn't have typhoid after all, thank goodness. "It's too hot and tiring here; you're not used to it. It's too much for you."

But I won't hear of it and explain to her that it's not the heat but the diarrhea and I that really I need to see a doctor. So she nags me to visit a doctor near the embankment. Despite Bina's heart-wrenching cries when I put her back in her cot, I go. I sense I won't be able to hold out much longer if I don't.

Even the few feet to the doctor's house are torture for me in this midday heat; I drag every step and have to keep stopping. I feel as though poison is spreading through my body. Eventually, I reach the house—well, really it's more of a shack. A short while later, I find myself sitting in the doctor's consultation room. It's a tiny space, just big enough for a chair, a couch, and a small table. Medical posters cover the walls. Once I've told the doctor my story about the amoebas and all the different antibiotics, she nods sagely. After tapping my back and listening to my chest, she gives me a stern look. She is extremely clinical and professional in spite of the primitive surroundings. Her opinion is that I have poisoned myself by taking so many antibiotics. I should never have taken so many. Then she writes something on a slip of paper and tells me to collect the tablets from her colleague; I'd soon feel better again.

I'm a little skeptical, but still head over to the young man sitting in the wooden hut where the tablets are kept. I slide the slip of paper the doctor had given me toward him and pay the few rupees for my consultation. When he returns some time later, I can hardly believe my eyes. He shakes a whole bunch of green, blue, pink, and yellow tablets out onto the table; they look like brightly colored jelly beans. He counts them carefully, sorts the tablets by color into little paper bags, and explains to me how many green, blue, pink, and yellow tablets to take each morning and evening. If I'd been at home, I would never have taken this mixture of tablets, but I feel so ill that I don't have a choice.

It takes me forever to return to my hotel. All at once, the heat and the grimy street are too much for me, and I ask myself how anyone can possibly spend a lifetime living here and manage to work as well. I sink down on the bed in my hotel room and use my last ounce of strength to swallow one green and two pink tablets with a mouthful of water. Then I fall into a deep sleep.

I'm out for the count for the rest of the afternoon, so I don't yet know that the social worker has decided Bina's squint is bad enough for us adopt her. Apparently, she was very moved to learn that I came to the orphanage every day; Sister Lena told me the social worker had said she wished more adoptive parents would do this.

In the coming days, I swallow my pink, green, yellow, and blue tablets as written on the slip of paper, and I am surprised to find that I soon feel well again. The diarrhea is almost gone. I feel noticeably better—something the doctors at home hadn't achieved in five months of treatment.

Chapter 26

WHAT A CHRISTMAS SEASON

Christmas has arrived, and Andreas tells me that there's snow back in Germany. We talk on the phone every day, and he's just as impatient as I am for the court date at the Mumbai High Court. If things go well, he's going to fly straight out here, as we'll be able to take Bina out of the orphanage. We'll need to spend a few weeks in a hotel with her while we wait to receive her passport and visa so that we can take her back to Germany, but Andreas will get time off from work for this.

I still can't quite get my head around the fact that in a matter of days, we'll be a family of three; I never thought we'd make it this far. I'm already tense and don't yet dare to picture us leaving the orphanage with Bina in our arms. All the same, I've been to the bazaar and stocked up on the banana-and-apple–flavored porridge they feed the children here in the orphanage. I've also bought the same powdered milk, the same coconut oil, and the white powder used prevent heat rash, as well as some disposable diapers—I'm afraid Bina will just have to get used to those.

So far, Mumbai doesn't feel very Christmassy, although the sisters have put up a crib among the palm trees. I've never been in the tropics at this time of year before, and it seems strange to think of Christmas in this heat. But there's a big celebration this afternoon: the American Consulate has organized an early Christmas party for the children.

I cross the yard to the side door of the orphanage, as I do every morning. I kick off my shoes and slowly climb the stairs to the second floor. I always get butterflies in my tummy as I climb these steps because I can't wait to see Bina.

Today, she bounces for joy in her cot when she sees me. I bend down and put my arms around her. I feel so moved by her enthusiasm; it gives me so much joy and courage.

She's already opened up to me. Things are so different from the early days when I'd just arrived. I lift her out of her cot. Soon, we're playing hide-and-seek with the older children. This time, Bina comes up with the idea for us to fall into each other's arms in amazement every time we find each other; the game is a great way for us to practice eye contact and physical closeness.

Bina runs playfully along the hallways, ducking behind doors and cots. Then she suddenly runs toward me, beaming, and throws herself into my arms. She makes me so happy. Just a few days until the court date! Then no one can argue with our adopting Bina, at least according to Indian law, and the adoption will soon be confirmed by a German court, too. Because India hadn't signed the Hague Convention on Intercountry Adoption, the appointment of parents as legal guardians by an Indian court is not automatically recognized in Germany, and the adoption hearing will need to be repeated in a German court. Nevertheless, the Indian court's approval would give us a high level of legal protection.

Our game sends me running after Bina into the older children's bedroom. At this time, I would have expected the room to be empty and for all the children to be playing in the big dining room. But I hadn't noticed that Aisha was missing; she stands here looking at a boy I've never seen before. Bina also pauses and watches the boy sitting on the floor awkwardly, fiddling with walking aids. He must be around seven years old. He gives me a hasty glance before turning back to his crutches. I notice he has a bad squint, but worse than this, he is paralyzed from the hips down. It looks like the effects of polio.

Clumsily, he tries to force his limp left leg into a metal splint, but it's not easy for him on the slippery tiles. The frame keeps slipping away from him. I bend down, grab the splint, and try to support him, but he pulls the splint from my hand and pushes me away. I stand back. "Just like Nirav," I think: *he doesn't trust anyone anymore. He has to do everything himself.*

With much determination, he finally manages to get his leg into the splint and pulls the leather strap incredibly tight, as if he has done it so many times before. He then repeats the process with his right leg. It takes him a long time, and it would be so easy for me to help him. "How damaged must a child be to reject adults this vehemently?" I wonder.

At some point, the boy will have to stand up, but he can't do this unaided on this slippery floor. He gives me a short, wary look, but along comes Aisha, the good fairy with the sad eyes. She goes over to him gently. He looks as if he had been waiting for her. With her weak body, crooked back, and spindly legs, she's just able to support him in such a way that he can pull himself up between her and a cot. He takes his crutches from her and then, with his splints and crutches, hobbles slowly into the corridor. Aisha, the girl with the heart condition, supports him, and together, they limp and shuffle off down the corridor.

"How could anyone neglect and abuse a child so badly that he feels this utterly betrayed by adults?" I ponder, sadly. I stand, lost in thought, at the end of the corridor, watching their silhouettes as they hobble away, arm in arm.

Yet, compared to Aisha, the boy is lucky: he's on his way to Switzerland, Sister Martha tells me later. He came from the orphanage in Kolkata and is just passing through. Tomorrow morning, one of the nuns will fly with him to Switzerland and his new adoptive parents.

I follow Bina, Aisha, and the boy back into the big ones' dining room. An incredible commotion greets us, as Sister Martha has just handed out a whole box of confectionary. Anita dances around excitedly with her red lollipop, while the other children's faces are smeared with sticky red goo and caramel syrup. Sister Martha beams with joy at the children's excitement and pushes a lollipop into Bina's hands. I pretend to be just as thrilled with the sugary, sticky, Christmas excitement as Sister Martha is; I know that someone has been kind enough to donate the candies, and Sister Martha only wants to make the children happy, to bring a smile to their faces and help them forget their sad lives for a moment. But I also know that half the older children's teeth are so rotten and black that their adoptive parents' will have to take them straight to the dentist or orthodontist. Of course, many of the children would have already had bad teeth when they arrived at the orphanage, but the daily handouts of candies don't help. And particularly now, at Christmastime, every visitor to the orphanage seems to think that the children have never seen cookies, lollipops, or candies before. No one thinks to give books or tapes of songs, even though the orphanage has an old cassette recorder. Instead, it's always confectionary.

Of course, the children love Sister Martha for giving them candies. I often think she needs this love just as much as they need her affection and cuddles. She needs to be needed—it's her purpose in life. The young caregivers never give out confectionary and don't show any affection. There seems to be a clear division of duties: the staff is responsible for feeding, washing, and changing the beds, while the nuns are there for the special moments of love and tenderness. This ensures the children are more attached to the nuns, even though they spend far less time with them than the caregivers. Perhaps it made sense; Sister Martha had once told me that the younger children couldn't always tell them apart but reacted to the white cotton sari. Because all nuns wear the same sari, the children fling their arms around every nun they see. I've already seen this with Bina.

Just before Sister Martha heads downstairs to help with the preparations for the Christmas party, we all play Ring a Ring o' Roses. I like to get out my video camera on occasions like this. I already have almost an hour of film of the children being fed and changed, playing and swinging in the yard, and being kissed and cuddled by the sisters. This time, even Sister Martha patiently plays along; she knows this video will be important for Bina later on.

Once Sister Martha has left, I take my camera back into the cot room, where I leave my bag during the day. There, I see the little ones, still in their beds, clutching pearl necklaces. Someone must have donated the necklaces. Sister Martha had hung them around the children's necks, but they must have pulled them off again. Manika and two other children are now stuffing the pearls into their mouths. Didi and Sivana are downstairs fetching the porridge and aren't there to intervene. I rush to take the necklaces away from them. As I'm fishing the pearls from the screaming mouth of a scratching Manika, I curse Sister Martha. She showers the children with candies and glittering pearls, buys their love, and then leaves the little ones with mouths full of pearls and rotten teeth. I know I'm probably being unfair, but really I'm still very insecure. I worry that I won't succeed in winning Bina's love. The gifts other mothers receive automatically when their children are born—their attachment and trust—are things I'm having to fight hard for. So I can't help but feel jealous when Sister Martha wins Bina's heart with candies and cheap tat.

On the other hand, I know how hard it must be for the sisters to stand by and watch as Bina slowly turns away from them, despite their offerings. Two days ago, Sister Alissa had Bina on her lap as we sat chatting in the yard, when suddenly, Bina slid off the knees of the sister she had always been so fond of and came toddling over to me. As she snuggled up to me, Sister Alissa and I exchanged astonished glances because a few weeks ago, this would have been unthinkable. I noticed how Sister Alissa kept calling sadly after Bina, and while Bina did go to her, she immediately ran back to me again. Sister Alissa is no longer everything to Bina.

It must be difficult for the nuns to care for these little children—to spend over a year protecting them from sickness, tears, and despair—only for them to leave. Most of the time, they don't even know where their charges have ended up or whether they're well looked after, loved, and happy. They never see the children again, apart from perhaps a few photos at Christmas.

Once lunch is over, the orphanage turns into a madhouse. "Jingle Bells" is already blaring over the loudspeakers in the yard, and the stairwell echoes with loud voices. The corridor and the dining room are packed with people I've never seen before, Americans from the consulate and Indian guests. I have to squeeze my way through the party to reach the dining room, where someone is standing at a microphone spreading cheer to the Christmas party, telling stories of Santa Claus, and giving out balloons while "We Wish You a Merry Christmas" drones from his stereo. The noise is deafening. The room is packed with so many guests that the nuns can barely be seen.

Then I spot Sister Martha standing among the madness with the children, surrounded by guests. Everyone's clearly expecting the children to celebrate Christmas with their eyes aglow. A little plastic Christmas tree sits on the table, garlands hang from the wall, and balloons bob across the room. The American with the microphone tries to encourage the children to sing along, but Aisha and Nirav just stare at him, speechless. The man doesn't seem to understand that the children can't speak a word of English and have no idea what all this is for.

The little ones are absolutely terrified—they've never celebrated Christmas. They don't know who the old man with the white beard and the red coat is. They don't know what to make of this strange brown horse with funny sticks on its head and are wondering what all these people are doing here. The American and Sister Martha struggle to keep the children in the middle of the room; most of them are too frightened and try to hide against the wall behind the guests or cling to the sisters.

The older children, however, have realized that there are more treats to be had and are grabbing as much candies, cookies, and chocolates as their hands will carry. They manage to collect so much that they even share it with the little ones, who have gone completely nuts by now and are just cramming themselves full of sweet food. Nirav fills the pockets of his thin pants and disappears into the bedroom with his spoils. Anita has vanished, too. The little ones are so hysterical and fractious that Sister Martha has to take some of them into the cot room.

Amid the pandemonium, I finally find Bina running around like a headless chicken among the other children, her mouth covered in chocolate. I pull her out of the crowds of guests and try to calm her in my arms. The droning music and the chattering guests are so loud that I can't take it anymore, so Bina and I sneak off to the roof.

On the way, I grab one of the little baby baths that are used for dirty laundry, quickly fill it with a little cool water, and carry it upstairs. Bina beams and trots straight over to the tub; this is one of our favorite things to do at the moment. I undress her and place her in the cool water, which she really enjoys, because it's thirty-four degrees Celsius in the shade. She splashes merrily with her hands in the water and squeals with joy as it sprays in her face. I think she's going to be a real water baby. I crouch in the shade, enjoying her fun. And so we celebrate our "Merry Christmas," as the song drones from down below, in a cool baby bath on the roof between the palms and the railway tracks.

The court date is just a few days away, and then Andreas will arrive. I'm so excited to see how Bina reacts to him. Hopefully, she'll take to him and accept her new daddy!

The weeks I've spent here have been wonderful. Admittedly, they were often hard, exhausting, and dreadfully sad, but it was the most relaxing and valuable time of my life.

Chapter 27

CASE NO. 236

Another hour to go. I'm so worked up that I set out far too early. Today is the day of the court date for our adoption—or more accurately speaking, our guardianship—of Bina at the Mumbai High Court. There, a judge will decide our fates: Bina's, Andreas's, and my own. I hope and pray that he will grant us custody, but it wouldn't be completely out of the question for him to decide against us and for Bina and I to have gotten to know each other for nothing. Because of this uncertainty, Andreas has decided not to come to India yet. He won't fly out until he hears that everything has gone to plan; he'll be sitting at home with his bags packed, waiting for my call.

At eleven o'clock, I've arranged to meet my lawyer, Mr. Pandey, at his offices in Colaba so that we can make our way to the court together. It's only ten now. The porter of the building where Mr. Pandey has his office won't let me in because the lawyer hasn't arrived yet. But the old man does push a chair out into the shady porch, so that I can rest after my journey.

I took the train to Churchgate, an enormous station in the center of Mumbai a short walk from Mr. Pandey's office. The office is in an ugly, weather-beaten building in a shady alley lined with mighty tropical trees. It's a bustling scene: business people and traders hurry across the street. The area is home to countless legal chambers, businesses, and sales agencies, and the consulates aren't far away. The beating heart of the district is Churchgate, one of Mumbai's two huge stations. Every day, millions of commuters pour into the city, and many of them work nearby in the grand old Victorian buildings that hark back to British colonial times.

I pull my chair a little further into the shade and take out my favorite Indian novel, *Sister of My Heart* by Chitra Banerjee Divakaruni. Could it be a coincidence that today I've come to the chapter where the young woman learns that the child she's carrying is a girl and her mother-in-law insists that she have an abortion because it's not the son everyone had hoped for? In the story, the young woman dreams of running away, but even her own parents tell her she must stay with her husband's family and have the abortion because this is her duty as a loyal wife. But the girl loves her unborn daughter and tries to find a way to save her.

Stories like this make me think of Bina and her mother, Ragini. Who knows how desperate Ragini's situation was? She was unmarried, had got involved with the "wrong" man, and had suddenly fallen pregnant, with a girl at that. What kind of pressure had she been under? And yet she hadn't aborted Bina; she had brought her into the world. She had saved her child's life and perhaps even managed to give her a promising future. Maybe that was the best she could do in her situation. We will never know what things were like for Ragini, so we mustn't be too quick to judge her decision.

The porter signals that I can now go up to Mr. Pandey's office. As I follow the old man into the dark corridor, I'm amazed that a lawyer could have his chambers in this building with peeling plaster walls and a rickety old metal elevator. But the floors of the building seem packed with the offices of many different companies.

Perhaps they can't afford anything better. Property prices in central Mumbai are sky high. Mr. Pandey probably isn't making much from our case: we're paying him twenty-three hundred rupees for handling the adoption and applying for the passport, while the court fees are sixty-five hundred rupees.

This is a ridiculously small sum compared to what we had paid back at home for the lawyer alone. In total, the adoption has set us back twelve thousand rupees on the Indian side—not even three hundred dollars—while at home the figure is more than ten times that.

As we reach the third floor, the porter stops the rickety elevator with a bump, pushes the metal door aside, and leads me to Mr. Pandey's office, which consists of two tiny rooms. The lobby, where the lawyer's young colleague greets me politely and offers me a cup of spiced tea, is only just big enough to squeeze in a filing cabinet, a fax machine, a narrow table, and a chair, so I'm invited to take a seat in Mr. Pandey's room. The chambers are so small that my chair is right up against his desk, but the room is clean and bright, thanks to the sunlight that filters in through the frosted yellow window. A photo hangs above the desk; it must be Mr. Pandey and his father, both dressed in lawyer's gowns. Someone has hung a garland of flowers around the photo as a mark of respect. Tiny statues of Krishna and Ganesh sit on a little side table, where Mr. Pandey's colleague has already lit some incense. Soon, the scent of sandalwood mingles with the steam of my tea.

I peer curiously at a tall stack of files; every folder has a rubber band around it. These must be the files for today's case. At that very moment the door opens, and Mr. Pandey enters. He is a tall, powerfully built man with thick curly hair. He greets me politely, but the look of serious concentration on his face tells me he's in no mood for chatting. He sits straight down at his desk and looks through the files. Because I'm sitting right in front of him, I can easily make out the number of our case: 236.

At last, he lets out a sigh and looks at me. "We have fourteen cases today, some of them from other orphanages. There won't be any problems. Judge Singh is responsible for adoptions at the moment. He's good. We're in luck. A few months ago we had a different judge. He was nothing but trouble—adjourned every case."

He runs through the process with me. I then gather my courage. I ask him whether it's true that Ragini gave Bina to the orphanage, whether her name really is Ragini, and whether she signed the confirmation to give up her child.

"But of course." He looks at me in astonishment. "The case would have no chance otherwise. Every woman has to sign a standard letter in which she confirms that she gives up her child and that she understands that after three months she will lose all legal rights as a mother."

Mr. Pandey confirms the few biographical details I have for Ragini and Bina, but when I press him further, his answers become monosyllabic. So I decide not to ask any more questions.

He's quite right of course; he isn't allowed to tell me anything about Bina's mother. All the same, it's so hard not to ask. It would be so easy for him to flip open the file in front of him and give me her name and address. Then, in theory, I could visit her and ask her if the story was true—whether she had really given Bina away and wanted her to be adopted by other parents. But it's impossible. According to Indian law, the mother's identity must be kept secret.

That's the hardest thing for me about the adoption. I have to trust the sisters, the lawyer, and the court when they say that Ragini signed this letter. I will never see it for myself; that's just the way Indian law is. Even the German court, which will need to confirm the adoption under European law, won't get to see this letter. It will stay in the Indian courthouse, under lock and key.

Sister Lena will later give me a letter to present to the German court, which states, "We are unable to provide the current address and formal consent of the biological parents, as in most cases such children are born to unmarried mothers. In India, women who have children out of wedlock face great stigma. For this reason, this document is strictly top secret and will only be presented to the relevant court in deciding the case. The court will consider this document and the parents' circumstances in making its decision and will then retain the document for safekeeping."

I have to trust that they are all doing their jobs properly, and in this case, I am convinced that they are. Mind you, even in Germany, I can think of several shocking cases of adoptions from India from a few years ago in which it turned out that the biological mothers had never given their consent; the papers had obviously been forged. These were older children, who had apparently been placed in the orphanage to be looked after, but not put up for adoption.

Although these are one-off cases from the late 1980s, they still worry me, in particular because since arriving in India, I'd read in the paper about a recent adoption scandal in Hyderabad. Here, too, it emerged that an orphanage had been giving babies away for adoption without the knowledge of their biological parents. This case, however, concerned domestic adoptions, not international.

Sister Lena had brought the case to my attention and grumbled because it had led to special audits by the authorities in New Delhi. She told me she had great respect for these audits, which were also carried out when an orphanage renewed its license. "They leave no stone unturned." She had sighed as she told me about the auditors. They had to close the office for days and couldn't get any work done.

"Do mothers ever come back wanting to know what has become of their children?" I ask Mr. Pandey cautiously.

"No, never," he replies matter-of-factly and looks at me shaking his head. "We never hear from them again. They're glad that everything's over and they can make a fresh start. Come on, we should go." He grabs his robes and the big stack of files and we leave his office.

My heart is pounding in my chest. It's eleven o'clock, and we're making our way to the high court. I trot after Mr. Pandey through central Mumbai in the baking heat. We can barely hear each other over the roar of the multilane traffic. Mr. Pandey bounds across the crosswalk in giant steps; I struggle to keep up with him. Then he leads me toward the correct entrance to the court. If I hadn't already been nervous enough, this mighty Victorian building would have done the trick. The British had certainly shown India who was in charge with this imposing architecture.

We're just a few steps inside the building, and I've already lost my bearings. Mr. Pandey, on the other hand, storms ahead of me down corridors and passageways, across courtyards, leading me through crowds of lawyers, judges, and assistants to a spiral staircase. I struggle to keep up with him on the stairs and find myself staring at yet more corridors and passageways in confusion. The place is dripping with impressive Victorian features: arches, balconies, columns, and gables.

I have a quick peek inside one of the colonial courtrooms, with its massive tables, leather chairs, and wood-paneled walls lined with bookshelves. A pleasantly cool wind wafts through the building.

"The British designed the building like this for a reason," Mr. Pandey explains. "The balconies and alcoves are exactly the right width so that the sun never shines directly into the courtrooms. The building is constructed so that the sea breeze from the coast blows through the rooms when all the windows and doors are open." This construction method was clearly ideal for the Mumbai heat, and it gives the massive, dark building a feeling of space and openness.

Finally, we come to our courtroom. A sign hangs above the door: "Singh." Mr. Pandey greets a woman in the crowd waiting outside the room and introduces her to me as Mrs. Metha, the representative from the Ministry for Social Affairs. She is practically our opponent, in that she argues against adoptions in the interest of the children. Her chances are slim against Judge Singh, however, as he's well known as a supporter of international adoption. With the previous judge, things had been more difficult. He was a traditionalist who was against inter-country adoption, had always upheld Mrs. Metha's objections, and had kept adjourning cases.

"If that happens, there's nothing we can do. Ultimately, the judge's decision is at his own discretion," Mr. Pandey stresses.

The Mumbai High Court operates on a rotating system, with judges switching places every few months. This means that the judge responsible for international adoptions often changes. Parents who are hoping to adopt from India often worry whether they'll get a "sympathetic" judge or a "rejectionist." For example, there are certainly some judges who will refuse an adoption if the adoptive parents haven't provided evidence that they are unable to have any biological children; they won't grant an adoption where there is a "risk" that the adoptive child might end up with biological siblings.

Suddenly, Mr. Pandey signals to me to follow him, and he leads his colleague and an elderly Englishwoman, whom he greets, into the courtroom. The English lady is accompanied by an Indian girl—a teenager—who follows her into the room. Mrs. Metha trots after us, clutching her files.

Judge Singh is already sitting at an oversize desk behind a mountain of files. The doors of the balcony are wide open beside him, and the wind blowing into the room is so strong that it almost blows the documents off the desk. Then again, it could be the draft from the enormous ceiling fans, clattering away at full speed.

Judge Singh peers at us sternly over his glasses. Mr. Pandey, his colleague with the files, and Mrs. Metha have taken their seats directly in front of him. The judge and Mr. Pandey exchange a few words, and then Judge Singh gives the sign that the hearing can begin.

The judge, Mr. Pandey, and Mrs. Metha work through the files and cases at breakneck speed. The ceiling fans rattle so loudly that I can barely make out a word. So, instead, I stare at the file that Mrs. Metha has open diagonally in front of me. The format soon becomes clear: Mr. Pandey briefly presents each case, and then the judge asks Mrs. Metha for her objections. Then a quick nod of the head and a few remarks from Judge Singh tell me whether the case has been approved or not. This is periodically interrupted by the judge nagging his own assistant to bring him the files more quickly. "You're as slow as an oxcart driver," he scolds the timid man.

Our case has yet to come up, but my eyes are fixed on a document that Mrs. Metha has just turned to in the file. It's just a few sentences in English. It is a form filled out in some bits in handwriting, which I cannot read, but it goes like: "I hereby confirm that on…I gave birth to the girl… and I hereby state that…" But at that moment, Mrs. Metha snaps the file closed and moves on to the next case.

Suddenly, it comes to a discussion among the judge, Mr. Pandey, and Mrs. Metha.

"And where is the mother?" the judge asks. The hearing is in English. Now that everyone is speaking with raised voices, I'm able to understand.

"We don't know," Mr. Pandey replies. "She's disappeared. The father insists that she ran away two years ago. He wants to give the child up for adoption, but of course we can't get the mother's signature because she isn't there to give it."

"But the woman must be found! The case is too uncertain," Mrs. Metha contests.

"Have they looked hard enough for her? How long did they search?" the judge presses. They discuss back and forth.

"I'm afraid that's not good enough. The case is adjourned. More effort must be made to find the woman first; they'll have to keep searching," the judge explains.

I breathe a sigh of relief as I hear this, because it's clear that Judge Singh is very particular about having the mother's written consent. It sets my mind at ease to know that even a staunch supporter of adoption like Judge Singh won't let a case through without it.

Another discussion has started.

"May I see the child? She should at least show her face for a moment," says the judge, and he nods to an assistant standing by the door. A shy little girl enters, perhaps eight years old; she stands there obediently in her prim dress and stares up at the judge with huge eyes. She has no idea what's happening.

"My God, the poor thing's terrified. How awful!" the judge exclaims, and with another nod toward the door, the girl disappears again. Later, Mr. Pandey explains to me that a child of her age must appear before the court in person.

My heart leaps into my mouth when I see the file Mrs. Metha opens next—number 236. Our case.

"Have you come here especially for the hearing?" the judge asks, giving me an encouraging look.

I blush and answer, "Yes."

"I know Europe well. My parents lived in England, and I myself lived in Barons Court, where I also studied," he adds, not without a touch of pride. He must have studied at one of London's venerable old law schools.

"So, you write about finance? What's your opinion of the financial situation in India?" he suddenly asks. I stare at him blankly and have no idea what to say. I'd expected to be asked almost anything—whether I found the Indian elephant-headed god funny, for example. I'd already been asked this by social workers at home. However, I'd never dreamed that the Mumbai High Court would want to test me on my financial knowledge of India. Sheepishly, I manage to stammer something, but Judge Singh gives me a grin and calls out, "Good luck, and enjoy your little one!"

It's not until the English lady, who had been sitting beside me, suddenly grabs my hand that it dawns on me—I'm a mother. The lady gives me a hug. An enormous weight is lifted from my shoulders. I'm overwhelmed, and my eyes well with tears. "We did it!" rings through my head. "Finally, we did it!" But there's also a new weight on me, a sense of responsibility. There's no going back now. I'm Bina's mother—forever. We're her parents; from today, she is entirely our responsibility.

As we come to the next case, there's another discussion, but this time I'm unable to follow it because the fans are rattling loudly again. Then suddenly, the English lady next to me beams, puts her arms around the Indian girl, and smiles at me. It's obvious that her case has been successful as well.

Later, Mr. Pandey explains to me that until recently, Indian law did not allow a foreign national living in India to adopt an Indian child, meaning that for fifteen years this English lady had been forced to remain the Indian girl's foster mother. After a change in the law, she was now allowed to adopt her.

Suddenly, everyone stands, for the hearing is over. Judge Singh gives me a look that is almost a little patronizing. I signal my thanks from my seat. He responds with the typical Indian headshake, this time a version that means "You're welcome; my pleasure." He clearly revels in the power he has and the pivotal role he plays in deciding the fates of others.

As we leave the courtroom, Mr. Pandey, the Englishwoman, and even Mrs. Metha from the Ministry of Family Affairs all congratulate me. Then Mr. Pandey asks one of the court assistants when he can expect the certificates; he will need ours to apply for Bina's passport and visa.

Mr. Pandey explains that the certificate will take around ten days to prepare. Later, when I receive it, I'll be astonished. It's stamped with a grand red seal. The text requests payment of twenty-five hundred rupees in court fees and social worker expenses and outlines the obligations that we now have toward the child and the law. It states that the applicant "is to care for and raise her, as if she were the applicant's own child." Furthermore, we are to "treat her equally in respect of maintenance, upbringing, and succession." It also states that we must adopt Bina within two years according to German law and that we are to provide the Indian authorities with social reports on her development for five years.

The entire text is one long sentence in convoluted legalese spanning three typewritten pages.

The third page contains a clause stating, "and herewith I further agree that the applicant…is now the legal guardian…of the herein named minor" and "is authorized to take the herein named minor from this esteemed court…and to transport the minor to the applicant's foreign country of residence at will, wherever or whenever this may be…."

After I've said good-bye to Mr. Pandey and left the court building, I feel like I'm walking on air. As I glide through the crowded streets, I feel like hugging everyone I see. I'm so proud and emotional. I look around me at the traffic on the grand, wide streets of old colonial Mumbai, at the great grass lawns, at the young men playing cricket, and at the traders at the crossing, hawking old books on one side and cheap men's shirts and kitschy plastic toys on the other, and I think about how much I love India. This country has given us a child, and I'm grateful for this show of trust.

Despite the noise of the traffic, I call Andreas on my cell.

"You're a father!" I scream down the phone, and I tell him about the hearing. I can tell it's a load off his mind, too. It's such a relief for both of us. What a fight it has been! Now that our case has been legally settled and nothing else can go wrong, in a few hours he will drive to the airport and arrive in

Mumbai this very night. Tomorrow, we'll be a family at last.

On the train back to the north of Mumbai, I stare out of the window, misty eyed, and enjoy the view: the cricket club by the embankment, the long bay along Marine Drive, the shabby blocks of apartments, the brackish sewage drains, the landfills, the building sites, and the slums. Then finally, I reach my station, the one I can see from the orphanage. I can hardly wait to get there and take *our* daughter in my arms.

Bina is thrilled to see me and pulls me along behind her by my finger. Slowly, we make our way to the yard and pay a visit to the nuns, who congratulate us right away. Mr. Pandey has already called to tell them that all the orphanage's cases had gone through.

I've decided to keep Bina in the orphanage for two more days so that she can get used to Andreas and so that he has time to settle in and get to know her properly. After that, I've made a reservation at a hotel in the north of Mumbai by the beach, because we will have a few weeks' wait until Bina's passport and visa are ready for us to take her out of the country.

As I walk along the bustling market street late that afternoon, I stop in my tracks, fascinated. Other passersby stop, too, look up in surprise, and smile. A work elephant is making his way down the street, in the middle of the busy traffic, his head swaying. He is so enormous that his head towers above the cars, the auto-rickshaws, and the people hurrying by. The elephant plods slowly past the little shops and stalls, stretching out his trunk to everyone he meets. He's collecting money on his way home from work and deftly passes the coins that passersby throw into his trunk to a wiry young man sitting up on his neck. I've often seen elephants here. Recently, two of these imposing animals were here at once.

I take the fact that the elephant was here today as a sign and decide that the elephant god Ganesh will be Bina's personal Indian god. *We plan to raise her with Christian values, but a little Indian mysticism can't hurt*, I think. So in the bazaar, in addition to new bangles for Bina and more powdered milk and porridge, I also buy a holy portrait of Ganesh.

Back in the hotel, I go straight to bed. I'll be up in the middle of the night to drive to the airport and pick up Andreas. Now we really have a reason to celebrate!

Chapter 28

GOOD-BYE TO THE ORPHANAGE

What a merry, joyful Christmas Eve! Andreas has arrived, and we sit happily on the bed in the hotel. The room is hot and stuffy. The mosquitoes seem to have increased in numbers recently. The sound of the trains drones through the hotel as ever. But in spite of all this, it's one of the most wonderful Christmases I can remember.

"Cheers—to Bina and our happy family!" cries Andreas festively. We raise the glasses we've had brought up from the kitchen. We toast with the champagne Andreas had brought from home especially for the occasion. We chat and open the Christmas mail Andreas has brought while we tuck into a ham—another Christmas surprise from Andreas. It's the first time I've had meat and alcohol in weeks.

"I did think about bringing a plastic Christmas tree. You can even get folding ones these days, but I wasn't sure if you'd approve," he says jokingly. How adorable. He's right. I wouldn't have approved. I've had enough of plastic Christmas trees and caramels.

After the long weeks alone in Mumbai, I really enjoy Andreas's company. As we chat and I go through the Christmas cards and letters from friends and family, I realize how much I've lost touch with home. And there's so much I can't put into words. I talk about Bina, full of excited anticipation, but how am I supposed to tell Andreas about the children's despair and the terrible things I've seen in the institutions I've visited, particularly on Christmas Eve, when we've been apart for so long and should be celebrating and enjoying ourselves? Years later, it will occur to me that I never talk about these horrors. At home, people aren't prepared for this level of misery; life is so different that there's no frame of reference to discuss the pain and suffering I've witnessed in India. So I just keep it to myself. Many years later, at parties and celebrations, Andreas will ask me why I'm not getting into the spirit and having fun. He will ask whether parties aren't my thing anymore. Even I myself won't understand why I'm so withdrawn.

The next day, we visit the orphanage. The whole day is one long celebration. The nuns give Andreas a warm welcome and seem relieved to finally have the chance to get to know Bina's father a little better.

Sister Lena brags about her heavy workload. Sister Martha shows off how much the children need her. The sisters are so proud, and I'm happy, because now that Andreas is here, I can sense that our time in the orphanage is nearing its end. This helps me to enjoy the last few days all the more.

I take Andreas up to the cot room where Bina bounces in her little bed and reaches out her hands with purple thumbs—yes, purple thumbs! This morning, Sister Lena dipped her little fingers in blue ink and pressed them onto the application form for her passport.

Bina looks at Andreas in amazement as I lift her out of her cot. But when I place her in his arms, her expression changes to one of alarm. She wants to come straight back to me again. I take Bina into the diaper changing room to change her and return to find that Andreas has attracted a crowd of fascinated older children. I can tell from their gestures that Anita and Nirav are excitedly explaining to the younger children that this is Bina's father. They're happy to see Andreas and laugh and play with him; it's as if they're delighted to see a man for once—as if they're thinking, "So, this is what a Western father looks like." They're beside themselves with excitement and seem to be genuinely happy for Bina, rather than thinking of their own fates.

Yet, I sense Aisha looking at Andreas a little wistfully. I know that she would like nothing more than to go with us. Nirav, too, has a glimmer of hope in his eyes that I've never seen before. He's different with Andreas than with me; he'd dearly love a father. But I bite my tongue. How am I supposed to ask Andreas if we can adopt Nirav as well? And how would we manage it? We'd have to be assessed by the social workers again. The whole bureaucratic process would tumble down on us like an avalanche. Every social worker would warn us how ridiculous it was to take on an older, emotionally disturbed boy with behavioral problems so soon after adopting Bina. They'd say it was a recipe for disaster. And I know they'd be right. I wouldn't be able to make it work. Nirav needs to be cared for in an incredibly sensitive way; he would require professional therapy and an enormous amount of love from his parents. It wouldn't be fair on either child, Bina or Nirav. So I say nothing. Later, I will talk to Andreas about Nirav—but just talk.

Now Bina, Andreas, and I disappear to the roof and the shade of the corrugated iron hut; we need some time alone. Andreas is fascinated by Bina. He is more tender and considerate with her than I'd ever hoped. He respects that she needs lots of time. He hands her a little paper package. Bina huffs and puffs with exertion as she rips the paper and slowly pulls out a rag doll my mother-in-law had given Andreas. Bina is so proud of her prize.

"Her squint really isn't that bad anymore," Andreas suddenly says. "And she's much bigger and more outgoing than before." Being around Bina every day, I hadn't really noticed these gradual changes, but Andreas tells me there's a huge difference.

So we sit outside on the roof and watch as Bina hugs and cuddles the doll, pops it in her mouth, and chews on it. We don't need to say anything; we're happy just being there. It's the first time we've been together as a little family, and it's such an exhilarating new feeling that we need time to get used to it. The joy Bina brings us, the pride that we've finally made it at long last, and the knowledge that we belong together blows over us like a refreshing breeze. It's one of the happiest moments of my life. The day our family began, up on the orphanage roof next to the wailing trains and cawing crows, is one I'll remember forever.

Suddenly Sister Martha calls us downstairs. When we get there, we see that all the children are dressed in their Sunday best. Sivana and Didi have even put the babies in pink, frilly tulle dresses in honor of the occasion. Before we have time to blink, Sister Martha stuffs Bina into a pink, slightly too-small dress as well. The children are sweating; these synthetic clothes are far too hot for the thirty-four-degree heat and 58 percent humidity, but Sister Martha knows no mercy. The priest is waiting downstairs to hold a short Christmas mass for the children and to bless them.

A little later, the sisters carry the babbling, screaming pink bundles downstairs to the big room where the babies sleep. Soon, the room is so packed with sisters, babies, and toddlers that we can barely force our way in. But the sisters make it clear that attendance is mandatory. The priest's sermon is actually very moving.

It's a day of much prayer. When Andreas goes back to the hotel to catch up on a few hours' sleep because of the time difference, Sister Alissa, Sister Martha, and Sister Lena ask me to come to the chapel to pray with and for Bina as she leaves the orphanage. Even after the court date, they had refused to baptize Bina; they said she wasn't definitely our child yet—after all, the German court date was yet to come. However, final prayers and blessings are still a must. So, that afternoon, I find myself standing with Bina in the little chapel next to the orphanage as Sister Alissa shows me to my seat.

Holy statues of the Virgin Mary, candles, flowers, and a sanctuary lamp adorn the altar ahead of me. Jute mats lie on the stone floor in front of the altar, where I'm asked to kneel. The prayers seem to go on for an eternity—for one and a half hours, the nuns and I kneel in front of the altar in the baking heat while mosquitoes buzz around us. I really do pray to God, thank him for Bina, and ask him to protect us, but I only pray for a few minutes before I lose my concentration.

It had been a very different experience when I took Bina to Sunday mass at the church next door to the orphanage. At first, I had only gone there out of boredom. Before the court date, I couldn't take her out of the orphanage without the sisters' express permission because legally she wasn't my child yet. The one place I was allowed to take her was to church. So, I took Bina to mass. On Sundays, the priest's voice and the congregation's singing could be heard in the orphanage. The church was packed. Men filled the pews on one side of the aisle. On the other side sat the women, with their clean saris and neatly oiled, braided hair. They had woven jasmine into their locks especially, put on their jewelry, and dressed their children in fancy Sunday dresses, lacy socks, and shiny patent leather shoes. The priest stood at the front preaching. The sisters sat in the front pews. The fans rattled over it all. Every door was open, so that a tropical wind blew through the building. The rustle of the palms in the light sea breeze and the squawks of the green parrots that circled the church wafted in from outside.

I spent many a Sunday sitting in a pew with Bina, listening to the singing of the congregation. The hymns were so much more joyful and heartfelt than the ones we have at home, and the atmosphere was so much warmer and more intense. I couldn't sing along, not only because I didn't know the hymns, but also because I was so moved, thankful, and surprised to be here—in a church in the middle of Mumbai, with a baby in my arms—our baby, little Bina, chewing on the corner of a prayer book. Sometimes I wondered whether perhaps God was helping us after all—if there was a God. He hadn't forsaken us—although I was only beginning to realize that now—and I was thankful for that. I joined in the Lord's Prayer, and prayed that Bina would never be unhappy and that I would never have to see her die before me.

I can't find that kind of peace in the chapel. I'm only staying out of politeness and because the nuns have made it clear that Bina and I have to get through the full hour and a half. It doesn't matter one bit to them that Bina won't sit still and has started flicking through the prayer books, playing with the sisters' rosaries, and tugging on their crucifixes.

Still, the nuns pray every day, and it's clearly at least as important to them as their service to the children, the sick, and the disabled. So, I really do kneel in the chapel for the full ninety minutes until my skin begins to itch from the mosquito bites and my knees are exploding with pain. Toward the end, I'm hardly sure how to position myself. Unlike me, the sisters show no sign of pain as they kneel; their thoughts are only on their softly murmured prayers. I notice how different our lives are, and I'm suddenly aware just how much I focus on the outside world, while behind the orphanage's high walls, the sisters concentrate on their prayers and their work—and the sense of peace this brings them.

Later, Sister Martha ties a little pendant of the Virgin Mary round Bina's neck. I will let her keep it on until she decides for herself that it's time to remove it. This will be many years later. But even then, Bina will only go off the pendant when other children tease her about it in the playground. A few weeks later, she will ask me to put it back on again.

Over the next two days, we stay with Bina from morning to evening. In the afternoons, we even take her across to our little hotel room near the orphanage. This goes so much better than I had anticipated. Bina clings to me when we leave the orphanage and still doesn't want to be held by Andreas. However, she's happy to spend time on our bed in the hotel. She drinks a bottle of milk and merrily unravels a roll of toilet paper and tears it into tiny pieces. What fun!

Of course, getting used to Andreas will take time. From Bina's behavior, I can tell that she's going through the same process she went through with me a few weeks ago, except now I've taken on the role of the sisters as her trusted person. She seeks refuge in my arms; she wants to be close to me. Her interactions with Andreas are slow and tentative. I feel sorry for Andreas. I try to explain the situation to him. He seems to understand, even though it clearly hurts him when Bina rejects him, keeps wanting to go to me, and follows me everywhere.

This is a critical and difficult time for Bina. Her last few days in the orphanage have begun. The fact that we're taking her to our hotel for an hour here or there is disturbing her normal daily routine and unsettling her. When we arrive back at the orphanage with Bina, she's overjoyed and runs over to hug the sisters. Then she wants to come back to us again. When we leave at the end of the day, she screams and cries after us.

"It's as if she's being torn in two," says Andreas. "She doesn't know where she belongs anymore."

He's right. Bina is much more unsettled, tearful, and wound up than usual. For her sake, we need to make a clear and final decision—she needs to leave the orphanage. So we tell the sisters that we will be taking Bina out of the orphanage in two days' time.

In the end, our departure seems to be harder on the sisters than Bina herself. We promise them that we will pop in again before we fly home, as the hotel by the beach is some distance from the airport. So, it's not a final farewell, but it is a firm "good-bye for now."

Sister Martha dresses Bina one last time, in the dress that I had brought with me a few weeks ago that Bina has worn quite a few times now. Then she takes out a few more bangles for Bina, takes extra care painting the bindi on her forehead, and ties her hair into a topknot even more lovingly than usual. She hunts in her cupboard for more Virgin Mary pendants and gives them to us in case Bina should lose the one round her neck. Then she wishes us and Bina the very best for the future, gives Bina a hug, says, "God bless you," and traces the sign of the cross on Bina's forehead. She hesitates a moment, and then with an abrupt "good-bye," she turns away. She doesn't come down into the yard to see us off. I can understand why.

Then we say our good-byes to the big ones. Anita and Aisha cling to me, but it's just their way of showing me that they care. As I hug them and take Bina out into the corridor, they stay behind and gaze after us, almost as if they understand. In many ways, they're already so grown up, so experienced, hardly children anymore. Thus, they always knew that I would become Bina's mother and that they would be left empty-handed, as usual.

Bina doesn't understand that we're saying good-bye. She lets me carry her down the steps into the yard as I have so many times before. My heart is pounding in my chest. What does the future hold for us? Will Bina settle into our family? Will I be able to handle her, or will she cry desperately to go back to the orphanage? All of a sudden, I feel insecure and find myself dreading the next few days. Will I be able to cope? There'll be no one around to help us anymore; we'll have to muddle through with Bina one day at a time. And we're not talking about a newborn baby who sleeps peacefully in his or her cot for hours every day, but a toddler, who needs to be entertained, parented, and supervised all day long. I feel weak in the knees, but try not to let it show.

"We'll manage," Andreas whispers and puts his arm around me. He can tell I'm worried. I'm so glad he's here.

When we arrive in the yard, Sister Maria, Sister Lena, and Sister Alissa are already waiting for us. Sister Maria hands me a bag with milk, porridge powder, and medicine. Then each sister takes Bina in her arms, kisses her, traces the sign of the cross on her forehead, and wishes her all the best. Bina lets them, but wants to come straight back to me again.

Then we go. We wave to the sisters and say bye. As I slowly turn away, Bina suddenly begins to wave, too, a little clumsily, and says, "Da-da-da," her word for good-bye, which she sometimes said when I left the orphanage at night. Sister Alissa is closer to tears than Bina. My wish has been granted; it would have been so painful to have to drag Bina away from the orphanage screaming and crying. As long as she's in my arms, Bina feels happy and safe. We're off to a great start! And I'm so glad we're finally able to begin our new life together.

Looking back, I see Nirav, hanging high up on the window bars. He waves after us until we vanish through the gateway. I'll never forget him.

I'm tearful and emotional as we leave the orphanage behind us. This time will never come again.

In spite of all the sadness, there are so many things I've loved about the orphanage. I loved playing with Bina up on the roof in the first moments we spent alone together—the warm tropical wind blowing through the tops of the palms around us—and Bina begging me to pick her up so that she could see the trains go by. I loved the peaceful afternoons spent down in the yard, sitting with the sisters and laughing as the children rode their tricycles with caramel dripping from their mouths while Aisha and Anita whooped with joy on the swing. I loved the quiet time at midday, while the children dozed in their cots with the bottles of rice water slowly sliding from their mouths and the curtains billowed in the breeze. In those moments, everything was at peace, the children slept innocently, and we could all relax for a moment. I also loved the time I spent downstairs with Bina in the infant room, where we peeped through the window bars and Sister Maria let us watch as she gently massaged a baby who was just a few days old.

I've so enjoyed the way the sisters laugh and beam with joy, how peaceful and balanced they are. I've enjoyed their unwavering commitment and their tolerant forgiveness of human failings. I've learned a lot here, and it's changed me. I've learned to appreciate different values and, perhaps, become a bit less superficial. Most important, I've witnessed Bina's transformation from a shy, anxious orphanage child to a happy, open, and cuddly girl—our daughter, our pride and joy. I love her more than anything, and no one will come between us again. What a gift!

Chapter 29

INTERLUDE IN PARADISE

The lawn fine, plush, firm, and deep green—like a carpet. Everything here is green, shining brightly in the glistening rays of the sun. Around the manicured grass, towering king palms sway in the warm sea breeze that caresses the blossoming bougainvilleas, oleander bushes, and other tropical plants. The garden is beautifully tended. Through the trees I can see the beach and the sparkling sea. I wish Andreas would hurry up checking in at reception. The blue of the swimming pool glistens through the nearby palms. I turn my face toward the sun and take a deep breath, trying to fill myself with its light, joy, and radiance. I feel the energy flowing into me. Looking back, the orphanage seems so dark and oppressive, the last few weeks gloomy and suffocating.

Our taxi ride had taken us almost an hour outside of Mumbai, to the northern coast. We left the behemoth of a city far behind us. We passed the monsoon- and dirt-weathered apartment blocks; the building sites where sweat-drenched women in dusty saris shovel throat-burning tar while their naked babies play nearby in the dirt; the concrete cores of new tower blocks where scaffolding sways on slender bamboo canes; the billboards for violent-looking Bollywood movies, computers, and cell phones. All the while, we were surrounded by motorcycles, which overtook us at breakneck speed, the saris of the women on the back flapping in their wake. Then we were stuck behind a smoking tanker, slowly weaving its way between the potholes. At some point, the outskirts of Mumbai turned to swampland as the road wound its way toward the coast.

The hotel is right on the Arabian Sea. Wide beaches where wealthy Indians jog stretch along the coast. The lights of fishing boats glitter on the horizon at night.

The taxi ride couldn't have gone more smoothly. Bina spent the whole journey asleep on my tummy. Now I hold her in my arms, and, because she's getting a little heavy, I set her down on her little feet on the lawn. She stares at me in disbelief, hops from one foot to the other in confusion, and begins to cry heart-wrenchingly. She looks at her feet in terror and tries to climb back into my arms. It's the first time she has felt anything other than tiles beneath her feet.

Over the next few hours, I will realize just how small Bina's world has been. Upstairs in our room, when I go to take a shower after the hot journey, she breaks into panicked screams. Why is Mommy suddenly standing behind a wall? Why is it suddenly loud? Why is Mommy wet, and why does she look completely different? Bina screams like a banshee. It will be many weeks before I can take a shower without her standing nearby, distraught and in tears.

But other than that, things are going amazingly well. As long as she can hold on to me or climb into my arms, she's calm. But she won't go more than a few feet away from me, which means that I have to take her everywhere I go, even to the bathroom. Even there, she tries to climb into my arms. She won't let me out of her sight.

We spend a blissful first day together. At lunchtime, Bina sits happily between us in the restaurant in a high chair, greedily stuffing chips into her mouth. Afterward, I feed her a yogurt, which she joyfully smears across her face, positively bathing in the fragrant mess. She sighs peacefully. In the afternoon, we visit the swimming pool, where Bina charges straight into the water without hesitation. Andreas can't hold her back. She's just as I thought: a water baby.

The day goes far, far better than I had expected—no crying, no whining, no stress. I can hardly believe our luck. That afternoon, as the shadows of the palms slowly creep across the lawn, the gardener turns on a sprinkler. Bina squeals with joy as we run through the jets of water in the muggy afternoon heat.

Later, she cries a bit because it's time for her porridge; but even then, I'm able to make it up and feed it to her in our room without a problem. That evening, Andreas and I sit on our hotel bed while Bina sits nearby in her own little bed. She should really be sleeping, but instead she grins at us and chortles with glee. Then she raises her little hand, waves, and says her version of "bye-bye"—"da-da-da." But we don't go, which amuses her. She can hardly believe that she's supposed to sleep with us here. Again and again, she waves at us from her little bed, calling "da-da-da," and giggling when we stay sitting on our bed. Eventually, she becomes so tired that she curls into a ball and falls asleep. Andreas and I can hardly believe our luck. We order a delicious curry and Tiger beer from room service.

But once Andreas has disappeared into the bathroom to have a shower, there's a knock on the door. I open it to see a young man from reception standing there, hemming and hawing with a serious look on his face.

"I'm afraid there's a problem. May I speak with your husband?" he asks nervously.

"He's in the bathroom. Why? What's wrong?" I inquire, worried.

"I've got a message from management," he replies apologetically. Then his voice hardens and he says, "You are kindly requested to leave the hotel. You can't stay here. Your child is adopted, isn't she?"

I stare at him. I have no idea how to react.

"Um, why—What? Yes, she's adopted. What's the problem?" I stammer.

"We no longer accept couples with adopted children. It's house policy," he says, looking a little sheepish. The conversation is clearly uncomfortable for him. "I'm going to have to ask you to leave the hotel. We would never have let you stay here in the first place if we'd known about the adoption."

My blood pressure rises. A wave of confusion, anger, and resignation begins to build inside me.

"But why? Why do we have to leave?" I ask in desperation.

"Madam, you have to understand," the young man begins again, "a few weeks ago, we had another European couple staying here with two adopted children. Suddenly, the police turned up, and we discovered that the couple was making dreadful videos with the children in their room. Do you see what I mean? It was absolutely terrible. The press had a field day, and the papers claimed the hotel had been in on it, that we'd known what they were up to all along. So the manager decided that the hotel will no longer accept parents with adopted children. We really must ask you to leave."

"But we're not pedophiles!" I scream back. "I won't let you make me out to be a criminal! I'm not going to just take my child and leave as if I've got something to be ashamed of. We went through all the proper legal channels. We went to court. I have all the papers. I didn't buy my child in a back street!" I yell in his face. I begin to shake and cry. Not this—this is exactly what I was trying to avoid. That's why I jumped through all these bureaucratic hoops in the first place, so that everything was legal and above board and we could look our child and the world around us honestly and openly in the face. And now, here we are, being thrown out of the first hotel.

"What's going on?" Andreas calls through the open bathroom door. He must have heard me shouting.

"They're throwing us out," I sob.

"They can't be serious!" says Andreas. Then he calls to the young man, "Wait outside. I'll be there in a moment." I stand there while he gets dressed, tearful and terrified that all this commotion will wake Bina.

Andreas steps into the corridor. There are raised voices. Then he comes back inside and slams the door.

"They're crazy. I'm going down to see the manager," he tells me.

"Andreas, we can't leave," I plead. "We won't find another hotel around here at this time, for one thing. But most importantly, we mustn't let them get away with this. We haven't done anything wrong! We can't let them treat us like this."

"Yes, yes, I know that. Don't worry. We're not going anywhere. They won't know what's hit them!" he grumbles and leaves.

I sit down on the bed and stare at Bina, who is sleeping innocently. I can't believe people are already making things difficult for us, on our very first day! What will the future bring?

After a long time, Andreas finally comes back up to the room. He's obviously managed to convince the manager that he can't just kick us out.

"We're staying. They seem pretty embarrassed about it now. It's a disgrace. Really, we should leave right now on principle," Andreas rants.

I whisper, "Hush, we don't want to wake Bina."

But she doesn't wake, not tonight. Tonight she sleeps peacefully because she hasn't yet realized that her entire world has been turned upside down. That will soon change, though.

We stay in the hotel. The staff can't do enough for us. The only other guests are a few businesspeople here for meetings, so we mostly have the pool to ourselves and can enjoy our new family life with Bina. It warms my heart to watch her paddling among the waves on the beach, to watch her having fun splashing in the kids' pool with Andreas, and to see her amazement at the flea-bitten dog on the beach and her four puppies. Little by little, Bina is discovering the world. She spends most of her time playing between our sun loungers in her little sun hat. But every day, she moves a few feet farther away from my lounger. After a week, she's happy to spend a few minutes alone with Andreas. At last, I'm able to go for a swim, even if Bina does call worriedly after me. Her trust in Andreas is growing day by day.

Things are going very slowly. It's demanding, especially for me, because Bina never leaves my side and mostly wants to be in my arms. She has diarrhea, too; perhaps the change in food and water was too much for her.

In spite of this, there hasn't yet been a situation where we can't calm her down. As soon as I pick her up, she's happy. We even get the feeling that she understands us better all the time because, apart from the few Hindi words I had learned, we always speak German with her. She has a lot to say for herself, although it's only baby talk so far. She's getting more used to us every day, except that, in the evenings when she's tired, she goes wandering, as if she's searching for something. She runs to the door of the hotel room. I think she's looking for the familiar surroundings of the orphanage—her porridge and her cot.

All the same, her nighttime panic attacks do worry us. For three nights running, we've had the same scenario: at seven o'clock, Bina falls asleep relatively easily in our hotel room, while Andreas and I quietly eat our curry, read, and watch over our little one. But then toward late evening, something strange happens. Out of the blue, Bina stands up whining, looking for something, her eyes wide with horror. She stares into space as if she can see something terrible, her little face and eyes full of utter fear. The panic in her eyes is so sickening that I can hardly bring myself to look at her; it's as if she's staring at a monster right behind us. I start to feel scared myself.

She's having bad nightmares, so-called night terrors, during which she is still asleep, despite her wide-open eyes. This is why Bina doesn't react to our attempts to calm her; she simply doesn't know we're there. After a few minutes, the panic attack is over, and she goes back to sleep. These attacks are a clear sign of the effects that the huge changes in Bina's life are having on her. What I don't yet know is that the most difficult period of adjustment is yet to come—it will begin when we arrive home—and that it will test me to the limit, both psychologically and physically.

After our three weeks at the beachside hotel, the time finally arrives for Andreas to collect Bina's passport from the sisters at the orphanage and her visa from the consulate. This, too, had to be arranged weeks in advance because the consulate required a large pile of original documents. Basically, they wanted to ensure that the social workers at home had vetted us as adoptive parents, and of course they also needed the court documents from the

Mumbai High Court. Only after receiving all these documents would they prepare the visa. This is a special one-year visa for adopted children, issued under the condition that we apply for adoption under German law as soon as we arrive home; indeed, the Indian Embassy would send a notification to this effect to the authorities and the Youth Welfare Office.

Finally, the night when we will leave India with Bina is nearly here. The flight will be almost nine hours long and will depart in the early hours. I'm dreading it. The airport is always insanely busy, and waiting for the flight in the middle of the night is exhausting. And with a newly adopted, terrified child, the nine-hour flight is eight hours too long.

We move back to the little hotel next to the orphanage. Straightaway, Bina becomes unsettled and starts to scream. She screams and screams, but this time, there's nothing I can do to calm her. Even so, we decide to take her to say a last good-bye to the sisters, who welcome us with a big "hello" and open arms. But Bina is shy; she snuggles into me and seems not to want to recognize the orphanage, her room, the other children, or the caregivers at first. It takes some persuading before she will let Didi hold her. Even though she enjoys the sisters' loving welcome and kisses in the yard, she soon wants to be back in my arms.

The change of hotel has been too much for Bina, and she starts to scream again at the orphanage. The sisters decide she's dehydrated, and before we have chance to argue, they put her on a drip. Sister Maria reckons I haven't been giving Bina enough to drink, particularly considering the heat and her diarrhea. I'm not so sure she's right, though. Bina screams the place down. I suddenly wonder if bringing her back here was a huge mistake.

"She can sense the change. Children can tell when a great journey is upon them and their lives are about to change," Sister Martha tells me. "We had a young girl who came down with a high fever on the day she was supposed to travel to Europe, so we delayed her flight. This happened three times. The fourth time we sent her to Europe, high fever and all."

This time, our farewell is less idyllic. Bina sits in my arms, still crying from the trauma of the drip, while we adults are too busy worrying about the flight to be nostalgic. I don't notice the other children or the slum huts beside the street—the things that had been part of my little world for all those weeks. All I can think of is the journey because I don't know how Bina will cope with such a long flight or how we're going to calm her down if she does start to panic. I'm absolutely petrified that she's going to spend hours on the plane crying while we sit there, helpless. Our stay in the hotel had been an interlude in paradise, but now I feel that we are venturing into the real world with Bina and that our baptism of fire is about to begin.

The flight really is as much of a trial as I feared. As expected, the process of checking in our luggage in the stuffy airport and the long wait at passport control is exhausting. To keep Bina calm, Andreas and I take turns carrying her, but I'm left holding her until my arms and shoulders ache most of the time. I find myself dreaming of home and my bed. If I'm honest, I'm dreaming of a time when Bina has finally settled in and the struggle of this adoption is behind us.

Lining up for passport control is also our first experience of other passengers staring at Bina. Most Indians give us a friendly smile. "Did you adopt the little one here?" I'm suddenly asked by a kind-looking European woman in the line next to ours. Because she seems friendly enough, I engage with her and answer her questions.

After a while, I'll begin to notice that people ask us these same questions over and over again, and I realize that it's not always in Bina's interest to discuss the adoption in public like this. All the same, it will take me many years to be able to say in situations like this, "I'd rather not discuss my child's background in the middle of the airport. Please respect our family's privacy." Other times I might just stare at the other person's children and ask, "And where did you get these children—are they yours?" It takes a comment like this to make some people realize how much their questions intrude into our family's private life.

But at this point, I'm happy to answer. She replies, "Oh, you know, we used to wonder whether we should adopt, and we still think about it from time to time. After all, we'd be helping these children, wouldn't we?"

Everything seizes up inside me. This belief that adoption is a completely selfless act, to help the children—it sounds so patronizing, as if the children should be grateful to their adopters in the future. And there's nothing I hate more than the two-faced assurances I get from so many people that maybe they might adopt, too. Why can't they be honest enough to admit that they don't really want to, which is perfectly OK?

As we approach the officials at passport control with Bina in our arms, another official comes over—clearly their superior. As well as Bina's Indian passport, which still calls her "Baby Bina" with no offical last name, and visa, the officials also want to see the documents from the Mumbai High Court and her birth certificate. Finally, a decisive nod and the loud thud of the stamp in our passports make it clear that we're allowed to leave the country.

But once we get to the departure lounge, Bina really lets it rip. The people, the noise, the luggage, our uneasiness—it's all too much for her. Bina runs around between the passengers and their luggage like a headless chicken, grabbing frantically at random cases. Neither Andreas nor I can hold her or calm her down. I can see she's going completely out of control. She won't listen to us, and I get increasingly worried. Eventually, I run out of ideas and get out the magic medicine Sister Maria, who's responsible for the orphanage's pharmacy, had given me—a concoction to make Bina fall asleep. I take her to the ladies' restroom and pour a spoonful of the syrup down her throat. I don't feel good about doing this to my child, but I don't know how else I'm going to cope with Bina on the crowded plane.

When we join Andreas in the line for boarding, an Indian father turns to us and says, "I know how glad you'll be when this trip's over!"

"Yes, we're hoping she'll sleep as much as possible," I reply.

"Come and see me if you have any trouble," he says and points to his two young children with a grin. "I have a fantastic drowsy cough syrup; it never fails."

Genuinely relieved, I thank him. I can only hope that I'll be able to find his seat aboard the jumbo if I need him.

It's time for us to board. I carry Bina in my arms, so worked up and tense that I can hardly walk. As we make our way past the flight attendants onto the plane, a single question hammers in my head: Are we doing the right thing, taking her away from India? We squeeze ourselves awkwardly into the narrow seats with Bina, her blanket, milk powder, bottle, extra diapers, and cuddly toy. It's so cramped that we can hardly move. I sigh my deep sigh again, and Andreas squeezes my hand.

"We can do it," he says soothingly.

"Yes, I know," I reply absentmindedly. Then the flight attendant comes to tell us that they will hang a cot for Bina in the bulkhead in front of us once the plane reaches flying altitude. In fact, Bina will spend five hours of the nine-hour flight time asleep, while I stare at the tiny airplane icon on the screen in front of me as it slowly creeps across India, and then Iran and Turkey. Everyone on the plane is asleep and snoring. It's still dark when I push up the window shade. What a shame. On the flight out, I could make out the Ararat in the far east of Turkey—a massive, extinct volcano, where Noah landed his ark. I try to catch a glimpse of it on every flight to and from India; it's the highlight of the flight for me.

But now, the plane is still at the gate. The flight attendant is spraying the plane with insecticide while the safety briefing plays on the screens in front of us. Bina stands between my legs, flicking through the in-flight magazines. But as the plane taxis down the runway, she begins to yawn and crawls onto my lap, where I'm able to strap her in with the baby seat belt without a problem.

She has no idea what's happening to her. She falls asleep on my tummy before the plane has even left the ground and climbed into the dark night sky. I look out of the window and try to make out the lights of Mumbai while tears roll down my face. We're taking her away from her home, but she doesn't even realize. She's so incredibly small, naive, and innocent. I can only pray that we've made the right decision, that her life will be a happy one, and that we will have the strength to support her.

Part Four

Chapter 30

MY FEAR OF LOSS

Four years have passed. Bina is now a healthy, friendly, and happy five-year-old. Her squint improved on its own after the adoption—she doesn't even need glasses now—and I have to stress (not without a touch of sarcasm) that the circumference of her head is clearly large enough. She is very bright, loves school, and is growing up bilingual—we speak both English and German with her.

She lights up our family with her friendliness and her radiant smile. We love her more than anything and are so thankful to be able to experience the wonderful joys of parenthood with her. There's no greater pleasure than running alongside a little bike on the empty Sunday-morning streets and teaching your child to ride without training wheels. Andreas and I ran breathlessly up and down the street until she finally wobbled nervously out of our reach, and we held our breath, hoping she wouldn't crash into the parked cars. Then there was the time when Bina was brave enough to swim into Andreas's outstretched arms without armbands. She spluttered, only just able to keep her head above the water. Her big dark eyes grew even larger, and then suddenly, her beautiful smile spread across her face as she reached the safety of Andreas's arms. At times like these, when I see the pride in her eyes and see how eager she always is to try new things, I know the long struggle of our adoption saga was worth it a thousand times over.

Bina enriched our lives so much that two years after bringing her home, we decided to adopt a second child from the same orphanage run by the Catholic nuns in Mumbai—Sushmita, our little daredevil, who buries my silver candlesticks in the sandpit and throws books down the toilet. Sushmita, who drops Andreas's favorite towel into a bathtub full of water, who pulls the tape out of Bina's story cassettes, who cuts our tape measure up with her plastic scissors and then looks at me, shakes her head, and says "No, no, no!" because she knows this is exactly what Mommy will say. Bina and Sushmita love, tease, argue, and kiss each other the way only sisters can. It's a joy to see.

We might have adopted a third child, too, if it wasn't so incredibly exhausting. It wasn't much easier with Sushmita than it had been with Bina; the highs and lows of the bureaucratic process and the stay in the orphanage were very similar.

It's evening, and I'm putting the children to bed. I tuck Bina in nice and snug under her favorite quilt—red with yellow elephants.

"Mommy—kiss," she says and puts her arm round my neck. I give her a goodnight kiss and stroke her long, silky hair, which I have just braided in the bathroom, otherwise it gets knotty when I comb it in the morning.

"Will you come back later?" she asks. She always asks me this.

"Yes, yes, I'll come back. Think nice thoughts about tomorrow. You've got PE at school."

I go over to Sushmita's bed, where she is busy hunting under the covers for her little teddy. She'll be three soon. I bend down over her and go to give her a kiss, but she turns her face away, rolls into a ball, and buries her face in her pillow.

"Sleep well," I whisper in her ear. I know that during the night both children will sneak into our room and crawl into our bed. Andreas leaves every morning because he says it's too cramped and he can't sleep. My body has gotten used to it, and although I wake up several times in the night, I've learned to go straight back to sleep again.

Things weren't so easy just after we'd adopted Bina. I remember the first few weeks and months after we brought her home with us from the orphanage. It was by far the worst phase of the entire adoption. My nerves were shot. I was at the end of my tether because it was simply too much for me.

The nights were the worst. Bina had stopped sleeping through after just a few nights in the hotel in Mumbai. But it wasn't the terrifying nightmares that bothered me, because after a few nights, they disappeared. What really wore me down was Bina's nightly whining and screaming. And it only got worse once we arrived home. At first, we tried her in her own bed in her own room, but she was frightened because she'd never slept alone in a quiet room in her life. The concept of sleeping in a room by herself was completely alien to her.

She cried and wanted me to stay with her, but I could hardly go to bed at seven in the evening. So I tried staying with her until she fell asleep. But then, she would just wake up and cry in the night. The more I went to her to settle her, the more she woke up. After ten days, she was crying almost every hour. We felt as if we'd been hit by a bus. Andreas retreated to the spare room because he had to get up for work the next day. By five o'clock the next morning, when Bina wanted to get up, I hadn't had a wink of sleep and was utterly exhausted.

Things went just as badly when I tried having Bina in bed with me. Of course, she wasn't used to sharing a bed either. For her, my presence meant it was time to play. When she did finally drop off, her sleep was so disturbed that I hardly got a wink myself. By four in the morning I couldn't sleep any more.

It was a vicious cycle, one I couldn't find a way to break. The nights were a disaster, and by morning I was so tired that I was praying for Bina's midday nap to come. And that lasted only twenty minutes, because Bina couldn't stand to be in bed for any longer. The more tired I became, the more irritated I was when she cried, which only made her more whiny and clingy. And of course that wore me down even further.

On top of this, Bina was also very nervous to start with. For the first few weeks I couldn't put her down for a moment or she would begin to scream heart-wrenchingly. In the early days, I had to brush my teeth with Bina in my arms; she would even clamber onto my lap while I sat on the toilet. I found myself almost crying with frustration; I felt trapped because she'd completely taken over my life. For weeks, I couldn't take a single step without Bina clinging to me for dear life. If I pushed her away or put her down on the floor, she would appear next to me a few moments later shaking like a leaf.

It was too much for her, even though I was her trusted person and she'd known me for weeks. Sushmita would react in a similar way. I visited her for weeks in the orphanage, too. Yet, once we arrived home, she seemed traumatized. She pulled faces, hit herself in the face with her fists, and banged her head against the tiled kitchen floor so hard that I worried she'd crack her skull. These extreme signs of trauma vanished within a few days, thank God.

But the screaming remained—with both children—for many weeks. I remember being so upset by Sushmita's screaming at one point that I ran out of the house and slammed the door behind me. Sushmita stood upstairs in her cot and screamed incessantly. I reached the end of my tether and ran sobbing down the street to the nearest café, where I sat drinking a cup of coffee with shaking hands. I felt like a terrible mother for leaving my child screaming alone at home, but I just couldn't take it anymore.

In the early weeks, I felt like I was being held hostage by my child. Because I was the one who had been there in the orphanage, both Bina and, later, Sushmita were obsessed with me; they wouldn't accept my mother-in-law or our housekeeper. Andreas was the only one who could care for the children at the weekend so that I could finally get a full night's sleep. However, there were times when I was too wired to sleep, even when I had the chance to do so. My sleep patterns were completely messed up; in one of those early weeks, I typically slept no more than three or four hours a night.

In the end, my only option seemed to be the "controlled crying" method that some doctors recommend. I left Bina crying in her bed and went in to calm her at gradually increasing intervals until she fell asleep. It took three days, during which I often stood in the hall outside Bina's room, barely able to stand her miserable, forsaken cries, but it worked wonders.

After a few days, she was falling asleep within minutes and sleeping through the night. We'd made it; the worst was behind us. At last, I was able to get a good night's sleep myself. I felt well rested in the morning and could deal with Bina more patiently. Because she was also sleeping better and I was calmer with her, she began to blossom. Before long, we had a cheerful, friendly little girl who was the very picture of happiness. We'd finally broken the vicious cycle. We began to make progress. Our home became a happy place.

Four months later, we were back in our usual daily routine, and Bina had mostly settled in. She quickly became more secure. Because she now slept much better, I was able to let her spend the night on a mattress beside our bed. In the morning, she would creep into our bed and fall asleep again on my tummy. It was moving to see how important this bodily closeness was for her, how much she needed to make up for the lack of human contact she'd had in the past. I still love it when she cuddles up to me with her cold little feet.

Even now, I find it hard to follow a rigid parenting strategy with the children. I think perhaps this is easier with biological children. Because Bina was so starved of tenderness and closeness, I needed to encourage a close bond between us, which meant I "spoiled" her at first. I would hold her all the time, carry her around, sit her on my lap, and let her sleep in our bed. At an age where other parents generally insist their children learn to sleep alone, I was teaching Bina, and later Sushmita, the opposite. Later, we'd be forced to turn the clock back and bring the children back into line with a "normal upbringing," which of course upset them.

Also, we tended to put any bad behavior down to their time in the orphanage. Parents aren't tempted to do this with biological children; it's easier for them to tell whether their child has a genuine problem or is simply in a bad mood. For us, it's more difficult.

I turn my attention from Sushmita, who has fallen asleep under her covers, and go back to Bina.

"Mommy, another kiss?" Bina begs. I kiss her on the cheek and on her long, black eyelashes. She has become more beautiful than I could have possibly imagined—a gift from God.

"I love you, Mommy. Where are you going?" she asks.

"I'm going to sit in the living room. Daddy will be back tomorrow. I'll be working on the computer, like I always do."

"Where will you be?"

"In the living room, Bina."

"Can I hear you in there?"

"Yes, of course. But you need to sleep, darling."

"But will you hear if something happens?"

"Yes, but nothing's going to happen. Sweet dreams."

"Can you leave the door open?"

"Yes, of course." I walk slowly out of the room, leaving the door open as I do every evening.

"Will you leave the landing light on?"

"Yes," I say, and I leave the light on—like every evening.

"Mommy, will you come back later?"

"Yes. Now it's time to sleep."

"But you will come back later?"

"Yes, of course. I always check on you before I go to bed," I say. Every night, the same ritual. Bina is always a little uncertain; she always asks the same questions: "Mommy, where are you going? Will you stay?"

Other mothers think I'm reading too much into Bina's behavior; they tell me that their children also beg them to leave the door open every evening. I'm sure that's true, but that's exactly my point: we will never know which aspects of Bina's behavior are just her natural character, which stem from her time in the orphanage and the trauma of her adoption, and which are a result of our parenting. It's so hard for us to distinguish.

This is why I'm careful. I remember a conversation with a father who had adopted three children, who are much older now. He told me, "Don't let your friends convince you everything is normal. We made that mistake for a long time. Then years later, we realized that everything wasn't normal after all and that the children had problems we needed to deal with properly. We should have done it much sooner."

With this in mind, I always keep a close eye on the children. In Bina's case I notice that she's still very clingy. Even now, I can't go from the backyard to the kitchen without Bina jumping down from the swing and running after me.

"What's the matter, Bina?"

"Oh, nothing, Mommy. I just wanted to know where you were."

"I'm just in the kitchen making dinner."

"OK."

"Don't you want to go and play on the swing? Sushmita is still out there." But Bina pulls a face and stands waiting in the doorway.

"No, I'd rather be with you." She won't go out to the yard alone—not even with Sushmita. She's watching to make sure I'm really there and don't leave.

I love Bina and Sushmita more than anything. They are my world; I would be devastated if something were to happen to them. I know Andreas feels the same way. It melts my heart to watch him with the girls; he is much more loving, tender, and concerned than I had ever hoped—more than other fathers I've seen. We know the children will never be able to completely shake off their past. We will always have to live with the consequences of the shock of their mothers giving them up and the scars on their souls from their time in the orphanage. These will fade with time, but some traces will always remain.

Some problems take longer to correct: the lack of eye contact; the difficulty with being close to people; the initial inhibitions; Sushmita's desperate refusal to eat, which took several months to disappear; the sleep problems; the excessive clinginess; and the difficulty in dealing with emotions. The professionals all say the same thing: the children need time, calmness, security, and routine. Everything else will fall into place—or not. There's nothing adoptive parents can do to change that.

"There's only so much you can do," a friend who was adopted herself tells me. "If you're adopted, at some point it dawns on you that your mother didn't want you and rejected you, and that knowledge goes right to the core. It creates a deep sense of insecurity that you will never be able to make up for as an adoptive mother." She says that as a result of this rejection, she had spent her life looking for security, especially in her relationships with other people. She always went for reliable boyfriends. "Looks aren't as important to me," she says.

"The problem comes when you experience rejection from another person—for example, when a boyfriend breaks up with you. It confirms your deep-seated fear of being abandoned, and it's very hard to cope with," she warns. "As an adopted child, you're terrified of being rejected by others." That's why, she tells me, a good education is so important, so that the child at least has the chance to achieve stability and recognition in his or her working life.

"And you need to live a long life, be there for the children for a long time as a calming influence, a figure of security," she says. She also tells me that due to her fear of being abandoned again, she particularly craves harmony in her relationships with others. She doesn't want to risk upsetting people for fear of driving them away.

"The worst thing is, as an adopted child, you've done nothing to deserve this misery; after all, you can't help that your parents gave you away." She tells me that this has instilled in her a heightened sense of justice, as she knows just how it feels to be an innocent victim.

These warnings are a bitter pill for me to swallow. Although they matched what I had always read in my adoption books, I had thought I could nip Bina's and Sushmita's fears and insecurities in the bud and make up for them. Other, older adoptive mothers had also told me, "They will always feel insecure deep down." I see echoes of this in Bina's daily questions.

Yet, children have the amazing ability to regenerate, to a certain extent. I've learned that our children seem to develop in spurts and suddenly reach developmental goals that make up for the delay. At the beginning of her adoption, Sushmita had a much harder time tolerating close contact with other people than Bina did. She would hit me in the face with her fists if I got too close to her and would turn away and refuse to look at me if I didn't keep a minimum distance away. I could feed her an entire bowl of semolina without her giving me a single glance. I read her stories without her once looking me in the eyes. Often, she would stand in the kitchen asking me for apple juice while staring out the window.

We soon realized that this was not "normal" behavior and that it was a result of her time in the orphanage. We were under no illusions, unlike, perhaps, an acquaintance of mine, who adopted a two-year-old from an orphanage in the former Eastern Bloc. One day, she was seated on our sofa, telling us how fantastic her child was—so independent already! Meanwhile, her daughter was walking around, her head held low, not looking at any of us, even for a second. I gently asked my acquaintance if she'd read any books about the effects of orphanage life on adopted children, but I think she was too busy at work to have time for this. She couldn't see the warning signs in her child's behavior, or perhaps she didn't want to see them.

"Look at me if you want something!" I would sometimes tell Sushmita. I was so fed up with her staring out the window instead of looking at me. Then she would force herself to look me in the eyes for two seconds, but I could tell how reluctant she was to do it. It was almost two years before things began to improve a little. This behavior reminded me of a post I read on the Internet by a mother who said that after more than two years, her adopted son had finally looked at her for the first time.

Children who have spent a long time in an orphanage are slow and cautious to open up. A few days ago, I caught a look on Sushmita's face that I had never seen before. It was tender and loving. In that moment, she seemed almost shy and vulnerable. Andreas had always said that Sushmita was a very sensitive, warmhearted child and that her rough behavior was just something she'd adopted to protect herself from her cruel, harsh surroundings. I think he was right. Sushmita had just never dared to show this side of herself before. When we took her out of the orphanage, she showed almost no feelings or facial expressions; she was stone faced—even more so than Bina had been. It was as if Sushmita had built a shell around herself and had locked away her emotional core like a dormant bud. On the outside, she was aggressive, rude, and provocative. She would literally wait for us to lose our patience with her and for our behavior to confirm her feelings of suffering, rejection, and dislike. But now, the bud was slowly beginning to open, and the outer layers of her shell were falling away as if in slow motion. Bit by bit, we could see her true soul, her real feelings and personality. It will take some time before we really get to know her. She's not giving much away. We'll have to work for it.

It was the same sort of thing with Bina. When they came to us, each of our girls was a closed book, which we had to open very slowly, carefully turning the pages one by one. We often wonder what surprises there are in store for us—what new personality traits, both cute and quirky. Our girls will always be an adventure for us, a voyage of discovery.

For a few weeks now, Sushmita has been climbing into our bed. She flings her arm round my neck, gives me a sloppy wet kiss, strokes my cheek clumsily, and proudly announces, "That was a big kiss!" I'm so thankful for this slightly soggy proof of her love. Two years ago, it would have been unthinkable.

Tonight, Bina actually manages to sleep alone in her bed. In the morning, she will get a sticker on her calendar. When she has collected fifteen stickers, we'll buy the new summer shoes she's been longing for—red patent leather ones.

Chapter 31

NOT THE REAL MOTHER

The sky is overcast and gray. I'm starting to get cold. It hadn't occurred to me that there would still be snow up here in the mountains. So, I'm standing here in the McCraigs' garden in slip-on shoes, peering through the viewfinder of my camera. It's the school holidays, and we are in Scotland visiting friends.

"Lakshmi, push your hat out of your face!" calls Paul from behind me. But the children are too busy horsing around. Indira and Lakshmi jostle and tumble together into the snow; Sushmita soon joins them. Only Roshini, who has been struggling with kidney problems for quite some time and even now looks sickly and pale, is standing nicely in the snow waiting for me to take the special photo.

Finally, I manage to get a good shot of the four girls, all in woolly hats, gloves, and wellingtons, standing in front of a snowman that Paul and Andreas helped them make. It's so special to have a photo of Lakshmi, Roshini, Bina, and Sushmita together. We two couples adopted all four of them from the very same orphanage next to the railway tracks in Mumbai within the past two years. We met by chance through a group for adoptive parents.

Although Lakshmi and Bina were never at the orphanage at the same time, at least not in the same room (Lakshmi is a year older than Bina, and Roshini is a year older than our Sushmita), they understand that the orphanage is a bond between them. We as parents have decided that we want to cement this bond, because there may come a time when it could help the girls to know other children who have been through the same experience in their lives.

"Come on, it's getting cold! And we wanted to watch the videos, didn't we?" calls Shanon, Paul's wife. At this, we all troop inside again. While we drink tea and hot chocolate and indulge in Shanon's homemade muffins, we put on the videos. First is the video that Paul and Shanon made when they went to collect Lakshmi from the orphanage. It's not long—they were there for only two days—but there are a few clips of Lakshmi with Sister Alissa. The sight of her gets Bina very excited. Then it's time for our video, which brings back precious memories for the adults, too. The girls, of course, don't manage to sit still for long and are soon letting off steam in the playroom. We don't mind; it's more important that Lakshmi, Bina, and the two little ones get to know one other. After all, they've already seen the videos plenty of times at home.

At first Bina would watch the orphanage video nearly every day, dancing along in front of the TV when it got to the part where Sister Martha sings "Ring a Ring o' Roses" with the children. She rarely asks for it these days—only when she's homesick for India. At those times, we put on the video, and I dig out a bag of keepsakes I collected from the orphanage for Bina: her first little bottle, one of the handmade cotton diapers, all the Virgin Mary pendants from Sister Martha, Bina's very first new dress, the tiny bangles the sisters placed on her wrists, and a baby's rattle that I found with her in the cot. For all her childhood, Bina still enjoyed her memories of her stay in the orphanage in Mumbai with the sisters; only as a teenager would she realize more and more that it was really a sad time.

It will take Bina a long time to understand what being adopted from India actually means. In fact, she still doesn't know quite what to make of it. Recently she surprised us with her own logic. She pointed at an Indian man in town and asked, "Mommy, is he from the orphanage, too?" She'd quickly worked out that all Indians must be adopted. In this kind of situation, I explain adoption to her in simple, short, and carefully chosen sentences; I've learned to keep it to the bare minimum and to answer just the questions she asks. In any case, I generally find that she only asks one or two questions about adoption before changing the subject; a child will only ask he or she can handle, and that's usually just a tiny bit more than they already know. At bedtime, I read her one of the storybooks we have that are written for adopted children—the one about the baby elephant searching for love and security, who is adopted by Mommy and Daddy Bush Pig, or the story of Choco, the funny little bird, who finds a new home and lots of other adopted brothers and sisters with Mommy Bear. I have no idea what Bina makes of it all, but children understand more than we think.

That's the very reason why it leaves such a bitter taste when I see how insensitively some people speak to us on the street, clearly believing that Bina can't follow an adult conversation; some nosy people even think she doesn't understand German. "Oh, she knows German?" comes the surprised response, and I think, *Of course she understands German. Why on earth shouldn't she?*

So poor Bina is left looking on in amazement as the customs official in Frankfurt airport asks me, "And what relationship do you have to that child there?" He has examined our passports, but appears to have overlooked the part that says she is our daughter and that she shares our last name. It's even more hurtful when I'm asked in the middle of the street, "Couldn't you have children of your own?" I wrap my arms around Bina and say, "I'm sorry? But these are my own children." With that, the discussion stops. I'm asked the same question over and over—"Where are they from?"—to which I reply, "Oh, we're from Germany." Some remarks are so rude they take our breath away, like the time a cyclist yelled from behind us, pointing at our daughter, "Where did you hire her from?" I would have liked nothing better than to chase him down and pull him off his bike; even Andreas, who is usually much calmer than I am, was hurt. What is Bina supposed to think when people ask us where we "hired" her from?

A few days after that, Bina was very quiet after she came back from the playground. Although I could tell something was bothering her, it took her until dinnertime before she opened up to me.

"Mommy, the other children said that you're not my real mommy. I told them you are my real mommy, but they said that's not true." Bina was three years old then. I cuddled her in my arms as I had many times before and explained it to her again. I tell her that she has an Indian mother called Ragini, that she was in Ragini's tummy, but that Ragini couldn't care for her baby, so she brought her to the nuns in the orphanage. Then Sister Lena asked us if we wanted to be Bina's parents, her mommy and daddy. So that's how I became her mommy. Ragini was her Indian mother from before, and I'm her mommy now; people call that "adoption."

This answer seemed to satisfy her. All the same, for the next few weeks she must have told me at least twenty times a day, "You're my mommy. You're my mommy." She said it so often and with such certainty; it was as if she was arguing with a voice in her head. One day, I decided to turn the tables, and reassured her myself twenty times a day, "I'm your mommy. You're my darling Bina." Sure enough, after two days she didn't mention it again; she just wanted to hear the words of reassurance from my lips.

These days Bina is able to speak really quite confidently about adoption. Sometimes when we're all sitting together at the breakfast table on a Sunday morning and Andreas and I are spreading peanut butter on the girls' rolls, they'll suddenly call out, "Hold hands!" So we all join hands and the girls chorus, "We're a family!" To this day, we still have no idea where they picked that up from.

Bina only really began to fully comprehend her adoption on our trips to India. Before our first trip back to Mumbai, she was absolutely petrified. She was three then, and really she was looking forward to meeting Sushmita, the new little sister we had told her so much about, for the first time. Sushmita was nine months old. The plan was that we would all fly to Mumbai together to visit her. But shortly before we were due to fly, Bina became sickly and feverish. That evening, she suddenly burst into tears and sat on the living room carpet in a sad little heap; it was the first time in a long time that I had heard this deep, lonely "adoption" crying. "Mommy, Mommy," she cried, yet she wouldn't let me touch her. I sat helplessly by her side, not knowing what to do. I was devastated because it was the first time in so long that she wouldn't let me help her, even though she was clearly overcome with fear and sadness. Eventually, she sobbed that she didn't want to go to India. Andreas could go on his own; she wanted to stay at home with me. Only later would she let me comfort her. The next day, she was well again.

We flew to India together after all. In the first few days, Bina literally couldn't set foot in her native land. She clung to Andreas's arm, threw her arms round his neck, and stumbled as soon as he set her down on the ground. So Andreas carried her for the first two days, through the bazaar, through the streets, and finally to the orphanage. She was afraid of the orphanage, of the sisters, and most of all of the rooms; it was as if she couldn't sort through her feelings. In her memory and our videos, the orphanage was a pleasant place that triggered feelings of security and familiarity, yet when she entered the room with the barred cots, feelings of fear from the past must have surfaced in her subconscious—fear of the loneliness of the cots, the screams, the crying, and the bleakness. Bina couldn't stay in that room for long.

Still, we spent three weeks in India, balancing our visits to the orphanage with a leisurely, peaceful holiday in Kerala. When we returned to Mumbai from our boat trip along the canals and through the leafy groves of the backwaters, Bina had become more trusting. She had had time to get used to the sisters again. In the end, she did sit on Sister Alissa's lap, letting her feed her caramels and pour her fruit juice. All the love and affection she had felt for her first mother figure came flowing back; it was as if she had come home, as if a longing had been satisfied for both of them. Sister Alissa, for her part, was clearly moved at seeing Bina again, well grown, healthy, and happy. It was rare that children came back to visit the orphanage or that their visit would reawaken such affection and warmth in them toward her. To this day, we still have a photo on display at home of Sister Alissa holding Bina lovingly in her arms; it's a picture full of intimacy and fondness.

Six months later, when we traveled to India to collect Sushmita and spent another few weeks in

Mumbai next to the orphanage, it was clear that Bina found visiting the orphanage much easier. She even looked forward to seeing the sisters and quickly made friends with the other children in the orphanage; she played on the swings with them down in the courtyard and cuddled her new little sister, Sushmita, excitedly.

A year later we returned to India again. This time, Bina was almost five and Sushmita was two. We went on a cross-country tour of India, from Mumbai to Kolkata, where we hoped to visit Sister Alissa. She had been posted there, and Bina was determined to see her again.

"Mommy, when we get to India, can we see Ragini and give her a hug? Ragini is nice, isn't she?" asked Bina before our trip. I stared away, stunned with surprise.

"Yes, of course Ragini is nice," I stammer. "But no, we won't be able to see her because she's gone away."

"Where to?"

"Home, Bina. But we don't know where that is. That's why we can't see Ragini. We'll never be able to see her, but we can still think about her," I say, feeling Bina's disappointment.

"Isn't she coming back?"

"No, Bina, she isn't. She's never going to come back."

It hurts me to have to say things like this. Every time Bina asks me questions, I have to disappoint her a little bit more; every time I have to tell her a little bit more of the truth, that will hurt her. I know this, and yet I feel it's better to give her small doses of pain than a rose-tinted world built on lies that will one day turn into a huge disappointment she won't be able to deal with. That's why we try to talk about her adoption as often and as naturally as possible; it shouldn't be a secret or a taboo subject, but instead, a natural part of our lives. It's the only way to make sure that Bina feels able to ask questions, and the only way that we can help to ease her sadness about our answers.

When we arrived in Mumbai, Bina was very aware of why she was there. The sisters even laid a baby in her arms to show her how tiny she had been when Ragini brought her to the orphanage. They showed her the first little cot they had put her in. Bina asked if she could take a photo of it with our camera. She photographed the room and wanted to return to the orphanage that afternoon. "So that I'll recognize it again later," she said. We could hardly believe how serious and sensible an almost-five-year-old child could be. And yet, it was still too much for her; she couldn't comprehend how she had been alone in the orphanage for so long or how she had somehow come to live with us in another country—the unsettling journey through the different worlds of her childhood.

"Mommy, I've got four sisters," she announced one evening. "They were here in the orphanage, too, and were adopted as well. They live in different countries now, but they've come today to visit the orphanage like us. They're coming over soon to have dinner with us."

We were speechless. Was this a way of asking whether she had biological siblings? Or did she just need to feel that she wasn't alone in this difficult situation?

That evening before dinner, she went out to the front of the hotel and looked down the street. When I tiptoed up to her, she pointed down the street and told me that her sisters would be arriving soon by rickshaw. And so the imaginary sisters came and sat at the table with us; Bina even told them where to sit. They ate with us, and when it was time for Bina to go to bed, they went with her. Bina was living in a fantasy world, and her sisters stayed with us throughout our entire three-week trip to India, slowly merging into one friend, Sophie. Sophie eventually left as well.

At six years old, Bina was asking different questions; she still hadn't quite grasped the order of events in her adoption.

"Mommy, when you were with me in the orphanage back then, did you forget to bring your camera with you?"

"No, I had my camera. Why?"

"Well, then you could have taken a photo of Ragini when she brought me to the orphanage."

"My love, when Ragini brought you, I hadn't arrived yet. You spent a year on your own in the orphanage with the sisters. I didn't come along until later. I never saw Ragini," I explain, knowing that this is another little stab in her heart.

"Oh, OK, then," she says, disappointed, "because then I would have known what Ragini looks like."

Bina asked the questions I had expected her to ask much sooner than I thought she would, using her imagination to help her. A few days later, she tells me, "Mommy, I can remember that Ragini was wearing a green sari with a white pattern on it."

I just smile and say nothing.

"And she had black hair, too," Bina adds.

"Of course she had black hair; she is Indian, after all. I'm sure she had a long, black braid and was just as brown as you are. And you're very pretty, so she must have been pretty, too; maybe she even had lovely cupid's bow lips like you do." I play along with her fantasy and suddenly catch myself speaking in the past tense, which is really the wrong thing to do. Ragini is almost certainly still alive; she would only be in her early twenties by now.

Bina keeps trying to get closer to her Indian mother, to build up a picture of her. One day, I speculated out loud whether Ragini might have been a vegetarian and perhaps that was why Bina ate so little meat. Since then, Bina mostly refuses to eat meat, saying she is a vegetarian like Ragini. I hold my tongue, though, wary of breaking the delicate web that Bina has spun between herself and her mother. Why shouldn't she hold on to these fantasy facts about her mother when we don't know anything about how she really is?

Still, Bina has another means of connecting with her mother Ragini—she loves India. Learning about her cultural identity will bring her infinitely closer to her Indian mother. It is a never-ending journey that will reveal new secrets and answer her questions about where she came from.

Chapter 32

INDIAN DANCE

Mrs. Kapoor sinks slowly down onto the gray linoleum floor of the Indian Cultural Institute. She tucks her legs under herself in the lotus position and straightens her green-patterned salwar kameez. Then she peers carefully at the five students in front of her with her big, dark eyes. The girls are standing attentively in a row before her, dressed in T-shirts and leggings, barefoot, their hair neatly braided. Bina and her new friend Aisha can hardly contain themselves; they were playing around in the corridor before the dance lesson and now need to focus.

"Let's start with the prayer," Mrs. Kapoor tells the girls in English. She's from Tamil-Nadu, but she now lives in Germany with her husband and daughter. She is the only teacher in our town who offers *bharata natya*, one of the six traditional forms of Indian dance.

Bina and the other dance students raise their hands and begin: "Aangikam Bhuvanam Yasya…" They pray to the Indian god Shiva, and in a short ceremony they ask Mother Earth for forgiveness as they will soon be stamping around on her. The rhythmic stamping is so loud that the dance lessons have to take place on a Sunday so as not to disturb the other courses held at the Indian Cultural Institute. It's quite a long drive for us, which isn't ideal, but it's important for Bina to have some contact with Indian culture, even if only for one hour a week. Here, surrounded by the Indian teacher, the Indian girls, and their Indian mothers who sit at the edge of the room waiting together, I'm the outsider for once, not Bina.

The Indian dance lessons teach Bina a great deal about her heritage. Even the hand gesture the girls use to signal the beginning of the dance has a specific meaning. Hindus put their palms together in greeting, but whether the hands are placed over the head, in front of the forehead, or at the chest denotes the level of respect they wish to show toward the person they are greeting.

By following the steps and coordinated leg, feet, arm, hand, finger, eye, and head movements she learns in her dance lessons, Bina will learn to tell stories from Indian mythology through the medium of dance.

The lessons connect her with her heritage and the traditions of her Indian mother and father. I still think of the "Indian Nefertiti" I met, Inka, who was twenty before she realized that she wasn't just Swedish but Indian as well. She had had difficult times figuring out what this meant for her, as she had no opportunities to connect with India and its people. We want to spare Bina this. We try to let our girls experience some of their Indian heritage. Only then might they be able to discover, understand, and respect their roots.

If at some point during puberty the children decide they've had enough, that's absolutely fine. Perhaps one day I'll hear "Mother, stop with all the Indian stuff!" because the children have grown tired of their exotic roles.

The girls are growing up with us, German parents. They have me—an emancipated, independent woman who is not afraid to challenge others—for a mother, and they have Andreas—who not only accepts that it's fine for a woman to be this way, but actively encourages the girls to become independent, open, and confident—for a father. Will this eventually lead to issues with Indian culture and people and, above all, with Indian men's perception of women? We will raise Bina and Sushmita to be the kind of girls who certainly wouldn't accept a marriage arranged by their parents, but who will want to choose their own husbands and who might choose to continue working all their lives.

Will they be so Western that they are automatically excluded from some parts of Indian society? It's highly likely that they will always live in the Western world. Before long, Bina and Sushmita will be sure to work this out for themselves. Perhaps then they won't be so keen on the "Indian stuff" for a while.

That doesn't matter, of course. We will respect their decisions if and when the time comes. If the girls do want to learn more about Indian culture in the future, at least we will have given them the foundations. It will be easier for them to pick it up again if they wish.

We take Bina and Sushmita to Indian dance performances and temple festivals whenever we can. I spend time in the kitchen with the girls, letting them smell ginger and garlic, cooking Indian curries, and getting them used to the sweet taste of mango chutney. We read to them from the Bible, but we also read stories about Krishna, Rama, and Sita. We play Ludo—which, incidentally, is based on the Indian game pachisi—as well as Snakes and Ladders, originally an old Indian board game. We celebrate Easter and Christmas, but we also go to the Indian temple at Diwali, the symbolic celebration of the triumph of good over evil. We wear jeans, but in high summer, we get out our salwar kameez and wear those, too. Our home is a mixture of European and Eastern style, with some pieces of Indian furniture and photos of India on the walls. And sometimes I practice yoga with the children on the floor at home.

At the beginning of the school year, Bina's teacher came to me and said, "The children will be doing a presentation to the rest of the class in a few days' time. Does Bina see herself as Indian?"

This wasn't just a random question; there are children from eleven different countries in Bina's class. Many of them come from mixed-nationality families and have spent many years living abroad, like us. It's important for the children to explain who they are and for their classmates to learn to respect every child and his or her different culture, heritage, religion, or language.

"Bina comes from India," I tell the teacher. "It's part of her identity."

"That's all I wanted to know," she replies. "You see, some adoptive parents don't feel that way. They tell me, 'My child is German now.' They don't want me to complicate matters."

A few weeks later, during the Indian festival of Diwali, Bina and I find ourselves standing in front of her class. Her teacher has asked us especially, so we put on our salwar kameez and use Indian leather puppets to tell the story of Sita's abduction and her rescue by Hanuman and Rama. It is a resounding success. The boys like the gruesome demons in the story and the smoking incense sticks we'd lit. The girls are fascinated by Bina's gold-and-red shimmery salwar kameez and jangling bangles.

At the Diwali festival at the Indian Cultural Institute, we are greeted warmly by Mrs. Kapoor, her husband, and their daughter; the other students from the dance class are there with their families, too. The room is packed with large Indian families, neatly turned-out mothers in their saris, fathers in their best suits, children in frilly dresses and little lace socks. Around the edge of the room are the young people, who aren't so keen to sit with their parents anymore. The girls from more conservative families wear salwar kameez, but there are also girls with daring makeup who have been brave enough to show up in tight jeans and T-shirts. The young men stand an appropriate distance away, with extravagant haircuts and panache borrowed from the posters of Bollywood stars that hang in their rooms at home.

Andreas and I watch the dance display. We manage to keep Sushmita entertained with cookies, but Bina sits proudly two rows in front of us with Aisha, an Indian friend she met at dance lessons. During a pause in the program, Mrs. Kapoor calls the two girls backstage. They've been asked to present the flowers at the end of the performance. Bina stands in front of the dancers in their finery, her eyes wide with joy and excitement. The women are dressed in colorful saris, which hang in stiff folds, as is the tradition; theatrical makeup adorns their faces, and they have woven silver chains into their hair and attached their long braids to their saris. The bells on their feet jangle with every step. They look so magical that Sushmita points excitedly at the stage crying, "Princess! Princess!"

As I watch Bina among all the Indian women and dancers, I suddenly sense her diving into her very own Indian world and beginning to move freely within it. I think to myself that perhaps we can only follow her so far down this road, otherwise we'll get in the way; it is a path that Bina needs to walk alone in order to fit in properly.

Will it lead to a conflict between our Western, Christian way of life and the Eastern, Hindi way? I ask myself this question every time we visit Hindu temples, like the grand Mandir Temple in Neasden, an area of London. We travel there, watch the prayer ceremony, look at the statues of the gods, and buy Indian children's books and music cassettes in the little temple shop.

Bina loves lying flat on her back in the big hall in the temple. "Like a big flower!" she whispers, pointing to the dome high above her. The flowerlike shape of the marble dome soars above us; it is like a paper cutout, as fine as lace. It's peaceful here. The only sounds are the quiet footsteps of the temple priest on the marble floor. He goes from altar to altar, using a clanking key to open the doors in front of the statues of the gods. Soon, it will be time for prayers; more Hindus are already quietly padding into the hall.

The priest signals to us to take our seats in the women's area at the back of the hall, as the men will sit and pray at the front.

"Mommy, how do you do that?" Bina asks.

She is watching the ceremony that the Indians perform when the priest brings the offering bowl to them. I'm not sure what to tell her—I don't know the ritual. But the priest seems to understand our situation at once. When he comes to Bina, he shows her how to pass her hands over the holy flame to honor the gods and how to stroke her hair symbolically.

Then he gives Bina a friendly nod and moves on to the other worshippers. He seems to know that I don't pray to Hindu gods. Even Bina appears to understand this now and no longer expects me to lie down on the floor and pray as some Hindus do.

Yet, Bina wants to imitate the Indians in the temple because she feels a sense of belonging with them. I won't hold her back, even though we are raising the children as Christians and even though, as a nod to the nuns in Mumbai, to whom Bina's mother had brought her after all, we had her baptized into the Catholic faith. I would never stop Bina from showing her respect to the Hindu gods in the temple, because that's all it is. I have explained to her that we respect all religions, and that also goes for Hindu gods. In any case, the basic moral values all major world religions expect from their believers aren't really so very different. In the long run, Bina will have to decide for herself how much she wants to involve herself in Indian religion and how strong her ties will be to our Western, Christian world.

Language is a similar matter. Bina has Hindi lessons in the afternoon with a small group of Indian children. She's only in the beginners' group at the moment, but when we last visited an Indian restaurant, the waiter gave us the menu and asked Bina her name—in Hindi. Imagine my surprise when she replied slowly and deliberately—also in Hindi. I was thrilled, of course, but then it dawned on me what I had started by arranging these lessons for her. We would have to accept that, as well as English and German, our daughters might one day speak a language we couldn't understand. We wouldn't be able to follow their conversations! At her young age, Bina learns Hindi in her lessons much more readily than I can by learning pages of vocabulary. Down the line, we may even have to face one or perhaps both girls going back to India, at least for a while. Who knows where their careers will take them. Who knows which men they'll meet and fall in love with.

Andreas has always stressed that in today's world people should build bridges between cultures and religions; he calls it being a "citizen of the world." Bina and Sushmita will always be a combination of both West and East. I find the remarks that we often hear from adoptive parents to be almost cynical: "The children must be so glad to have left all that poverty and dirt behind."

Of course they may be glad to have left, but that's not the point; there's more to India than poverty and dirt. I think it's a shame when adoptive parents wait until their children are much older to take them to India for the first time. By that stage, it's too late, and it's highly likely that they'll simply write India off as strange, dirty, and poor.

Some of our happiest memories are of the early morning hours we spent on our boat trips through the canals and swamps of Kerala. Andreas and Bina sat on a soft mat on the deck, and the peaceful sight of the sunrise wrapped around us like a warm towel. The cook handed us steaming tea as we watched the swarms of parrots circling in the palm trees and the herons beating their heavy wings as they flew over the shimmering rice paddies. Every now and then, a blue kingfisher darted across the canal while the water lapped leaden and heavy against the bow of our boat. I took a photo of Andreas and Bina just as one flew by; it now hangs in Bina and Sushmita's room.

There are other precious memories, too. There was the time we visited an enchanting maharaja's palace in the middle of India, where a servant led Bina through the overgrown gardens. He knocked fruit down from the trees with a long stick to show them to her, breaking them open and handing them to her to eat. Later, Bina and Sushmita ran barefoot on the cool marble floors of the palace hallways, while in the dining room a dalmatian wagged his tail lazily in the heat and the thunder of a coming monsoon rumbled on the horizon.

Or there was the time in Khana National Park when we were riding in a jeep through the jungle at dusk with the children and some rangers. The car suddenly came to a stop as a herd of brown bison crossed the dusty road ahead of us. One of the rangers picked Sushmita up to show her the massive animals and then put his hand over his mouth and roared like a tiger. The bison stared in amazement, as did our daughter!

Of course, India isn't all romantic boat trips, maharajas' palaces, and national parks. Bina has also seen the children in the slum huts in Mumbai with their matted hair and rags. She observed that even her doll's dress was nicer than anything these children would ever wear. Later, she asked Andreas what the boy wanted—the son of the cropped-haired mother from my first trip—who kept touching Andreas's arm, pointing at his pant pocket, then putting his dusty hand to his mouth in a pleading gesture. I explained to her what begging was and why, sadly, people need money to buy bananas and rice at the bazaar.

At a crossing in the middle of Mumbai, she witnessed a beggar shoving the stumpy remains of his arms into our motor rickshaw. She asked me for days afterward why he has no hands.

We hope we aren't asking too much of our children, but Bina's reactions give us comfort that we're not. As we sat in the motor rickshaw in one of Mumbai's heavy traffic jams, sweat running down our backs in the heat, almost suffocating in the diesel fumes from the buses, Bina suddenly whispered in my ear in amazement over the clatter of the motor rickshaw, "Mommy, India is *so* beautiful!"

I knew then that all our efforts had been worth it.

Chapter 33

BROWN BABY, GO AWAY!

The New York subway train rocked rhythmically down the tracks and slowly made its way over the bridge across the East River. Bina was on my lap. We were on our way back from Queens, where we had visited the shops in the Indian quarter, bought spices and music cassettes, and eaten a curry. The train was just pulling out of the station when a Rastafarian slumped down into the seat in front of me. He was impressively tall and powerfully built, his dreadlocks stuffed into a red, yellow, and green hat. Many gold rings gleamed on his fingers. He was so tall that his knees stretched right out into the aisle, and he had to bend forward in the narrow seat, as there was no room for his broad back between the other passengers.

Bina was tired of sitting on my lap and was standing between my legs, directly in front of the man's knees. She watched him, and after a while the

Jamaican gave her a smile. She must have grinned back because he pulled a funny face, and Bina giggled. He pulled another silly face and Bina tapped on his knees excitedly. From then on, he entertained her with tongue clicks and all kinds of silliness. Bina loved it. I was grateful for the distraction because she could be very impatient on long journeys. It was a long train ride back to Manhattan. Many stops later, he smiled at Bina again, gave her a gentle pinch on the cheek, and got up from his seat. He got off at the next stop. In twenty minutes he had not looked at me once, not even for a second.

I've often experienced this in New York, where we had lived for a while with Bina. Once, I was standing there in the subway, helpless, with the stroller, bags of shopping, and Bina, wondering how on earth I was going to make it up the stairs (there are no escalators or lifts on the New York subway). Before I could blink, an African-American man had grabbed the stroller and was carrying it, Bina and all, up the steps in front of me. I had to rush to keep up with all my bags of shopping. Upstairs, he'd put the stroller down on the pavement without saying a word and turned away before I'd had chance to thank him. After all, it was Bina he'd helped, not me.

Incidentally, it was almost always African Americans who had helped me in this way and only very rarely investment bankers from downtown who probably didn't have time in their busy schedules for kindnesses like these. During my time in New York with Bina, I realized that the world there is very much divided into black and white.

Bina couldn't have known at the time how much of an impact the topic of racism would have on her life. However, even at her tender age, she recognized that there was a difference between us.

Bina wasn't even two years old when she grabbed my hand while I was giving her a bath and said, "Paint." To her, this word usually meant smearing paint around with her fingers on a piece of paper, but now she grabbed my hand, rubbed my skin, and kept saying, "Paint." She wanted to wipe away my pale coloring, assuming that she would see brown skin underneath.

At that age, whenever I showed Bina light- and dark-skinned dolls and asked her, "Which one is Bina?" she would always grab the brown or black doll. And when I showed her a United Colors of Benetton ad, she would always tap decisively on the dark child—never a white one—to indicate herself.

When we first adopted Bina, Andreas and I didn't know how much racism we'd have to face;

because we'd never been subjected to this kind of discrimination ourselves, we had no way of knowing how things were going to be. And now I know that it doesn't even make sense to discuss racism in society as a white person. We will never be confronted with it ourselves, and so we are in no position to judge.

One of the nannies in New York warned me about it. In the mornings, I liked to take Bina to one of the amazing playgrounds in Central Park, where the children played on the climbing frames while their Caribbean nannies sat on the benches in the shade, watching their employers' offspring. I had made friends with Rosie, who had twins to look after and had become very fond of Bina. She despised the family she worked for; both parents were investment bankers who worked in downtown Manhattan, usually until late in the evening. At the weekends and on holidays, they wanted time to themselves to recover, so Rosie would bring the children down to Central Park, even on Sundays, when the playground was otherwise full of fathers enjoying precious time with their kids. Rosie told me that the twins cried out for her in the night; they never cried for their mother.

"That's why some employers change nannies after a year—otherwise the bond between us and the child grows too strong," she had moaned.

It made me think of our neighbor in our eighth-story apartment in Manhattan. I had congratulated them on the birth of their baby and told them about our adoption, mentioning that under German law I was entitled to three years' parental leave.

"How dreadful!" she had replied. "I'm taking two weeks, and then I'll be back at the bank. Children do nothing but eat, drink, and sleep in the first year anyway. What do they need me there for?"

I bit my lip and said nothing. Words fail me sometimes.

One day, Rosie had said something that had taken me aback.

"It's so good of you to adopt a black child," she said. "Not many people are brave enough to do that."

I was surprised to hear her say this—both that she saw Bina as a black child and that she had warned me so explicitly about racism. But perhaps she was right that other adoptive parents didn't want to take this risk. In the playgrounds of New York, I had met lots of parents who had adopted foreign children, but the children were almost always from China.

A few days later, Andreas came home from a trip to the playground with Bina and told me a child had said to Bina, "Brown baby, go away!" That was just the beginning. Today, we know that racism is a topic that goes much deeper, and it has hit us and our children much harder than we ever expected.

Bina must have been about four when the questions started. "Mommy, it's such a shame that I'm the only brown child in the class," she said once. "Why aren't there more brown children where we live? Then I wouldn't be the only one." I held my breath at first, but then I was relieved. She hadn't wished to be white herself; instead, she wanted other children to look like her. That meant she was happy with her own appearance. She had self-confidence, which was important.

Our upbringing had obviously paid off. We'd always taught Bina that being Indian was something to be proud of and that she should be proud of her appearance, too. We keep telling her how beautiful her skin color is and that she's extremely pretty. The children have brown and black dolls as well as white ones. We're doing everything we can to show them that "beauty" doesn't just equal blue eyes and blond hair.

Where I have the choice, I try to make sure the illustrations in any children's books I buy are as international as possible, which is easier with British and American books than German ones. In a mixed family like ours, it suddenly matters that there are nonwhite newsreaders, that adverts include people from ethnic minorities, that minorities are integrated into and reflected in every aspect of society.

That's why our vacations to India are so important. In those times, Andreas and I become the outsiders, while the children blend in with others like them. For a few weeks, people stare at us parents and not Bina and Sushmita.

Almost everyone we know is open, tolerant, and has actually gone out of their way to be nice to the children. On the street, too, more often than not, people are friendly and accepting of us and the children, which is very encouraging. So far, we haven't encountered any malicious racism where we've been attacked or insulted, although this certainly exists in our society. Instead, the children are confronted with thoughtless comments; they are not meant unkindly in themselves, but taken as a whole, they make our daughters insecure because they draw attention to and attach value to their skin color.

Bina was hurt during a fight in the playground when her best friend suddenly blurted out, "I'm not playing with you anymore! I don't like brown faces."

It was typical little girl teasing, but Bina looked around in disbelief. We mothers had overheard, and my friend went nuts at her daughter.

"Apologize now—right now!" she scolded. I knew how embarrassing it must be for her. She loves our children, this Swedish-born woman, married to an English diplomat, and she is anything but racist. I reassured my friend and comforted Bina. That evening, I read her one of her children's books about racism; I've built up a collection of appropriate books for times like these.

But just a few days after that, Bina came home from school in tears. "Mommy, my teacher says she doesn't like my brown skin. She says it isn't pretty," she told me.

I stared out of the kitchen window, frozen with horror. This was something I hadn't expected. It couldn't be true, not in this small, good English school. My suspicions were correct. When I delicately brought it up with Bina's teacher the next morning, she was flabbergasted and hurt. We quickly worked out what had caused Bina to say it. Bina was clearly so insecure about her appearance that she was worried her teacher didn't like her. It was this fear that Bina had tried to express. The teacher decided to deal with Bina's fear in a lesson.

The next day, every child had to stand up in front of a group and give a detailed description of his/her appearance and where he/she came from, and then each child would be given lots of praise. Bina had given a long presentation on herself and India, the teacher later told me. Her plan worked. From then on, Bina seemed much more self-confident.

Much to our dismay, insulting comments are something we often encounter. Once, we were sitting in the airport on an island in the North Sea, waiting to be called for boarding. The little departure lounge was packed full of average German tourists. Bina was pushing her doll's pram past an elderly couple and looked up at them, as curious little children do when they're surrounded by strangers.

"My God, just look at her!" said the husband and pointed to Bina. "Look at her eyes! They're so dark. She looks as if she's about to gobble someone up!" A few passengers gave me a shocked look. I called Bina back to me. The conversations around us died down; there was an awkward silence for a few moments. Then everyone carried on chatting. My heart was racing, though I tried not to let it show. I was upset, particularly after we'd already been stared at so openly on the beach in a way I'd never experienced before.

Another time, on the train, we were sitting with Bina at a table in an open-plan carriage. Bina was playing, drawing, laughing, and happily babbling away when suddenly, a woman leaned over from the table next to ours and said, "You know, all children are the same underneath." It was clear that she meant it in a nice way, but I said nothing. She repeated herself, though, thinking I hadn't understood. "All children are the same underneath, aren't they?" I ignored her until finally she gave up.

Another time at the drugstore, I was standing with Bina at checkout, and the pharmacist said, "Wow, aren't you pretty? Your skin's such a great color. I'd have to use a tanning bed to get a tan like that!"

We have even encountered comments at our pediatrician's office. Both children had terrible colds, so I'd dragged the two of them to the kind pediatrician who had been recommended to me by many other mothers. As he was listening to Bina's chest, he suddenly said, "Wow, you've got such a brown tummy! What does your mommy do to make you so brown? Does she rub chocolate sauce on you at bedtime?"

"No!" Bina laughed.

"Does she rub raspberry sauce on you at bedtime?"

"No!" Bina squealed with joy.

"Does she rub shoe polish on you at bedtime?"

"No!" Bina laughed, barely able to move now.

"Does she rub…"

The doctor was standing with his back to me, so he couldn't see that my mouth was wide open in shock. "This is unbelievable!" I thought. I was stunned. What should I do? Make a scene? Grab the children and storm out of the surgery? Or say nothing and never go back? Or perhaps I should say something, but what and how? I felt helpless. Here was another situation where I had no idea what to say. When the words finally came to me, the moment had passed, as usual.

Do American social workers have a point when they advise white couples not to adopt children of color because they aren't equipped to deal with precisely these kinds of situations? At the end of the day, we've never been treated like this ourselves and have never learned how to react to it. How, then, can we teach our child the correct way to respond?

The pediatrician and the pharmacist thought they were paying the children a compliment; they meant it nicely and are fond of the children, in fact.

They don't realize that their comments turn the color of our daughters' skin into a talking point—in the drugstore, in the doctor's office, in the airport, and on the train. And it hurts the girls when people keep commenting on the color of their skin. Technically speaking, it's a form of racism.

Sadly, this type of naive, casual racism isn't yet seen as a problem in Germany. Neo-Nazis beating up Turks in the streets, painting swastikas on the walls of their houses and chanting "Foreigners out!"—this is the German idea of racism. They haven't yet realized that racism also comes in more subtle guises. If the color of a person's skin is the subject of constant comments and questions and affects the way he or she is treated, then it is racism. This is because it continually forces one to justify one's appearance. One is never left in peace, is never treated like everyone else; one is stigmatized and alienated.

When the immigration officials at Frankfurt airport smirk and ask my friend, who comes from Korea, to show them her return ticket and establish whether she has enough money to pay for her stay in Frankfurt, that's racism. She isn't a high-class Asian prostitute; she's an investment banker on her way to a conference in the financial metropolis of Frankfurt.

In that respect, Germany is more racist than the United Kingdom or the United States; people there are more careful about these things. A New York pediatrician would never dare ask a child if her mother rubbed chocolate sauce on her; he'd have a lawsuit on his hands if he did. But we live in Germany, so I will have to learn to protect my children from racism, in whatever form we encounter it.

One day I was out with my children when an eight-year-old brat asked me, "Are those your children?"

"Yes, they are," I replied, because I always answer children's questions; they need to ask to learn.

"But you're so pretty, and they're so dark!" I tensed up and hoped that Bina, who was holding my hand, hadn't heard.

"That's right; they're very dark and very pretty, aren't they?" I said, picking Sushmita up.

"But you don't *love* them, do you?" the brat asked. He wasn't trying to be mean; he didn't know any better. By then, Bina had pricked up her ears, so I had to answer him.

"Of course I love them. Just as much as your mom loves you," I explained. And I realized that, yet again, I'd let the conversation go too far.

"But you don't *kiss* them, do you?" he asked. Bina stared at me.

"Of course I do," I said, giving Bina and Sushmita a kiss on the cheek to prove it. I was hurt, so I added angrily, "Now get lost and leave us alone!"

I can't be this rude at Bina's school. One day while we were having lunch, Bina had told me in a quiet voice, "Mommy, Lisa in my class says I'm brown like poo. Now some of the children call me poo-poo. Can you tell them to stop, please? I don't like it."

I got up and started fussing around by the sideboard so that Bina wouldn't see I was close to tears. How could someone liken my child to a piece of shit and use this to make fun of her, even making it her nickname? What upset me even more was how Bina had asked me so politely if I could get them to stop; she didn't even seem angry about it, which she had every right to be. I comforted Bina and promised to speak to the child and the teacher. That evening, we read together the book *Chinese Eyes*, in which an adopted child from China is teased at school for the way she looks and is comforted by her mommy.

The next day, I spoke with Bina's teacher, who confirmed the teasing. She spoke to Lisa's parents, then Lisa herself, and finally Bina and Lisa together. We parents and the teacher are disappointed that this has happened. Hadn't the children just learned to respect each other with all their different backgrounds, races, and religions? Is this so quickly forgotten in the playground?

At least the teacher's reaction is reassuring. She really involves the children in the topic and shows them a book about different skin colors. The book has a palette of every possible shade of brown and she asks the children to put their hands next to it. They soon see that every child's skin color is on the scale of shades of brown and that no child is actually white or black.

But just a few weeks later, Bina comes home with another complaint. "Mommy, the boys say I look like chocolate, and now they keep coming over and licking me and saying I'm going to melt." I can hardly believe my ears. Not again. How often must Bina put up with this, and how long will it take before these comments stick and begin to change her? It scares me to think that Bina will hear many hundreds of comments like these. Will she be able to cope? How much can a person take? When does one give in, begin to doubt oneself, lose one's self-confidence or shut oneself away in frustrated rage?

How much humiliation must the Rastafarian have faced that he would completely ignore me while he played with Bina? How often had he been called "pothead" or "drug addict" or "nigger"? How much resentment and hate had built up in him that he no longer bothered to look at whites?

I would dearly love to spare Bina this kind of hurt. Nothing makes me as angry as when people humiliate our daughter because of her appearance. It's so unfair. As adoptive parents, we feel powerless against it.

The sad thing is, one day Bina and Sushmita will understand that their skin color was actually one of the reasons they were put up for international adoption and why no parents could be found for them in India. I already know that this will be another bitter disappointment for them. They'll feel let down by their own country, their own culture, their own heritage. Bina and Sushmita will not only face racism in the Western world, but will also experience a similar problem in Indian culture, where people still believe that fair skin is clean, pure, and beautiful. What's particularly nasty is that Western companies adapt their marketing accordingly and further reinforce these judgments.

I wanted to buy Bina an Indian Barbie doll for her birthday to show her that beauty isn't all about long golden hair, blue eyes, and white skin. I found a beautiful Barbie in a sparkling sari with long black hair, a bindi on her forehead, and Indian facial features. But then, I decided not to give it to Bina after all—the Indian Barbie's skin was white as snow.

Sushmita, too, will learn to recognize these subtle things, although at the moment she only half understands the topic. Once, as I climbed into the tub shivering and turned the shower on hot to warm myself, Sushmita stood in the bathroom, watching me curiously. All of a sudden, she stroked her hands and announced, "Sushmita has brown hands." Then after looking at her feet, she added, "And brown feet." Then she looked at me, looked down at my feet, thought for a moment, and said, "And Mommy has cold feet."

I let out a huge laugh and would have hugged her tightly if I hadn't been standing under the shower, because she was absolutely right.

Part Five

Chapter 34

TEENAGERS

The finish is in sight. "Give it your best! Watch your timing!" Laura yells as the boat shoots through the water. Bina pushes the painful blisters on her hands, her wet shoes, and her burning thighs to the back of her mind. She's staring intently at the back of the rower in front, pulling her oars through the water of the Thames in time with the rest of the four. Suddenly, she hears Indian music over on the riverbank.

"Cool, a wedding!" Bina hears Ashan shout in front of her, before the rest of his words are drowned out by the wind and the slapping of the oars. She spies the wedding party out of the corner of her eye; she sees the colorful saris and can even make out the groom among them as they glide by on the bank. It's just like the weddings she's seen on our vacations to India. As quickly as it appeared, the celebration vanishes among the reeds. The music dies away.

Bina is now fourteen years old and is already taller than I am; I even wear her hand-me-downs—an old pair of size five winter boots that were hers two years ago. Now she takes a size seven. She's certainly a lot fitter than I am, too. I couldn't row up and down the river the way she does. Her eyes have recovered well from her operation; they're not as red as they were just a few weeks ago.

When Bina was seven, her squint suddenly came back. The first operation wasn't a success. As time went on, she had increasingly more problems with reading and the hours of homework she had for school, so she was operated on for a second time. This time, we'll see how things go if she wears reading glasses.

Bina sinks onto the passenger seat exhausted, takes her headband off to let her long black hair fall onto her shoulders, and goes straight for her cell phone to check for new text messages.

"Things are going really well with the boys; we got a great speed going today. Shame there's no mixed races for girls and boys," she says. She loves her rowing; the team spirit really motivates her.

How the years have flown. Not long ago, Bina's school held a little celebration to mark the fact that the girls had completed middle school and would be starting high school after the summer vacation. Bina got up in front of the whole school, as well as teachers and parents, and took the microphone to make her first speech. Dressed in a smart suit and shiny high-heeled shoes, she seemed almost grown up as she read out her speech. Then the applause came, and she took her seat among her classmates.

At first, high school was tough for Bina because she wasn't quite sure of her true identity. Was she Indian, German, or English? This question troubled her most of all on the day when all the girls at her international school were allowed to come dressed in their national costume.

"I don't know what my identity is, but that doesn't bother me. It's other people who always want to know where I belong," Bina complained. "Why should I have to pick one? I'm whoever I want to be at the time; it depends on the situation." Once she went as a German football fan. Then again, she was just as proud when she stood in front of the class and did a presentation about "her" country, India.

All the same, it pains her that she can't chat in Hindi with her other Indian classmates, and she's aware of her very Western upbringing. Andreas and I brought Bina and Sushmita up to be self-confident young girls. Since our divorce, both girls have grown up living with me, a full-time workingwoman. It really matters to Andreas and me that the girls are well educated and are able to use their education to take control of their own lives, so Bina is stunned by the occasionally deeply conservative atmosphere at the houses of some of her Indian friends.

It must be said, of course, that many of her classmates also have identities that are not exactly clear cut. What is the identity of a child living in London who has an Italian mother, who grew up in Kenya, and a Norwegian father? A child whose Mexican-German father grew up in Asia and whose German mother grew up in Australia, and who is growing up in London himself: where does he belong? What about a child with a Swedish mother, who grew up in France and Peru, and an English father? And after twenty years in London, where do I consider home?

Now, sixteen years old, Bina sees herself as a German; at least, she wants to be accepted as a German and was deeply hurt when a girl at school told her, "You are not German. You will never be German. You are Indian." Bina did not want to stir a fight. She would never do that. She tries to explain, as she just wants to be accepted the way she is, but this girl does not want to understand. I feel that it hurts Bina.

It reminds me of the situation she experienced at the hotel one summer. Bina joined a group of teenagers, hanging out, playing sports, enjoying a disco in the evening. They started growing fond of each other, until one German girl told Bina, "Forget it. This guy will not be interested in you. You are black!" It stunned Bina—and all the other teenagers. Bina, with all her self-esteem and being proud of who she is, was furious and openly challenged the girl. She is so strong that she did not waver. Many of the other teenagers took her side and rebuffed the girl.

I am not sure whether Sushmita would react the same way. For Sushmita, her color is much more of an issue—it always has been. Her school turned out to be much more of a pure-English, mostly white school than Bina's International School. Sushmita's school is a mixed school, and all the girls are obsessed with how the boys judge them. It is all about having lovely, long straight hair, perfect eyebrows, short skirts, long legs, a nice figure, and a cool outfit—all this in our age of confident working mothers and women's rights. I think some of the teenage girls today are more insecure than teenage girls of previous generations. Sushmita is really worried about her looks. I can tell, and she often speaks about it.

"You know, Mommy, boys first look at your outer appearance. You must be blond and pretty and fair.

Only then do they get interested, and only then will they talk to you and realize that you are a nice person." I am shocked by her deep insecurity. Whatever I say to reassure her how pretty she is, it does not count. What Andreas tells her does not count. All that matters is the view of the other girls—probably not even the boys. The important thing is the girls' perceptions of what society wants. I start to cut out black and Indian models from fashion magazines and stick them to a door in the kitchen. There are some fashion houses that are happy to use black or dark models—for instance, Burberry and Chanel—but the list is not long. There are fewer black models in fashion magazines now than in the 1970s.

This summer, Sushmita will change schools. She will move to Bina's International School, where a girl from Nigeria just gave a speech about the chances in life of aspiring young women. It is a school where a Chinese girl plays an old Chinese string instrument in assembly. It is a school where Bina and a group of (mostly black) girls surprised the parents with a jazz performance, Bina on her saxophone. They all accept each other, no matter how different their culture, their looks, or their experiences in life. That is the school ethos. Later, I will discover that changing Sushmita to that school was liberating for her. In only a few weeks, her self-esteem will rise, as she laughs with other girls from all over the world, mascara and hair straightener forgotten.

The modern lifestyle of the West has crept into our lives and has turned Bina and Sushmita into two modern, Western teenagers. Not much remains of my Indian passion from our early years; with school, homework, sports, music lessons, choir practice, student council, netball, Sushmita's street dance, doctor's appointments, birthday parties, friends, garden, dog, and Andreas's and my work commitments, our lives are already busy enough. We kept up the Indian dance for as long as we could, but we were spending every Sunday traveling right across London for lessons. At some point, we had to give it up. After that, an Indian student, Nija, used to come to us and teach the girls in the kitchen, although admittedly it was a bit cramped. Nija looked like someone out of a fairy tale when she performed at the Indian Cultural Institute in her beautiful dance sari; she could have passed for a temple dancer. But she won a biochemistry scholarship at an American university, so our lessons had to stop.

Nothing really came of the Indian flute lessons either. Bina loves to play the piano—the usual teenage repertoire and *Für Elise*—as well as the saxophone; sometimes the house even sways to the bossa nova beat of "Desafinado." There was just no time for the flute as well. We dropped the Sanskrit lessons when the grammar became too complex; German, English, French, and Latin lessons at school were quite enough. But at least when we're in India, we can decipher the street signs and the names of the stations on the suburban trains in Mumbai. It's fun, too!

But at home, in our day-to-day lives, we stick to Indian curries, Bollywood movies, and museum exhibitions featuring Indian bronze statues and miniature paintings from Mogul times. Very occasionally we still visit the Indian area in Wembley, wander round the sari shops, buy bright clunky bangles and a new Bollywood DVD, or gaze in wonder at the Indian temples. We have even forgotten to celebrate Diwali some years; these days, I'm the only one in the family who remembers. This year, even I forgot. And when we were invited by Indian neighbors, we went, all dressed up in Indian outfits, only to find our Indian neighbors and relatives celebrating as if it were any other Western party, no sari in sight.

In the hustle and bustle of daily school life, the topic of adoption has been pushed right into the background, too. We've always been honest with the girls from the start, and the start was the hardest time. When Bina was little, she asked if she could meet the woman whose tummy she had been in. She wanted to know why I didn't have any photos of her. I gave her honest answers to her questions, and every time it hurt her a little. The girls would only ever ask as much as they wanted to know, and

I learned to tell them only that much. As soon as I went too far, they would block it out. When they were little, they could only work through the topic in stages.

Sushmita takes her adoption much harder than Bina. I noticed this when she was young, so I read her a little story about birds, which is basically about adoption. Although Sushmita could only have been about four, she wouldn't forgive the mother bird and explained to me, in her rigorous logic, that the mother bird could have built the nest differently and could have made more effort. Then she wouldn't have had to give her baby bird away. No matter how I tried to explain things to her, she still thought the mother bird was "mean." She still thinks that to this day.

Sushmita went through a phase where she tried to use her adoption against us. It was her way of testing our relationship. "You're not my real mother! You don't love me and don't want me to be happy. Anita was my real mother; she would want me to be happy. If I still lived with Anita, she would let me watch TV now!" I had to turn away so she didn't see me smirking at her silliness.

An even better one: "Mama, you love torturing me; that's why you're making me do my homework! You only adopted me so you could torture me!" What am I supposed to say to that kind of nonsense?

"Torture or not, I want you to do exercises five through eight in your math book. They're due tomorrow." The result is furious sobbing and more muffled moaning about "torture."

Sushmita would always play on her adoption and Indian identity when it suited her: "I'm not eating that broccoli. Indians don't like broccoli, you see; we have completely different taste buds."

Bina read the first edition of this book during her summer vacation. "For the first time, I feel I really understand what happened," she told me afterward. Her friends asked her about the book and her adoption, and she appreciated their interest. Yet, sometimes the girls find people's interest in them difficult to handle, Sushmita more so than Bina. It even stops Sushmita from inviting friends over for a while. At times, I even get the impression that she finds it embarrassing when I appear, because she knows questions will immediately follow about why I'm "white" and she's Indian. I need to be careful here, though. How many parents are told by their teenagers that they're "embarrassing" and are asked to wait out of sight when their friends are around? Not everything is about adoption.

For years the girls loved it in summer when we had the same skin color, when I was "brown," too; young children long to form a symbiotic bond with their mother. This has completely changed, as far as the girls are concerned. Andreas and I are their parents. I once asked Bina, "Would you rather have an Indian mother?"

"No, why? What a stupid question!" came the annoyed answer.

Bina tries to forgive. "I don't blame my mother for giving me up; if I'd been in her situation and didn't have any choice, perhaps I would have done the same thing. I don't want to judge her," she tells me. "But I am cross that I can't find out more about her," she admits, having a dig at the Indian authorities, who still don't allow any contact between adoptive children and their birth mothers. It must be said that Bina isn't interested in finding or meeting her birth mother at the moment, which she thinks is kind of strange. It would be easier for her to at least know the option was there, though.

She only really thinks about the adoption when she's sad. "Sometimes, I wonder what it would have been like if I had been adopted by a different family. Where would I be then? What country would I live in? What would my life be like there?" thinks Bina. She would love to know if she has biological brothers and sisters. Questions about her father haven't come up yet.

Still, fourteen years on, she is happy with her life, with her school, with her friends, and with girly gossip and Facebook, and she is usually more concerned with making sure her hair looks nice, with the e-mails her friends send, and with how our dog is doing than with the issues surrounding adoption.

Our love is as deep as it possibly can be for parents and their children. There was one Saturday that I realized how much I loved the girls, loved Sushmita. That morning, before she went to German School, I had told Sushmita off—really told her off. I was angry and shouting, and she was upset. I cannot even remember what typical, stupid argument it was. I should have picked her up from German School, but I came late—too late. Sushmita was not there anymore. I called her cell phone, but no answer. I asked the teachers and parents; nobody had seen her leaving. I searched the building, but Sushmita was not there. I drove home and waited. She did not come. I got scared and went back to school—no Sushmita. The school was near an extended parkland and nature reserve, close to the Thames River. I got scared, very scared. I drove back home and back to school—still no Sushmita. Then I panicked, called Andreas, and completely freaked out. What if our argument had been too much? What if she had walked away, out of her life with this horrible mother? A wave of guilt almost suffocated me. What if she walked into this nature reserve with all these lone joggers, bikers, and dog walkers? I got so frightened I could barely breathe. Andreas told me to wait a bit more and then drive again the way back from school to our house and then call the police. I nearly caused a traffic accident just staring at the pavement and people looking for her jacket, her green jacket. And there she was, a few hundred feet away from home, walking home. I stopped, and she got into the car.

"Where have you been? Why did you not come to school? My phone had no battery left. I could not call you. I did not have enough money for the bus. I had to walk; it is so far…" I just kissed her—cried and kissed her—over and over again. My baby, my darling.

We belong together, like any other family. "When I tell people I'm adopted, they always feel sorry for me," Bina complains. "They should find out more about it; then they'd realize it's really not that bad."

There was a time when I worried it could be different for Sushmita. So I asked her, "If you could meet your mother in India, what do you think you'd say to her? I mean, of course, that's not really an option, but just in case, what would you say?"

Sushmita hesitated. Then she said, "I would ask her if it's true that I was born in April 2000 and whether I have brothers and sisters. And I'd ask who my father is and where the mother lives."

"Anything else?"

"I'd ask her if I could come back and visit her again sometime." She said this as if it was the most natural thing in the world. It was one of the most beautiful sentences I've ever heard.

Chapter 35

HAPPY HOUR IN MUMBAI

In the shadows at the roadside, almost invisible in the headlights of the passing cars, the scrawny man takes off his prosthetic legs and sinks down onto his ragged blanket. All day long he's begged for alms in the blistering heat, yet now, during the early evening "Happy Hour," when the luxury hotels try to tempt guests into their bars, begging will do him no good. The "beautiful people" in their chauffeur-driven, climate-controlled luxury cars don't even notice him; there are too many excuses to celebrate: weddings, birthdays, receptions, and even the Formula One Grand Prix.

Crews of workers with heads for heights spend their days weaving bamboo cane and coconut fiber into ever-changing backdrops for functions that bring in the big bucks for the hotels. Yesterday's big event was a wedding reception. The receiving line lasted almost two hours as a steady stream of guests paid their respects to the happy couple, the ladies in their magnificent saris and the men in sharp suits. Meanwhile, up on their dais, the couple glittered and glowed like heavenly beings. Sporting my "Indian hippie" look, I felt quite out of place in the hotel and found myself wondering if I should have packed a cocktail dress instead.

Over our nightly curry, we watch as rich, middle-class guests from northern Mumbai come into the hotel.

"She's wearing those high Christian Louboutins!" whispers Bina, as her eyes follow an Indian beauty teetering toward reception on her husband's arm. This evening, there's a birthday party for the eight-year-old son of a leading figure in the petrochemical industry. There is bungee jumping, a band, a bouncy castle, and acrobats to entertain the little ones beneath the palms strung with fairy lights. The highlight is a fireworks display large enough to impress even the glitterati on Juhu Beach.

"The father has his son's party here every year," a waiter whispers confidentially.

As an emerging nation, India is going from strength to strength, and this is particularly true of Mumbai's middle classes. With Diwali a week away, computers, iPads, and cell phones are flying off the shop shelves in a way we Europeans only see at Christmas.

I barely recognize the city. Even the stray dogs on Juhu Beach are fatter than before, and it's no wonder in a city that produces nine thousand tons of trash a day. To the north, Aksa Beach, where we once drove through sprawling slums and swampland, is now home to glass shopping malls and towering thirty-story apartment blocks; the air is thick with smog; and the peaceful beachfront hotels have vanished without a trace.

To be honest, the girls weren't wild about coming to India. "Not again!" they groaned. "It's too tiring, too hot, and we've seen it all before anyway." Yet this time, coming back is more important than ever. It's more important than the time we traveled India by train, more important than visiting the temples in Varanasi or tea picking in the Nilgiri plantations. We may be in Mumbai for only a week, but we're bringing our view of India into the here and now.

Since I was last here, the official population of Mumbai has swelled to eighteen million. Even the neighborhood around the orphanage has changed drastically. The auto-rickshaws and motorbikes that once swerved along these streets have given way to climate-controlled sedans, barging their way through the traffic, bumper to bumper. The streets have become so dangerous that special pedestrian bridges have been erected high in the treetops. Like sprawling tentacles, they spread throughout Mumbai, and even in the bazaar street near the orphanage, the trees have been brutally lopped to make way for another "skyway." The vegetable sellers struggle for space on the pavement; the small, open-fronted shops have given way to glazed and air-conditioned businesses. Instead of Indian sweet shops, we are greeted by McDonald's, Kentucky Fried Chicken, pizzerias, and patisseries with windows full of chocolate cakes.

We pass the little hotel where I stayed on my visits to the orphanage; it has been extended and renovated. The tea stand has vanished, street kitchens being generally forbidden these days for health reasons. At the train station, the slum huts have also disappeared; parked cars now stand in their place. Just one slum family lives on the street at the station entrance.

I lead the children through the streets to the orphanage. Bina doesn't want to go. She still remembers, and she's afraid it will make her sad and that she might cry. Sushmita, on the other hand, is curious. As we arrive, I notice that many things are still the same: suburban trains still thunder past on the tracks, the orphanage buildings are still painted pink, the gate is still sky blue, and the little ones are still fighting over the few battered tricycles in the yard.

I can hardly believe my eyes. Fifteen years later, Sister Lena is still at her desk, making phone calls, plowing through the grueling paperwork for domestic and international adoptions. At the sight of Bina and Sushmita, her face lights up. She can hardly believe that fifteen years after our adoption journey began, two of her children have come back. Bina has just turned sixteen and Sushmita is thirteen.

With a little more effort than last time I saw her, Sister Lena gets to her feet and hugs us all, joyfully and just a little too tightly; she doesn't often get a chance to see what's become of the little children she entrusts to European parents. Generally, she never sees them again. Sushmita only has vague memories of Sister Lena, though Bina remembers her a little better. The plan was really just to stop by and see the orphanage one last time. Yet, unannounced as it is, I suddenly realize how important this reunion is for all of us. It's as though Sister Lena has been waiting for the girls all these years, and seeing them again has finally put her mind at ease. With emotion, she marvels at how much the girls have grown and how Bina's squint has vanished. She wants to know how they're getting on at school—"Are they working hard, taking it all in?"—and she checks that we're being good parents. "Don't worry about being too strict," she says, but then her expression becomes serious.

"I'm glad you're here, because now I can tell you to your faces," she begins, turning to the girls. "I never sent you away. I didn't just pack you off," she says, checking that Sushmita is listening. "I couldn't be a mother to you. I couldn't give you a proper home. I could never replace a family. Every one of my children has a place in my heart, and that goes for both of you, but you needed a mother and father, a family. So we chose your parents. Your Indian mothers couldn't keep you, of course."

I notice now that she is hesitating, wondering whether sending children all over the world is really what's best for them. She, too, is plagued with guilt and hopes to justify herself to the children; she wants them to understand what she did so she can lay her guilty feelings to rest.

She tells Bina and Sushmita the story, a story I have heard before, told just as bluntly as she tells it today. "Your mothers conceived you illegally, outside of marriage. That's not acceptable here. Here, when a woman has a child out of wedlock, her life is over; no one in her family will look her in the eye, not to mention the child. Mothers and their children are cut off, rejected; no one will have anything to do with them."

I gulp a little at the term *illegal*. As she speaks, the girls listen. Bina is emotional; Sushmita listens more out of politeness as she stares blankly at the baby photos that decorate the gray filing cabinets, family photos from Europe and America.

"I looked for parents for you in England because no parents here would have you on account of Bina's eyes and Sushmita's dark skin," Sister Lena goes on. At this, I cringe again and cast a nervous glance at Sushmita, who is focusing on keeping her composure, trying not to show any emotion. "Now you have good parents, who care for you lovingly," I hear and can't help but look at Sushmita again, thinking of the not quite so "loving" shouting matches we sometimes have over homework and other petty things.

"I know that not having known your biological mother means there will always be something missing from your life; this will never change," the sister says, and I'm stunned by her directness. "But when you feel this emptiness, you must pray to God, you must ask him for his help, and this will help you to come to terms with it." I can't help but admire her for the no-nonsense, direct way she uses her beliefs to help the children through life; her faith deals with the questions I cannot answer. Tears well in Bina's eyes, while Sushmita lets hers focus on the baby photos for the first time. "Is she even listening to me?" Sister Lena wonders.

The office phone rings. Over what is obviously a bad line, Sister Lena speaks to an adoptive mother-to-be in Spain who is longing for the day when she can collect her daughter from the orphanage. With the national and regional Indian adoption authorities challenging every overseas adoption and with the new, more complex procedures, the majority of children are now several years old before they leave India.

"These days, we just can't do it as quickly as we did with your adoptions," the sister tells me after the phone call. "It takes years now; last year, I only got three overseas adoptions through."

She turns to Bina and Sushmita again. "I see how terrible things are here for young mothers who have to give their babies away, and because of this, you must make me a promise. Promise that you'll wait until you can stand on your own two feet and look after yourselves before you get a boyfriend," she cautions. "No boyfriends until you're twenty-two years old, when you've finished your studies, when you're adults." I keep quiet on the matter. Sister Lena busies herself with her files. Suddenly she says, "Sushmita, straighten your T-shirt." I notice that Sushmita's T-shirt has slipped off her shoulder, and the strap of her vest is showing. "You must dress properly! What you're made of and how you look is nobody's business but your future husband's." Both my daughters continue their silence, so I let the situation run its course; after all, how often do young Western girls get an old-fashioned Indian talking to?

Afterward, we head up to the second floor to the room with the cots. Fifteen years on, the same pictures hang on the walls, and the little beds are still painted sky blue. I can still hear the crows, the helicopters, and the local trains rattling past—so many memories. The cots are empty now, as the children are playing downstairs, and there are no sisters or helpers around. So we stand around aimlessly. Almost immediately, Bina wants to go. She says she finds it depressing. Sushmita, though, appears to be drinking everything in, as if trying to etch the scene in her memory. We visit the office one last time and take our leave from Sister Lena and the other sisters, none of whom I recognize. Whether the girls will return one day without me, I couldn't say; they seem to be drawing a line under that chapter of their lives.

Once we're on the other side of the gate, Sushmita lets out her thoughts. "Someone should really tell her how things are these days. No boyfriends until I'm twenty-two!"

"Mama, do I really look that bad?" Sushmita whispers later. It hurts me to hear this, and I try to tell her that some Indians probably just don't want to adopt darker children because it would make the adoption more obvious and then they wouldn't be able to sweep it under the rug. With her thick hair, big dark eyes, and graceful, sporty figure, Sushmita is stunning, but she won't accept compliments. It's not easy for Sushmita, even in our Western world—or perhaps especially there. Although no one comes out and says it, there is still such a thing as being too dark; from Madonna to Lady Gaga to Miley Cyrus, fair and blond is the ideal, even for young people. Western marketing just can't break away from images of flowing golden hair, which, of course, is also always perfectly smooth with a silky shine. To help her achieve this look with her "frizzy" hair, Sushmita's friend gave her some hair straighteners for her birthday, which she dutifully uses every morning, despite my protests.

Being Western teenagers, there's only one word for how Bina and Sushmita would most like to spend their time in Mumbai: shopping. They've both seen the girls in their modern clothes on the Indian suburban trains, tapping away on their iPhones with their henna-painted hands, and they've already spotted the big Western-brand stores in the shopping precinct in Juhu Beach, where items can be bought for a fraction of London prices. Before I know it, I'm shopping in a Mumbai branch of Tommy Hilfiger with my daughters, and it suddenly hits me how bizarre this all is. Tomorrow, however, will be a total contrast.

When I asked Sister Lena about Sushmita's mother, she kept biting her lip. "Yes, yes, I know where she lives. She's from over there," she said, while vaguely pointing somewhere beyond the railway tracks. It could have meant a lot, yet at the same time nothing at all. But in that direction lies Dhavari, one of the largest slums in the whole of Asia. Over one million people live and work there in conditions that are almost unthinkable by Western standards. Over many decades, refugees and migrant workers have settled there, many of them from Bengal and the south of India, including a large number of Tamils.

I've booked us a tour of Dhavari through an aid organization that puts the money they collect from tourists into slum projects. The scenes that greet us are not unlike how I imagine things would have been during the industrial revolution. Young men shred aluminum cans in a cramped, pitch-black room, their brows shining with sweat. With no masks to protect them, they struggle for breath in the chokingly thick aluminum dust. We see the migrant workers, who melt the aluminum in ovens. For ten hours a day, they work and breathe the toxic fumes, and, as they sleep in their poisoned workshop, they breathe it all night, too. They live like this for six months, only to be paid a pittance. Refuse is sorted here, plastic shredded and cleaned, metal painted, leather dyed—all without mouth protection or ventilation of any kind. At thirty-seven degrees Celsius in the shade, the stench is so revolting that I have to keep holding my breath. Slums aren't camps of people sleeping, eating, and whiling away the day under plastic sheeting; nowhere else on Earth do people work so hard and in such devastatingly inhumane conditions. Yet, this is the very reason the Indian authorities tolerate their existence, they provide thousands of jobs, albeit of the most primitive kind imaginable.

Conditions for the families here are just as miserable. They live in windowless rooms no bigger than one hundred to two hundred square feet. The huts are so tightly packed together that in some places there's barely room for a crouched person to squeeze down the narrow passages between them. Some of the slum huts even have second stories of huts on top, meaning that the lower huts never see the light of day. Toilets and bathrooms are an unknown luxury; sewage flows right past the doorstep. The damp conditions are a hotbed for mosquitoes, malaria, and dengue fever. How the people here manage to stay healthy and clean is a mystery to Western tourists. Yet, the place is abuzz with children, who spend their time playing in the landfills when they're not heading off to school in their neat uniforms.

Bina and Sushmita trot valiantly along behind the tour guide, observing everything almost stoically. Suddenly Bina grumbles, "What really bugs me is that everyone at home goes on about how terrible poverty is and says they want to help. But they have no idea how hard it really is."

I let the kaleidoscope of scenes around us speak for itself. I can't explain everything to them; in fact, I don't think I should. Seeing and experiencing it for themselves is all they need to learn about India's many sides, as well as its many surprises.

As we sit in the restaurant on our last day, my attention is drawn to the young Indian family at the table next to ours. Their little daughter is toddling around the table; she is perhaps fifteen months old, the age that Bina and Sushmita were when they left the orphanage. The little one reminds me of Sushmita so much so that I become emotional and tell the young mother about her adoption. At this, she beams at me.

"To tell the truth, our daughter is adopted, too," she says, lifting her into the high chair. "We already have a son, but I wanted a daughter as well. So we adopted her." The parents are visibly happy. The mother looks at her daughter, full of pride, as she tells me, "She has added so much positive energy and happiness to our lives in the past year with us. It was one of the best decisions of my life."

Bina is not even listening. She is again on her cell phone—probably on Facebook, writing to a "boyfriend" that she met, I think from that summer vacation. But that is another story I am not writing about.

ACKNOWLEDGEMENTS

This books tells the story of the adoption of our two daughters from an orphanage in India. I must offer my sincere thank you to the Sisters and their warm welcome in the orphanage. They never thought I would write a book about our experiences. They always treated me as a mother, not a journalist or author. I deeply respect their trust and therefore keep the name of the orphanage confidential. I have changed all the names of the people in the book, especially the children, as I want to keep their privacy.

I offer my sincere thank you to Trevor Hook and Kate Horne, who gave so much support and help with translating, editing, and advising on how to get the book published in English. A big thanks to the team of CreateSpace and Amazon helping and supporting me with their editing, design, valuable advice, and technical help to get the book published. Again, a big thank you to the team of the German Marion von Schröder Verlag and Ullstein for the edition of the German Book. Major thanks to Thomas, who always supported me in writing this book, and Andrea Schruff and Dorothee Grueter-Fröhlich, for their great help and encouragement. And last but not least, a kiss to my daughters, who endured their mother sitting endless hours in front of the computer and gave all their support, help, wit, and humor to make the book happen.

Made in the USA
Charleston, SC
06 May 2015